W9-BXE-474

LUTHER AND KATHARINA

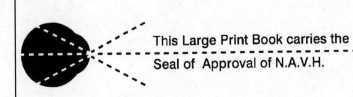

This Large Print Book carries the
Seal of Approval of N.A.V.H.

LUTHER AND KATHARINA

A NOVEL OF LOVE AND REBELLION

JODY HEDLUND

THORNDIKE PRESS

A part of Gale, Cengage Learning

GALE
CENGAGE Learning·

Farmington Hills, Mich • San Francisco • New York • Waterville, Maine
Meriden, Conn • Mason, Ohio • Chicago

GALE
CENGAGE Learning®

LIBRARY OF CONGRESS CATALOGING-IN-PUBLICATION DATA

Hedlund, Jody.
    Luther and Katharina : a novel of love and rebellion / Jody Hedlund. — Large print edition.
        pages cm. — (Thorndike Press large print christian romance)
    ISBN 978-1-4104-8502-1 (hardback) — ISBN 1-4104-8502-1 (hardcover)
    1. Luther, Katharina von Bora, 1499–1552—Fiction. 2. Luther, Martin, 1483–1546—Fiction. 3. Reformation—Germany—Fiction. 4. Large type books. I. Title.
PS3608.E333L88 2016
813'.6—dc23   2015036316

Published in 2016 by arrangement with WaterBrook Press, an imprint of Crown Publishing Group, a division of Penguin Random House LLC

Printed in Mexico
1 2 3 4 5 6 7 20 19 18 17 16

This book is for you, Dad.
As a Lutheran pastor you embodied
Martin Luther in so many ways: in
personality, love of family, devotion to the
gospel, and passion for your flock.
You were well loved everywhere you
served. As you look down from heaven,
I hope you're proud of your little girl.

MAIN CHARACTERS IN LUTHER AND KATHARINA

Katharina von Bora — a daughter of noble birth, but raised in convents from the age of five; also called Kate

Martin (or Martinus) Luther — once an Augustinian monk but excommunicated by the Catholic church; nailed his Ninety-Five Theses to the door of All Saints' Church in Wittenberg on October 31, 1517, sparking the Reformation; renowned minister and writer of the sixteenth century

Abbess Margareta (Reverend Mother) — at Marienthron, she disciplines Katharina for Baltazar; also Katharina's aunt

Abbot Baltazar — Abbot of Marienthron

Amsdorf — friend to Luther

Aunt Lena/Aunt Magdalena (von Bora) — remains at Marienthron after Katharina escapes; serves as a mother figure to Katharina

Charles V — historical figure, lived 1500–

1558; emperor of the Holy Roman Empire 1519–1556

Cranach family — Lucas Cranach, one of the wealthiest men in Wittenberg, owns a printing shop and prints most of Luther's writings; a famous painter; his wife, Barbara, befriends Katharina

Dr. Glatz of Orlamünde — lives in Wittenberg; a rector

Elector Frederick — Luther's benefactor and protector, who has his home palace in Torgau; also known as Prince Frederick, or Frederick III, Elector of Saxony

Greta — maidservant to Katharina; escapes with her from the Marienthron convent; in love with Thomas

Hans Luther — father of Jacob and Martin; a smelter

Jacob Luther — Martin's younger brother

Jerome Baumgartner — friend of Elsa Reichenbach; comes to stay and develops a relationship with Katharina von Bora

Johann von Staupitz — Augustinian vicar and a mentor to Luther

Justus Jonas — close friend of Luther's

Margaret von Schonfeld — a nun who escaped from the Marienthron convent; a close friend to Katharina and is interested in Luther

Merchant Koppe — a supporter of Luther;

helps the nuns escape

Pastor Johannes Bugenhagen — pastor of the Stadtkirche in Wittenberg; a friend of Luther's

Philipp Melanchthon — friend of Luther's; father to little Anna

Reichenbach family — the family Katharina initially works for in Wittenberg; Elsa is wife and mother; her husband is the mayor

Thomas — Merchant Koppe's servant; in love with Greta

Wolfgang — Luther's manservant at the Black Cloister

Zeschau sisters — Fronica and Etta; were tortured at Marienthron but escaped with Katharina

ONE

Before dawn on Easter morning, 1523
Saxony, Germany

Time to jump.

With trembling legs tangling in her scapular, Katharina crouched on the stone ledge of the window and peered down at the matted grass, still hard and untouched by spring. She blinked back a wave of dizziness and hoped the two-story drop wasn't as far as it looked.

The blackness of the barren cloister yard spread before her — the neatly trimmed hedges, the gardens, and the thick stone wall beyond. Nothing moved. No one was in sight . . . although anyone could be hidden in the thousands of shadows the April moonlight couldn't reach.

"Jump, my lady." Greta nudged her. Her tight wimple framed delicate features showing the strain of anxiety. "We've waited long enough."

"You must help lower me." Katharina clutched her maidservant's arm to steady herself. She took a last deep breath of the familiar mustiness of the abbey, then swung her feet over the edge.

"No," came Margaret's strained whisper behind her. It echoed against the bare walls of Katharina's cell, gripping her and threatening to immobilize her. "We mustn't leave without Sister Ruth."

"We've been back from the vigil too long." Greta spoke urgently. "We can't wait anymore."

In the scant moonlight Margaret's thin face was as pale as the plain white band wound around her forehead. Her narrow nose and pointed chin were pronounced and severe but belied by the kind worry in her eyes. "Something must have happened to Sister Ruth —"

"It doesn't matter," Greta said, nudging Katharina further to the edge.

Katharina glanced over her shoulder to the other sisters, some huddled against the wall shivering, others resting on her straw-filled pallet. She had the feeling they were shuddering more from fear than from the frosty air that had swept into the narrow, unheated cell.

If she delayed any longer, she'd put everyone at greater risk and possibly ruin their chance of leaving undetected.

"Just a few more minutes." Margaret's fingers quivered against Katharina's arm. The tall woman, who was like a sister to Katharina, had one fault — too much compassion.

Through the barred aperture on the cell door, Katharina glimpsed the outline of Aunt Lena's head. But there was no sign of anyone else and no sound — just the utter silence required both day and night. Katharina prayed that all the other Marienthron sisters were sleeping heavily, especially after staying up much later than usual celebrating the Vigil of Easter with the consecration of the Easter fire outside the church. It was the one occasion each year that changed the routine of their carefully prescribed worship hours, the one occasion when they were permitted to stay up late, the one occasion when escape might be possible.

Katharina's chest tightened with agony. She didn't want to abandon Sister Ruth, but they had run out of time. "I'm sorry, Margaret." She squeezed her friend's cold, bony fingers. "But Greta's right. We need to be far away by the summoning for Prime. We must leave now."

Katharina tugged up her habit and

gripped the rough stone. Did she dare jump? Did she really think she could sneak all nine of them out of the abbey without getting caught?

She'd prepared for this moment for days, considered every detail, from the time they would leave to the exact route. She'd even spent days prying loose the lattice window in her cell so she could remove it soundlessly on the night of their escape.

In spite of such careful planning, something could still go wrong. Anything could happen between her window and the cloister wall. And if they made it over the outer wall, Abbot Baltazar would hunt them down like hares.

The skin on her back prickled at the memory of Abbot Baltazar's whip whistling through the air and slapping against the bare flesh of the Zeschau sisters. Only yesterday he'd beaten the young women because of a letter he'd discovered hidden in one of their pallets. Communication with the outside world was severely limited to help maintain their proper focus on God. But lately the abbot had restricted their visitation rights and missives even more. He was no fool. He knew the rumors about Martin Luther and his writings had begun to make their way into convents. And after intercepting the Zeschau sisters' letter, the abbot was well aware of just how much Luther's teachings had infiltrated Marien-thron.

Of course, through the beating, the abbot had hoped to discover who had given the Zeschau sisters the letter and how. But the young women had remained silent, much to his frustration.

Katharina's stomach lurched. If a mere letter could incite him to violence, what punishment would he devise for their attempting to run away?

Fingers squeezed her shoulder tenderly. She pivoted on the ledge and found herself looking into the tear-filled eyes of Aunt Lena. The thick cell door stood open, and another one of the nuns stood guard.

"God will be with you, child," Aunt Lena whispered. Her black veil shadowed the tiredness and sadness that always seemed to etch her plump face.

"Come with us." Katharina knew her request would do little good. Aunt Lena had insisted that at age forty she was too old to leave the convent, get married, and start a new life. And now Katharina had run out of time to convince her otherwise. She stroked the woman's fleshy cheek, knowing if she escaped to freedom, she wouldn't see Aunt

Lena again.

Aunt Lena cupped Katharina's chin and pointed her face toward the plain wooden cross, the single adornment allowed in the barren cell. "Don't forget to pray."

"I won't."

She pulled Katharina's head against her ample bosom and pressed a kiss to her temple. "I love you, Katharina von Bora."

Katharina's throat constricted with an ache that rose from her chest. When had she last heard anyone speak those words? Certainly not in all the years she'd lived at Marienthron, where stoicism was commanded and affection forbidden.

Aunt Lena stepped back, her features reflecting embarrassment at her bold words. Although none of the nuns were supposed to show favoritism, Katharina had always known that her aunt cared about her. But this was the first time she had spoken words of love.

Katharina wished she could express her feelings for the woman who had replaced her mother. But even if she found the words, they couldn't slip past the tightness in her throat.

Go. Aunt Lena motioned in the sign language they often used. *No more good-byes.*

Please. Come with us. Katharina signed back.

Aunt Lena shook her head and pointed at the window.

Katharina hesitated. As the nun on night watch, Aunt Lena would be questioned about the escape. Eventually Abbot Baltazar would guess her aunt's involvement in aiding them and would discipline her. How would she survive his wrath, the beating he would surely give her?

Greta gripped Katharina's arms, her fingers digging through the layers of her habit to pinch her skin. "My lady, we're wasting time." Panic laced the servant's whisper.

Katharina nodded. The time for thinking was over.

She turned back to the window, and then with Greta's assistance she hoisted herself over the ledge so that she was hanging down the cloister wall, her cheek brushing against cold stone. Her soft leather shoes dangled just above the arched window of the first floor.

After Greta released her hold on Katharina's arms, she clung to the rocky edge for a moment, the jagged ledge scraping the tender skin of her fingers. With a whooshing breath she closed her eyes and let go.

In an instant she found herself slamming against the hard earth, the air forced out of her lungs. For a long moment in the darkness, she gasped for breath. At a thud and grunt next to her, she lifted her head to see Greta crouched beside her, struggling to catch her breath too.

"You should have waited for my assistance," she softly chided her servant as she pushed up from the ground. Pain jarred her legs and radiated to the rest of her body.

"Time is running out," Greta rasped, staggering to her feet. But the moment she straightened her petite frame, she clutched her stomach, bent over, and retched.

"What's wrong?" She touched the maidservant's arm. "Did you hurt yourself with the jump?"

Greta shrugged off her hand and spit into the grass but not before dribbling on herself. As a servant, her plain, colorless habit and wimple were not so finely woven as the habits worn by Katharina and the other nuns. But that was the only difference. They were all attired alike, their shorn hair was tucked securely out of sight, and their womanly curves were well concealed. Every bit of flesh that could be hidden was.

Only Greta's pretty face distinguished her, except now it was twisted with pain. "I'm

18

not hurt, my lady." But the moment the words were out, she bent over and retched again.

"Something ails you." Katharina cringed as her whisper echoed in the air around them. The first-floor windows of the common room in front of them were dark. Now that the nights were not so severely cold, she and the sisters had less need for the abbey's only heated room.

Nonetheless, Katharina rebuked herself to remain quiet and to communicate with signs as they'd planned, lest she alert one of the gatekeepers the abbot had charged with keeping the keys to the main gate. Even if she knew what ailed Greta, she could do nothing to help her servant now. She would have to tend Greta's need later, after they were secure.

Once again her gaze flitted to the shadows that cloaked the cloister yard. A cool breeze lifted the length of her veil. The air slithered underneath and sent chills up the back of her neck. The full moon that marked the coming of Easter hid behind a thin mist of clouds. They would be safer if it stayed there.

Greta wiped her mouth on her sleeve and turned to the window where several others stood, their white wimples gleaming too brightly against the dark building made of unevenly chiseled rocks cut from nearby hillsides. The rough stones lent an austereness that was appropriate for their Cistercian order, which affirmed poverty and banned all luxuries, including statues and colored-glass windows. Even their church was unadorned and indistinguishable from the other buildings in the complex.

Hail Mary, full of grace, the Lord is with thee. Katharina lifted the silent prayer to the Virgin Mother, the Latin words as familiar as breathing. They would need a special measure of divine help if they were to reach the walls without detection.

With quiet urgency she and Greta assisted the others being lowered from the window. All the while Katharina watched the other dormers, waiting for a flicker of candlelight. Faces seemed to lurk in the diamond lattices of each one. But every time she looked closely, she saw nothing.

When everyone was finally down and clustered around her, she motioned them to follow her. With the soft tread she'd perfected over the years, she ducked along the path between the hedgerows and led the women under the brick archway in the wall that opened into the convent's three main gardens. They kept to the outer edge and passed the latrines positioned near the vegetable beds.

She stayed as far away from the Predigerhaus as they could get but continually scanned the narrow windows of the priests' house, waiting for a flicker of light to appear behind one of the leaded panes, the signal that the two monks who lived at the convent as confessing fathers had heard them. Abbot Baltazar was still visiting and was staying in the Predigerhaus too. Although he oversaw the Pforta monastery, where the two monks had come from, he was the spiritual supervisor over Marienthron and visited regularly.

Every nerve in Katharina's body stretched tight as she willed the windows to remain dark. If nothing else alerted the monks to their presence, the pounding of her heart would. It was loud enough to awaken the saints in the graveyard.

She reminded herself again, as she had a hundred times that day whenever fear or doubt had assailed her, that she had no choice but to escape from her empty life. Of late, the desire for marriage and a family had grown so strong she was sure God Himself had put the longing there. Even stronger was the desire to know the truth about her purpose in life. She'd always been told that becoming a nun was the surest way to get to heaven. But Luther's writings that had been smuggled in spoke of faithful women, even the Virgin Mary, who had served God outside of convent walls. Luther claimed that cloistered life wasn't necessary for their souls' salvation. His words had resonated deeply within her, unearthing long-buried questions she'd never dared to ask before. Like some of her sisters of the cloth, she'd begun to ask those questions, unable to deny them any longer.

The chill in the air nipped her cheeks and nose, and the dew on the grass seeped into her shoes, stiffening her toes. Behind her the sisters moved as silently as angels. These sisters who had been her closest companions felt the same desires and pondered the same questions. They too were willing to risk everything to get what they had been denied.

She could not fail them.

When they reached the physic garden, Katharina allowed herself a breath of relief. They crept behind the low hazel fences that supported the raised herb beds, each woman slinking through the maze, following Katharina's steps. She knew the garden better than anyone. Every new bud carried her touch; every tender plant of cumin and fennel and comfrey and dozens of other herbs had seen her hand.

A sweet waft of blossoming cowslip lingered in the air as if it had come to say good-bye. Who would tend her herbs once she was gone? No one would be able to take care of them the way she had.

She wanted to linger, but she slipped by silently, past the well, until they finally reached the safety of the orchard with its canopy of apple and pear trees. Once they were concealed among the tangled branches with their tiny buds to shield them, Katharina stopped and held up a hand.

She stayed motionless like the others and hardly dared to breathe, straining to hear any indication they'd been noticed. Next to her, Margaret shifted and cracked a twig underfoot. Her cold fingers found Katharina's, and Margaret squeezed them as if to say, "Almost there."

Only the grove stood between them and the outer convent wall.

The guard at the rear gate would be breaking his fast with the beer that Merchant Koppe had given him. She hoped he'd be too busy imbibing to hear them. But they would need to be wary of the extra watchmen the abbot had appointed from among the laborers who lived and worked at the convent. Although the abbot had tried to keep their Marienthron community ignorant, they had heard whispered rumors and bits of smuggled news about other monks and nuns who'd left their convents, giving them hope they could do the same. Katharina had no doubt the abbot had increased his vigilance at both his monastery and the abbey, especially now that he'd discovered the Zeschau sisters' letter.

"This way," Katharina whispered, giving Margaret's fingers a return squeeze before letting go to sweep aside a low twig. She led them deeper into the orchard, winding through the trees, thankful most of the winter's windfall had been raked away, leaving only moist earth and moss and the scent of damp soil. She ducked under limbs and dodged low branches until they reached the thick stone wall that surrounded the cloister.

She peered up at the patchwork of stones, despairing that the wall rose higher than she remembered. A distant bark of a hound echoed in the eerily silent morning. And she crossed her arms to ward off a shiver.

Greta edged past her and pushed aside a tangle of currant vines and brush to reveal a small mound of earth. "Here," she whispered. "We climb the wall here, my lady." Greta had managed over the past week to form a hill with brush and dirt. If they worked together, they could scale the wall aided by the small mound. Greta motioned she would go over first and assist with the descent on the other side.

Standing on the mound, Katharina linked hands with Sister Margaret, and they formed a step and hoisted everyone up, first Greta and then the others. She tried not to think about the dangers that awaited them on the other side — wild boars and foxes, thieves, and unfamiliar terrain. Instead she reminded herself of the future — the real lives they would be able to lead, the noble men they would marry, the children they would bear, and the families they would finally have after so many years without.

When they finished helping everyone else, Katharina signed to Margaret. *Your turn.*

Margaret shook her head and stared into the orchard, her eyes widening to the size of Gulden coins.

Katharina followed her friend's gaze, and at the rustling and crackling of branches, her body tensed. *Holy Mary, Mother of God . . .* Someone was after them. With a burst of panic, she yanked Margaret toward the mound. "Quickly. I shall boost you over. Then you must lead the others north along the river."

Margaret's thin face pinched with worry, and she clutched Katharina's arms. "I can't leave you."

Katharina steered her toward the wall. "You must."

"We won't make it without you."

"I shall stall them and give you time."

"Wait," came a low, urgent call behind them. "It is I, Sister Ruth."

Through the tangle of branches and budding leaves came the stooped figure of a broad-girthed nun. She moved cumbersomely and was dragging something with her.

It was indeed Sister Ruth, the one she'd thought they must leave behind for want of time. Katharina barely had a second of relief before she recognized the burden Sister Ruth brought with her. The Zeschau sisters clung to the nun in their effort to walk, their faces ashen, their bodies trembling.

The two girls were young, hardly more than novices, having taken their vows of obedience, poverty, and chastity just the previous Lenten season. How much had changed in a year so that they were now forsaking those vows.

Katharina reached for Fronika and Margaret for Etta. Sister Ruth, although as strong and wide as any peasant farmer's wife, relinquished her hold on them and staggered backward, her knees buckling. Katharina slipped her arm around Fronika to hold her up, and her fingers felt the stickiness of blood oozing through the girl's habit. She reeked of the mold in the cloister prison and the sourness of urine. Her glazed eyes met Katharina's, reflecting pain and confusion, just as they had when Abbot Baltazar had forced her to kneel in the courtyard, then had bared her back and lashed her mercilessly.

Katharina swallowed her frustration at feeling helpless, just as she had when she'd been required to watch the beating. She could do nothing to assist the Zeschau sisters then. And she could do nothing now, although everything within her demanded that she do so.

"Once we are free," she murmured against Fronika's ear, "I shall take good care of you. I promise."

Under the weight of the girl, Katharina stumbled toward the wall. "How did you get them out without being seen?" she whispered to Sister Ruth.

"I don't know," the woman said, her chest heaving.

Dread pricked Katharina. She suspected Sister Ruth had not used enough caution during her trek through the cloister grounds.

"I couldn't leave without them," the older sister said, as if reading Katharina's thoughts. She sagged against the wall and mopped her brow beneath her damp forehead band.

"Everything will be all right," Margaret whispered, tenderly kissing Etta's bent head. "If we have compassion on others, surely God will have compassion on us."

Katharina couldn't answer. Even if the abbot didn't know, they all were aware of who had been smuggling the Zeschau sisters the forbidden writings of Martin Luther: Prior Zeschau, their uncle who resided in the Augustinian monastery in nearby Grimma. Most of the time during his visits, he'd only been allowed to speak with his nieces through a lattice window that was too finely meshed to permit the passage of any documents. But on several occasions he'd brought them gifts and had slipped the manuscripts and notes inside.

Of course, the Zeschau sisters had then secretly passed the documents along to others. If not for the two young women, none of them would have dared to dream about leaving the only way of life they'd ever known. But how could they expect their escape to succeed with Fronika and Etta slowing them down?

Greta's hoarse whispers from the other side of the wall urged Katharina to action. Whether or not they reached safety, Katharina couldn't abandon these sisters. For better or worse, she would help them. And if the two couldn't keep up, then she would stay behind with them and send Margaret ahead with the others.

Katharina was the last one over the thick stone wall. When her feet touched the opposite side, relief surged through her. She fell to her knees and signed the cross. *Glory be to the Father, and to the Son, and to the Holy Spirit.* She bent her head into the long grass until her lips connected with solid earth. The freshness of the recently thawed soil filled her senses with promises.

Her father had taken her away from her home when she'd been only five. For the first time in nineteen years, she was outside cloister walls. She took a deep breath of freedom, but along with the breath came a tremor of fear. An unknown world spread before her with its way of life so foreign to all that she knew.

Greta tapped her shoulder and with a jerk of her arm motioned for her to hurry. Her fair, unblemished face flashed with worry as she peered at the severe stone wall, the only thing that separated them from recapture. "Someone's awake," she whispered.

Katharina stood and listened intently. In the distance, from inside the convent, came an urgent shout. Her heart slammed against her ribs, and Greta's gaze met hers with a gravity that confirmed her worst fears.

Their escape wasn't a secret any longer. Abbot Baltazar would gather a search party. They would have horses. And they would scour the countryside for them.

How far could she and the others get before they were caught?

Two

Luther stepped out through the arched portal of the Church of Saint George, and the faint streaks of dawn greeted him in the sky above Mansfeld. The soft chatter of other parishioners exiting the Easter service swirled around him.

He drew in a deep breath of the chilled morning air and allowed himself to enjoy a rare moment of peace. Although he hadn't preached, the message had been one of grace, and the Eucharist had satisfied his hungry soul. For just a few minutes, he'd been able to forget about the constant troubles that were closing in like a net around its prey.

A hand clamped on his shoulder, and he heard the gentle voice of Melanchthon, his traveling companion for this journey. "Are you ready to break your fast?"

The rumbling in Luther's stomach told him it was past time to end his Lenten fast, although he knew he could go much longer if he wanted to. He'd done so many times during the years he'd spent in the Erfurt monastery. There he had fasted until his strength was depleted. He'd locked himself in his cell and remained there to pray until he'd grown so exhausted that his fellow brethren had to break in the door. Thankfully, those days of fear and judgment and terror over his sin were in the past.

"Let's go eat," he said, starting across the narrow street that was already busy at the early hour. The tall two- and three-story buildings were crowded together, their shutters mostly closed against the cold spring morning. The businesses and storefronts hadn't changed much in the years since he'd been a boy and had roamed the streets and gone to the common school with aspirations to become a lawyer. That urchin never would have guessed that nearly four decades later he'd return as an excommunicated monk.

Melanchthon fell into step next to him, his curly reddish hair poking out from under his low-crowned, broad-brimmed beret.

He was slightly shorter and much thinner than Luther. But what he lacked in physical endowment, he made up for in heart and intelligence.

Melanchthon's lean face and hollow eyes lent him a scholarly aura that was rare in one so young. At twenty-six Melanchthon had to keep a scruffy goatee in order to prevent others from mistaking him for one of Wittenberg's students rather than the distinguished professor of Greek language that he was.

"We must be on our way back to Wittenberg before the ringing of Terce," his friend said. "I told my wife and child I would be back to feast with them this eve." The worried glimmer in his eye revealed his words for what they were — an excuse.

Luther nodded and went along with him. "We shall get you home to your family as soon as possible, my good friend."

The truth Melanchthon didn't mention was that Luther was in grave danger everywhere he went. Although he'd limited his travels since that fateful Diet of Worms two years ago when he'd been branded a heretic by the emperor and pope, he'd decided he couldn't cower from his enemies forever, even though they still wanted him captured, dead or alive. One year at Wartburg Castle disguised as a knight had been enough hiding for him. Now that he was free of the confines, he'd begun to travel again, much to the chagrin of many of his friends.

Ahead on the street corner, a crippled beggar sat in a pitiful heap of dirty rags and lifted skeletal arms at the many people passing him by. Luther's fingers went instinctively to the purse hanging inside his scapular. The leather pouch was weightless and empty. As usual.

"I have nothing to give," he grumbled to Melanchthon.

"You're like the holy apostles," Melanchthon responded in the same conciliatory tone as always. "You may not have silver or gold, but you give something much better. Hope."

Melanchthon's words were meant to comfort him, but Luther had to stop before the beggar anyway. "Come." He lifted the man to his feet. "I know where you can get a meal."

"Doctor Luther!" called several people passing by. "There's Doctor Luther!"

Melanchthon sighed and Luther knew his friend was worried about the attention he'd drawn to himself. Nevertheless, Melanchthon stood back uncomplaining while Luther shook hands and spoke to those who surrounded him.

"Is it really true that I don't need to buy an indulgence to free my son from purgatory?" called a stoop-shouldered man clothed in rags almost as filthy as the beggar's.

"It's really true," Luther responded. "The archbishop charges you so he can increase his coffers. But God's mercy is not for sale. It's free."

Only with Melanchthon's gentle prodding did Luther finally move forward with the beggar still firmly in his grasp. When they entered the inn, Luther settled the man at a corner table but was himself once again surrounded by crowds. As he seated himself next to Melanchthon on a bench, the table rapidly filled with townsmen eager to speak with him.

After quenching his thirst, Luther lifted his tankard, signaling the innkeeper for a refill. In the dimness and haze of hearth smoke, the innkeeper nodded and began to squeeze his way through the swell of bodies around Luther's table.

"I agree with what everyone is saying," Luther said to his companions. "There's no easy solution to the problem. But we can't let the devil stop us from doing the work of God."

"What if emptying the cloisters is merely the work of Martin Luther and not of God?" asked one of the Mansfeld provosts sitting opposite him, his fur-trimmed

Schaube hanging loosely over his shoulders. The question sparked another round of loud remarks.

The room had a low-beamed ceiling and dark walls and was lit by several flickering sconces. A cool breeze attempted to make its way through two small windows whose shutters were thrown open to the early morning, but it couldn't penetrate the air around Luther, which had grown stale and sour.

Irritation nagged him as it did every time he had to discourse with wealthy noblemen who thought they knew best. Why did they think their titles made them better than an average man like himself?

"If emptying the cloisters is merely the work of Martin Luther," he said above the boisterous voices that filled the inn, "then you won't have to bear the guilt for dumping two of your daughters in the Wiederstedt convent. Right, Herr Kohler?"

"I've sacrificed them to God for a life of service and worship. How could that be wrong?"

"Did you ask your daughters if they wanted to worship in such a way?" Before they could respond, he continued. "God wants worship that is given freely, not forced." The innkeeper reached the table and pushed a plate of cold salted herring, bread, and cheese before Luther and then refilled his mug. The man wouldn't expect payment. He never did. Luther knew the extra customers he attracted with his visits were payment enough.

The greasy odor of fried fish made his stomach gurgle. He nodded at Melanchthon next to him, but his friend shook his head, declining the invitation to share the meal.

Melanchthon was content to sit back and let Luther do all the fighting and take the fame and the food. His friend's kind eyes begrudged him nothing.

Luther wrapped his cold hands around his mug. He couldn't deny he relished the fight that Melanchthon was all too willing to abdicate.

"The cloistered life is one of privilege for our daughters," another wealthy burgher said. "Where else will our daughters learn to sing the psalms, read and write, and speak Latin?"

"They're mostly learning that the church will use them to fulfill the lusts of the priests who oversee their souls." Luther's remark brought guffaws as well as loud protests. But he'd seen firsthand enough abuse to know the men protested in vain. They blinded themselves in order to soothe their guilt — guilt for subjecting their daughters to the whim of every priestly overseer while they freed themselves from financial obligation.

He took a long swig of his beer and then spoke over his comrades again. "Everyone knows the abbeys have become nothing more than common brothels. You would do well to risk your goods and your life to get your daughters out of such places."

"Then we're back to our same problem," said Johann Ledener, vicar of the Church of Saint George, who'd preached the Easter message. "What shall we do with the monks and nuns who wish to leave the cloistered life? The monks have no skills. The nuns have no marriageable prospects."

"As I said, there are no easy solutions." Luther picked up his knife and stabbed it into his herring. "But I will say this: let the monks learn a trade and let the nuns marry whom they will."

One of the barons slammed his hand on the table, rattling tankards. Several other men roared oaths.

Luther lifted the piece of fish and twirled it. He knew what he was proposing was radical. The unbreakable boundaries between classes had been in place for centuries. But just as he'd questioned so many other practices, perhaps it was time to question this one as well. "What's wrong with arranging a marriage for your daughter outside your class? If you can't afford a dowry that will bring a noble match, then you must consider other godly men even if they are humbler in status."

Melanchthon nudged him and nodded in the direction of the door.

Luther followed his friend's gaze to the broad shoulders of his father, who was making his way through the crowd. His stomach cinched as tight as the cincture he wore over his tunic, and his knife slipped from his fingers, the piece of fish untouched. He slid the plate into the hands of one of the young merchants sitting near him. "Eat it. It's yours."

He pushed himself off the bench and stood, trying not to hang his head like an errant boy in need of the rod.

"*Ach,* so here is my son." The voice of his father carried above the clamor as he elbowed his way past those standing around the table. "I should've known he'd eat at the inn instead of going home to break fast with his family."

"Good day, Father."

"You didn't say good-bye to your mother." His father peered up at him, his brows puckered together above his long nose and his lips pressed into a tight line. His face was washed and free of the soot of the mines, as were his hose and cloak. At such an early hour, however, there was a haggardness in his expression that made his jowls droop.

Born the son of a peasant, Hans Luther had labored hard over the years to better his position in the community. His marriage into the burgher middle class and a relative's money had afforded him the opportunity to invest in the copper mines. With the endless hours and sweat of his back, his father had eventually leased mines and smelting furnaces. For a time the mines had made him a wealthy man. That had helped pay for Luther's education to become a lawyer, the education he'd thrown away when he'd entered the monastery.

But the mining industry had fallen on hard times in recent years. Now the output of the smelters wasn't enough for his father to pay his debts. Hans had grown more disgruntled. And Luther's visits to Mansfeld had become even less pleasant and filled him with more guilt for all the ways he'd failed his father. Though his father had long ago grudgingly accepted his life being devoted to the church, first as a monk and then as a professor of theology in Wittenberg, Luther had never been able to shake the feeling that he'd let his father down. Just this past weekend during his visit with his parents and extended family, he'd felt his father's censure, though he doubted his father realized he'd given it.

"Join us, Hans," said the vicar, making room on the bench next to him. "And tell us your opinion on the matter of monks and nuns leaving their convents."

For several long moments the conversation buzzed again, and Luther had no choice but to resume his spot at the table, even though his head had begun to pound. He respected his father too much to abandon him, but such conversations usually left him keenly aware of his shortcomings all over again.

"Other monks are getting married. But my son, will he?" Hans Luther said, smacking his lips after a long drink of his beer. "If only he knew the pleasures he is missing."

The men laughed.

Blood rushed to Luther's face. "I'm too busy."

"My son's always too busy. Too busy to give his old father an heir to pass on the family name."

"Should a man condemned to death take

a wife?" Luther strained to keep his tone respectful. "Once I'm captured, my enemies will burn me at the stake. Why would I want to leave behind a widow and children? The devil only knows what kind of torture my enemies would devise for my family."

At Luther's words his father's face blanched. Hans took a sip from his tankard, his Adam's apple protruding as he struggled to swallow the drink.

Guilt ripped through Luther, and he bowed his head. He knew his father loved him and only wanted the best for him. But it seemed as though their relationship was forever to be one of disappointment and hurt.

At the clatter of a tankard and a strangled cry, Luther's head jerked up in time to see the young merchant to whom he'd given his meal fall backward off the bench. The crowd parted to make room for him on the ground as he convulsed, his lips white and his face turning blue from lack of air.

"Get the physician," someone called.

A man kneeling next to the merchant reached for the piece of fish discarded among the rushes. He sniffed it, tasted it with the tip of his tongue, then flung it back to the floor. "It's poisoned."

The pounding in Luther's head came to

an abrupt halt. Silence held him captive as he stared at the lolling gray tongue and bulging eyes of the merchant, each ragged breath possibly his last.

Luther's hands began to shake, and he tucked them into his cuffs. "God have mercy." He looked at the mass of flushed faces, searching each one. The devil was there somewhere.

"Poison?" His father's voice boomed over the clamor. "Why on God's green earth would anyone want to poison Herr Muller?"

A small drum began tapping in Luther's head again, growing louder, beating against his temples until he wanted to groan with the pressure. Death stalked him everywhere he rode, in every town he visited, at every corner he turned. His enemies never ceased plotting his demise.

But this time death had come too close . . .

It had been only one bite away.

THREE

In the faint light of dawn, Katharina examined the unfamiliar landscape, the newly plowed fields, the peasant huts in the distance. It had been years since she'd viewed the world surrounding the convent.

Now she could see that Marienthron was situated in a lush valley, protected by hills on one side and dense forest on the other. She knew the abbey owned most of the land in the surrounding countryside, gained over the decades as payment from noblemen who had placed their daughters at the convent. The abbot commanded compulsory labor from the peasants who lived on it. He ruled over them like a prince and brought in a steady income to support the convent.

"Merchant Koppe's message instructed us to travel through the forest," Katharina whispered, glancing across the pasture. Along its edge tall evergreens jutted high against the thinly veiled moon. "We need to follow the river Mulde north of Grimma. He'll meet us at the crossroads."

The yells within the cloister yard echoed louder in the crisp air. The other women had plastered themselves against the convent wall and now watched her with frightened eyes. They were like sheep with her as their shepherd. She wasn't sure how she'd gained that role, but she was determined to lead them as best she could.

"Run." Katharina's muscles tensed. "Run as fast as you can for the woods."

Greta bolted forward, leading the way. With their scapulars and veils flying behind them, the others ran after the maidservant, losing all concern for silence in their haste.

Sister Ruth hoisted one of the Zeschau sisters onto her wide back like a sack of kindling wood. Katharina reached for the other. She was too petite to carry the young woman, but she slipped her arm around the sister and half dragged, half carried her forward. After only two dozen paces, Katharina's breath came in gasps, and the woods loomed no closer.

"Faster!" Greta called over her shoulder, far ahead of the others.

Like Katharina, the other nuns had never moved beyond the slow, thoughtful walk that behooved the contemplative life of a nun. They couldn't help but trip over clods of soil, stumble through the tangle of their tunics, and sob in fear as they raced for the cover of the woods.

Under the weight of Fronika Zeschau, Katharina lagged behind. She didn't want to put Margaret in more danger, but she was grateful when her friend rushed back to her and silently took the other side of the girl, easing Katharina's burden. Even if Katharina had wanted to admonish Margaret to stay with the others, she couldn't speak past the burning in her lungs.

Finally the forest swallowed them. Branches slapped and roots snagged. But Greta, in the lead, didn't slacken her pace. Panic gave them momentum to fight the undergrowth that clawed at their habits and the sharp rocks that bit through their slippers.

The river Mulde served as their guide. Although they could no longer hear the shouts, they knew that Abbot Baltazar was somewhere nearby and that he wouldn't rest until he tracked them down.

When the forest gave way to a clearing around the cloister pond, they crumpled to the ground, unable to go on without a rest.

Katharina couldn't feel the chill in the

grass past the heat roaring through her blood and the sweat dampening her face and plastering her tunic to her back. Her muscles cramped, and her arms and legs shook. Margaret sprawled next to her, silent of any complaints, but each wheezing breath was a testimony to the exertion. For endless seconds they lay unmoving, their cacophony of labored breaths mingling with the croaking of the recently awakened spring frogs.

Katharina pressed the ache in her side and felt for the pouch she'd hidden under her habit. It contained her only earthly treasure, the one gift she had of value and her only connection to the life that had been snatched from her so long ago.

In the vast sky overhead, the clouds were tinged with the pale pink glow of dawn. Would this finally be the beginning of a new life? Did she dare to believe it was within her grasp?

Nearby branches crackled, then crashed to the ground.

Katharina's blood froze as several men lurched into the clearing.

Margaret sat up and started to gasp, but Katharina cupped a hand over her friend's mouth.

The first hints of pale light outlined the hard countenances of the men beneath their straw hats. They wore the coarse linen of a laborer: short belted tunics and low boots secured with laces. Since they were carrying hoes and spades, she guessed they were the peasants who worked the fields surrounding the abbey.

"Well, well," said one of the men, stepping forward. "What do we have here?"

There was something hard and dangerous in the man's tone that made Katharina's limbs tremble. Nevertheless, she stood as gracefully as she could and straightened her shoulders. "You may continue on your way. We are not your concern."

"Not our concern?" The man chortled as he lumbered closer. "Of course we're concerned." With a lunge he grabbed Margaret and jerked her to her feet.

A whimper slipped from Margaret, and her frantic eyes found Katharina's.

"Unhand her and leave her be," Katharina said, attempting to keep a quaver from her voice.

" 'Leave her be,' she says." With a curse the peasant threw Margaret aside and stalked toward Katharina.

She didn't have time to react before the laborer gripped her arm and jerked her against him so that his breath bathed her face with the stench of strong beer. "You telling me what to do?"

"We are nuns, the brides of Christ. It's your God-given duty to protect and honor us."

"Did you hear that, boys?" The man tossed his friends a gap-toothed grin. "It's our *duty* to protect these rich, thieving church whores."

The other laborers hooted with laughter and crept nearer, forming a half circle around the nuns, who had clustered into a shivering huddle.

Church whores. Katharina's insides twisted at the insult — twisted because people thought of them that way and twisted because she knew there was some truth to the accusation. As much as she wanted to ignore the whispers of indiscretions, there had been too many stories along with unexplained disappearances of sisters and workers. None of her closest companions spoke of such abuse happening to them, but she was sure more of them had experienced the pain than had admitted to it.

She wouldn't let her friends experience abuse. Not here. Not this way.

"Be on your way," Katharina commanded, hoping her voice sounded more confident than she felt. She cast a frantic glance to the thick brush and woods beyond the pond. Could she find a way to escape these men, or were the women destined to be ravaged and abused on the doorstep of the convent?

"You won't be going anywhere." The peasant's fingers groped her habit, sinking into her soft flesh and sending revulsion to the pit of her stomach. "Not until we have a little fun with you."

He yanked on her scapular, ripping it free of her habit with a sickening tear. The rending of linen incited the other men, and in an instant they landed upon her helpless sisters. Their laughter mingled with the women's cries.

Panic twisted Katharina as tightly as flax fibers on a spindle. She pummeled her captor. The horrified calls of the others spurred her — she had to rescue her weaker sisters. "Take me, but let the others go!"

The peasant's knuckles slammed into the side of Katharina's face. Excruciating pain forced her to her knees. Blackness swirled in front of her. Before she could move, the peasant forced her backward so that her head slammed against the ground.

"For the sake of His sorrowful passion," she screamed, "have mercy on us and on the whole world." A familiar powerlessness blanketed her. She'd been at the mercy of

50

others her whole life, and here she was once again without the ability to control her own fate.

"Stop!" A voice rang through the chaos. A tall man with a pike strode forward out of the brush and crossed through the long-dried grass, his face a mask of fury. He swung his pike at the peasant holding Greta with such force that it hit the man's arm with a crunch. The peasant yelped and fell away.

"Get off the women!" the newcomer shouted.

"Why do you care?" The man holding Katharina peered at the tall man but didn't seem surprised to see him. She seized the moment of hesitation and clawed her captor's face. He cried out and reared back.

She scrambled away from him, and her fingers closed around his discarded hoe. Grasping it, she heaved herself up. With a fury born of desperation, she lunged at the other men, beating them away from the sisters.

Howling and cursing, the laborers backed to the edge of the clearing. Katharina gasped for breath and turned toward the tall man, who was holding Greta against his body and was smothering her lips with his.

"Release her at once!" Katharina demanded, lifting the hoe and aiming it at the man's head. Her breath came in gasps.

Greta broke away from the kiss. "Don't hurt him, my lady," she said, turning and shielding the man with her arms. Her wimple had fallen off so that her short-cropped hair was free of constraint. The soft, fair waves fell around her face, adding a fullness that made the girl even prettier.

"This is Thomas, Merchant Koppe's servant," Greta said, glancing over her shoulder with tenderness. The man was muscular and had chiseled features that were rugged and handsome for a commoner. Thomas stroked Greta's cheek in response.

Katharina shifted her attention away, embarrassment making a swift path through her. She'd heard rumors of Greta forming an attachment to the merchant's servant during his deliveries to the convent, she but hadn't imagined such familiarity. She'd wanted to believe her servant was as chaste as herself, although she wasn't naive enough to think that such liaisons couldn't happen.

At the grumbling of the other peasants, Thomas shot them a narrowed look, one that silenced them. "We're done with our meeting for the night," he said bluntly. "Time to go home."

Katharina lowered the hoe and twisted the wooden handle made smooth from years of hard use. It was Easter morn. These laborers certainly weren't heading to work today of all days. So why did they have their hoes and spades? At such an early hour of the morning no less?

"We should go," Greta whispered with a furtive glance in the direction of the convent.

"Yes," Katharina said. "Take us at once to your master, Thomas."

Through the growing light of morning, he regarded her with a piercing coldness and animosity she couldn't begin to understand. She tried not to shiver, even though all she wanted to do was sink to the ground and give way to violent trembling. Instead, she began pulling the others to their feet, encouraging them softly.

They had lost too much time. And with all the noise from their encounter with the peasants, surely they'd alerted Abbot Baltazar to their whereabouts. As if sensing the same, Thomas bade a curt farewell to the laborers and then led the women rapidly away, taking them deeper into the woods. If not for Thomas's sure steps, she wouldn't have noticed the nearly invisible path. She couldn't keep from wondering how Thomas was so familiar with the woods and what his connection was with the other peasants.

As she struggled along, her lungs burned and her legs grew weak. Under Fronika's weight, she was tempted to drop to the ground and rest, and she had to keep reminding herself why they were risking so much. They'd destroyed Doctor Luther's smuggled writings as soon as they'd read them, but his words were seared into her mind: *Priests, monks, nuns are duty bound to forsake their vows. . . . Their vows of chastity are contrary to God and have no validity. Marriage is not only honorable but necessary. . . . Men and women, who were created for it, shall be found in this estate.*

Those words had awakened desires that had been forced into slumber when she'd understood the reality of her destiny those many years ago — the reality that she'd lost her family and would never have one again. The closing of the convent gates had slammed shut the possibility of having a normal life or any semblance of freedom. She'd known she would live and die a virgin, without ever experiencing the joys that came from married life and bearing children. And she'd done her best to accept the fate that had been handed to her. She'd believed that becoming a nun was the surest way to reach heaven.

But the power of Martin Luther's writing had resurrected her desires. Now they burned inside, pushing her forward, compelling her into danger, urging her to risk even death.

When Thomas finally halted, they collapsed to the ground once again, breathing hard and perspiring from the exertion that was uncommon for their sedentary life.

After a moment voices carried through the foliage. Katharina strained to hear above the ragged breathing of the others.

"Then I guess you won't mind my servants searching your wagons." It was the nasally voice she had hoped never to hear again.

Holy Mary — she signed the cross and fought rising panic — *Mother of God, pray for us sinners now and at the hour of our death.*

Abbot Baltazar had tracked them down.

Katharina's fingers dug into the moss. Daylight was growing, but within the thick shelter of spruce and fir, darkness covered them. She could only pray that morning would take its time in arriving.

"All we've got are empty herring barrels," Leonard Koppe was saying. "I've been delivering goods to your convent for years, Father. Haven't I been trustworthy? What have I done to make you think I'd be party to a capital crime now?"

"One of the escaped is your niece." Abbot Baltazar's tone was condescending, just as it had been when he'd admonished the Zeschau sisters to repent.

"My brother's child isn't my concern."

"Perhaps you're the holy saint I've always believed," Abbot Baltazar said. "If you haven't sinned and have nothing to hide, then you won't mind lifting the tarps and letting us take a look."

"Then perhaps you won't mind finding a new merchant to bring your beer."

"Now, Merchant Koppe, don't take offense. Salvation is at stake. I know you wouldn't want to be a party to sending souls to their eternal punishment."

"Of course I wouldn't."

Katharina glanced around the dense tangle of branches and brush, gauging the best way to escape if they should need to run. Next to her Fronika Zeschau whimpered softly. Sister Ruth, crouched on the other side, quickly cupped a hand over the girl's mouth.

"If you aren't here at this hour helping my nuns escape, then why are you here?" At Abbot Baltazar's pointed question, Katharina closed her eyes and prayed Merchant Koppe had a ready excuse.

"I gave my servant the night off to go about his pleasuring," the merchant said, sounding frustrated. "He's agreed to meet me and my nephew here at first light, and then we're to be on our way. We've a long day's ride if we're to reach Torgau in time to feast on the sow my Frau is roasting."

"Then while you wait for his arrival, you surely can't oppose my men searching your wagons."

Merchant Koppe grumbled through the noise of Abbot Baltazar's men boarding the wagons and overturning barrels.

Katharina knew she would need to thank Martin Luther for sending Merchant Koppe. Apparently the man was not only a trusted supporter but a good actor.

Thomas put a finger to his lips and motioned for them to remain where they were. Then he retreated soundlessly through the woods the way they had just come. A moment later Katharina heard him break through the brush down the road from where they hid.

"There's Thomas now," Merchant Koppe said. "Get out of my wagons, and tie down the tarps. I hope you're satisfied. Maybe from now on you'll believe my word."

"You're truly a good man, Merchant

Koppe." Abbot Baltazar's voice was tight. "But for the sake of eternity, I know you won't mind if I question your servant."

Katharina scrunched her eyes closed and began another round of Hail Marys. Next to her Margaret shivered, and Katharina guessed it was from fear more than from the lingering chill.

"Thomas, Abbot Baltazar claims some of his nuns have left the cloister tonight. If you know anything about the matter, I'm sure our abbot would reward you handsomely."

"I saw a group of nuns back by the pond," Thomas replied, "and some fellows were having fun with them. 'Course I didn't want any part of causing those sisters to break their vows of celibacy, so I gave the men the tip of my pike."

"I've listened to confessions long enough" — Abbot Baltazar's tone grew impatient — "that I can recognize a lie when I hear one."

"It's God's honest truth."

"God knows peasants out at this time of night are either fornicating or plotting rebellion," the abbot insisted and then barked orders for his men to get off the wagons and to remount their horses. "Merchant Koppe, if I find out your servant has fornicated with my nuns, I'll personally castrate him."

"If he's fornicated with your nuns, I'll castrate him first."

From the diminishing clatter, Katharina knew Abbot Baltazar and his men had turned their horses in the direction of the cloister pond. In another moment the forest was silent except for the distant echo of horse hoofs in the air.

Katharina held her breath and waited, her empty stomach growling like a wolf. What would Abbot Baltazar do when he discovered they weren't at the pond anymore?

"All's clear," Thomas called from the road. "Get on the wagons. Fast."

They climbed through the thicket and ran to the wagons. The teams of stout draft horses stomped, ready to be away from the dark forest with its constantly moving shadows.

"Hurry, hurry," Merchant Koppe urged as he, his nephew, and Thomas lifted them into the wagon beds. Beneath the brims of their berets, their eyes darted to the road and woods. Katharina was sure they were thinking about what would happen if they were caught aiding the escape of a nun. They all knew the punishment could be death.

The last one aboard, Katharina crawled behind the barrels. She sat next to the others and waited as Merchant Koppe finished tying down the tarp. With the heavy covering it took only minutes for the air to grow stale with the smell of salted herring and beer, but after the harrowing trek through the woods, the rest was welcome.

When the wagons began rolling across the rutted road, Katharina whispered the Glory Be. They'd made it. They'd done their part. Now the rest was in God's hands. She could only hope that the bruises from the bumpy wagon ride would be the worst of the trouble to come in the long day ahead of them.

They had not gone far when Greta began to retch with dry heaves. When she finished, Katharina brushed a finger against the girl's cheek, signing, *What ails you?*

Greta shook her head, then leaned back.

Katharina rubbed Greta's arm, hoping to convey her concern. But Greta only released a long sigh and closed her eyes, clearly weary. As when they'd jumped from the window of the abbey, Katharina again had the sense that something was wrong with Greta.

Margaret leaned closer, her angular chin bumping Katharina's ear. "I've heard rumors." Margaret's voice was so soft that Katharina could barely hear it above the clanking of wagon wheels. "It's said she has baby sickness."

Katharina glanced at the silhouette of her maid. Greta was with child? Katharina shook her head. She wanted to deny that it was true. And yet she'd witnessed for herself the intimacy between Greta and Thomas. It was possible that they had found ways to be alone, however challenging that would have been in the busy convent.

In the dimness caused by the tarp, Katharina gazed with fondness at the slight wisp of a girl who'd been her servant for many years, one of her father's gifts to her when she'd taken her vows. They weren't friends, not in the least. That wasn't to be expected of a nobly born woman and a peasant. Nevertheless, she cared about Greta as a teacher would for a student.

If Greta truly was with child, she would have a difficult time ahead of her. She certainly wouldn't be able to continue as Katharina's servant. In fact, she likely wouldn't be able to find work anywhere. She'd become an outcast with little chance of survival. Unless of course she married the father of her child.

Katharina's spine stiffened with resolution. If they made it to safety without being captured and if they lived to see the dawn of another day, she would make sure a wedding was the first order of business.

FOUR

They were going to kill him. It wasn't a matter of *if*. It was a matter of *when*.

The cold wood floor pressed against Luther's hot cheek and against his trembling limbs. If his enemies had almost succeeded with a piece of poisoned fish, then they would surely get him with drink next time.

Another wave of dizziness crashed over him. A black tide swept him under, pulling him further into the abyss.

"Brother Martinus, can you hear me?"

The voices above him sounded faint, far away.

If only he could just die now and forgo the torture and public display he was sure to endure.

"He's having one of his episodes."

Luther struggled to push himself upward, but the devil stomped down on top of him. He fell again to the floor, its solidness his only comfort.

He had barely escaped the attempt on his life — but for what? He'd just returned from Mansfeld when he received a letter informing him that his benefactor and protector, Elector Frederick, was ill. Luther knew his archenemy, Duke George, was waiting just over the Saxony border, biding his time until the old elector died. The duke was interested in more than increasing his land holdings. He wanted Martin Luther — dead or alive.

Maybe Luther had been a fool to think he could withstand princes and pope alike. What mortal man had ever accomplished such a feat? Not the martyrs of the past. Not Hus or Savonarola. The pope had tortured them and burned them at the stake for much less than he'd done.

Besides, even if the elector survived another illness, lately all they'd done is disagree. It wouldn't take much more for his benefactor to hand him over to his enemies.

The burden was heavy — much too heavy. Too many people depended on him, looked to him for answers, for direction, for help. What if he failed them?

Luther caught his breath. *If God is for us, who can be against us?* The words from Romans whispered through the deafening noise that filled every corner of his mind.

"Doctor Luther, can you hear me?" The voice of his faithful manservant sounded nearer.

Luther raised himself to his elbows and shook his head, trying to clear the dizziness and the clamoring. *"If God is for us, who can be against us?"* The words grew louder. The thudding of his heart against his chest began to slow to a steady tap.

"The merchant Koppe and his nephew are here." Wolfgang knelt beside him, his dark bushy brows furrowed into a scowling V. "I told them to come back later when you're feeling better, but they insist on seeing you."

Luther pushed himself up. His black habit was coated with dust from the floor. Wolfgang and Brother Gabriel crouched shoulder to shoulder over him, their faces etched with anxiety.

"It's the devil again." Luther dragged in a deep breath of the chilled, musty air. "He's wrestling me down."

Brother Gabriel placed a warm mug in his shaking hands. "Take this." With his wrinkled, veined hands, he guided the mug and steadied it as Luther took a sip. The light fruity flavor burned as he swallowed, but it was a comforting heat.

The darkness in Luther's head began to

fade, and the reality of where he was began to push into his consciousness. "I despise myself for this weakness."

"You're a great threat to the devil's work, Doctor Luther," Wolfgang said. "And the greater the threat, the greater his attack."

Brother Gabriel cupped his hands around Luther's, raised the mug again, and supported it as he put it to Luther's lips. "Another sip." His voice never rose above a whisper.

Luther obeyed. Brother Gabriel had distilled the *Obstwasser* in the monastery's brewery. He'd brought the secret recipe with him when he'd arrived at the Black Cloister. Luther didn't know what the drink contained other than apples and pears. He didn't care as long as the old brother kept making it. The drink seared his throat and chest and chased the lingering demons from his mind. How long had he fought the devil this time? A glance at the small, high window told him darkness had settled.

Wolfgang rose. "So what would you like me to tell Koppe of Torgau?"

"Merchant Koppe is here?"

The servant nodded, his thick black hair poking up in disarray.

"Well, why didn't you say so, Wolfgang?" Luther stood and groaned at the stiffness of his limbs. Brother Gabriel took an arm and stabilized him. In the narrow cell Luther had converted into his study, there was hardly room to maneuver, especially with his stacks of papers everywhere.

"How long has Koppe been waiting?"

Wolfgang brushed rapidly at the dust that covered Luther's habit. "They arrived at the ringing of Vespers."

"They?"

"Koppe and his nephew." Wolfgang straightened the hood of Luther's cowl. "I told them to go away."

Luther batted at Wolfgang's hand. "Let me go make my apologies, and let's all pray he'll still be kind enough to leave us the usual supplies."

His back ached. His legs moved too slowly. At forty he was an old man.

Wolfgang picked up a thick candle that dripped tallow on the floor and then started into the hallway. "Merchant Koppe has more than supplies this time."

"We'll gratefully take whatever he has," Luther replied.

The servant shook his head firmly. "We shouldn't take his delivery. Not this time. Merchant Koppe has brought a wagonload of illegal cargo."

Illegal cargo? The stiffness evaporated

from Luther's limbs, replaced by excitement. After his plea for help, had Koppe finally turned himself into a criminal? With the beginning of a grin, Luther passed by his servant and started toward the winding steps of the tower.

"I don't think they should stay," Wolfgang called.

Luther's footsteps echoed off the high ceiling and stone walls as he descended the stairs two at a time.

"Any one of them could pose a threat to your safety."

"Come now, Wolfgang," Luther called over his shoulder. "I thought I was the only one with a wild imagination."

Wolfgang chased after him citing a dozen other reasons why he should send the merchant on his way. But when Luther reached the bottom of the three flights of stairs, he pushed aside the voice of reason warning him, calling him to sanity. He strode down the hallway toward the front entry of the monastery, passing the infirmary and the refectory. Both were in disarray because they were seldom used anymore, much like the rest of the building.

He stepped into the square parlor with a ready smile. "Merchant Koppe, my partner in crime —" He halted so abruptly that

Wolfgang bumped into him from behind.

The plain, sparsely furnished room was crowded with nuns. Some sat on the stone floor, some rested on benches, and others stood.

"Our Lord have mercy." Luther gaped at the pale faces that greeted him. "How many are there?"

"Doctor Luther, it's about time." Koppe hefted his bulky frame off one of the wall benches, removing his beret.

The women rose to their feet too, quickly tucking their hands out of sight and diverting their eyes to the floor. Black veils still covered their tight wimples and starkly outlined faces coated with the grime of travel. Their once-white habits were now disheveled and dusty.

"As you can see, we have finally arrived. By no small miracle, mind you." Koppe approached Luther and pumped his hand. The merchant's jerkin was stylishly slashed to reveal the leather doublet underneath. Bright lining bulged out of the splits in his plunder pants. His ostentatious attire provided the only color in the room.

Luther rapidly counted each head and swallowed his astonishment. "Are there nine?"

"We started with twelve. But three, including my own niece, I've already delivered to the safety of their families, who are willing to take them."

Luther nodded. He would write letters and pray that more of the fathers would heed his advice to take back their daughters. For what would he do with nine runaway nuns? Two or three he could help. But *nine*? How would he find homes and husbands for all of them?

One young girl swayed, clearly tired or injured, and a petite nun next to her slid her arm around the girl's waist, bracing her. The petite nun murmured a word of encouragement before turning startling blue eyes wide with expectation upon him.

Compassion stirred deep inside. He would do all he could to help them. He was responsible for their predicament. He'd been the one to encourage them to leave. Had he not instructed all priests, monks, and nuns to forsake their vows? They'd only done what he'd preached.

The church had forced them to deny the God-created desires and dreams woven into the very fabric of their bodies. Luther had come to the conclusion — contrary to the teaching of the church that praised a monastic life — that God had not made many for singleness. The nature and functions of their bodies testified to the naturalness of marriage, as did Scripture itself.

"I cannot deny I'm relieved it's over," said the merchant, mopping his brow and giving off a sour odor, a testimony to the amount he'd recently perspired. "There was more than one occasion when I feared I would not get my first taste of pork since before Lent."

"I commend you, Koppe." Luther turned to his friend. "You've done a new work that will be remembered by the country and the people."

"Now, Doctor Luther, we both know if word of my involvement in this escapade spreads, this could be very bad for my business."

"Certainly some will scream and consider it a great detriment, but others who are on God's side will praise it as being of great benefit."

"Let's hope our wise Elector Frederick will see it as a benefit."

Luther shrugged. Their ruler was never predictable or easy to understand. So far he'd tolerated the rebellion, mainly because Luther had brought notoriety to his Wittenberg University — not to mention more students and thus more money. If the elector handed Luther over to the emperor and the pope, the elector's dreams of having a great university would come to naught. Duke George's rival Leipzig University would be superior.

"We'll leave the consequences of our crimes in God's hands, Koppe." Luther clamped a hand on the man's thick shoulder. "In the meantime the least I can do is offer you and your companions a meal."

"We've traveled hard all day and would be grateful."

Luther grinned. "I can *offer*. But you must do the providing."

Koppe's brows shot up, and he rubbed a hand over his beard.

"We have nothing," Luther admitted, "except for the new provisions you have brought us."

"What happened to the stores I gave you last time?"

"He gives to any poor soul who comes to the door," Wolfgang grumbled. "And now apparently he's planning to shelter them as well."

"If Koppe has dared to risk his life for these women who have been wronged," Luther said, "then I can do no less myself, especially if Koppe will bless us with the provisions we need."

Luther waited calmly in the silence that

followed. How long would it take for Koppe to give in this time? His friend was generous, although perhaps not as openhanded as he himself. But Luther could always count on Koppe for aid.

"Very well," said Koppe. "I was planning to sell my load tomorrow at market. But I'll give it to you instead."

"We're grateful for your generosity."

"Mind you, as long as I get a mug or two of Brother Gabriel's Obstwasser."

Luther nodded at the stooped, frail form of Brother Gabriel in the gloom of the hallway as silent and unobtrusive as always. "Obstwasser we have."

As Koppe gave instructions for his men to unload the wagons, Luther took a deep breath and turned to face the nuns. In the years since he'd taken his vows, he'd had almost no contact with women and even fewer occasions to converse with them. He'd never been good at talking with the fairer sex. In fact, he had memories of making a donkey of himself, especially during his law school days. But the compassion that swelled again prodded him to issue some words of comfort.

"My sisters in Christ," he began, "welcome to Wittenberg and to your freedom."

A few heads lifted with slight traces of

smiles. Although the petite nun with the blue eyes remained serious, she boldly met his gaze again from where she was settling the lay sister on a bench.

"It took great courage to break free of the chains that have held you in bondage," he said. "And although you're safe for the present behind the walls of the Black Cloister, I don't know what will happen once word of your presence here spreads." They were all in grave danger and would likely face excommunication and persecution. But he wouldn't scare them with that news yet.

"Dear sisters, I promise to do my best to help each of you. If your families are unable or unwilling to receive you back, then I'll attempt to find you suitable husbands or homes of employ."

More of them smiled.

Some of the tension eased from his shoulders. Maybe he wasn't so bad at relating to women after all. There was no sense in frightening them with the facts that most of the former monks had already married and that very few noblemen would marry them without a dowry.

"In the meantime you'll stay here. And while we have meager supplies, whatever we have is yours."

"Forgive me, Doctor Luther." The blue-eyed nun stepped forward. The light from the wall sconce illuminated a purplish-green bruise coloring one of her cheeks. In spite of the mar, she had a pretty, heart-shaped face with high cheekbones and an elegant nose. "I cannot help but question the wisdom of housing a group of nuns in a place belonging to men. Would it not be scandalous, even sinful?"

Wolfgang cleared his throat as though to agree.

The nun's gaze was unrelenting and made Luther squirm like a schoolboy. At least he wanted to convince himself that it was her intensity and not her loveliness that made him squirm.

"I'm the only one left here at the monastery, along with old Brother Gabriel and my manservant, Wolfgang." He nodded first at the wrinkled old monk and then at his dark-haired manservant, who hovered nearby with the ferocity of a mother bear. "We'll sleep in the loft in the barn while you're here."

She nodded. "Very well."

Just "very well"? No "thank you"? Perhaps he should have told her that she and her friends could sleep in the barn. He swallowed the words.

"Since you're willing to share whatever

you have," she continued, "then I must ask for a few specific medicinal herbs."

Her tone pricked him.

"I must have comfrey — a fresh cutting if possible. And also herb Robert — the whole plant minus the root. And if not the whole plant, then I would have dried yarrow instead."

Luther stared at her. Even if her lips had a pleasant curve, the set of her mouth and chin had the bearing of aristocracy.

"Further, I shall need a small amount of honey and chamomile."

Did she think that she was better than he was, that she could come into his home and order him around? He straightened to his full height and puffed his chest. "What's your name?"

She hesitated, then lifted her chin. "Katharina von Bora."

"Ah, von Bora. A knight's daughter?"

She nodded without casting down her glance as the others had done.

"A noble knight," he continued, unable to keep the sarcasm from his voice. He might not fight with his fists, but he'd perfected his words. He could easily show this titled woman that she was no match for him.

"No doubt," he continued caustically, "your knightly father could no longer collect his rents or pay his debts. To ease the burden of his failing wealth, he dumped his young daughter into the nearest convent. So impoverished was he that his only choice was to cut off his flesh and blood rather than worry about the burden of a dowry."

The nun's eyes flickered for an instant, the only acknowledgment of the painful truth of his words.

"So . . . is there anything else you'll need?" he asked. "I am, after all, your humble servant." He knew he was being a donkey again, but he had little patience for the upper classes putting on airs.

Her gaze had hardened and shifted to Koppe's servant, who had returned to the room, his arms laden with supplies. "As a matter of fact, most honorable and revered Doctor Luther, I do need one more thing."

His ire continued to rise at this young woman's audacity. "And what might that be?"

"We're in need of a wedding ceremony as soon as one can be arranged. Tonight if possible."

The parlor grew silent.

"Wedding ceremony?" Luther glanced at the others, but their unwillingness to meet his gaze was in stark contrast to the boldness of their leader. "For whom?"

"For my servant, Greta." She nodded to the young lay sister she'd situated on the bench. The girl's wimple was askew, and her hair hung loose. At the sudden attention, her eyes filled with fear, and she tried to melt against the wall. "Greta has been compromised. And as her caretaker, I insist that she marry with all haste since her body swells with child."

Greta groaned and buried her face in her hands.

"And you must do your God-honoring duty, Thomas." Sister Katharina spun to speak to Merchant Koppe's servant. "You must marry her without delay."

First surprise, then concern flitted across Thomas's face. He dropped the bundles he'd been carrying and stalked across the room toward the maidservant. He lowered himself to one knee in front of her and took her hands in his.

Sister Katharina faced Luther again. "It's my responsibility to see that Greta is as well cared for now as she was at Marienthron. Therefore I insist Thomas marry her."

Luther wasn't surprised when Koppe's young servant cast Sister Katharina a glance dark with hatred — the kind he'd noticed lately in thin peasant faces when he'd gone preaching, one that warned of the growing unrest among the lower class.

"What is this?" Koppe asked, stepping through the front door, bringing a gust of cool air with him. "Has Thomas fornicated with one of the sisters? Will I need to castrate him after all?"

"A marriage ceremony would suffice, Merchant Koppe," Sister Katharina said. "Thomas must accept responsibility for his actions."

Thomas stood, his body as straight as a lance. "I'll gladly marry Greta. I'll even take responsibility for raising her child, but I'm not the father."

"We've all witnessed your passion with my servant." Sister Katharina's voice was hard. "How can you expect us to believe your claim?"

Thomas turned again to the servant girl and murmured something to her. But she refused to look at him or answer him.

"What have you to say for yourself?" Koppe asked, striding into the middle of the room, his expression severe. "Have you defiled this girl or not?"

Thomas quietly pleaded with the girl, ignoring his master.

"I ought to whip you for insubordination." Koppe's doublet strained at the buttons, and a ruddy stain crept into his cheeks.

"Tell me who," Thomas demanded louder, trying to make the servant girl look at him. "Was it *him*?"

With tears streaking her cheeks, Greta pushed Thomas away and threw him off balance. Before he could react, she scrambled toward the door and ran outside into the darkness of the coming night.

"I've put up with your surliness long enough," Koppe said, crossing to his servant and grabbing his arm. "Maybe I should give your job to someone more worthy."

"Very well. Take my job away. I don't want it anymore." Thomas jerked away from Koppe and turned to follow Greta. His gaze narrowed on Sister Katharina. "And you won't have to concern yourself with Greta much longer." He spat the words. "I plan to take good care of her myself. And maybe for once she'll finally be safe."

Luther saw confusion play across the nun's face as she watched Thomas stride outside. "Will you still need a wedding ceremony tonight, Sister Katharina?"

Her gaze swung to his. For a brief moment he could see the frightened little girl once abandoned and forgotten. Sorrow beckoned him to rescue her, to reach out to her, to comfort her. Her vulnerability stirred a place deep inside him, evoking a strange urge to cross the room and touch her cheek, to feel its smoothness.

"We shall postpone the wedding ceremony," she said, a mist in her eyes. "Perhaps on the morrow. For now we would like you to take us to our rooms."

It wasn't often someone could render him speechless, but her command did just that. He hadn't expected the years in the abbey to diminish her aristocracy. Although the cloistered life might be austere, most of the women still retained the protection and prestige afforded to their class, and they spent their days in relative ease and comfort. However, he hadn't anticipated quite so much forthrightness or entitlement from one of them, and it rankled.

"And you may let us know when your servants have a meal ready for us."

"Do you think I'm running an inn and I'm the innkeeper?" He didn't wait for her to respond. "Let me make something clear. This is no inn. And although I'm a humble servant of Christ, I'm not *your* servant."

Her blue eyes frosted like the water in his wash basin most spring mornings.

"Unlike the convent you just left," Luther continued, "here you'll no longer have anyone to cook your meals, mend your garments, or scrub your rooms. You may still consider yourself among the elite and privileged of society, but you'd do well to remember that the rats in the cellar possess more riches than you. And due to your advanced age, I would likely have greater success in marrying off my old horse."

"Doctor Luther," she replied, cocking her head at the others, "you'd *do well* to refrain from discouraging these women."

He took in the weary lines of their faces, their eyes wide at the implication of his words, and his heart sank.

How was it possible that with just one sentence Sister Katharina could reduce him, the doctor of theology, the great preacher, the learned professor, to an errant boy in need of a thrashing? How could she make him want to hang his head in shame and at the same time fill him with such annoyance that he neglected to restrain his tongue?

He would have to pray that this woman's family would take her back, or God pity the man who would end up as her husband.

FIVE

"He's not what I expected." Katharina skimmed her fingers along the red welts that crisscrossed Fronika Zeschau's back. The girl winced but said nothing. Katharina tried to wash as gently as she could, but she couldn't keep her doctoring from causing pain. Etta rested on another pallet patiently awaiting the herbs that would ease the discomfort on her back.

"Oh, Doctor Luther is much more than I ever dreamed," whispered Margaret, a smile softening the angles of her face. She sat next to the pallet on the cell floor and bruised more of the herb Robert with a pestle and mortar. The bitter odor of the leaves permeated the cell. "I wonder what it would be like to marry a man like him."

"Probably more trouble than it's worth." Katharina covered her patient's wounds with a clean bandage.

The others watching from the doorway

stood in absolute silence and stillness. Even after a week away from the abbey, they couldn't shed the practice of communicating with whispers and signs. Though Katharina's voice sounded loud and foreign against the bare walls of the monastery, she was attempting to adjust.

Doctor Luther had encouraged them to discard their tight wimples and veils, but none of them had been able to shed the head covering yet. They may have run from the abbey, but it wasn't so easy to run from a lifetime of customs that were somehow comforting among all the other changes in their lives.

Katharina continued to awake during the night at the prescribed Divine Hours even though the bells didn't summon her to the chapel for prayer. Her body was attuned to the rhythm of the prayer hours, a practice that had been as much a part of her daily routine as eating. Kneeling in her cold, dark cell and chanting the Latin prayers brought a measure of peace amid the uncertainty.

"He doesn't appear as old as I would expect for a man of forty years," Katharina continued, "but he also doesn't have the sensibility and demeanor of a professor." He wasn't the lofty professor she'd imagined when she'd read his smuggled writings.

She'd pictured the erstwhile monk to be quiet, contemplative, perhaps refined. And he was none of those things.

"He's entirely kind and generous and helpful," whispered Margaret. "I think him divine."

"I'll admit he's been more than generous with us. But I think *divine* is too extravagant." Katharina helped situate Fronika more comfortably on her straw pallet, the only furnishing in the unadorned cell. Then she stood and took the pestle and mortar from Margaret. "I grant you first claim to marrying him, Sister Margaret."

The others tittered. Her friend blushed.

Katharina tried to muster a smile. She wouldn't remind them of the growing hopelessness of their situation. From all appearances the coffers of the Black Cloister were empty. Doctor Luther did not have enough provisions to feed them or house them properly. And worse, there weren't any suitable men for them to marry, at least none that she'd seen. No one had said as much, but it had become obvious that most of the monks who had once resided in the monastery had already married. The eligible were taken. Those left were too old or beneath the nuns' social status.

Had she been wrong to lead her sisters

away from the security and ease of their lives at Marienthron? There they always had plenty to eat, clean clothes to wear, every need met. They didn't have to worry about anyone forcing them into a marriage with a man they didn't love, a man who might mistreat them. But now with so few choices available, what would become of them?

She stirred the crushed herb mixture and then dipped her fingers in and tested it.

Had she too readily accepted Doctor Luther's writings condemning cloistered life? He'd said that there was nothing uniquely spiritual about monasticism, that the work of a monk or nun stands no higher in God's eyes than the normal work of a farmer or housewife performed in sincere faith. He'd urged them to renew their natural companionships without delay and get married while they were still young enough.

Even if his words had resonated and urged them to awake as though from a great slumber, had she done the right thing to leave and to encourage her friends to do the same? What if they couldn't find proper husbands? What if they remained alone, uncared for, rejected? Worse, what if they were forced into loveless marriages?

Katharina shuddered. "I must go pick

more leaves to thicken the poultice before tending Etta."

Margaret moved to follow, her gentle eyes probing her, all too seeing of late.

"Stay," Katharina said. "I shall not be long." Surely a few minutes alone in the herb garden would help clear her mind and put their situation back into perspective.

The other ladies parted to let her pass into the long, windowless corridor. She tiptoed past the deserted cells, which had once housed monks but now sat dusty and full of cobwebs. True to their word, Luther and the remaining men had moved to the barn. She was grateful for his hospitality but had asked that he at least send one of his servants to clean and freshen their rooms.

Her request had been met with the same indifference, almost scoffing, that he'd given her requests the night they had arrived. She supposed she ought not to expect more from a man of Luther's common background. But it had been disappointing nevertheless.

She paused outside Greta's cell, the only closed door among the cells the nuns were occupying. Katharina grazed her fingers across the coarse wood and peeked through the barred window. Greta hadn't moved since the last time she'd looked in, when the bells had rung at the noon hour for Sext.

Katharina had tried to reason with the girl, had implored her to repent of her sins, had entreated her to reveal the father if it was not Thomas. But Greta had met her words with only despair and growing sullenness. Although Thomas had said he'd marry Greta and take care of the baby, regardless of who the father was, he'd disappeared the very next day without even a good-bye to the maidservant. With every passing day of his absence, Katharina knew, Greta's hopes for a better life for her baby and herself were passing by too.

Katharina sighed and continued down the hallway.

Although she wanted to hold fast to the idea that Thomas was responsible, that he was to blame for all that was happening to Greta, she couldn't forget the anger in his expression the night she'd demanded he marry her servant. His anger had been directed toward her, as though she'd had a hand in Greta's misfortune.

Katharina didn't want to think about the other possibilities for Greta's pregnancy, but the peasants' words beside the cloister pond came back to haunt her. *Church whores.* What if someone within the convent had taken advantage of Greta? One of the lay workers? Perhaps even one of the priests? As much as she wanted to deny such happenings, she suspected they were all too real, if not at Marienthron, then elsewhere.

An unbidden memory stole into Katharina's mind. When she'd been only twelve, having just started her monthly courses, one of the priests during confessional had commanded her to come to the Predigerhaus after Vespers in order to do more penance for one of her sins. Aunt Lena had intercepted her on the way. Dear Aunt Lena's face had filled with fear when she'd discovered where Katharina was going and why. She'd ordered Katharina back to her cell and had promised to speak to the priest on her behalf.

What had Aunt Lena feared? Had her aunt warded off a priest who purposed to abuse her?

Katharina shook her head to free herself of such thoughts and then tucked her hands into her sleeves, put her head down, and rushed toward the stairwell. *Hail Mary, full of grace, the Lord is with thee.*

Her slippers trod silently on the winding stairs. Her habit swirled the dust in a whirlwind about her feet, along with dirt, dried flies, and only the Lord knew what else. At the landing of the stairwell, she opened a narrow door that led to the cloister courtyard. She stepped into the cool spring afternoon, and her gaze swept over the empty yard with a few stone benches situated around the open square, which obviously at one time had been a beautiful and peaceful resting spot with several well-placed shade trees. Now the yard was yellowed and was in as much disrepair as the rest of the monastery.

Seeing no one, she strolled slowly along the stone path, careful to avoid tripping over straggling weeds that had grown between the cracks. She dodged broken bricks and stones that littered the pathway, fallen from the walkway walls. The outbuildings were crumbling. The grounds were overgrown. The blossoming fruit trees were in desperate need of pruning.

Nothing about the Black Cloister could begin to compare with the Marienthron abbey.

How could she endure the monastery much longer?

"You'd do well to remember that the rats in the cellar possess more riches than you. And due to your advanced age, I would likely have greater success in marrying off my old horse."

"Saints have mercy," she whispered. Doctor Luther's words were caged in her mind.

They stalked back and forth, taunting her. What if he was right? Was her future as bleak as the Black Cloister?

An ache pulsed through her chest. No one in her family except Aunt Lena loved her. Everyone had abandoned her. Even her mother had left her helpless when she'd died, making Katharina easy prey for her father's new wife.

Katharina fumbled under the layers of her robes for the pouch tied at her waist. Her mother's paper was still tucked inside, the last gift to her, a costly indulgence that could reunite them some day. It was a treasure, and yet it couldn't make up for the years of not having a mother's love.

Katharina wound through the beds of herbs, the ache pushing harder. All she wanted was a family, a real family to love, one that she would always have and never lose. Surely God wouldn't have given her such a desire if He didn't mean to fulfill it?

Among the disorderly garden beds, she finally found the raised box she needed and plucked the fernlike leaves that surrounded the opening pink petals. She twirled one of the leaves between her fingers, then folded it in her palm and crushed it.

Sunlight bathed her head, soaking into the black of her veil. After the damp cold of the stone monastery, the warmth was a welcome change.

"As usual, you're helping yourself to all we have, I see."

With a start Katharina straightened and peered over the low fence of a raised bed nearby.

There among lush new growth, Doctor Luther was kneeling and clutching a pale yellow carnation, his black habit twisted about him. He pressed the bloom against his nose and sucked in a deep breath. His face had a pallor and tautness she hadn't noticed before.

As with the first time she'd seen him, she couldn't keep from acknowledging there was something striking about his face, something strong and passionate that gave him a deep intensity. She had the feeling he was the sort of person who was always thinking, so that one could never have a dull conversation when he was involved.

His brow rose, revealing his steady, expectant gaze.

"This isn't for myself," she replied, hoping he hadn't read the direction of her thoughts. "It's for two sisters who are recovering from a beating."

"Prior Zeschau's nieces?"

"Yes."

Doctor Luther's forehead was damp with sweat and plastered with a wave of his thick dark-brown hair. He'd given up his tonsure, going from a bald head with the groomed ring characteristic of an Augustinian monk to a shaggy, tousled full head of hair.

His eyes, too, were brown. It was another feature that had stood out to her when he'd walked into the cloister parlor the night she'd met him. They'd sparkled with enthusiasm one moment, darkened with sadness the next, and glittered with anger just as quickly. She had to admit she found them rather fascinating.

"Why were they beaten?" he asked.

"The abbot discovered a letter. Flogged them. And then locked them in the cloister prison."

He was quiet for a moment, searching her face as though attempting to piece together all that she hadn't said. "I'm very sorry to hear it, Katharina. Then I'm partially to blame for their pain." His simple statement was laced with anguish. In the sunlight his expressive eyes were filled with a sorrow that moved her.

"We have only ourselves to blame for any pain," she said. "We may have been forced into the convent, but we willingly read your teachings, Doctor Luther."

"I'm glad you read them," he said quietly.

"We did more than read them," she admitted. "We lived and breathed your words."

He smiled, and it softened the deep grooves in his forehead. "I can't take credit for the words. Most of them are straight from the Holy Scriptures."

A thousand questions flooded her mind, questions about prayer and salvation and heaven and the church, questions that had left her restless to know more and to seek the truth. Did she dare ask him about some of the issues that troubled her? He pressed the carnation to his nose but then doubled over.

"Doctor Luther?" Frowning, she swiftly crossed to him, climbed over the sagging wattle fence, and knelt beside him.

He rocked back and forth on his knees, his body taut, his head bent to the ground.

"Herr Doctor, are you ailing?"

A groan was his only answer. He continued to rock back and forth for a moment and then finally pushed himself back up. He breathed in heavy gulps. A fresh sheen of perspiration glazed his face.

"How did you get your bruise?" He thrust his carnation back to his nose.

Startled at his abrupt change of subject, she touched the tender spot at the ridge of her cheekbone. "Tell me your symptoms."

"You tell me about your bruise first."

She was near enough to feel him shaking. "I'll make you an infusion of chamomile to soothe your aches."

"I don't need anything." He clenched his jaw, obviously fighting pain while stubbornly intending to make her share her story whether she wanted to or not.

With a sigh she told him about the night of the escape, climbing over the convent wall and running through the forest. "As we rested near the cloister pond, we were attacked by a group of peasants. One of them hit me."

He stilled. His gaze skimmed over her bruise, then over her face before coming to rest on her eyes. His dark-brown eyes penetrated, probed deep, saw more than her words had expressed.

"Your turn to tell me about your sickness," she whispered, suddenly aware that he was a mere hand span away. His size, his presence, his personality — they were magnetic, pulling on her heart in a strange way.

His gaze didn't waver from hers. "You've all been very brave, Katharina."

Her throat clogged with sudden emotion. The escape and the ride to Torgau in the back of the wagon with the endless hours of jostling and fear was a nightmare she didn't wish to remember.

"You'll have to be brave in the days to come too." He winced and grabbed his stomach. "Our debtors aren't paying their dues. They hold their purse strings too tightly."

Once again he doubled over, and this time he retched violently. She held his robe out of the way. Whatever his ailment, surely she could find the right ingredients to help him.

"Come, Doctor Luther. I shall take you to the infirmary and make a drink to ease your pain."

He lifted his head but then dropped it again. "Don't fret over me. I'll survive as I have before. The devil won't kill me like this. It would ruin his plans to see me burn at the stake."

"Come." She stood, careful to avoid the new buds and blossoms of the first spring flowers. "If the devil wants you, I cannot stop him. But I can stop your pain."

He heaved himself up. "If your drink is as strong as your bossiness, then I'll be cured."

She smiled. "Of course I shall cure you."

She walked with him to the infirmary, a small room behind the kitchen. One side of the room was lined with shelves filled with tinctures and ointments and a variety of medicines the monks who had once lived there had created with great care. Next to the other wall was a long, narrow bench and a raised bedframe filled with stale straw. She had already taken stock of the supplies and found them lacking, but she had located a few of the herbs she regularly used.

Doctor Luther settled himself on the bench, leaned against the wall, and closed his eyes while she steeped dried chamomile flowers in boiling water and added catnip, lavender, and honey.

Once the sweet aroma filled the room, she handed him a hot mug of the drink. "How often do you have this stomach ailment, Doctor Luther?"

His hands trembled around the mug. "More than I'd like."

"What causes it?"

"No one knows. Only that I'm an old man with too many ailments to count." He lifted the mug to his lips.

"Don't drink it!" Wolfgang appeared in the doorway, his overlong black hair askew and his thick brows outlining fierce eyes. "It could be poisoned."

"Absolutely not." Katharina narrowed her eyes, refusing to be intimidated by the man. In the short time she'd been at the monastery, she'd already noticed the way the manservant hovered about Doctor Luther as if the professor were one of the rare and holy relics of Christ.

"We don't know these nuns." Wolfgang crossed with long, swift strides toward Doctor Luther. "They could be working for Duke George."

"Nonsense," she said. "I'm only trying to ease Doctor Luther's discomfort."

"Doctor Luther's life is always in jeopardy." Wolfgang towered over her, his proximity too near for comfort. "We can never be careful enough."

Though tempted to back away, she held her ground next to Doctor Luther and glared back at the manservant. "You certainly have an elevated opinion of your master. Surely the whole world isn't trying to kill Doctor Luther."

Doctor Luther blew on the hot steam rising from the drink, a faint smile quirking his lips, as though he was enjoying the spat between the two of them. "You'd be surprised at how many death threats I receive. Many more than I can count."

"No wonder your servant exaggerates. He's only imitating his master."

Any trace of Doctor Luther's humor evaporated, and his eyes darkened at her underhanded insult. "You're right, Wolf. We must be careful. Sister Katharina might be trying to kill me."

She wouldn't encourage him by responding, nor would she encourage the paranoia of his servant. She took the mug from Doctor Luther and swallowed a drink. The hot liquid burned the roof of her mouth and scalded her throat. "There, Wolfgang." She returned the mug to Doctor Luther and finally allowed herself to take a step away. "Now Doctor Luther and I shall die together."

Wolfgang's black scowl lifted for only an instant before resuming its typical deep crease.

"Your claws are out," Doctor Luther said, his expression as murky as the liquid. "When you're riled, you're a hissing *Katzen*."

"If I'm the hissing cat, what does that make you, Doctor Luther? Are you the growling hound?"

The gleam in his eyes hardened, and the muscles in his jaw visibly tightened. Without taking his gaze from hers, he took a sip of the drink.

Wolfgang gave a cry of protest and tried to pry the mug from his master's fingers. But Doctor Luther shrugged the manservant away and took another sip, his eyes unrelenting in their censure of her.

A sharp needle of guilt pricked her. After Doctor Luther's kindness to her and the other sisters, not only in aiding their escape but now in providing shelter, she knew he was no growling hound. She ought not to have spoken so forthrightly. Should she apologize?

He spoke again before she could find the words. "If I'm the hound and you're the cat, then it would appear we'll have no camaraderie except quarreling. In that case, spare me your presence since I already have far too many enemies and need no more."

At his rude dismissal any thought of an apology disappeared. She turned her back on him and started toward the door. "You may spare me your presence as well, especially since it appears your servant is doing such a superb job of caring for you."

"I pray for the poor man who must marry you," he called after her.

"You can rest assured, I will not marry a *poor* man."

"You don't have many choices, Katzen."

"I shall choose whom I wish," she said as she retreated into the corridor and moved away from him with haste, unwilling to listen to any more disparaging remarks.

She didn't have a dowry, but she was of the patrician class. Surely that still counted for something. Surely a man of equal status would find value in her stock and in the qualities she'd acquired from her training at the abbey.

But even as her footsteps echoed down the deserted hallway, fear tapped a hollow rhythm in her chest. What did her future really hold?

Six

The lid of the parish chest fell, and its three keys clanged. It was empty except for a few Gulden.

"Uncharitable." Luther's voice boomed through the dimly lit vestry. He hoped the lingering congregants in the nave below could hear him. "Ungrateful."

The vestry with its low ceiling and stone walls was as barren as the nave of the ancient Stadtkirche. All the statues of Mary and the altars in the galleries had been removed during Luther's year of hiding at Wartburg Castle. He'd returned to Wittenberg to calm the tempest, but he'd been too late to stop the destruction of many of the beautiful old artifacts that had once graced the churches.

Unfortunately Karlstadt, his fellow professor and one-time friend, had led the smashing and burning of the decorations and even now had a growing following of reformers who were willing to use force. Karlstadt's followers criticized Luther for being too conservative and for continuing to love the church with all its ancient customs.

Somehow he'd made enemies with everyone — both inside and outside the movement.

"Eventually the townspeople will give as they have in the past. We must be patient with them." Melanchthon spoke quietly and calmly, watching Luther pace the length of the narrow room. For once his placid expression did nothing to soothe the turmoil rolling through Luther.

"They're thickheaded," Luther added. "If they won't give generously after hearing an entire sermon on the fruit of the Spirit, then they never will."

"I agree with Martinus." Jonas leaned one shoulder nonchalantly against the wall near the open door and waved irritably at Melanchthon. The motion opened his fur-trimmed cloak, revealing the fine linen of a new black robe, a sign of wealth and status that was foreign to Luther. Unlike the humbler Melanchthon, Jonas was tall, had a darker complexion, and had a regal bearing that was formidable at times. Nevertheless, both men had become brothers to him.

"The people have been stingy and rude,"

Jonas continued. "After all Martinus does for them, the least they can do is provide for his needs."

Pastor Bugenhagen, the pastor of the Stadtkirche, locked the small wooden chest. "The people are reacting in fear. Everyone knows the danger in helping the nuns, especially now that they've been excommunicated."

"We've all been excommunicated, and the town hasn't suffered." Frustration forced Luther's voice to a higher decibel. The stores of food at the Black Cloister were low. They had used the last of the malt for brewing beer. The supplies Koppe had given them had dwindled to nothing. And now the situation was desperate.

He needed money.

Pastor Bugenhagen stood behind the counting table and folded his hands across his well-rounded chest. His wiry hair and long beard gave him a nomadic quality, causing Luther more than once to consider giving this shepherd of the congregation a staff to complete the picture.

"The men of this town know the elector doesn't support your efforts to empty the monasteries," the pastor said. "If Elector Frederick implicates you in the escape of these nuns, they could face charges too if they help you."

"Amsdorf's at the elector's court. He'll smooth things over with him as he usually does. Besides, I only need enough supplies for another week or two." Luther stopped to face their wise pastor. "It shouldn't take much longer than that to hear back from their kinsmen."

"Two weeks is too long." Pastor Bugenhagen rubbed his long beard thoughtfully. The sunlight streaking through a round window at the peak of the slanted ceiling seemed to form a halo above his head. "You've already put yourself in a compromising position by having the nuns live with you at the Black Cloister. If you keep them any longer, they will bring you more disgrace."

"I'm already disgraced!"

"Have you heard the rumors?" Jonas flashed a crooked grin.

"There are always rumors."

"Not like these," said Pastor Bugenhagen with a sad shake of his head.

Jonas's grin widened. "You're the debauching monk with a household of vestal virgins to use at your lustful leisure."

Luther lowered himself to the bench next to Melanchthon and grinned at Jonas. "My enemies have given me the same privileges as the pope."

Jonas snorted. Melanchthon gave a soft chuckle.

"This isn't a joking matter." Pastor Bugenhagen frowned at them. Then he picked up his Bible from the table and flipped it open. "In all things showing yourself to be a pattern of good works —"

"Titus two," Luther interrupted. "That one who is an opponent may be ashamed, having nothing evil to say of you."

"Exactly."

Luther understood the pastor's admonishment, but he shook his head. "By helping the nuns, I'm only doing what's right. I won't live at the mercy of the slander of my enemies. They want me to cower and hide. But I'm determined to stay true to God's calling to bring change to the church. I only wish that I could rescue all captive consciences and empty all the cloisters."

Pastor Bugenhagen's expression remained troubled.

The small upstairs room grew silent. The rolling carts, clomping of horses, and calls of passersby from the market square outside the Stadtkirche seemed to fill the vestry.

"I'll write to Amsdorf," Jonas finally said. "He'll find a way to wring Gulden from the nobles at court. He always does."

"I'll send him a letter too," Luther said.

"If we both ask him to take up a collection from the courtiers, he won't be able to resist."

"In the meantime I must insist," Pastor Bugenhagen added, "that you do your best to get the nuns out of the monastery as quickly as possible."

A sharp knock on the open vestry door brought Luther to his feet.

To his surprise Sister Katharina stepped into the doorway. Her shoulders heaved and her breathing was labored as if she'd just been running. She was still cloaked in her habit and veil. Even so, he was struck again by the loveliness of her face, the unblemished skin, smooth cheeks, and finely drawn mouth. In contrast to the stark white of her wimple, her blue eyes were keen, and they swept around the room, touching on each of the men before coming to land on him.

"Doctor Luther, you must come with us this instant."

Luther bridled at her command. Why did she have the ability to make him feel as if he were beneath her every time she spoke? "You can be certain, my good men, that this Katzen will be the first one to go from the monastery."

Sister Katharina's expression was cool, but he caught a flicker of urgency in her eyes that tempered him. "We're in need of an escort back to the monastery," she said. "It would seem some of the townspeople dislike us."

"What happened?" Melanchthon asked, rising, his face tightening with concern.

"After the conclusion of the service, we crossed the market square and headed down Collegienstrasse," she said. "As we walked, we attracted a crowd. We tried to pass through quietly and calmly, but the taunts and comments frightened some of the sisters."

Sudden anxiety swelled inside Luther, propelling him across the room to her. "Did anyone hurt you?"

"No, we turned around and hastened back to the confines of Saint Mary's. But we would feel safer with your escort."

He stopped in front of her and caught the sweet and spicy scent of herbs that lingered around her. Her eyes were unyielding, but at the slight tremor of her lip, a strange protectiveness surged through him and made him want to reach out and touch her and reassure her that she would be safe.

"We're at your service." Melanchthon stepped next to him, pushing him aside, and gave Katharina a customary bow. "I'm Philipp Melanchthon. These are my friends,

Pastor Bugenhagen and Justus Jonas."

She curtsied at the men and then offered Melanchthon a tentative smile. "Thank you. You're very kind."

Melanchthon is kind? What about him? Irritation replaced all thoughts of concern. Didn't he merit a compliment and a smile? "Sister Katharina, I'll escort you and the others home. But you'll have to wait for us in the nave. We'll be down when we're finished here."

Melanchthon raised an eyebrow at him.

"Aren't we done?" Jonas asked bluntly.

"No, we're not." Luther glared at his friends, daring them to challenge him. Melanchthon and Pastor Bugenhagen looked at their boots. Jonas stared openly between Luther and Katharina, his eyes narrowing in what appeared to be nonchalant appraisal.

Sister Katharina curtsied again. "Very well, Doctor Luther. We shall be waiting."

After she left, the men were silent and stared at him.

Luther flipped through the pages of his Bible and tried to ignore the embarrassment gaining momentum in his gut the longer they stared. Maybe he had overreacted to Sister Katharina just slightly. But he wasn't accustomed to speaking with women. They, of all people, should know that.

Melanchthon finally cleared his throat. "If they're all as fair and fine as Sister Katharina, then you'll have no problem finding husbands or homes for them."

Luther wished he had Melanchthon's moderation and peace. He couldn't deny that at times he envied his young friend's ability to see the good in every person and situation.

"Martinus will be the first to take one of them as a bride," Jonas said with a teasing guffaw.

"Absolutely not." Luther knew his protest was too loud, but it was fueled by the swirling heat in his gut. "You can be the first, Justus. You need a woman to tame your crankiness."

"I won't ever marry, and you know it. I'm one of those rare Paul types, those one-in-a-thousand individuals who would rather work on the kingdom of heaven and beget spiritual children."

"Then we're alike."

"Hardly." Jonas's voice dripped with sarcasm. "The blood runs too hot through your body. You won't be able to resist marriage forever."

Luther began to deny it.

"A feisty cat might be just what the old

gander needs."

"Ach." Luther moved toward the door, ducking his head and praying his face wasn't as red as it felt. "Let's go."

Seven

The sweet smell of the steeping malt filled the brewery. Katharina sprinkled more heated water into the vat, covering the grist as Brother Gabriel had instructed her.

The old monk was stoop shouldered and watery eyed with age. He wasn't a man of many words, but he had been the kindest to them since their arrival and treated them with a gentleness that made her think of Aunt Lena. And, of course, every time she thought of Aunt Lena, her heart ached with the guilt of leaving her.

"The sparging's almost done," Brother Gabriel whispered, pumping a bellow on the flame to raise the temperature. "We must get the last of the sugar out of the grain if we want to have the kind of beer Doctor Luther likes."

"Now we have our wort?" she asked.

"Very soon."

"Make ready the hops, Margaret."

Her friend sat on the dirt floor of the shed on a thin scattering of hay. She leaned against the rough-hewed plank wall, her blank gaze on the open door and the steady drip of rain outside.

The brewing process obviously didn't hold the same fascination for Margaret as it did for her. Especially now. Only that morning another of the sisters had left the monastery. Magdalene von Staupitz's younger brother had accepted her into his home. Earlier Lanita von Golis had gone to live with her sister and would regain the title Lady of Colditz. Then Elsa von Canitz had left to stay with relatives. The good-byes had been harder than Katharina had imagined, and she could completely understand Margaret's melancholy about being left behind.

Six of them remained. But they'd heard rumors that Ava Grossin would likely be the next to leave since her family was still prosperous and her parents had agreed to let her live on their estate until they arranged a marriage.

Of course, there was still the problem of Greta's pregnancy. While the servant had finally arisen from her pallet and had begun performing some of her duties again, Katharina was at a loss about what to do for the girl. Katharina had tried to probe further, to discover the truth about the father of the baby and about Thomas, but Greta only shook her head and refused to speak of the matter.

"Margaret." Katharina spoke gently. "Something will work out for us soon. You'll see."

The young woman turned sad eyes on her. After the scant rations they'd endured at the Black Cloister, Margaret's thin face was gaunter and her narrow nose more defined.

Doctor Luther wouldn't get letters from their families. Margaret's family, the von Schonfelds, and her own family, the von Boras, lived in Duke George's territory in the part of Saxony where preachers who followed Luther's teachings were imprisoned and Luther's books were burned. Why would their families put themselves in danger to help the daughters they had discarded so many years ago? If they hadn't wanted them then, they weren't likely to change their minds now. Especially with the threat of persecution.

Katharina didn't harbor any hope of hearing from her family. She expected what she'd always gotten from them — silence. Even so, each letter that arrived for someone else pricked at the hurt buried deep inside and made her wish she'd been born first instead of her sister. Then she would have been the one already married and having babies.

She knew Margaret's forlorn feeling; it reflected her own.

Margaret reached for the basket of hops next to her but tipped it, spilling plants onto the floor. She stared at them listlessly, her usual cheer having blown away.

Katharina knelt and picked up a hop. She brushed off the dirt and placed the hop in the basket.

"I'm sorry, Katharina." Her friend's voice wavered, and her eyes brimmed with sudden tears. "We're hungry. We've no change of clothes. The townspeople harass us every time we venture out of the monastery. And to make matters worse, our families won't claim us."

"We knew that would be true when we made our plans to leave the abbey."

"But no one likes us. And it appears no one will have us."

"We'll find husbands. I'll make sure of it." Katharina had no plans for how she would accomplish her mission, but she wouldn't give up hope yet.

"Do you ever wonder if we should have stayed?" Margaret asked. "What if God is displeased with us? What if He's punishing us for forsaking our vows?"

"We had no choice in making our vows; therefore God won't hold us accountable."

"But what if we've thrown away our best chance at salvation?"

Margaret's words were barely distinguishable above the bubbling pot. Nonetheless, Katharina heard her friend's doubt as loudly as if she'd shouted it. "Remember that Doctor Luther has spoken about the priesthood of all believers. He says that Scripture doesn't set apart clergy as being more holy than anyone else. Being a nun or monk doesn't bring us closer to salvation. We're just as sinful and in need of God's grace as anyone else."

His teachings had been freeing. But she spoke to reassure herself as much as to comfort Margaret.

Katharina scooped the rest of the hops into the basket and stood. Brother Gabriel had begun straining the wort through the false bottom of the mash tun, separating the liquid from the crushed barley and wheat and draining it into a large copper kettle.

"What do you think, Brother Gabriel?" she asked. "You've heard Doctor Luther speak more than we have. Share what you've learned."

Something flashed in the old brother's eyes that Katharina didn't understand. "I cannot since I'm only a humble man." His whisper was barely audible.

Margaret released a winded sigh. Her wimple was askew, her habit gray from lack of washing. "What if we were meant to be set apart as the virgin spouses of Christ? How can the marriage union of a mortal man and woman be better than a marriage union to Christ?"

All their lives they'd been taught that celibacy was the highest calling for a man or woman, that it was far superior to earthly matrimony. Who were they to question what the learned and holy church fathers had believed for centuries?

Of course, Doctor Luther had warned that they might have these doubts about what they'd done, and he'd encouraged them to study the passages of Scripture that recommended and praised marriage. But studying the Bible was another new concept. The holy saints of the past had written interpretations of the Bible to instruct them. Reading the holiest book itself wasn't necessary or safe for the common person. Even attempting to read the commentaries of the saints was better left to the cardinals and pope. Did she dare try what her superiors

wouldn't do? How could she hope to understand Scripture if the most educated men
couldn't?

Doctor Luther had given them one of his
recently printed New Testaments — the illegal version he'd translated into common
German. But Katharina had determined
that if she ever needed to read the Bible,
she would do it properly, in Latin.

She reached over and gave Margaret's
shoulder a tender squeeze. "Remember all
we've read and heard? We have to continue
to believe we're doing the right thing."

Margaret lifted her head, and Katharina
was relieved to see a spark in the woman's
eyes again. "You're a true friend, Katharina.
And I have no doubt God will bless you
with a wonderful husband in reward for all
you've done."

"He'll bless you too." She grasped her
friend's cold fingers; the warmth of the
brewery fire had not taken the chill off the
day.

At Brother Gabriel's beckoning, Katharina
returned to the kettle. "Shall I add the
hops?" Katharina asked.

Because of her prodding during another
brewing session, the old monk had reluctantly shared his story — how he had arrived at the Black Cloister the previous year,

after Doctor Luther had returned from hiding in Wartburg Castle. Brother Gabriel's monastery in the south had closed when the monks there had followed Luther's advice to get married. As an aged man with no skilled trade and no place to go, he'd sought the mercy of Doctor Luther.

Brother Gabriel moved the kettle to the flame. "It's ready."

Katharina dumped the hops into the wort, careful not to splash the liquid.

"Gabriel, get the Obstwasser!" Wolfgang burst through the door of the shed. He heaved for breath, his black hair wild from the wind and rain. "Quick! Doctor Luther is having one of his melancholy episodes."

Brother Gabriel hesitated and glanced from the bubbling kettle to the assortment of jugs on the lone shelf on the back wall of the shed.

"Stay." Katharina wiped her hands on her habit. "You finish the wort. I shall go with Wolfgang and take Doctor Luther the Obstwasser."

"Oh. No, no." Wolfgang backed to the door and spread his arms wide to block her exit, his thick black brows crooking into a deep scowl. "Doctor Luther needs Brother Gabriel."

"Which is the Obstwasser? This one?" She

reached for the closest jug, a small one with a slender neck.

Brother Gabriel shook his head and pointed to the identical one next to it.

"I can help." She grabbed the jug and spun around to face Wolfgang. "Now take me to him."

Her command allowed no argument. She was, after all, a noblewoman and he only a commoner. He had no authority over her, and he should do as she bade, whether he liked it or not.

She stopped in the infirmary and prepared an infusion of St.-John's-wort. All the while Wolfgang muttered and complained and scrutinized every jar she opened and every ingredient she added.

"Maybe *you* are working for Duke George," she said as they wound up the spiraling steps to the dormer rooms. "He could hire you just as easily as he could hire me."

Wolfgang's fierce expression twisted into horror. "We all admire and respect Doctor Luther." The shock in his voice echoed off the walls. "None of us would be here if we weren't willing to stake our lives on him and his reforms."

Although she hadn't seen Doctor Luther since he'd accompanied them home from

Saint Mary's, she had grown to appreciate his kindness to them more with each passing day. Their presence at his home had surely brought him only more censure and hardship, and yet he'd borne it regardless of the cost.

The least she could do was lend him her doctoring skills. It made no difference to her that the last time she'd aided him, he'd told her to spare him her presence. He'd only said it in anger — at least she hoped. And surely now in the midst of his discomfort he would appreciate her knowledgeable assistance.

When they reached the cell Doctor Luther had converted into an office, Katharina swept into the narrow room that was nearly identical to the ones she and the other nuns occupied on the next level. She stopped short at the sight of him sprawled facedown on the floor, motionless except for the trembling in his hands. With the recent rains the air was dank. The room was lit by a lone candle upon Doctor Luther's writing table.

She stepped around his long, lanky body. Her foot knocked a stack of pamphlets into the papers already spilled across the floor. "How long has he been in this condition?"

"Nigh an hour," Wolfgang replied, kneeling next to his master, his hands fluttering over Doctor Luther.

"What's the cause of his melancholy?" Katharina pushed aside dried inkhorns and broken quills, then lowered herself beside Doctor Luther and across from Wolfgang. "Tell me what sends Herr Doctor into his episodes. I must know if I am to help."

Wolfgang hesitated, glanced at Doctor Luther's stiff, prostrate form, and then released a sigh. "An envoy of the elector brought him the results of the Diet of Nuremberg. The princes are having discussions with the pope's nuncio, Chieregati. He's calling upon them to enforce the Edict of Worms."

Katharina had heard only a little of Doctor Luther's open rebellion two years prior against the pope at the Diet of Worms, where he had stood before the Holy Roman Emperor, Charles V, and refused to recant his writings against the church. The emperor had issued the edict, condemning Doctor Luther to death.

The tales of Doctor's Luther's courage had amazed her. How could anyone dare to defy the emperor and the pope? Thus far Elector Frederick had protected Doctor Luther from the emperor's death warrant. But now if all the other princes decided to enforce Charles V's Edict of Worms, surely

Doctor Luther would soon face death.

"The princes have presented to Chieregati a list of one hundred grievances Germany has endured from Rome," Wolfgang whispered. "It's called the *Centum Gravamina.* The nuncio says the pope will consider the grievances if they'll promise to hand over Doctor Luther for immediate execution."

A chill rippled through Katharina. "And will they?"

"They're deliberating."

Katharina stared with compassion at the black hood that hid Doctor Luther's face. How many more days before he was captured and put to death? "Then he has episodes because he's afraid of dying?"

"Fear of dying?" Wolfgang shook his head. "I don't think so. But fear of failing? Yes, he doesn't want this reformation to fail in any way."

Katharina tugged at Doctor Luther's hood, her mind spinning. What could she do to ease the melancholy of a man facing prison and death? "Wolfgang, you must bring me Doctor Luther's lute."

The manservant didn't move.

"Doctor Luther likes music?"

He nodded.

"I've heard him playing the lute?"

Again he nodded.

"Then fetch his lute and a cool rag."

She slipped down Doctor Luther's hood. His eyes were pinched closed, and his face was pressed against the cold floor with one of his cheeks facing her. The line of his jaw was taut and his skin dark with stubble. His hair fell over his forehead, reaching almost to his eyes, but a vein in his temple throbbed.

She lifted her fingers to soothe the vein but hesitated. Did she dare touch this man? Her insides quivered at the thought. In the infirmary at Marienthron, the older sisters had allowed her to care only for the women. She'd never intentionally touched a man before.

A quick glance around the room told her she was alone. Thankfully, for once Wolfgang had done her bidding. She turned her attention back to Doctor Luther, and before she lost all courage, she pressed her palm against his hot skin. Her hand shook at the contact, and a strange heat formed a closed fist deep in her belly.

She skimmed her fingers across the scratchiness of his cheek and then pressed the pulsing vein on the side of his head. She gently massaged it, her knuckles brushing against his hair. The softness was unlike anything she'd felt before. And the fingers of heat in her middle began to unfurl one by one.

He gave a long sigh, and the warmth of his breath bathed the sensitive skin of her wrist.

Her face flushed with sudden warmth at the scandal of her closeness and the familiarity of her touch.

Wolfgang cleared his throat loudly, irritably.

She jerked her hand away from Doctor Luther and glanced up to see that the manservant had returned with the items she'd requested. She set to work, trying to ignore the new and confusing longings.

When she applied the cool cloth to Doctor Luther's temple, he groaned. She picked up the lute and plucked at the courses with a quill. The soft notes awakened memories of her childhood, the hours watching and listening to her mother play the lute — before her mother had grown ill. Katarina's fingers found the strings she needed even though her mind had forgotten. She hummed a simple tune, one her mother had often sung to her. *"Schlaf, Kindlein, schlaf. Sleep, child, sleep. Your father tends the sheep. Your mother shakes the branches small. Lovely dreams in showers fall. Sleep, child, sleep. Schlaf, Kindlein, schlaf."*

During the third time through the song, Doctor Luther's eyes opened, and he rolled to his side. His pale face emphasized the darkness of his eyes. They focused with unwavering intensity on her face. And she couldn't look into them without having unbidden thoughts about his hair and skin and how they'd felt beneath her fingers.

When she finished, she set aside the lute and reached for the Obstwasser. "Take a drink."

"So, Sister Katharina, you're the one fighting the devil off my back this time." He struggled to sit up and let her hold the jug while he took a swig.

"You're lucky I'm here to help you, Doctor Luther. The devil cannot abide me."

"I can believe that." A faint smile brought light to his eyes.

She couldn't keep from returning the smile. "You must take St.-John's-wort." She held out the mortar.

He raised an eyebrow at the cloudy liquid.

"It will help ease the melancholy. Take it," she commanded, "unless you're afraid I'm trying to poison you again."

Wolfgang's low growl came from the doorway. But Doctor Luther's smile widened. He took the bowl and drank the liquid in one gulp. Then he handed the empty bowl back to her. "Anything else, Doctor Katharina? Perhaps another song on the lute?"

She shook her head. "No. A song from you perhaps but not from me. I've played the only song I know."

His expression turned suddenly serious. His gaze held hers, and the intensity stole her breath. "It was a beautiful song, and I thank you, Katharina, for your help."

The softness and sincerity of his words only added to the warmth in her middle. Once again she was keenly aware of how close she was to him, near enough to see the dark flecks in his brown eyes.

"You're gifted with medicine." He searched her face, making a slow circle from her forehead to her cheek to her chin. And then to her lips.

She was sure her face must be red. She lowered her head, knowing it was a vain attempt to hide herself, and she spoke rapidly to cover her embarrassment at reacting so strongly to his nearness. "At Marienthron I was responsible for the herb garden and making the medicine. I studied the ancient recipes well. Besides, I helped my Aunt Lena in the infirmary."

"I think we'll keep you here at the monastery to be our doctor." His voice was low.

Wolfgang stepped into the room and loomed above them, his reproach radiating from his tense posture.

"You may call upon me, Doctor Luther, anytime you are ill." She wished her voice didn't sound so breathy. "It's the least I can do in payment for the kindness you have shown us."

"The good news is that you'll soon have homes."

She handed him the Obstwasser again, nodding at it and indicating he should take another drink.

"Finally I may have convinced several of Wittenberg's wealthy families to take you and the others." He lifted the jug to his lips.

"Then there are no husbands for us?" Disappointment slithered through her. If Doctor Luther couldn't find noble husbands among the many people he knew, how would she accomplish such a feat when she knew no one?

"I'm still searching. But in the meantime you'll move out of the Black Cloister into homes where your basic needs will be met and you won't slowly starve to death." His eyes held an apology, as though he regretted his inability to provide for them better.

"You've done all you can," she replied. Of course, she'd wondered over the past week why he had so little. He was Doctor Luther. Surely he could command payment for his preaching, teaching, and writings. But from the way things appeared, he had no steady income whatsoever.

"My servant, Greta, must come with me," she said.

He regarded her solemnly. "In her condition I'm not sure if that will work —"

"I cannot abandon her when she's in such great need."

He paused as if considering her request.

"Please, Doctor Luther?"

A small smile quirked the corners of his mouth. "Ah, I see you are capable of asking when it suits you."

"Occasionally." She smiled in return. His brown eyes regarded her with rare pleasure. And that strange warm grip once again tightened in her middle. She felt her cheeks flush again and focused on the lute still lying in her lap.

Her mind returned to what Wolfgang had just told her about the revival of the death warrant against Doctor Luther. "These families" — she spoke hurriedly to cover her reaction to him — "are they sympathetic to your cause and willing to break the law to accommodate us?"

A shadow descended over his face. "They

support my reforms now. But I don't know how long they'll stay with the cause after I'm handed over to Rome. When the flames of the stake stand before them, it will be easy to recant rather than die."

And what would happen to her and the other sisters if the German princes finally arrested Luther? Would they be imprisoned and killed too?

"As servants in prominent Wittenberg households," he said, as if sensing her fear, "my hope is that you'll escape detection."

Servants? Her insecurities about the future evaporated. "You're mistaken, Doctor Luther. We're not intending to live as servants."

"But of course you will. What did you expect? To be entertained as royal guests?"

She stiffened. "We're nobility."

With narrowing eyes he took another swallow of Obstwasser, then wiped the back of his hand across his mouth. "The burghers have agreed to take you in as servants in their households. Be grateful, Katharina, that they're willing to risk having you at all."

She stood and shook the dust from her habit. "I've not put my life in great peril to end up as a common laborer."

"Well, your majesty, I'm sorry you'll have to descend from your throne." He struggled to rise. Wolfgang rushed to his side and helped him to his feet.

"I will not work as a servant," she stated with more calmness than she felt.

"You don't have a choice."

A scream of agony came from a far part of the cloister and ricocheted off the walls.

EIGHT

Without a word of leave, Katharina rushed
to the stairwell, to the sound of slapping
footsteps. Several of the nuns were racing
down the steps, their habits flying behind
them.

"Tell me who is screaming and why!" she
called to them.

"It's Greta," one of the Zeschau sisters
responded over her shoulder. "Abbot Baltazar has captured Thomas."

"Ave Maria." Katharina's heart slammed
against her ribs. She raced after the others,
the drumbeat of dread increasing with each
step she took. As much as her mind
screamed to lock herself away in her cell
rather than face the abbot, she stumbled
out the front door of the cloister into a
gathering of onlookers standing in the
drizzle. She shouldered her way to the front
but then stopped short, next to Margaret
and Greta.

"And there is our Sister Katharina." Abbot Baltazar stood next to a wagon. His loose tunic and scapular couldn't hide his bulky middle. And his black hood couldn't hide his bulbous nose and overlarge blood-shot eyes that were now trained on her. Rather than covering his hands in the wide mouths of his sleeves, he had them folded at his chest, revealing abnormally long fingernails. "Your Aunt Magdalena sends her greetings from the cloister prison."

Although the news about Aunt Lena didn't come as a surprise, regret pooled rapidly inside, making her wish she'd tried harder to change Aunt Lena's mind about escaping with them. "You must release her, Father Abbot. She's not to blame for our leaving."

Standing next to the priest were several peasants who had worked in and around Marienthron. Their weathered faces were hard and unsmiling, and they kept glancing at Abbot Baltazar as if awaiting his orders.

"Oh, but Sister Katharina, she has already confessed her transgressions." Abbot Baltazar's smile was thin; the fatherliness of his voice was too sweet. "We also have custody of Leonard Koppe's servant, and he has made many confessions too."

Greta sucked in a quivering breath.

Margaret put a steadying hand on the girl, whose face had the pallor of death.

Abbot Baltazar nodded to his men. They turned to the back of the wagon, lifted out the body of a man, then tossed him into the muddy street. He lay unmoving, hands and feet bound.

An anguished cry slipped from Greta's lips, and she lunged forward. Margaret clutched the girl's robe. Greta resisted for only a moment before she twisted away and retched.

Katharina stared at the man, and her stomach churned with revulsion. It was merchant Koppe's servant, Thomas, but he was barely recognizable. His feet were blackened and charred, evidence of foot roasting. His fingers had been smashed by the thumbscrew, his back mutilated by hot irons. The once-handsome face was bruised and smeared with blood.

How had the abbot managed to capture Thomas — unless Thomas had gone back to the abbey to seek out the father of Greta's baby and to avenge her?

"What good is a dead witness?" Doctor Luther called from behind her as he elbowed his way forward, trailed by a breathless Wolfgang.

"Martin Luther?" Abbot Baltazar eyed

134

him, then raised his brow at his servants.

"I am he," Doctor Luther replied. He hadn't pulled up his hood against the cold drizzle and instead exposed the full fury in his eyes and the anger in his face. "I don't need to ask who you are. I can already guess."

Abbot Baltazar's fleshy lips curved into a smile.

"You're a servant of the devil," Luther continued. "Only the devil's servant could torture a man the way you have this one."

Abbot Baltazar's smile turned brittle, and with the flick of his fingers and long fingernails, he motioned to the peasants he'd brought with him.

The laborers began to creep toward Doctor Luther. Their hands touched their sheathed knives. Katharina's body tensed with the same urgency she'd experienced the night of their escape. "Beware, Doctor Luther," Katharina said with a nod toward the men. Abbot Baltazar wouldn't dare attempt to seize Doctor Luther, would he? Not now in the daylight in front of a growing crowd.

Doctor Luther eyed the men, then pinned a steady gaze on Abbot Baltazar. "You've killed one man. Isn't that enough?"

"Koppe's servant isn't facing eternal

damnation yet." Abbot Baltazar kicked Thomas in the back. The bloody mass grunted. "But we castrated him, and he'll soon face judgment."

Castrated? *Holy Mary, Mother of God, pray for us sinners.* Katharina crossed herself and tried to push down the bile in her throat.

"Why are you here? What do you want?" Doctor Luther demanded, straightening his broad shoulders and rising to an imposing height. Wolfgang had unsheathed a knife and had it pointed toward the peasants moving nearer.

"I want my nuns back." Abbot Baltazar's bulging eyes swept over the women.

Katharina fought against the urge to flee and made herself stay where she was.

"They're not yours," Doctor Luther said.

"They belong to Marienthron, and it's my sacred duty to see that they return to their Bridegroom Christ and the Mother Church. If I don't attempt to bring these prodigals back, I'll stand accountable when they suffer the torments of hell."

"You're the only one here who needs to worry about the torments of hell."

Abbot Baltazar started to answer, but Doctor Luther continued, clearly accustomed to waging war with his words. "I think you want them back," he said loudly enough that the growing crowd could hear him, "so you can defile more of them in your common brothel."

"I've heard rumors that you're the one with the brothel these days."

Katharina cringed at the abbot's accusation. Was that really what people were saying about Doctor Luther and her sisters? If they lived through this encounter with the abbot, she resolved she wouldn't hesitate to move out of the Black Cloister, no matter where Doctor Luther sent her.

Baltazar's men formed a half circle, like a net drawing tighter.

Wolfgang moved in front of Doctor Luther and waved his blade at the peasants. But they responded by raising their knives. Dread pulsed through Katharina, turning her blood to ice. No matter his good intentions, Wolfgang wouldn't be able to ward off all the attackers. Perhaps they'd been unwise to rush out of the monastery without a plan for how to prevent an attack. Should she usher her sisters back inside now while they still had a chance? But how could she leave Doctor Luther at the mercy of the abbot and his men?

Several young men in the crowd elbowed their way forward. Their cloaks and berets signified them as university students. "Do you need help, Doctor Luther?"

Abbot Baltazar's men froze.

Half a dozen more scholars armed with spears and halberds moved out of the crowd. "We don't take kindly to anyone threatening our Doctor Luther."

He gave them a grateful nod. "Yes, let's give Abbot Baltazar a hand back into his cart and usher him from Wittenberg. Those who prohibit marriage and force perpetual celibacy on young women against their will have neither the authority nor the right to be here in our town."

Abbot Baltazar eyed the students, who were closing around him. "Are you putting yourself above the pope and the laws of Christendom, laws that have been followed and accepted by saints and scholars for hundreds of years?"

"The Archbishop of Mainz is selling licenses to his priests to permit them to keep concubines. Shall we stand by and accept such a twisted practice even if our forefathers did the same?"

Abbot Baltazar scowled and again assessed the armed citizens of Wittenberg before his gaze lingered on Greta.

The girl paid no heed to the abbot and instead stared at Thomas with blank eyes.

A sickening thought lodged in Katharine's

mind. Was Abbot Baltazar the father of Greta's baby? Katharina closed her eyes briefly to fight off the nausea that rose swiftly at the idea. As much as she wanted to deny that the abbot would do such a thing, she knew it was possible. He'd visited Marienthron all too frequently, and Greta had a comeliness that wimples couldn't hide. It made sense that the abbot would have noticed her. What if he'd taken advantage of the young woman?

Suddenly Katharina knew with certainty that he was the father of Greta's unborn babe. That's why Thomas had returned to Marienthron — to punish the abbot for abusing Greta. Apparently the abbot had captured Thomas before he could accomplish his revenge.

"Get our primary witness back onto the cart," Abbot Baltazar ordered his men as he returned to the safety of his wagon. "We'll take him to Elector Frederick. Once the elector hears this worthless peasant's confession, he'll have no choice but to turn Martin Luther over to me, along with these wayward nuns."

The men gathered Thomas without care and dumped him into the wagon bed. The man's cry of pain echoed through the silent crowd.

"I've heard rumors that Bundschuh peasants are holding secret meetings and plotting revolt." The muscles in Doctor Luther's jaw were rigid, his eyes black with contempt. "Now I know why. They're treated worse than dogs by the very men who should shepherd them."

The Bundschuh peasants? Katharina's mind spun back to their escape from the convent, to the peasants they'd encountered at the pond, to the strange circumstance of their early morning meeting. Had the men been meeting to plan a rebellion? Had Thomas been a part of that?

Abbot Baltazar climbed onto the seat of the wagon and settled his tunic about his large frame. "I'll get my nuns back one way or another. You won't be able to stop the work of God."

A chill crawled up Katharina's spine. God help her if Abbot Baltazar ever carried through with his threat.

"It's my sacred duty as confessor and overseer of Marienthron to restore all the sisters who've abandoned their vows." The abbot looked directly at her.

The chill penetrated to the very marrow of Katharina's bones.

"I will not cease my vigilance," he said, "until they are back where they belong."

NINE

Overwhelming helplessness seeped through Katharina as she scrubbed the tiles in the entry of the Reichenbachs' home. For all her brave words to Doctor Luther about being nobly born and not doing the work of a common laborer, she hadn't been able to prevent the fall from dignity.

A week ago, at the beginning of May, she'd had no choice but to leave the Black Cloister and go to live in the home Doctor Luther had arranged for her. With her escape from the convent, she'd hoped she might take a hand in shaping her own destiny, but the truth was, as a woman, she was merely a pawn to be shuffled about by the men in her life. Whether controlled by her father or Doctor Luther or someone else, she had little freedom to go where she pleased or do as she liked.

She sat back on her heels and kneaded the ache in her neck. The vaulted ceiling

and leaded-glass windows afforded brightness in the room, illuminating the glossy
loose threads in the tapestries hanging on
the paneled walls. In some ways she felt as
though her life was like a tapestry. With each
passing day the silk was unraveling further
and floating neglected in the dusty air. Her
neatly ordered life had come undone. Her
plans for the future were left hanging. And
now here she was, reduced to the life of a
servant, no better than Greta.

Poor Greta. Katharina shuddered every
time she thought about Greta being violated
by the abbot. Beyond the revulsion, it
stirred something deeper in her that she
couldn't name. All she knew was that she
was greatly disturbed by the fact that
someone who was charged with being their
protector had not only failed to keep them
safe but had been the one to violate the
fragile beauty needing protection.

With a heavy sigh she lowered the scrub
brush back to the floor. Now Greta was
gone. She had vanished in the night. Without a word. And despite Katharina's inquiries, she hadn't been able to locate the girl.
She'd asked Doctor Luther for help, but
he'd had no success in his inquiries either.

A door banged open behind her, and the
heavy footsteps of wooden pattens clomped

across the floor.

Katharina kept her attention fixed on the diamond pattern of the tiles.

The footsteps came to a halt in front of her, and the velvet hem of a richly embroidered gown swished across the narrow, pointed shoes. From the corner of her eye, she could see the path of dirty prints that now trailed across the floor — the floor she had been washing since the bells of Saint Mary's had pealed for Prime.

Humiliation pulsed through her again, as it did every time she had to face Elsa Reichenbach, her new mistress. The woman was the wife of the town mayor, of burgher class, not titled as she was. But Elsa acted far above her status, and Katharina had quickly learned that the woman relished treating her as if she were no better than a peasant. She had no doubt Elsa had neglected to remove her muddy wooden shoes at the door, as was customary, just to make more work for her.

Katharina sprinkled more sand on the floor and rubbed it with the wet brush, loosening the dirt. Her hands were chafed from the lye soap; they were no longer the soft, smooth hands she'd always had in the abbey.

Elsa tapped her patten as if trying to draw

143

Katharina's attention to the special hem on her gown, a clothing privilege Katharina wouldn't have now as a servant.

Katharina scrubbed harder, letting her anger at the injustice of her situation give her fresh vigor — anger at herself for getting trapped into the position, anger at Doctor Luther for leaving her no other choice, and anger at the Reichenbachs for allowing her to be treated as a servant. Part of her knew that she was being irrational, that she couldn't blame anyone, that she couldn't stay at the Black Cloister any longer, especially in light of the horrible rumors about the cloister becoming a brothel. Even so, her chest ached at all that had happened not only to herself but also to Greta.

"Katharina." Elsa spoke haughtily. Her dark hair was pulled back severely under a short veil, and her hairline had been plucked to create a higher forehead as was the custom of some women who indulged in vanity even though the church considered it a sin. "It's come to my attention you know Latin."

"Yes, you're correct."

"It's my understanding that you were instructed in Latin at the convent. Do you know it well enough to teach the children?"

"Of course."

"When you're done with the floor, I'd like you to go to the girls' room and begin teaching them Latin."

Teaching Latin to the children? The thought sent a shimmer of hope into the gloom that had clouded her mind of late. At Marienthron she'd always loved having one of the young postulants shadow her in the herb garden or infirmary.

"You're fairly useless as a servant, not that I needed another one anyway," Elsa continued, waving airily to another servant, who was descending the spiral staircase. "Perhaps by tutoring my daughters, you'll finally be able to earn your keep here in our household."

Katharina reached for the rag and wiped the sand and dirt away, revealing a shining tile. The mayor's wife had already made it quite clear that she'd opened her home to Katharina only out of obligation to Doctor Luther and to her husband. Nevertheless, it stung Katharina to know she wasn't wanted even as a servant. But she couldn't let Elsa see her distress.

Elsa tapped her shoe again.

"Very well." Katharina slid her pad toward the next tile and rearranged the faded green skirt, one of Elsa's castoffs. The edge was ragged, evidence that Elsa had ripped away the ribbon and removed any traces of class status. "I shall teach your daughters, Elsa. You may let them know I'll be with them shortly." She sloshed water onto the floor and returned to her work with what she hoped was an attitude of dismissal.

After a moment Elsa retreated the way she'd come, leaving another trail of dirty footprints. When she disappeared through the door into the main hall, Katharina blew out a shaky breath and hugged her arms across the lacing of her bodice. She'd known she must eventually give up the comfortable familiarity of the habit, but she couldn't shake the feeling of nakedness. Compared to the loose flowing tunic she'd worn all her life, the tight sleeves and bodice of her new clothing constricted her movement and showed much more of her figure and skin. Despite the wide collar over her neck and shoulders shielding her bust, she felt exposed.

She'd also discarded her nun's wimple and donned a thin head cap that didn't conceal her hair. After years of wearing the linen wrapped tightly around her head and neck, the barrenness was strange. From time to time she found herself fingering a strand of the blond hair that came loose from the simple ribbon she used to tie it back. Its silky fairness was foreign, and although she didn't want to fall into the sin of vanity, she secretly longed for the day when her hair would grow past her shoulders and cascade down to her waist, the way a virgin's ought to.

A thumping sounded on the front door.

She started, her body tensing. What if Abbot Baltazar was returning from his visit to the elector to capture her?

A servant hurried to the door. Katharina wanted to command him to bar it and post a plague sign, but what good would it do?

Her gaze darted around the empty room, searching for a place to hide, somewhere to run. But where? She had no place to flee to, no one to help her, no one who cared whether she lived or died.

The servant opened the door, spilling sunshine across the tile and revealing the busy clatter of Mittelstrasse at midday — a passing carriage and calls from the nearby Marktplatz. Before Katharina could move, a young man elbowed past the servant into the room. His tabard, rimmed with lynx fur, flapped around his legs and revealed slashed breeches. One leg was yellow, the other black, with taffeta forming bands in differing patterns on each.

"Don't delay." He tilted his velvet beret

and revealed a sharply featured face. "Take me to the nun."

Katharina shook off the apprehension. A woman of her status wouldn't cower. She would face adversity with dignity. Wiping her hands on her linen apron, she stood and pulled her petite frame to its fullest height. "I'm Katharina von Bora. You're seeking me?"

The man's attention shot to her, and his eyes widened as he took in the length of her. A sudden smile lit his clean-shaven face.

At his perusal she had the urge to fold her arms across her too-defined chest. Instead she forced herself not to fidget but to be composed, as a lady should be.

He crossed the space between them. "Ah, at last I get to meet one of the runaway nuns." The aristocratic lines of his face were softened by a boyish charm. His shoulder-length hair, neatly cropped in the style of Emperor Charles V, added to the aura of his youth and noble status. He didn't look like anyone Abbot Baltazar would hire.

"If you have any intention of persuading me to return to Marienthron, you may as well know I won't go back," she stated.

"Persuade you to return to Marienthron?" Thick lashes blinked at her, and his gaze lingered over her bare skin making her wish

148

for the protection of her veil. "No, I won't take you to Marienthron. Instead, I believe I'll take a pretty lady like you with me to Nuremberg."

His words sent a wave of emotions through her — relief, surprise, embarrassment.

They hadn't been properly introduced. She had no skill in exchanging banter with men. Who was he anyway?

"I beg your pardon," she said, stepping back. Proper etiquette demanded formal introductions before they spoke.

"Is that you, Jerome?" A door opened, and Elsa's voice came from behind Katharina.

"My dear Elsa." He flashed a brief smile at the mayor's wife but brought his attention back to Katharina.

Elsa crossed the tiles once more, her pattens clunking with undisguised eagerness. She brushed past Katharina, pushing her aside, and held out her hand to the man. With a flourish he reached for her fingers and brushed them with a kiss.

A delighted smile transformed Elsa's plain face — the first smile Katharina had seen. "I thought I heard your voice. And I'm glad I wasn't deceived."

"I've only just arrived in Wittenberg." The man's voice was almost a purr. "And I've come here first to see you."

Rosy pink circled Elsa's high cheeks. "How long will you stay this time, Jerome? Last time was too short."

His smile flashed wider, and he shrugged. "I'll stay until your husband gets tired of my flirting and kicks me out like the last time."

Elsa's blush deepened. "He's too stodgy."

"He cannot be too stodgy, Elsa." He winked at Katharina. "Everyone in Nuremberg is talking about the mayor of Wittenberg's new distraction."

Katharina gasped at the same time as Elsa. Jerome threw back his head and laughed.

Katharina could only stare, too astonished by his brashness to speak in defense of herself.

Elsa, however, spoke rapidly. "We didn't have a choice. When Doctor Luther asks for a favor, who can say no?"

"Of course," Jerome said smoothly. "Who can say no to the great Martin Luther? Now introduce me to your guest, my dear Elsa. I'm dying of curiosity."

Elsa tucked her hand into the crook of Jerome's arm and smiled up at him. "She's not my guest. And she isn't worth your time."

"I have all the time in the world." Jerome

slipped out of her grasp. Then he shouldered out of his tabard and held it out to a waiting servant. "Humor me."

Elsa hesitated, but when he smiled at her, she sighed. "Jerome Baumgartner, meet Katharina von Bora."

He reached for Katharina's hand and lifted it to his lips. His deep blue eyes locked with hers, and there was a flash of desire in them that quickened her pulse — whether with fear or anticipation, she knew naught.

The instant the soft moistness of his lips grazed her fingers, her breath stuck in her throat.

"I'm very pleased to meet you, Fräulein Katharina." His voice was soft and inviting. "I'd heard you were lovely, but the words of praise did not do you justice."

She pulled her hand away from him, but his gaze wouldn't let her go. She'd never had anyone speak to her so intimately, and she had no idea how to respond. Although Elsa apparently had learned the art of beguiling a man, the abbey had never schooled her in such matters.

Flustered, all she could manage was a shy smile.

TEN

"We all agree," Melanchthon said. "You should go into hiding as soon as possible."

The shade of the sprawling maple covered the faces of Luther's friends, but the heat of the May afternoon had wilted him. He'd thought the cloister yard would serve as a cool spot for their meeting, but the spring temperatures had grown unseasonably warm.

The innocent giggles of Melanchthon's young daughter, Anna, drew his attention to the center courtyard, where she was running and chasing a butterfly. At two she was hardly taller than the long grass that had sprung up in the cloister yard. Her fair hair with tints of Melanchthon's red shone in the sunlight, the wispy curls blowing in the warm breeze. Compared to the current dismal state of things, she was a buttercup in a field of weeds.

Luther rubbed his sleeve across his forehead and wiped off the sheen of perspiration. "I can't leave. I won't slink away like a whipped dog with its tail between its legs."

"It's not defeat," Pastor Bugenhagen said as he paced behind Melanchthon and Jonas and rubbed his long beard. "It's only a new location where you'll be safe to continue to write and preach."

Luther blew a frustrated breath. How could he stand alone against the advice of his friends? Especially when they were right? The princes would likely sacrifice him to Rome. The recent news hadn't been encouraging. Elector Frederick might be willing to persuade the other princes in Luther's favor, but first Luther had to promise to stop encouraging monks and nuns to leave their monasteries.

"Elector Frederick knows I won't stop helping my brothers and sisters escape the bondage of their convents any more than I'll stop preaching against the relics that fill his Castle Church." Luther took a swig of his beer, trying to ignore the unsettled rumble in his stomach.

"Our elector has shown great patience with you already, Martinus." Pastor Bugenhagen paused his pacing, and his kind eyes regarded Luther. "He could have turned you over to Abbot Baltazar instead of claiming that he was ignorant in the matter of the nuns. The elector knows as well as any of us that you helped them."

Luther shifted on the cool stone bench. "Prince Frederick is sly. He plays the political game well enough by keeping out of the thick of the conflict." A courier had brought word from Torgau, from the home palace of Elector Frederick, that Abbot Baltazar had demanded the return of the nuns. The wise elector had informed the priest that he never interfered in such matters and that he would leave judgment to the church authorities.

"Even in hiding you'll still be able to give us your guidance," Pastor Bugenhagen said.

"Just as I did when I was hiding in Wartburg?" Luther couldn't keep his voice from rising with his ire. "And look what happened. Riots. Disorder. Iconoclasm. Near anarchy."

Jonas snorted. Sprawled on his bench, arms behind his head, he was the only one not sweating. "We didn't have doctrines as clearly defined then as we do now."

"If Martinus leaves," Melanchthon said from his spot on the long bench next to Jonas, "then every crazy Zwickau prophet will descend on Wittenberg claiming to have the newest spiritual revelation."

Luther raised his eyes to the blue sky that showed through the new leaves above him. He'd done nothing for which he should be ashamed. He'd proclaimed the truth — that indulgences wouldn't free souls from purgatory, that only God's grace could. But the pope needed the steady income from the sales of such false documents to support his extravagant lifestyle, a lifestyle Luther had been sickened by during his pilgrimage to Rome many years ago.

But the sad truth was, no one questioned the pope's authority and lived to tell about it. The martyrs who had come before him were proof enough of that. So far he'd taken cover behind the cloak of the elector. But he felt certain that God would not have him hide this time. He must boldly proclaim the freedom that came from a life lived for God. "I cannot hide from danger again. Once was all I can stomach. Now I must stand before death and look the devil in the face."

"If you die, what will happen to the cause?" Melanchthon's voice was somber.

Luther's stomach roiled. What would happen? That question had plagued him night and day for the past year. When he was killed, would these men, his closest advisors, be able to withstand the pressure to recant the truth? Would they stay strong together against adversity? What if everything they'd achieved was destroyed — everyone and everything burned, obliterated for all time?

Surely death would come only when God was finished with him on this earth — and not before. Until then he must not cower from the work that needed to be done.

He took a deep breath of the fresh spring air. "Since Christ shed His blood and died for me, how can I not, for His sake, place myself in danger? We must say, 'Satan, if you frighten me, Christ will give me courage; if you kill me, Christ will give me life.' "

A child's scream from the cloister yard interrupted the start of his sermon. Melanchthon arose at once and sprinted across the yard toward the area where his daughter lay slumped in the tall grass, crying.

Luther stood with a start at the thought that sweet Anna might be hurt. He rushed after Melanchthon, who now knelt next to the little girl and had begun examining her.

"What happened?" Luther asked. "How's she hurt?"

Melanchthon ran his fingers along Anna's leg, and when he pulled them back, they were coated in blood. The young professor stared at the blood, and his already-pale face turned ashen.

"What is it, my good man?" Luther towered above his friend. But Melanchthon's bloody fingers shook and he didn't respond. Luther knelt next to Anna, who turned her big eyes on him, the tears streaking her chubby cheeks, and her sobs tearing his heart. "Shh, darling." He brushed a hand across her feathery hair and smoothed it off her face. "You'll be just fine. You'll see." At the same time he gently shifted the hem of her skirt to reveal a jagged gash. One glance at the nearby bricks that had fallen from the crumbling ledge of the cloister walkway told him what had happened. She'd cut herself on one of the pieces of brick that littered the grass.

He studied the cut again, noting the way the tender flesh had split and formed a gaping white crevice amid the blood. The wound was deep and would need stitching.

Melanchthon gulped in a breath of air and looked at his daughter's leg again. But then covering his mouth, he turned and gagged.

If Anna hadn't been in so much pain, Luther would have been tempted to tease his friend for his weak stomach. But with Anna's pitiful, confused cries echoing around them, Luther scooped her into his arms and cradled her against his chest, careful not to bump her leg. As he rose, her wispy, fair hair tickled his chin, and her arms closed around his neck. At her complete trust and willing affection, his heart swelled with praise for the God who'd designed the beauty of infancy. And something else rose within him — a tender longing to experience the arms of his own child wrapped tightly around his neck.

"You'll be just fine, darling," he whispered and then pressed a kiss against her head. He started across the yard toward the infirmary. "I'll take good care of you. I promise."

Anna's sobs softened but her body still shuddered.

"Wolfgang," he called over his shoulder to his manservant, who was hovering in the shade of the arched walkway. "We'll need a physician to do some stitches."

His servant nodded gravely and bounded toward the gateway that led to the street. Luther carried Anna inside and situated himself on a bench in the infirmary. Although Melanchthon joined them minutes later, Luther didn't relinquish the girl, and Anna seemed content to rest in his arms as Brother Gabriel pressed a warm cloth against her wound.

As they waited for the physician to arrive,

Luther sang softly to her until she stopped crying. Melanchthon leaned against the wall with his head down, berating himself over and over for not paying better attention to Anna and for bringing her along in the first place. He'd only thought to give his wife, who was heavily pregnant with their second child, a break from the busy toddler.

"You're a good father," Luther said. "This was just an accident."

Luther stroked Anna's head, her hair silky beneath his fingers, and again the longing to hold a child of his own stirred within him. Before he could make sense of his feelings or formulate a response, he was startled by the sight of Katharina von Bora striding through the infirmary door with Wolfgang on her heels. He hadn't seen her since she'd left the Black Cloister to live with the Reichenbachs, and their parting hadn't been cordial in light of her displeasure over the new living arrangements.

As she hastened across the room toward him, Luther couldn't prevent himself from gaping at her new appearance. She looked like a different person in her worldly garments that did nothing to hide her slim waist, curved hips, and full bust that had once been concealed by her shapeless habit. Without her wimple and veil, he could see that her hair was a light honey color. She wore a linen cap and had attempted to tie back her hair, but strands still fell in soft waves around her face. Her features had been delicate and pretty even with the severity of the wimple, but now that her face was freed from the tight constriction, her skin glowed, and her cheeks and lips had a fullness that hadn't been there before.

Luther's mouth felt dry and his tongue heavy, as though he'd been fasting for days. He couldn't formulate the question to ask why she was there.

As if anticipating his question, Wolfgang spoke through heaving breaths. "The physician was busy tending the mayor's gout —"

"I offered to come in his stead," Katharina interrupted. With a swish of her skirts, she stepped around Luther's outstretched legs and lowered herself onto the bench next to him. She surveyed Anna, who was huddled against his chest, lifted the warm cloth on the wound, and studied the cut for a moment before replacing the makeshift bandage.

"I'm sorry, Doctor Luther." Wolfgang hovered above him. Sweat flattened his dark hair against his forehead, and his fierce eyes silently rebuked Katharina.

She ignored Wolfgang and instead caressed

Anna's arm. "You're a brave girl, *Liebchen.*" The tenderness of her expression, although meant to soothe the girl, had a calming effect upon Luther too. "I'm here to make you feel better," she assured Anna, who stared at Katharina with open curiosity.

Katharina lifted her gaze and finally met Luther's. Her eyes widened, and the pure blue seemed to flicker with confusion for a moment before she dropped her attention back to Anna, a flush moving up her cheeks. Was his reaction to her appearance that obvious? He shifted on the bench in sudden embarrassment himself.

"Maybe we should wait for the physician," Melanchthon said.

"He may not be available for another hour." Katharina rose and started across the infirmary toward the shelves, which still contained a few supplies. "I may not be a physician, Herr Melanchthon, but I worked for years in the Marienthron infirmary and am quite competent at doctoring."

She paused and looked at Melanchthon. When he finally nodded, she briskly collected several vials and set to work at the long table, concocting whatever it was she needed.

"I'll give your daughter a tincture that will make her sleep," Katharina said as she crossed again to Anna. "Once I know she won't awaken, I'll work on her leg."

Luther's shoulders relaxed at her words. And as she interacted again with Anna, coaxing her to drink the tincture, his admiration grew. He liked Katharina's tenderness, her gentle smile, and her ability to put Anna at ease. She was a good doctor. His thoughts traveled back to the time she'd doctored him during one of his episodes. A warm ache stole through him at the memory of her touch that afternoon. The feel of her skin against his had awakened a longing for a woman in a way he couldn't remember experiencing before, even during the days of his youth.

It didn't take long for Anna to fall asleep. Katharina made quick use of the window of opportunity to work on the girl. She cleaned the wound and sewed several small stitches. When she finished, she bent over Anna and stroked the girl's cheeks. He couldn't stop staring at the bare stretch of Katharina's neck and the loose tendril floating there. The skin seemed to beckon him to graze it, but the very thought of such brazenness made him squirm.

He cleared his throat, hoping he didn't look as foolish as he felt. "I didn't know the color of your hair was so fair."

She smiled. "Neither did I."

"Then you're adjusting to normal life?"

"Well enough." Something in her tone told him she would have complained about her living situation with the Reichenbachs had they been alone.

Anna was still asleep, but Katharina continued to stroke the girl's cheek. "I suppose it must be a relief to be out of the barn and back in your own bed."

"I didn't mind staying in the barn for you." His voice came out breathier than he'd intended. What was wrong with him? His mind scrambled for something to say, anything that could cover the awkwardness of his admission.

She spoke before he could. "You seem to have a natural way with children."

He loved the way Anna was snuggled against his chest, and he couldn't resist caressing her hair again. "I've been with her since she was born. She's like a daughter to me; I suppose as close to a daughter as I'll ever get."

"Maybe you'll have your own one day."

As much as he wished he could agree with her, he could only smile wryly. "I think you're forgetting something."

She lifted her innocent eyes to his and quirked a brow.

"The natural God-given order is to have a wife before begetting children."

She rapidly dropped her attention to Anna, and her cheeks flushed a faint pink.

He wanted to pummel his palm against his forehead at his donkey-brained comment. Melanchthon's frown only confirmed the stupidity of his words and his inadequacy in talking with women, especially a refined woman like Katharina.

"Have you any news about my maidservant, Greta?" Katharina had the grace to change the subject and ease his discomfort. Her eyes held a hopefulness that made him wish he could give her good news, but instead he shook his head.

"Where could she have gone?" Katharina persisted.

"Unfortunately, there aren't many options for an unchaperoned woman."

Her shoulders slumped, and she released a long sigh that had a hint of chamomile.

"We must commit her into God's hands," he urged, wishing he could do more to help Katharina find this wayward servant, touched that she even cared.

She was silent for a long moment, and he had the feeling that his time with her was coming to an end. The thought filled him with more regret than he cared to admit.

"Thank you for coming," he whispered.

"I'll come anytime."

"Even when you're angry at me?"

She glanced over her shoulder. "Perhaps I'm not as angry as I once was."

Luther followed her gaze. A finely dressed young man leaned against the doorframe. His smooth face was familiar, but it took a moment to remember his name. "Jerome Baumgartner."

The man straightened and stepped into the room, then gave a slight bow. "Doctor Luther."

At the sight of Jerome, Katharina's lips parted in a soft smile, and light filled her eyes.

A weight settled on Luther's chest.

Baumgartner had the same dashing aura about him he'd always had. "What are you doing here, Baumgartner?" Luther demanded.

Baumgartner flipped Katharina a grin. "My dear Katharina needed an escort, and I very willingly offered her my service."

"Wolfgang was escort enough."

"Not for a lady like Katharina."

Her smile widened at his flattery. "He's staying with the Reichenbachs, and I've had plenty of opportunities to gain his acquaintance over the week since his arrival."

Plenty of opportunities? "Find another place to stay, Baumgartner." Luther glared at the man.

"He'll do no such thing." Katharina stood and Luther glimpsed the admiration in her eyes as she faced Jerome. "He's quite the gentleman in every way."

Luther snorted. "Baumgartner has a reputation, but it's not as a gentleman."

"And I suppose you're now the expert on what it means to be a gentleman?" Her words, although said with a smile, had a sting to them that he didn't like. Was she putting him down for his class?

He stiffened at the insult whether she intended one or not. "You're right. I'm not a gentleman. But at least I've retained my integrity."

She didn't reply in words, but her eyes told him everything he needed to know. Jerome Baumgartner was the kind of man a woman like Katharina prized. He was nobly born, wealthy, handsome, young, and he had an opinion of himself that was bigger than the Vatican.

Baumgartner would make the perfect match for a proud woman like Katharina von Bora. Indeed, he could think of no man more suited.

ELEVEN

"The rumors get bigger every day," Margaret said as she prodded the soaking linens with the handle of her battledore.

Katharina leaned into the cushion of grass along the shore of the Elbe River. The June sun bathed her face with its warmth. The companionable laughter of other women nearby mingled with the rippling of the wide but gentle river. The grassy plain that led to the walls of Wittenberg was dotted with children playing and running, free of the crowded confines of the city. She took a deep breath of contentment.

Margaret straightened and towered over her as tall and thin as a willow branch. Without her wimple and headband, her face had lost some of its severity, even though she still wore her short dark hair pulled back tightly under a head cap.

"I shall not mind in the least if the rumors come true." Katharina combed her fingers through her own hair that had come loose and tickled her neck, and she gazed at the brilliant blue of the cloudless sky. Although she offered extra prayers at the Divine Hours for considering her appearance, she still fought the new feelings of womanliness and couldn't deny she rather liked them. "Indeed," she said, relishing the breeze against the bare skin on her arms where she'd pushed up her sleeves, "I shall be a very happy woman should the rumors come true." Her time teaching the Reichenbach girls had only intensified her longing for daughters of her own.

"You wouldn't like the rumor I overheard this morning." Margaret's kind eyes brimmed with worry.

"The ladies are jealous, just like Elsa." But Elsa was more than jealous. She'd become unbearable. If Jerome hadn't made frequent use of his charming influence over the woman, Katharina was sure Elsa would have found a way to make her work as hard and as long as humanly possible.

"Some of the apprentices were talking in the workshop," Margaret continued, "and I couldn't help but listen."

"And why were you in the workshop? You're now taking up painting?"

A shy smile brought light to Margaret's

face. "I found a portrait of Doctor Luther. Master Cranach isn't finished with it yet, but the likeness is so astounding I can't stay away from it."

"Then you're truly smitten."

"Doctor Luther's the most amazing man I've ever known."

Katharina's thoughts returned to the last time she'd helped Doctor Luther. A portrait of him was painted in her mind — him sitting on the hard infirmary bench with Anna Melanchthon in his arms, his ink-stained fingers combing tenderly through the toddler's hair.

Inevitably Katharina's thoughts diverged to the way Doctor Luther had looked at her when she'd first walked into the infirmary. There had been something in his eyes, something intense, that had told her he was seeing her as a woman and that he liked what he saw. Her belly sparked with a strange heat just thinking about that moment.

She scrambled to conjure Jerome's face in place of Doctor Luther's, which should have been easy since she hadn't seen Doctor Luther often since that day in the infirmary. He was apparently busy traveling and preaching in the surrounding towns. She'd heard he was venturing out even though the risk was high. And yet she couldn't keep from wondering if his distance was due to more than just his travels, for even when he was in Wittenberg, he never sought her out, although she wasn't sure why she expected that he would.

"I would consider myself blessed by Saint Priscilla and the Virgin Mother herself for the chance to marry him," Margaret said wistfully.

Katharina sat up, and as she studied the eagerness in her friend's face, her muscles tightened in a protest she couldn't understand. "Has he shown you any interest?"

Margaret sighed. "Not in the least. I can't remember when he's ever even looked at me."

Strangely, a whisper of relief loosened the tension in Katharina's spine. At least she could say with confidence that Doctor Luther had looked at her. He'd looked at her long and hard and — dare she say — with desire.

With a shake of her head, she shoved herself off the ground and stood before Margaret could glimpse her thoughts. What did it matter if Doctor Luther had paid her attention on occasion? He wasn't looking at her anymore. And she didn't want him to. If Margaret wanted to marry Doctor Luther, then she should have him.

"We shall have to find a way to make Doctor Luther notice you." Katharina reached for her battledore and used the end of it to ladle her linens out of the shallow pool at the edge of the river where she'd been soaking them.

"How will he ever notice me?" Margaret rose and began to fish her linens out of the river too.

"We'll think of something." Katharina wrung the water out of the undertunic, then spread it on the washing stock, a small flat table Margaret had borrowed from Master Cranach's house.

"Now tell me the rumor about Jerome."

Margaret glanced around. The riverbank was crowded with clusters of women from the town who were taking advantage of the warmth and sunshine to launder bedding and undergarments. The townswomen had peered at them from time to time but had thankfully left them undisturbed on the fringe.

Margaret lowered her head and voice. "The other Cranach servants have placed bets on you and Jerome."

"Go on." Katharina rubbed her tunic with the heavy block end of the battledore, loosening the odor and grime that had accumulated since the previous washing weeks ago.

"Jerome has made claims that he'll bed the virgin nun before the feast of the Visitation."

"I've heard such nonsense already." Embarrassment infused Katharina as it had the first time she'd overheard the whispers.

"Then you don't think it's true?"

"It is complete and utter foolish talk." At least she desperately prayed it was. "Jerome has been kind and considerate in every way."

"Then his intentions toward you are truly honorable?"

"I have reason to believe he may propose marriage soon."

Margaret's eyes widened.

Katharina began pounding the linen. "He cannot stay in Wittenberg much longer. And he's hinted at taking me to his family estate in Nuremberg."

"Oh, Katharina, how divine." Margaret smoothed a pair of hose onto the washing stock next to her. "I know life with Jerome will be exactly what you've wanted. You'll finally have a family of your own." She paused and her voice caught. "But I shall miss you if you move to Nuremberg."

They'd been together since their families had abandoned them, scared little girls

172

who'd found comfort in their forbidden friendship amid the strange rituals and cold silence of the convent.

"I'm sure we'll visit Wittenberg from time to time. Jerome is always talking about how he misses his university days." Katharina's arms ached from sledging the battledore against the clothes. After only a few minutes, the bat had grown so heavy it felt as if it were made of bricks instead of wood. Her breath grew choppy until finally she stopped.

"How do the other women do this?" she asked. "I've laundered just one garment, and I'm already tired." She peered at the others along the riverbank, at the natural-ness and efficiency with which they worked. Servants had done the laundry for them at Marienthron, servants like Greta. She'd never realized how hard those lay sisters had to work, how much effort went into some-thing as simple as washing clothes.

She sighed. Maybe she'd made Greta work too hard. Or maybe she hadn't shown her servant enough appreciation for all the tasks she'd done daily. Perhaps if she'd shown Greta more compassion or if she'd reassured Greta that somehow they'd make things work out . . . She certainly hadn't treated Greta the way Elsa treated her, had she? What if she'd done more for her servant? Maybe then Greta wouldn't have run away.

Katharina narrowed her eyes at the sight of two men approaching a cluster of women near the wooden bridge that spanned the Elbe.

Margaret pounded her hose. "I rather like doing the washing and the other jobs Mistress Cranach assigns me. The work makes the hours pass more quickly. My days are much more interesting now than they were at the convent."

The men spoke with the townswomen. Then one of the housewives turned and pointed toward her and Margaret.

A shiver streaked up Katharina's backbone.

"I never realized the monotony of our lives." Margaret hammered her linens, raising her voice above the racket. "So much of our time was taken with services and prayers and embroidery."

The men nodded at the townswomen, then turned and began strolling forward again.

From a distance they were not recognizable. Their gaits were unhurried, and yet Katharina's pulse picked up speed. Should she order Margaret to gather their dripping linens and run? She glanced across the span of grass to the thick wall of the town and the gate leading inside. They could make it if they hurried.

"Do you miss anything about our life at the convent?" Margaret dropped the battledore and massaged her arms.

Katharina shook off the trepidation. Surely they had nothing to worry about — not when they were surrounded by so many people.

"Of course I miss Aunt Lena." Katharina wished she could discover how the dear woman was. She ached every time she thought of the words of love her aunt had whispered during the night of the escape, and she longed to hear them again. But attempting any contact would only put Aunt Lena in greater danger, and she wouldn't risk that again.

"I miss the other sisters." Margaret picked up another linen and began smoothing it out. "And I admit, there are times when I miss our devotion to God. Here, outside convent walls, it's too easy to get swept away in the busyness of our lives and neglect to give God the attention and prayers He deserves."

Katharina nodded, having felt the same tug. But her attention again strayed to the men drawing nearer. Something about them looked familiar. Too familiar. Fear slithered up her arms, making the pale hairs there stand on end.

"Margaret, collect your laundry."

Margaret looked at her with wide eyes and then followed her gaze. "Isn't that the woodcutter from Marienthron?"

Katharina's chest tightened. Margaret was right. The shorter man with thick arms *was* the woodcutter. The missing earlobe and scar along the jaw could belong to no one else. The other was one of the unskilled laborers who sometimes worked with the convent's sheep and goats.

"I wonder why they're here." Margaret let her linen dangle into the grass.

The woodcutter said something to his companion, and their strides grew longer and quicker.

"We need to run, Margaret. Now." Katharina grabbed a fistful of her skirt and scrambled up the bank.

"What about the laundry and equipment —"

"Leave it." Katharina spurted forward through the thick grass, stumbling in her haste.

A cry from Margaret froze her steps. She glanced back, and her heart plummeted at the sight of Margaret on the ground, tangled in the overturned washing stock, struggling to free herself.

"Hurry, Margaret!"

The men were running now too, closing the distance.

Katharina raced back and slipped down the bank. *Hail Mary, full of grace, the Lord is with thee.* With shaking hands she shoved the bench off her friend and yanked her to her feet. "Hurry!"

But Margaret was twisted in the wet linens and tripped again.

Katharina clawed at her friend's arm and dragged her forward. The pounding of her heart ricocheted through her head. *Holy Mary, Mother of God. Be with us now.*

"Where do you think you're going?" The woodcutter's greeting was followed by his pinching grip on Katharina's wrist. "It's not polite to leave without saying a proper greeting."

He spun her, forcing her to relinquish her grip on Margaret.

"Uh-huh, Cal, not polite at all."

The taller laborer hauled Margaret to her feet. In the struggle his broad straw hat fell off, revealing thin black strands of hair that didn't fully cover his balding scalp.

Behind Katharina the woodcutter pushed

closer. "I suggest you say 'good day' to Cal before he gets angry."

Katharina twisted and caught a glimpse of the woodcutter's puckered scar and gaping earlobe. She yanked hard, trying to free herself. "Let go this instant."

He made a clicking noise with his tongue and the roof of his mouth. "I won't be letting go until I get the payment I've been promised."

He didn't have to say anything for her to know who would be paying him. All she knew was that she had to escape. Now. Before it was too late. Her gaze darted around and landed on her discarded battledore. She turned on the woodcutter and began kicking and scratching.

He swore and backed away. His grip loosened for an instant.

It was the second she needed. She ripped free and lunged for the washing bat. Her fingers closed around it, and she swung it wildly, forcing the woodcutter to retreat.

"Cal's got a knife, don't you, Cal?" The woodcutter lifted his arms to protect his head. "And Cal won't mind cutting up your friend's pretty face with it, will you, Cal?"

Margaret cried out in pain.

At the sight of Cal pressing the tip of his

knife against Margaret's chin, Katharina
froze.

TWELVE

A dot of blood dripped onto Cal's hand, but his face was emotionless, as if Margaret were nothing more to him than an animal hide in need of tanning.

"Stop. Let her be." Katharina threw down her battledore.

The woodcutter pounced on her and yanked her arms behind her back with such force that hot pain blinded her, and a cry slipped from her lips.

"What do you say, Cal? Every time my gal don't cooperate, you put a slice in your gal's face?"

Cal grunted.

The blood on Margaret's chin glistened. Her friend stood absolutely still, her eyes scrunched closed, her face pinched.

"Put the knife away." Katharina could hardly speak for the burning in her arms. "I'll do whatever you say as long as you don't hurt Margaret."

The woodcutter chortled. "Now that's a good girl. No need for anyone to get hurt if you cooperate."

Cal lowered the knife.

Katharina exhaled. The drive to fight deflated. She couldn't chance Margaret getting hurt.

She didn't resist when the woodcutter tied her hands behind her back or when he shoved her past the townswomen, who watched silently without making a move to help. Did they dislike her and Margaret so much that they could stand by and let these men lead them away like sheep to the slaughter? Did they truly believe the runaway nuns should go back where they belonged?

The woodcutter pushed her along, up the grassy bank and over the bridge that led away from Wittenberg, and Cal followed behind with Margaret. The men directed them to a covered wagon concealed in a grove of willows. They made quick work of gagging them and binding their feet too. When they lifted the covering and shoved them into the wagon bed, Katharina's heart sank at the sight of Margaret's sister, Eva, already bound and gagged, curled into a ball with tears streaking her cheeks.

Margaret scooted over to her sister and

tried to comfort her as best she could.

Katharina listened to the woodcutter argue with the driver, and their words confirmed her fear — the men were working for Abbot Baltazar. They were looking for one more, Greta, and the driver didn't want to go until they found her. But the woodcutter insisted that she was gone, that the townswomen said she'd left Wittenberg weeks ago.

Eventually the wagon began to roll and jostle them mercilessly. Under the tarp the musty, damp odor of the wagon bed filled Katharina's senses. The sun beat down on the tarp and baked them beneath. Over and over she chastised herself for failing to protect Margaret, for not running when they'd had the chance. Her mind jumped between Ave Marias, Our Father prayers, and efforts to plan their escape. And she tried not to think about what was in store for them at the end of their journey.

The endless bumping was torture, but it was nothing compared to the dryness that had overtaken her mouth and throat, made worse by the dirty cloth filling it. The increasing desperation in Margaret's and Eva's eyes told her they were suffering in the same way.

Her efforts to loosen the rope binding her

wrists resulted in nothing but skin chafed raw. Finally she could only lie in utter exhaustion like her friends. Her mind screamed not to give up, but she grew too hot and weary to move.

Eventually the wagon lurched to a stop. She could hear the loosening of the tarp, and then sunshine fell across her and blinded her. She tried pushing herself up, but rough hands wrenched her forward, dragged her like a bag of barley, and tossed her to the side of the road.

The impact with the ground jolted her breath from her chest. But blessedly the men untied their gags and passed them a jug. Apparently, Abbot Baltazar wanted them alive. The only question was why. So that he could torture them to death himself?

The men returned them to the wagon and didn't stop again until darkness settled. By then Katharina was so sore and tired and weak she could only lie listlessly next to Margaret and Eva on dried pine needles and moss and watch their captors as they ate and bedded down.

Their kidnappers had located a secluded grove, thickly wooded with spruce and cedar. They hadn't bothered with a fire, and now the chill of the deepening night crept through the thick undergrowth and surrounded them.

She waited for even breathing that signaled the men were slumbering before she wriggled the binding on her hands. The skin on her wrists was already rubbed raw from her efforts in the wagon to loosen the rope, and the attempt was as useless now as it had been before.

With her gaze fixed on the motionless forms of the men half a dozen steps away, she pushed her hands into Margaret, hoping her friend would understand what she needed to do and would now have the strength they'd lacked in the wagon bed.

The tug of Margaret's teeth on her rope told her that Margaret was more alert than she'd realized. Margaret struggled until Katharina's wrists were hot and slick from her friend's futile efforts. Finally Katharina sidled behind Margaret and tried her turn at using her teeth to untie the rope. She had no other plan. If they failed, she wasn't sure she wanted to see another day.

At the snap of a twig behind them, Katharina tensed and pulled away from Margaret. But a large hand cupped her mouth and muffled her gasp.

The heat of the hand suffocated her. With a surge of fear, she jerked to break free.

A mouth pressed against her ear. "Hello,

hissing Katzen."

"Doctor Luther?" Her whisper was caught in the hollow of his hand.

"Yes, it is I, the barking hound." His lips grazed her earlobe.

Her body melted with overwhelming relief. The tension of the day pooled in her chest and rose on the edge of a sob. For a long second the heat of his breath filled the hollow of her ear. His hand remained over her mouth. And she didn't want to move; she wanted to stay safe in his hold.

Slowly he released her and reached for her hands. His knife sawed into the rope, pressing the binding into her skin. He worked quickly, and in only a moment her hands were free, and the cool night air bathed her raw skin.

He moved to her feet and tugged at the rope with his blade. His black cloak hid him, turning him into an apparition. Several other dark figures crouched nearby, and she could hear the slicing of their blades against Eva's and Margaret's bindings.

The tightness around her feet fell away. Before she could push herself up, Doctor Luther clutched her and then crushed her against his body, wrapping his arms around her.

She buried her face in his cloak and took

a deep, shuddering breath. The solidness of his chest and the strength of his grip surrounded her like the walls of a fortress. The fear of Abbot Baltazar and the horror of her capture faded into the distance.

"Are you hurt?" His whisper was low, and his lips grazed against her ear again, sending a shiver through her.

She shook her head, aware of the heat of his mouth, the hoarseness of his breathing, the softness of his lips against her skin. For a long exquisite moment, time stopped, and she had the deepest feeling of being treasured.

Shouts erupted near them, followed by scuffling.

Doctor Luther stiffened. "Stay here and don't move."

"I'll do no such thing."

"So the hissing Katzen has to give all the orders?" She could feel his lips curve into a smile against her ear. "Then what does her majesty command?"

"I'll lead Margaret and Eva away." She was thankful when he didn't protest but instead helped her to her feet.

Once they were standing, he hunched to keep the hood of his cloak from tangling in overhead branches. "Follow the moon toward the west." His face was shadowed, and she wished she could see his features. "When you reach the edge of the field there, wait for us."

She grabbed Margaret's arm and reached for Eva's hand. The darkness of the forest was thick and ominous, reminding her of the night she'd led the women out of Marienthron.

He held out a dagger. "Take this."

"Won't you need it?"

"Take it now and run."

She hesitated.

"This isn't the best time to pick a fight, Kate."

The shouts around them escalated. Scant moonlight slanted through the branches revealing men circling around one another and the glint of outstretched knives.

Doctor Luther grabbed a thick branch off the ground and wielded it like a weapon. Then he thrust the dagger into her hand. "Go."

She nodded and took the weapon. She couldn't jeopardize them again by her indecisiveness. She'd gotten Margaret into this predicament, and now she needed to get them to safety.

"Margaret, Eva, follow me."

They stumbled after her, slow and unsteady. After hours of the ropes cutting off their circulation, their numb legs could hardly carry them over the uneven wagon path. When they could no longer hear the din of the fight, Eva crumpled to the ground.

"Don't stop." Katharina clutched the girl.

Eva's chest heaved with the effort of breathing. "I can't —"

"Get up. We need to move farther away. If the fight doesn't go well . . ." Katharina didn't want to think of Doctor Luther and his friends sustaining injury, possibly dying on account of them.

Margaret took hold of the other side of Eva, and they worked together to drag her along. Their labored breathing and the crunching of twigs under their feet filled the night air. When they reached the clearing, Katharina guided Eva and Margaret into an overgrowth of brush, and then she hid behind a tree. A pasture spread out before them. A grazing doe and her fawn lifted their heads, their glowing eyes finding them all too easily.

They didn't have to wait long before they heard approaching voices.

Katharina shrank against the bark. *Our Father in heaven, hallowed be Thy name. Let it be Doctor Luther and his comrades.*

The words were the closest she'd ever

come to making up her own prayer. Did she dare? She'd heard Doctor Luther and his followers wording their own prayers, but were they right to speak to God with such familiarity? The holy apostles and saints had already written the prayers they needed. Surely she'd do better to pray as she'd been taught.

Thy kingdom come. Thy will be done.

The voices drew nearer, and dark-cloaked figures emerged into the clearing.

"Katharina?" came Doctor Luther's voice.

She exhaled and stood, relief weakening her knees. "Over here."

With long strides he crossed the distance, leaving his friends behind.

"I'm glad I won't need to use this." She held out his knife.

He took it and sheathed it. "Those scoundrels won't be going anywhere soon."

"You killed them?"

He threw back his hood. Moonlight illuminated the haggard lines of his face. His dark eyes searched hers. "My friends and I aren't men of violence. We couldn't murder — even though I've never wanted to more." Before she could respond, he reached for her hands and enclosed them within his.

"We tied them to trees and set the draft horses loose. If the men manage to loosen their bonds, they'll have a long walk ahead of them."

Under his searching gaze, the warmth of his hands spread through her arms and to her middle. "You saved our lives."

His fingers touched the scraped skin on her wrist, and he tugged her closer. His voice dipped low. "When I got the news that you'd been taken, I couldn't function. I thought I would go crazy. I very nearly did." His soft confession lingered over her like a caress.

She had the sudden longing for him to circle her in his solid embrace so she would feel treasured once more. But the movement of the others around her and their voices reminded her they weren't alone.

"How did you find us?"

He nodded to his friends, who were comforting Margaret and Eva. "We picked up your trail early. I wanted to jump the wagon right away, but the others forced me to wait until everyone was asleep."

"Your friends were wise. Abbot Baltazar's men were brutes." She thought of the slice on Margaret's chin that needed stitching and a poultice.

"The abbot is the bigger brute. He's the devil's sword."

"Let's go, Martinus." Jonas straddled his

horse. "You'll have plenty of time later for whispering endearments to Katharina."

A rippling of guffaws among the men sent heat through her.

Margaret was already mounted sidesaddle in front of Jonas, her wide gaze taking in the intimacy of Katharina's position with Doctor Luther.

Katharina snatched her hands away and hid them among the folds of her skirt. *Margaret, dear Margaret, this isn't what you think,* she wanted to say. Instead she took a step away from Doctor Luther.

He took the reins of his horse from Melanchthon and then reached for Katharina.

She backed toward Jonas and Margaret. Her mind whirled, her heart strangely conflicted about what she knew she must do. "Margaret needs to ride with you, Doctor Luther."

He stopped. His gaze bore into hers, searching, questioning.

"It would be for the best." She hoped the darkness masked her confusion.

"What's best, Kate?" His tone was suddenly tense.

She straightened her shoulders. Margaret was in love with him. If he didn't realize it, she must make him see it. And Jerome was best for her. Did Doctor Luther still doubt her choice?

As if he'd heard her thoughts, anger flashed in his eyes like lightning in a midnight sky.

He raised a hand toward Margaret, and his face turned into a stone mask. As Margaret eagerly slid off Jonas's horse into Doctor Luther's arms, Katharina looked away.

Only after Margaret was perched with Doctor Luther on his horse did Katharina attempt to speak. "I'm in debt to your kindness for coming to our rescue —"

"I didn't do it for you." Doctor Luther dug his heels into his horse.

Jonas snorted. "That's right, old man. You did it for your good health."

"Nevertheless," she called to Doctor Luther's retreating back, "I'm grateful for your intervention."

This time he didn't respond except to spur his mount faster.

THIRTEEN

"The Bundschuh again." Luther nodded toward the side of the road to the calf-length rawhide shoe tied by its long leather strips to the top of a crude post. With nothing around but fields and wildflowers, the tall beam and shoe were strangely out of place.

"As their numbers grow, they're becoming more daring." Melanchthon reined his horse next to the pole.

Luther wiped the perspiration on his forehead. What in heaven's name had ever compelled him to begin a preaching expedition around Saxony during the heat of the summer? All his friends had told him traveling was too dangerous. They'd warned against leaving Wittenberg. They'd pleaded with him not to go now. Not when the princes were ready to turn him over to Rome should the pope agree to address their grievances. Not when the princes had given Elector Frederick three mandates, the foremost of which was the prohibition of seditious preaching.

Word had reached Wittenberg recently that their greatest adversary, Duke George, had hoped the Diet of Nuremberg would strip Frederick of his possessions and his rank in the empire for not enforcing the Edict of Worms and for not dealing with heretics in his kingdom. But the only discipline Frederick had received was a scathing letter from the pope.

The outcome of the Diet had incensed Duke George, and now he intended to do everything within his power to destroy the heretics himself and devastate Frederick in the process. He'd already begun imprisoning the monks and priests in his territory who had forsaken their vows in order to marry. He'd recalled his students from the universities under the influence of the reforms. Worst, he'd ordered all copies of the recently translated New Testament to be given up to magistrates and burned.

Luther shifted wearily in his saddle as the high sun beat on his back. Deep inside he knew the real reason he'd left Wittenberg. He still keenly felt Katharina's rejection the night of the rescue a fortnight ago. He supposed it was a good thing she hadn't known how crazy her disappearance had made him, how he would have slipped into one of his melancholic moods except that he'd known he couldn't, that he had to find her first. His wildly beating heart hadn't slowed until he'd finally freed her bonds and pulled her into his arms.

She'd responded to him, or at least he thought she had. But perhaps she'd only reacted out of relief. Perhaps she would have thrown herself into any rescuer's arms. Whatever the case, he knew now that he'd made more of the encounter than he should have. When she'd turned down his offer to ride with him, she'd sent him a message with resounding clarity — she wasn't planning to encourage anything beyond simple friendship with him. She'd already chosen the man she wanted, and he wasn't that man.

Not that he'd offered himself. Not that he wanted more. He didn't.

Even so, he'd felt the sting of her rejection deeply.

With a sigh he stared at the peasant shoe — tattered with use, stained brown from the soil.

Melanchthon stared too. Perspiration plastered his rust-colored curls to his temple. "What message do you think the Bundschuh is trying to send?"

"Perhaps it's their call for peasants to unite in conspiracy."

"Who do you think is leading it? Karlstadt? Müntzer?"

Luther shook his head. "I think there are too many to count now." He'd reprimanded both of the former professors for their violent methods. But they had persisted and now appeared to be stirring the peasants with their preaching.

He lifted his gaze to a nearby field, to the laborers weeding among the new barley. Their bent backs and wide-brimmed hats soaked in the unrelenting sun. Their lot consisted of hard work, poverty, and cruelty. The burden placed upon them by bishops, abbots, princes, and nobility exceeded the capacity for endurance. Several years ago he'd chastised the leaders in his tract "To the Christian Nobility of the German Nation." But they hadn't heeded his advice.

The Bundschuh had good cause to resort to flails and clubs and pitchforks. Yet no matter how justified, rebellion was something he couldn't condone.

Melanchthon was watching the working peasants too. Anxiety clouded his pale features. "We'd best spur our mounts onward."

They dug in their heels and urged their

steeds down the wagon tracks that had worn a path through the long grass of the meadow. They had trotted just past the next curve in the road when a raucous group came into view, heading in their direction.

Luther slowed his horse and took in the peasant garb of most of the men — the shabby hose, long and patched doublets cinched by girdles with hooks for holding pouches and knives. Some had stockings on their heads. Others wore caps with turned-up utility flaps, combs and spoons tucked inside.

Their laughter died when they spotted the approaching riders and caught sight of Luther's habit, which signaled the clergy they'd come to despise. They halted behind the outstretched arms of a large, thick-shouldered man who was missing one eye, the puckered skin of his eye socket grotesquely empty. As if on cue, the group spread out, making the road impassable.

Luther pulled on his reins. Melanchthon's horse whinnied next to him.

The leader's face hardened with unfriend-liness, as did the other browned and weathered faces, some with scars, others missing teeth.

Luther slid his hand underneath his cowl and ran his fingers over the hilt of his dagger. Perhaps he should have shed his monk's garments as most of his friends had long since done — at least for the duration of his trip.

"Good day." The cheerfulness of Melanchthon's greeting was forced. The tightness of it matched the growing tautness in Luther's muscles.

Dark, angry gazes answered.

"Fine midsummer day, wouldn't you agree?" Luther remarked, peering around at the lush green of the countryside, searching for an escape route.

The one-eyed peasant at the head of the group unsheathed a knife. He held it out, its length surpassing the limitation of any city hall measuring knife Luther had ever seen. "You have to pay a toll to pass."

Luther inched his dagger out of its leather casing. "What kind of toll?"

"A monk's toll."

Their best way of escape was back the way they'd come. On their horses they could easily outrun the peasants. "How much do you want?"

"Everything you have." The peasant nodded at their horses.

Could these peasants be nothing more than a wandering band of rebels out to rob them of their worldly goods? "I don't think you know who I am."

"You're nothing more than a lying, cheating monk."

"I'm Doctor Martin Luther."

"How do we know you're Martin Luther?"

A man as thin as a skeleton cracked a gap-toothed grin. "That's him. I seen him preach over in Mansfeld once."

The leader stared at Luther for a long moment. Finally he lowered his dagger. "Martin Luther? Well, why didn't you say so?" The man turned to his companions. "I'll be quartered — it's Martin Luther."

Melanchthon breathed a heavy sigh, one that echoed Luther's relief.

Excitement wound through the group.

Melanchthon leaned toward Luther. "You're their champion, their hero."

Luther nodded, but his friend's words unsettled him. He championed their spiritual freedom, the liberation of their souls from the heavy chains the church had placed on them. He sympathized with their plight under the tyranny of the rich. He was of peasant stock himself. But he couldn't support violence to bring about the changes they needed.

When the leader asked him to join them for a meal and the others chorused their approval, Luther couldn't refuse. They traveled a short distance off the road to a makeshift camp with a scattering of tattered tents alongside a creek. The peasants had erected a flag of the Bundschuh in the center, and Luther realized these men were responsible for the other Bundschuh symbols they'd observed along the road.

At the barking commands of the men, a handful of women hurried to prepare a meal and serve their guests. In the cool shade of the woodland, the men relayed one tale after another of the injustices they had experienced, similar to stories Luther had heard all too often, stories of punishment for fishing in the elector's pond, hunting in a prince's forest, and gathering firewood in unauthorized land.

They were most upset about the case of one of their own, a forester who'd been gored in the leg by a boar while on a hunt for the elector. He'd lost his leg and his livelihood. But the magistrates had refused to give him any of the compensation they owed him.

Luther tossed the mutton bone onto the dwindling fire, then licked his fingers. He hadn't questioned where the peasants had acquired their feast. He didn't want to know.

"I understand your complaints," he said, rising from the log that had served as a bench for his meal. "And maybe I can intervene on behalf of your forester."

"We only want the lords to observe their agreements," the one-eyed leader said, then he sank his teeth into another juicy bite of mutton. The heavy haze of smoke drifting around them carried the lingering aroma of roasted lamb and water chestnuts.

"They aren't held accountable the way they need to be." Luther's attention returned to a ragged woman on the edge of the camp. He'd noticed her earlier and was still puzzled by her. She moved listlessly with vacant eyes. He assumed she was like the other women, a slave by day and a camp Jezebel by night. Yet somehow she didn't fit. Her features were too pretty, too fresh, too delicate to be those of a peasant woman accustomed to deprivation and hard labor in the fields.

"I'll leave you with one final word." He stretched. "A sensible ruler is rare, a good one even rarer. By and large they are the dumbest fools and greatest villains on earth. Still, the Lord expects you to honor and fear them."

They grumbled. "But you'll take up our cause, won't you?"

"Rest assured, I'll do whatever I can."

When he and Melanchthon were finally

on their way again, heaviness weighed him down.

"They're a despised and unhappy lot," Luther said, spurring his horse to a trot through the tall grass and the whir of dragonflies.

"I fear they're ready to act first and think later." Melanchthon wiped his pointed goatee, rubbing out the remains of their meal. "And the consequences of such rashness will be unnecessary bloodshed."

"Now that the light of truth, so long suppressed by the pope and his followers, has begun to shine brightly again, the tyranny of Rome and her followers has become visible. Unless they reform, I too fear revolt is imminent."

"Perhaps it's time for you to write another tract, one that addresses both nobility and peasants, imploring them to seek peace."

"You're right. And we'll pray. Prayer shall be our greatest weapon." Luther urged his horse faster. The long summer day was on their side, but they would be wise to reach the safety of Dessau before eventide.

They rode for several more hours in peace, discussing the merits of education and the need to develop tools whereby they could easily teach doctrines of historic Christianity to more people, perhaps through a catechism. "And perhaps when we finish with that," Luther said, his mind spinning with possibilities, "we could write a smaller catechism that would be designed for children, like Anna."

"I'd like that very much," Melanchthon replied wistfully, no doubt thinking of his daughter and the newborn babe he'd left behind to accompany Luther.

Luther had a momentary pang of guilt for pulling his friend away from his family. But the instant he thought of returning to Wittenberg, he could feel Katharina in his arms again, the crush of her supple body against his when he'd freed her from her bonds. He could feel the silk of her hair, the delicate curve of her ear, the warmth of her lips in his palm when he'd cupped her mouth to keep her from making a noise.

As quickly as the thoughts came, he pushed them aside. He didn't want to explore these new reactions to her. He wanted to keep that part of himself closed off as he had for so many years. But even if he tried not to think of how womanly she felt and looked, he pictured her anyway. He thought about her tenderness with Anna when the little girl had been injured, about how Katharina had come without being asked and had checked on Anna in the following days. He thought of how she'd doctored him. And he'd heard from others in town of her willingness to provide her physic services to anyone who needed them.

It appeared that no matter how far he traveled to get away from Katharina, he was destined to think of her wherever he went. He had to admit that although she was as proud as royalty, she was compassionate. And he respected her for that. She'd even shown considerable distress over her lost maidservant.

"That girl back at the peasant camp," he said after a moment. "What if she was Katharina von Bora's lost servant?" He tugged on his reins and checked the position of the sun. It hung low in the sky and lengthened the shadows around them. "Perhaps we should go back and check."

Melanchthon shook his head and slowed his horse. "It's much too far back. We'd never make it by nightfall. And besides, if it is her servant, I doubt she'd willingly leave the camp even if the Bundschuh allowed it."

Luther's mount came to a complete halt. He knew his companion was correct. Nonetheless, he could already feel Katharina's disappointment. "Katharina wouldn't let me live if she learned I allowed this opportunity to slip by."

"I'm sure she's too busy with Jerome Baumgartner to worry about a missing servant."

The mere mention of Baumgartner's name sent a rush of irritation through Luther. The sly weasel. The boy was full of flatulence and had been since his university days. And now he'd blown hot air in Kate's face just as he had countless other girls.

Why did she want a man like Baumgartner? What did she see in him? But even as the questions bombarded him, despair quickly followed. He knew exactly what Katharina saw in Baumgartner. He was the kind of man who could give Katharina the lifestyle she desired.

Well, she could have him. If she was shallow enough to care for the boy, then she deserved him. He didn't want Katharina von Bora anyway. Plenty of other women would have him. In fact, sixteen more nuns had just fled the Wiederstedt convent in Mansfeld. He could have his pick . . . if he wanted. But he didn't want a wife. He wanted a reformation of the church. And as long as he had breath, his one and only desire was to carry forth the mission God had given him.

He felt Melanchthon's intense gaze upon

him as though waiting for him to come to the same conclusion. He guessed Melanchthon had mentioned Jerome's name on purpose, had known the reaction it would elicit.

"Ach." Luther kicked his heels into his mount, prodding it to a gallop. "Make haste, Melanchthon!" he shouted over his shoulder. "Do you have balls and chains on your hands and feet?"

Run. The horse hoofs pounded faster. *Run.*

He didn't want to think of Katharina von Bora anymore.

Maybe if he ran farther and faster, he'd finally outdistance his thoughts of her.

Fourteen

Katharina placed her hands on the fine linen head coverings of the Reichenbach girls, her heart warm with contentment. After tutoring them for all of June, she'd grown fond of them. "You're doing well with your lesson today, *discipulae.*"

The young girls sat straight on the bench in front of a low table. Their dainty faces peered up at her, alight with smiles. "Thank you, *magistra.*"

She shook her head. "In Latin. *Gratias tibi, magistra.*"

"Gratias tibi, magistra."

"Good. We shall complete the Pater Noster, and then you shall finish memorizing vocabulary."

They nodded and bent their heads back to their wax tablets and styli. They understood what a privilege she was giving them by teaching them Latin. Not only were they of burgher class, but also they were girls.

While their brothers attended the school down the street, as girls they were lucky to be given any education, even at home in the hottest, dingiest dormer room of the house.

Katharina fanned herself with the lacy cap she'd pulled off her head. Today the low ceiling beams and normally cool walls seemed to radiate heat into the narrow room that was as small and plain as her cell had been in the abbey. In spite of the heat, she loved every minute she was able to spend with the girls.

She'd decided over the past month of tutoring that when she had children of her own, she'd never send them away from her home for any reason. She couldn't imagine how a parent could bear the parting. How had her father been able to live with himself after he'd sent her to Marienthron?

Here was a portrait of what having her own children might be like, and it stirred her with anticipation. This was exactly what she wanted — a family into whom she could pour her life and love. A family of her own. A family that would never leave her.

The door of the dormer room squeaked open.

"Katharina?" Jerome peeked in, his hair flopping over his bright eyes. He spoke in a singsong tone. "Where oh where is Katharina?"

The girls giggled.

He glanced around. Then as if having satisfied himself of their privacy, he stepped into the room, ducking to keep from bumping his head on the slanted ceiling. He wore a new ready-made gray jerkin trimmed with black velvet and was attired as usual in brightly colored plunder pants with fashionable splits. He was the perfect representation of nobility, and her heart quickened at the thought that she would be restored to her rightful status when she married him.

"Sophie, Anna, time to go." He cocked his head toward the door.

The girls started to rise.

Katharina had done her best to maintain propriety with Jerome. And against all rumors, he'd remained a gentleman. Still, she couldn't cast aside the niggling apprehension at the thought of being completely alone with him.

"Discipulae, stay where you are." She motioned for them to sit. "You're not done with your lessons."

Jerome smiled — one of his beguiling smiles that never failed to make her heart patter. "Of course you're done, aren't you, girls?"

Sophie and Anna smiled but turned confused gazes toward her.

"Start on your vocabulary," she instructed.

Their attention swung back to Jerome.

He winked at them with his thick lashes. "I've something very important to ask Fräulein Katharina."

"You may ask me now." She mopped the dampness on her neck, wishing the tiny window afforded more breeze and light.

"This is something very, very important, my dear." His eyes were filled with sparkling promises. "I must ask you in absolute privacy."

Her body shivered with sudden expectation. Would he finally ask her to marry him?

"Now, girls, go on." He propelled them toward the door.

They looked at her again, clearly wishing to please and obey her. The thought that they returned her affection warmed her heart. But how could she resist Jerome? "Very well. We shall finish our lesson later."

Once the door closed behind her students, a voice of caution urged her to follow them. Certainly Jerome couldn't make the customary visit to her parents to ask their permission to marry her. But shouldn't they have witnesses for so momentous an event?

As he neared her, his gaze strayed to her

neckerchief, to the dipping V that revealed her throat. His eyes were dark with a look she was beginning to recognize as desire. It was a look she'd seen there more frequently lately, one that filled her with a mixture of both wariness and strange anticipation.

She stepped behind the table, putting a barrier between them. "What do you need to ask me, Jerome?"

"I'm leaving for Nuremberg. My father and mother expect my return by the first day of July."

"Then you'll leave in the morning?" Her pulse sped. Would he take her with him?

His gaze slid down her body. "It depends."

"Upon what?"

"Upon you, my dear."

"You're conversing in riddles. Speak plainly."

He edged around the table toward her. "My dearest Katharina, it's no secret you have captured my heart. I want nothing more than to take you back to Nuremburg with me and make you my wife."

Her breath caught in her throat. Was this it? Was he asking her to marry him?

"You're beautiful, Katharina." He sidled nearer.

She couldn't move. Even when he stood before her, she could only stare and wait —

wait for the words that would finally give her everything she wanted.

He reached out and grazed her cheek. "Let's be betrothed today, right now."

"Now?" Her excitement over his proposal was tempered by his unusual request of urgency. "But we have no witnesses, no justice for the ceremony —"

"We don't need anyone." His hand strayed to her neck.

"You're confusing me again, Jerome."

He was close enough that she could feel his hot breath on her forehead. "There are many bishops who've been recognizing unions made in private."

"But custom dictates we should have witnesses."

"The customs are outdated. And that's why the church sanctions secret marriages."

Secret marriages? Katharina's heartbeat slowed to a stammering halt. "Certainly we can have a proper betrothal. There's no need to have one in secret."

His mouth hovered at the edge of her forehead. "I must have time to prepare my parents for the news of our betrothal. And I need to make arrangements for your arrival."

All the anticipation that had been mounting suddenly plummeted. "Then you'll be leaving without me?"

"Only for a short time. But I'll return for you."

"Your parents won't be pleased with me?" Was that it? Was her lack of a dowry a stumbling block after all?

"They don't know you the way I do." His lips grazed her temple. The pressure was hot and sticky in the heat of the room. "But if we've consummated our union, how can they disapprove?"

She was naive about many things concerning men and relationships but understood enough about the marriage bed to know what was required. "You want to lie with me and make me your wife in the truest sense?" As she spoke the words, embarrassment added to the stifling, stale air around her.

He smiled. "Exactly."

"And then this secret marriage will be approved by the church?"

"Eventually, when the time's right, we'll announce our marriage and find a bishop to recognize it." He cupped her chin. Desire had hardened the lines of his face, and he dipped toward her, aiming his mouth for hers.

Over the past month he'd tried to sneak a kiss whenever he caught her alone. But so far she'd always maintained boundaries with him, wanting to build a relationship based on friendship first. And it had indeed been a delightful month of talking, taking walks, playing games, visiting with Jerome's friends, and doing ordinary things she'd never been allowed to do in the convent. She'd finally grown more comfortable in the presence of men, especially Jerome.

She couldn't deny that she wondered what it would be like to finally kiss him. And now that he'd proposed, what was the harm in letting him kiss her, especially in light of his suggestion of a secret marriage?

As if sensing her acquiescence, suddenly his lips pushed against hers, slipping and sliding, hot with eagerness and passion. His body pressed toward hers. And she could feel her face flame with the embarrassment of not knowing how to respond.

If she gave herself to him, she'd secure her place as his wife. She'd get everything she wanted and more — a husband, children, a family, wealth, status. All she had to do was consummate their union.

His hands found their way to her back, roamed upward, and began to untie her laces.

With his lips still slippery against hers, she fought the urge to push away from him.

Kissing was much messier than she'd expected. How much longer must she let him press against her before she could politely pull away?

His fingers continued to fumble with her laces until her bodice began to slacken, to pull away from her overheated skin. Was he undressing her?

Ave Maria.

She squirmed, unable to resist prying herself from his grasp. His mouth on hers was suddenly suffocating. "Stop, Jerome."

His grip tightened.

What was the difference between fornication and a union made in private? She pushed against his chest. "Stop this instant."

"Don't stop me, Katharina." His breath against hers was hot. "If you want to secure our future together, then you must let me have you."

Was he giving her an ultimatum? With a deep breath she ripped away from him and hastily stepped back around the table. He stumbled toward her, and she held out her arms in warning. "I want you to stop, Jerome."

Irritation flashed across his boyish features. He ran his fingers through his cropped hair and combed it away from his face.

"If you care about my reputation and my

honor," she spoke breathlessly, "then you'll understand my need to betroth ourselves before God and witnesses as is required."

"And if you cared about me" — his voice was strained — "you'd understand how important this is for me."

"I do care for you." She glanced at the ceiling. "It's just that —" Just what?

Straggling cobwebs hung above her. The beams were dusty and rotting with mold. Lit only by the small dormer window she had opened earlier, the room was dismal — not the kind of place she'd consider appropriate for a marriage bed. Not here on the hardwood floor. Not with the fear of someone walking in on them.

"I can't, Jerome." In addition to the less-than-ideal conditions, she'd planned to be a real bride and experience a real ceremony. Since escaping from the convent, she and the other sisters had talked excitedly about what their wedding days would be like.

He blew an overlong breath which clearly communicated his exasperation.

"But I promise I shall wait for you," she continued, not wanting to disappoint him. "When you return for me, then we shall be betrothed and follow it not long afterward with the *Kirchgang,* the public wedding ceremony."

"I didn't think you'd be so difficult, Katharina. I knew you'd be chaste. But I expected that after years of suppressing your desires you would show more willingness, more curiosity about the ways between a man and a woman."

The boldness of his words made her duck her head in mortification. "I'm willing, Jerome. Just not like this — not for our first time."

"Tomorrow then? I'll find another spot, a private place." His eyes pleaded with her. "Please, Katharina, I promise you celestial pleasure."

She met his eager gaze. Her heart weighed each of his words. Surely she could give up her silly plans for a real wedding. Besides, she had nothing to lose by doing what he wanted. They must mate sooner or later. Why not now?

On the other hand she had everything to lose if she refused him. Perhaps he'd be angry with her and reject her. Perhaps when he told his parents about her, they would object. Perhaps he would find someone else.

But what of the rumors? What if his eagerness to bed her had more to do with winning a bet than consummating their secret marriage?

She allowed herself an inward groan at

her predicament before giving him a compromise. "I shall think about it tonight,
Jerome."

He grinned.

"But only if you promise that whatever I
decide, you'll marry me the very first day
you return to Wittenberg."

"That, my dear, I can promise."

FIFTEEN

Forgive me my sins, O Lord. Forgive me my sins.

Katharina unrolled the crinkled paper, her only possession of any value.

O my God, I am heartily sorry for having offended Thee, and I detest all my sins. Maybe if she prayed through the Act of Contrition often enough *and* did penance, God would truly forgive her for what she was about to do.

She smoothed the paper on her lap and fingered the fading ink. And if He didn't forgive her, she could always rely on her indulgence for help. Her mother's hands had trembled when she'd given it to her. Her voice had been a mere whisper when she'd instructed her to keep it with her always so that someday they could see each other in heaven. If she was making the wrong choice — if she was sinning by consummating her relationship with Jerome

— then surely the indulgence would keep her from condemnation.

Hurried footsteps clunked on the balcony outside the room in the servants' quarters that Margaret shared with her sister, Eva. Katharina rolled the indulgence and stuffed it into her pouch.

"Katharina?" Margaret swung open the door, flooding the narrow room with light. It revealed the sparseness and the lack of worldly possessions that plagued them in their current working situations.

Katharina arose from the straw pallet and tucked her pouch back into hiding beneath her underbodice.

"Eva said that you were here, that you needed to see me." Margaret's breath came in short bursts. "What ails you?"

"Close the door."

Margaret pushed it shut, snuffing out the sunshine and casting a cloak over the room. Because of Margaret's height, her plain skirt, a castoff from one of the townswomen, barely touched her ankles. But in the weeks she had lived and worked at the Cranachs', she'd begun to fill out so that her features were softer.

"I need you to come with me." Katharina straightened her own castoff skirt. "I'm to gather firewood this morn and am in need of a companion."

Margaret's breathing grew suddenly silent.

"We must make haste," Katharina said.

"But we did this work only yesterday morn."

Katharina picked up a large woven basket next to her and slipped her arms through the straps so it hung down her back.

"And, besides, I'm in the middle of making beds." Margaret held up a bed staff, the club used for smoothing the heavy linen sheets.

Katharina put a finger to her lips. "I shall not be collecting wood."

Margaret's eyes widened.

"I shall be meeting Jerome."

"Oh, Katharina." Dismay weighted her friend's words.

"He sent me a message that I'm to find the grove of quince on the south of the Elbe. I'm to meet him there when the bells ring for Terce."

Margaret's brow furrowed, and she shook her head.

Even though her friend's hesitancy mirrored her own, she refused to acknowledge it. "You must come with me."

"Do you realize what tomorrow is?"

At her friend's abrupt question, Katharina's thoughts tumbled like barrels in a wagon bed. "I don't care what day tomorrow is."

"But, Katharina, tomorrow's the feast day of the Visitation."

"What does it matter?" She spoke more irritably than she'd intended, and she blamed it on the fact that she'd tossed and turned on her pallet most of the night. Now her head ached. "Let's be on our way."

Margaret put out a hand to stop her. "Don't you remember the rumors? the bets?"

Katharina kneaded circles in her temple. Yes, she did remember the rumors. But after thinking about all her options, she'd come to the conclusion she must do as Jerome wanted. It was the only way to guarantee the future she wanted. If he won a bet by bedding her by the day of the Visitation, what difference would it make?

"He's promised to marry me when he returns to Wittenberg."

"Then why not wait?"

Katharina rubbed her eyes trying to ward off a faint headache. "I don't want to lose him, Margaret."

Margaret's eyes softened.

"He's exactly what I've wanted. He can give me everything I've desired and never had." At least that's what she'd tried to convince herself of all night. She kept telling herself that even if he had his faults, even if he was flirtatious and slightly insincere at times, underneath he was a good man. She couldn't expect to find a man who was perfect in every way. Jerome would have to do, especially in light of the fact she hadn't had many other options.

Margaret's long fingers found hers and squeezed. "I don't have a good feeling about this, but I'll come with you if that's what you want."

Katharina hesitated. The alarms began ringing in her head again. She'd tried silencing them, had thought they were done sounding. "We must go." If she couldn't quiet the warnings, she would ignore them. She stepped to the door. "He'll be waiting."

She followed as Margaret led the way out of the domestic quarters on the third story and down the stairway to the sprawling courtyard of the residence, a square, grassy area that had several fruit trees and a small vegetable garden and was surrounded on all four sides by workshops and living quarters. They wound their way unnoticed through the bustle of servants and apprentices, playing children, and clucking hens. Katharina had come to realize that the Cranach household was the largest private dwelling in Wittenberg and that it resembled a small village. With studios for painting and engraving, as well as the apothecary shop and printing press, the place was always teeming.

"Stop." Margaret flattened herself against the brick wall and pushed Katharina back with her.

"What is it —"

"Shh." Margaret put a finger to her lips. Her cheeks were pink and her eyes alight. She leaned forward and inclined her ear toward the open doorway in front of her. "Doctor Luther's here."

Katharina quieted her clamoring thoughts and listened.

"The publication of Scripture must in no way be fettered." Luther's strong voice was easy to distinguish.

"Chieregati's edict from the Diet asks that the printers and vendors of your books be punished." This voice belonged to Master Cranach. "If the princes carry out his request, the first place they'll come is here. Everyone knows I print whatever you bring me."

"You do it because you know it's God's work. And I'm sure you don't mind that in the process I'm making you a rich man."

Margaret leaned into Katharina and whispered. "Doctor Luther won't take honorariums on the sale of his books. He lets Master Cranach have all the profits."

Katharina raised a brow and thought of the poverty of the Black Cloister, of the financial want Doctor Luther had experienced when they'd arrived in Wittenberg. Surely he would benefit from taking something, even if only a pittance.

Doctor Luther's voice grew louder in his passion. "We're following the edict prohibiting the printing and vending of all materials that have not been inspected and approved by judges. But we cannot compromise the publication of Scripture. This is our only exception to the mandates."

Master Cranach's hearty laughter rolled through the doorway. "Ah, Martinus, I can always count on you to cheer my spirits."

"All right." Doctor Luther's voice hinted at humor. "I suppose printing Scripture isn't the only exception."

Master Cranach's laughter rang out again.

Margaret tilted toward Katharina with another whispered explanation. "They say the princes have commanded Doctor Luther to refrain from preaching. But he's been away from Wittenberg preaching everywhere."

If she was perfectly honest, Katharina had

to admit she had noticed Doctor Luther's absence from the Stadtkirche during the services. She'd seen little of him since the night he'd rescued her from Abbot Baltazar's men but had lived with an unsettled ache in her chest, wondering if her choice that night had hurt him.

Margaret sighed. "I wish he wasn't gone so much and I could see him more often."

Katharina's heart swelled with compassion for her dear friend and her lack of suitors. Already Eva had the attention of one of the young medical students working in Master Cranach's apothecary. But Margaret still had no prospects and kept her heart set on Doctor Luther. If only men didn't put so much stock in things like a dowry and age and outward appearances. If only they could see Margaret's heart, what a good, kind woman she was.

Katharina stepped away from the wall, determination stiffening her spine. She must ensure Margaret's marriage to Doctor Luther before leaving Wittenberg as Jerome's bride.

"You won't see him if you cower outside the door." She tugged her friend forward and then gave her a shove that sent her tripping into the printing shop.

Katharina heard Margaret's startled gasp

and then her stammering apology.

Ave Maria. The woman lacked all art in alluring a man. Not that she was so skilled herself, but at least she had already captured the attention of a suitor. It was becoming more apparent that Margaret would never attract Doctor Luther if left on her own.

Katharina pressed her lips together and stepped into the shop. The metallic scent of ink on wet paper filled the large room.

The two journeymen manning the press glanced her way. One was rolling ink with a long-handled ball onto the frame filled with type. The other had a dampened piece of paper and held it ready to spread over the frame. An apprentice stood by to aid them. The rest of the shop was strung with lines of drying paper, which hung above the heads of the bookbinder and typesetter at their benches.

"I'm sure Doctor Luther was just about to inquire how his runaway nuns are faring, Margaret." She touched Margaret's elbow to warn her against retreating. Katharina's attention leaped from Master Cranach slouched over a type tray to Doctor Luther towering above him.

For a second Doctor Luther's gaze met hers. There was a flash of something powerful in his rich brown eyes — something that barreled into her and made her catch her breath. But before she could make sense of the emotion, his eyes narrowed. "I've no need to ask about you, Katharina. The sordid news of you and your lover spreads through Wittenberg daily."

She stiffened. What did Doctor Luther know about her relationship with Jerome? Certainly not the truth. She glanced around the workshop and glowered at the others, who had stopped their work to watch her. They ducked their heads and resumed their tasks. Master Cranach, on the other hand, was peering quizzically back and forth between her and Doctor Luther. She'd learned in her previous visits with Margaret that Master Cranach was kind. He was a man with a quick smile behind his long, forked beard and a man who indulged in hearty laughter that shook his full belly.

Doctor Luther stood with arms crossed, clearly waiting for her to answer his challenge.

She returned his stare, unwilling to let him shake her confidence.

"Perhaps Baumgartner will have more news to share today," he said in a low voice. "What do you think, my dear Katharina?"

Her body froze. Did Doctor Luther know of her plans to meet Jerome? Her heart thudded with the thought that perhaps her impending secret marriage to Jerome was not so secret after all.

"Jerome has promised to marry me."

Luther raised his brow. "He promised?"

"He's promised to marry me when he returns to Wittenberg."

Surprise flitted through his eyes, followed by anger. "Then I congratulate you, Katharina. It appears that you've accomplished the job of finding yourself a wealthy and noble husband, just as you've desired. I pray that the two of you will be drunk on your happiness together."

"As a matter of fact, we'll be ecstatic to be together."

"Good."

"Yes. It is good."

Master Cranach let loose a roar of laughter that reverberated in the spacious room. "Go on, go on. The two of you are better entertainment than a hanging."

Katharina closed her mouth, but frustration pounded at the barricade, demanding release. What right did Doctor Luther have to be angry about her decision? Was he still peeved at her for turning down his offer to ride with him on his horse the night of her rescue? Perhaps there had been a spark of something between them during those tense moments. Or perhaps he'd only been extending the hand of friendship and she'd read more into his offer. Whatever the case, she didn't understand his opposition to Jerome.

"My future is well secured with Jerome." She forced a calm tone. "But you must remember Margaret. She's yet in need of a husband." She took hold of Margaret and dragged her forward.

Luther's attention shifted to the blushing woman. Margaret's long fingers fluttered in front of her, and she visibly swallowed hard.

"Margaret's been learning much from Mistress Cranach about running a large household. She'll make a good wife."

"And I suppose you're learning how to be a good wife too? Or perhaps you'll expect Baumgartner to provide you with a household full of servants to do your bidding." Doctor Luther's gaze was back upon her, challenging her once again.

Katharina sniffed. "Whether or not I have many servants isn't your concern. I'm concerned right now for my friend Margaret and finding a husband for her. She's as beautiful on the inside as the outside, and she should attract any number of men, don't you think?"

"Of course." But he didn't look at Margaret. He was surveying her instead in a way that sent a strange shiver through her, shredding her thoughts, prompting the memory of being in his arms and feeling treasured in a way she never had before.

"Doctor Luther?" A shout from outside the printing shop made her jump. "Urgent message for Doctor Luther!"

A young man careened through the doorway, heaving at the effort of breathing. His face was red and sweaty, his hair wind tossed. "Doctor Luther?"

"What is it?" He stepped forward to identify himself to the messenger.

"I've news from Brussels." The man gasped through each word. He reached for the pouch at his side, fumbled to untie it, then pulled out a rolled paper. "The inquisitors have condemned the young Augustinians Esch and Voes. They'll burn at the stake this very day, perhaps are burning at this very moment."

Katharina, like all of Wittenberg, had heard about the persecution that had broken out against the monks at the Augustinian monastery in Antwerp. The men had spent time in Wittenberg and had accepted Luther's new teachings. When they'd returned to the Low Countries, they'd begun preaching Doctor Luther's message about salvation coming from grace. The church leaders there hadn't liked the enthusiasm with which the townspeople had received the new teachings, so they'd destroyed the monastery and put the monks into prison. Some of the monks had escaped only to be recaptured. Now it appeared that their end had finally arrived.

With trembling hands Doctor Luther took the paper from the messenger. "The cause that we defend is not a game or child's play. It will have blood. It calls for our lives."

The shop hushed as he unrolled and silently read the letter. After a moment he spoke. "Hochstraten, that heretic hunter, asked if they would retract their assertion that forgiveness of sins belongs only to God and not to priests. But Esch and Voes said that they wouldn't retract anything, that they would not deny the faith, that they would rather die."

Luther fell silent as he read the rest of the letter. When he finished, he looked up, his face now the same pale gray as the paper.

Uneasiness wound through Katharina. They'd heard of monks and priests being imprisoned for following the new ways of Doctor Luther. But no one had been put to death for them — until now.

"The inquisitors told the monks to confess

they had been seduced by me. But they replied they had been seduced just as the apostles had been seduced by Jesus Christ." Doctor Luther remained motionless except the letter shaking in his hand.

No one spoke. The clucking of chickens in the courtyard and the innocent laughter of children wafted into the room.

"You're sure the monks will burn today?" Doctor Luther finally asked.

The messenger nodded.

Doctor Luther swayed but then steadied himself against the wall. "Then they're our first martyrs. It won't be long before the persecution spreads."

"Martinus, don't speak of gloom." Master Cranach ran a hand down his beard. "The Netherlands pay homage directly to the king. They don't have the benevolence of our princes to offer them protection."

Although King Charles V was emperor of all the Holy Roman Empire, including the German provinces and princes, apparently he hadn't been able to persuade the princes to cooperate with him in handing Doctor Luther over, at least not yet.

"King Charles is a butcher and all the Romish devils with him." Doctor Luther took a step away from the wall, but his knees buckled. Katharina raced across the room, but before she could reach him, he crumpled. His head hit the edge of Master Cranach's worktable, and then his body slammed into the floor.

"Herr Doctor!" The panic in her cry echoed the sudden burst of panic inside. She knelt next to him and quickly searched for the pulse in his neck. When the slow rhythm of his life moved under her fingers, she drew in a breath and tried to steady the strange frantic feeling that flowed through her.

"Help me roll him over." She took hold of one shoulder while Master Cranach grabbed the other. They maneuvered him onto his back on the ink-stained floor.

He groaned, then blinked hard and pressed a hand to his head. "The devil is trying to climb on my back again."

As he lowered his hand, Katharina snatched it. A sheen of bright blood smeared his palm. "You're hurt." She reached for his head, but he batted her hand away.

"It's just a little dizziness."

"No. You're bleeding."

He struggled to push himself off the ground.

Katharina gently forced him back. "Stay where you are."

"What would your royal majesty have me do?"

"Lie still. I shall examine your head." She bent closer to inspect the trickle of blood at the edge of his temple. She was unprepared for the warmth of his breath bathing her outstretched neck and even more unprepared for her reaction — the strange ripples in her belly. She lifted her hand to his thick hair and hesitated only a moment before threading the tips of her fingers into the strands.

He sucked in a soft breath.

A ribbon of heat wove through her. Perhaps she ought to send for the physician. Surely this intimacy with Doctor Luther wasn't appropriate.

Her fingers slid across a slippery split in the skin. Doctor Luther winced.

"You have a deep gash, Herr Doctor." It ran the length of her finger, and the blood was moistening his hair. "I shall need to sew you up."

He didn't protest.

Katharina turned to the hushed group watching them. "I'll need yarrow, fine silk thread, a small needle, scissors, a clean cloth, warm water, and strong wine."

Several scurried away to fulfill her requests, but the surrounding crowd had grown even larger.

"Master Cranach," she said, "send everyone back to their tasks. Doctor Luther will need privacy."

Doctor Luther managed a lopsided grin. "Do as the lord and master Kate commands. She's my personal physician."

When she had everything she needed, she hesitated. "I'll need to cut the hair around the wound before I can stitch."

"I don't think that'll be the worst of it."

There was no way to avoid causing him more pain. Even if she'd ordered a tonic from the apothecary shop, it would have little effect on a man of his size. "I'll do my best to be gentle."

"I know you will, Katharina." Gone was the antagonism that had just stood between them, and in its place was the honesty and kindness she'd grown to appreciate about him. "I saw your tenderness with little Anna Melanchthon. And there's no one else I'd rather have doctor me than you." He gripped the leg of the table. "Besides, this won't be the first time I've needed sewing."

"I'm beginning to realize that you need more doctoring than most."

Master Cranach squeezed Doctor Luther's shoulder with ink-blackened fingers. "Maybe Martinus is just looking for excuses to get your attention."

Doctor Luther snorted. "I can think of much pleasanter ways to do that."

"I doubt it. Not when you've got a pretty young nun running her hands over you and fairly lying on top of you."

Katharina pulled away from Doctor Luther. Heat stole through her.

Master Cranach laughed.

"I'm only doing my job," she said.

"Continue on." Luther grinned. "I won't complain."

She reached for the scissors, her insides betraying her with more of that pleasant rippling.

With Margaret by her side and Master Cranach holding a candle to provide extra light, she snipped the hair away from the wound, then cleansed it with wine and warm water. As she punctured his skin with the needle, she tried to ignore the pain on his face and the veins bulging in the tautness of his skin. She tried to take no notice of the clenching of his jaw or the agony in his eyes. But with each piercing of his flesh, her body coiled tighter until she could hardly breathe.

"I'm done," she said as she knotted the thread. Then with a long exhale, she finally sat back on her heels and wiped his blood from her hands.

He was motionless, eyes closed, a layer of perspiration above his lips and across his forehead.

Perhaps he'd blessedly lost consciousness. She leaned forward and wiped the blood and sweat from his brow, willing her fingers to stop trembling. "I need the yarrow now," she said.

Margaret handed her the mortar with the dried yarrow flowers mixed with hot water into a paste. Katharina scooped a small amount onto a cloth, folded it in half, and pressed it against the wound. The healing properties of the yarrow would hopefully keep the gash from swelling and festering.

Doctor Luther's eyes flickered open. His glassy gaze found her face.

"How do you feel?" she asked.

"Terrible."

"I'm afraid it will pain you for a while."

He thumped a hand against his chest. "It pains me the most right here."

Katharina frowned. Had she missed another wound?

"It should have been me, Katharina," he whispered. "I should have been the first to die." His pain-filled eyes reflected a deeper agony.

She knew about herbs and medicines and

treating sickness. What could she say, what could she do to ease this kind of hurt?

"They were so young." The lines of his face were drawn tight. "They were too young to die."

Katharina reached for his hand and squeezed it.

He clutched her hand as if he would sink into the abyss if he let go. "It's my fault they'll burn. It's all because of my teaching."

The contact of his long, sure fingers against hers made it hard for her to think. And yet she knew she must say something. "Watch your pride, Doctor Luther. For whose sake are they giving their lives? Yours or Christ's?"

He didn't say anything for a long moment, and she began to wonder if her words had angered him, if perhaps she'd overstepped her bounds in speaking so forthrightly about spiritual matters that she knew so little about compared with him.

"I'll take you back to the monastery," she said, "and you'll have Brother Gabriel's Obstwasser. Master Cranach will spare a manservant to assist us."

His grip on her hand loosened and the rough pad of his thumb skimmed the pulse at her wrist. At first she thought the caress was an accident, but when he grazed her wrist again, this time deliberately slower, the soft touch sent a shiver up her arm.

Remembrances whispered against her skin, and she could almost feel him holding her with his mouth pressed against her ear.

A sudden grin teased the corner of his mouth as if he'd read her thoughts, as if he'd gotten the reaction he'd wanted.

She snatched her hand out of his, but his reflexes were quick in spite of his injury, and he recaptured hers in a grip she couldn't escape.

"How did you come to be such a smart woman, my dear Kate?" His grin, now out in the open, contained a hint of censure. "You're very smart indeed. Except about one thing . . ."

She needed only to look into his eyes to understand his meaning. He was scorning Jerome again. She yanked again, and this time he released her. "I think Master Cranach can spare two of his men to convey you." She stood and wiped at the splotches of his blood on her skirt. It would be difficult to wash away.

What she really needed was to wash away all traces of Doctor Luther's presence, including those lingering thoughts that wouldn't befit a woman on the verge of marriage to another man.

"You don't need me anymore." She took a step away and refused to look at him where he lay on the floor, long and solid and strong. She avoided looking at Margaret and Master Cranach, afraid of what she would see on their faces after they'd witnessed her interaction with Doctor Luther.

She started toward the door. "I should be going anyway . . ."

To Jerome.

The words hung unspoken in the air, but from Doctor Luther's silence, she knew he understood.

Her destiny was already settled, and she wouldn't question it. Neither would he. Not anymore.

Sixteen

He'd fallen into the trap.

The sound of his horse's hoofs drummed in rhythm with the pounding in his head and the wild racing of his heart. Luther tossed a glance over his shoulder. The riders were not gaining ground, but neither was he losing them. He dug his heels against the flank of his mount and tried to spur the beast to move faster. But after running hard for the past hour, the horse had reached its limit.

"Not far now!" Jonas shouted, his tall frame hunched low over his steed, his dark hair flying in the wind, his cap long ago discarded.

The pointed turrets of Mansfeld Castle rose over the thick spruce and beech forest that blanketed the peak of the hill to their right. The castle was built into the rocky hillside and set on the highest point above the town. Its massive walls and towers overshadowed the small mining town of Mansfeld.

The imposing fortress was their signal that they would soon reach safety. If they made it through the gate, they would be alive for another day. The assassins wouldn't dare follow them inside the protective limits of the town.

Luther's body slammed against the horse with each stride, jarring his head, making him nauseous. *Father in heaven, You are our protector and defender. We need Your help.*

Ahead, above the trees, the dark smoke of the copper smelters beckoned him.

He tossed another glance over his shoulder. The cloaks of the riders flapped behind them. Only the span of several horse lengths separated him from the hands of murderers. Maybe it was his day to finally die for the cause. Maybe he ought to stop trying so hard to evade death and just hand himself over.

"Over there!" Jonas nodded toward the meadow ahead outside the city wall.

Luther raised his head. Two naked men hung by their necks from a long plank. The wind slowly pivoted them. Crows circled above them, then swooped near and pecked at their decaying flesh. Their caws filled the air with twisted jubilation.

Revulsion crawled through Luther's stomach. As they raced past the grisly scene, he focused on his steed's mane instead. Hangings were commonplace, but the sight of such desecration always caused the same sick feeling and raised the same question: What had they done to deserve death?

He could only pray they hadn't died on account of the reforms, like the monks in Antwerp. The persecutions were sweeping from the Low Countries into Germany. New stories reached him every day of fanatical Roman priests who seized followers of the reforms and threw them into dungeons. The zealots restored Romish rites, prohibited reading the Bible, and forbade sharing the gospel. The persecution was spreading throughout the German provinces, not just in Duke George's Saxony.

However, in the case of these two corpses, it was more likely that Count Albrecht in his hilltop castle had sanctioned the hangings due to the growing unrest with the miners. The miners were simple men — laborers and peasants — who risked their lives in the deep, dark tunnels, chipping away at the rocks and lugging ore to the surface day after day with little to show for it except illness and accidents. The Mansfeld count, like most of the nobility, demanded much but gave little in return. The town leaders had asked for Luther's mediation between the count and the miners. It was one of the reasons he'd ventured away from Wittenberg.

Jonas cast a glance to the two riders still chasing them. The lines of his face tightened. "Faster!"

The assassins' horses thundered behind them. Somehow his enemies had gotten word of his route, had set the trap, had tried to waylay him. He had the feeling someone in his circle of followers wasn't quite loyal. But he had no proof of it, and even if he did, he couldn't bear to accuse anyone.

The pressure in his head radiated to his aching bones. The gash that he'd sustained in Cranach's printing shop throbbed, even though it was healing. His breath came in gasps and caused a sharp pain in his side. At forty he was too old to be racing like a university boy.

He focused ahead. The smoke of the smelters billowed over the clay tiles of the crowded rooftops and seemed to roast the underbellies of the low clouds to a charcoal black.

"Almost there!" he called.

The familiar acrid tang of burning coal

and melted copper greeted him. The city gate loomed ahead, and the traffic on the road thickened.

"Make way for Martin Luther!" Jonas shouted. "Make way!"

Travelers and peasants stood back and stared as they galloped past.

Luther didn't slow the gait of his horse until he rode past the city gates. Only then did he draw the reins so that his beast pranced sideway and whinnied.

The dark-cloaked figures brought their horses to an abrupt halt outside the city wall, only a stone's throw away. They didn't dare ride inside a town where he was not only well loved but also under the protection of the count.

"This time was too close." Jonas slowed alongside him. Dust mingled with sweat along his brow.

The assassins watched from outside the walls. Their horses foamed at the mouth and snorted with flared nostrils. Finally one of the riders motioned to the other, then they spurred their beasts and began to canter away.

Jonas glared after them, his scowl sharp enough to flay a man alive.

"Doctor Luther!" A milling crowd surrounded Luther, and eager hands reached toward him.

"This is why you've come," Jonas said, turning to the crowd. "They need encouragement. They need to know that the death of the martyrs wasn't a defeat but rather a confirmation that the gospel is good and worth dying for."

Work-weary, haggard townspeople filled the street. Yet when the laborers looked up at Luther, their eyes filled with hope, and his heart strengthened with renewed determination. By now they'd surely heard about the death of the martyrs in the Low Country. If the news hadn't discouraged them, why should he let it weigh him down?

He took hold of the dirt-incrusted hand of a stoop-shouldered man who'd raised it to him. "God bless you, my man." He reached for another hand, then another and another. Slowly he made his way through the gathering, speaking words of hope to each person he touched, his heart welling up with compassion.

Jonas was right. He had to put to rest all fears and proclaim to their enemies they were not afraid, not defeated, not shriveling away. He had to stop blaming himself for the deaths of the young monks and the increasing persecution of his followers. He had to remember that death would be the ultimate cost of pursuing the truth of the gospel but that such a sacrifice was worth it if he could help set these people free from their bondage.

He finally made his way past the swell of townspeople to the inn. Johann Ledener, the vicar of the Church of Saint George, met him, as did a number of other important citizens who had accepted the gospel. They sat together at a long table, and the men updated him on the unrest. They informed him that Count Albrecht had wanted to make an example of any miners who associated themselves with the rebellious Bundschuh peasants. So he'd hung two and put more in prison. His move had only fueled the animosity.

"The count is holding the prisoners as leverage. He says he'll hang a prisoner every time there's an offense." Vicar Ledener gripped his mug, his knuckles white.

"The biggest offense is protesting his request for a larger share in the revenues from the mines," grumbled the man next to Luther.

Luther had already drained his drink, and he leaned against the cool wattle wall, grateful the pounding in his head had subsided. The dank, dimly lit inn provided a haven after the long, hard ride.

"You need to speak with the count and ask him to release the prisoners," said another one of the townsmen.

"Why haven't you done this yet yourselves?"

His question brought a chorus of angry replies.

Vicar Ledener's voice broke through the commotion. "We *have* already spoken with the count. And as usual he won't listen." Again the men's voices crescendoed.

"Ach, so here is my son," came a familiar voice from the doorway, "solving the world's problems once more."

Luther sat forward and his muscles tensed. His father pushed through the crowded room, making his way toward him. His brow was creased with lines of perpetual disappointment — the common look his father wore whenever they met.

"When word reached me that my son was in town, I hurried home. I thought surely my son would visit his family before conducting business." His father doffed his beret and crushed the brim in his soot-covered hands.

"Good day, Father." Luther stood and gave up his spot for his father, refusing to be drawn into old arguments.

With a long sigh and shake of his head,

his father lowered himself onto the bench. The others offered Hans Luther a round of greetings and passed a drink his way. His father, like other leaseholders, had already suffered enough losses in recent years. Their floundering profits would suffer even more if the count didn't lessen his demands.

Luther swallowed a lump of frustration. Perhaps he would bring himself more peace with his father if he attempted to wield a measure of influence over the count. As Luther watched his father take a swig, he wished, as he always did, his brothers hadn't died of the plague in their youth. His younger brother, Jacob, had survived and had become a smelter master like Father. But Jacob had neither the education nor the drive to give their father the success and prestige he craved. Nor had he given their father what he wanted most — a grandson to pass on the Luther name. If his other brothers had lived, perhaps his father wouldn't have placed so much hope in him.

Luther sat back and sipped from his mug silently, letting the conversation flow around him, watching his father's easy camaraderie with the men. Even if his life had taken a different course than the one his father had hoped for, Luther was relieved that his father had embraced the reforms or at least hadn't opposed him as he had with other things so many times in the past.

As though sensing Luther's attention and the tempest of his swirling emotions, his father's expression turned grave, and he set his mug on the table and let his thumb draw circles around the slick rim. "I heard you were almost caught today on your way into Mansfeld."

The other men at the table grew silent and stared at Luther. He squirmed at the sudden attention but nodded. "It was close. But apparently God isn't ready to take me home yet."

Jonas slapped him on the back. "You may be turning into an old goat, but you showed our dear friend Duke George that goats can tuck their tails and run when they need to."

Luther grinned, but the seriousness in his father's eyes cut short the humor of the moment.

"Then it was Duke George's men who were after you?" his father asked.

"We forgot to ask them," Jonas started, his voice tinged with his usual sarcasm.

Luther elbowed his friend but then looked squarely at his father, seeing all the fear and heartache in those brown eyes that were so much like his own. "We're fine, Father."

"Maybe if you settled down and had a

normal life now," his father began, "if you stay in Wittenberg and focus on being a professor and resume teaching your classes at the university . . ."

Luther tensed and braced himself for the litany of things he could be doing to please his father. In a deep place he knew his father loved him, worried about him, and wanted what was best for him. But what his father thought was best usually didn't match Luther's plans.

It was Luther's turn to stare at his mug and run his fingers around the rim, the swirling movement matching the churning in his gut.

"Perhaps if you got a real home instead of living in that big, empty monastery," his father continued, "and if you found yourself a wife and had children, then you'd be able to live a normal life."

Luther didn't want to respond and say anything that would hurt his father. He'd already done that enough in his life. So all he did was sigh.

His father responded with a deep sigh of his own. And for a long moment, the chatter and laughter of the other patrons overtook their silent table. Luther's men busied themselves with taking sips of their beer, seeming to want to ignore the awkward conversation between father and son.

"I'll go see Mother now," Luther said, pushing back, needing to put an end to the strained moment. His childhood home was down the main street, a short escape away.

"Good idea," his father chimed in. "She'll have heard the rumors too and will be wanting to make sure you're unharmed." Luther said his good-byes to the men, knowing the conversations about the count and the unrest among the peasants were far from over. But for now, at this moment, he needed to put distance between himself and the disappointment he was to his father. He stepped away from the table and, with Jonas on his heels, squeezed through the crowd.

"I don't know why you won't just tell him to shut up," Jonas grumbled when they were out on the narrow street. Tall buildings rose up, crammed close together, casting shadows on the street.

"If just once he could tell me one thing I've done right." Luther's throat tightened with the longing of wanting to please his father but never quite being able to do it.

"I think you'll shut him up in only one way," Jonas said as they dodged hens and dogs and picked their way through the dregs of garbage that housewives had dumped into the street. In the dampness of the day, the stench filled his nostrils. "Get married."

"Such a solution might temporarily placate my father, but it would set a thousand other malicious tongues to work."

Jonas snorted. "What worse things could they possibly say about you?"

"You know my position on the matter. And I won't change it, even to please my father."

"The Schonfeld sisters still need husbands. You must admit the tall one is rather taken with you."

He wouldn't admit anything. He wasn't in a position to pay attention to the whims of the nuns he was rescuing.

Jonas quirked an eyebrow. "Or perhaps you already have your heart set on Katharina von Bora?"

"Absolutely not!" He asserted his denial too loudly and startled the urchins nearby who were setting rattraps. Luther's mind suddenly filled with a picture of Katharina's face, the concern that had strained her delicate features as she'd tended his wound that day in Cranach's workshop. He could almost feel the gentleness of her fingers on his gash, and it brought a keen longing for more of her.

Jonas's brow shot higher, and a grin played at his lips.

Luther fought for control over the surge of emotions at the mention of Katharina's name. "She's a hissing Katzen." Again his tone was too strong.

What about Katharina had the power to blow through him like a thunderstorm? He took a deep breath and forced himself to respond calmly. "If I were taking a wife — *if* — Katharina would be the very last woman I would want."

This time Jonas gave an all-out hearty laugh, as though he'd never found anything more ludicrous.

"I'm serious." Luther stopped and sized up the brick facade in front of him that rose three stories. His childhood home hadn't changed over the years. "Katharina von Bora isn't the woman for me."

Besides, she was practically married to that weaseling, womanizing Baumgartner. If the rumors were true, then she was Baumgartner's in all but name. Irrational but familiar anger flashed through him at the picture of Baumgartner's hands on Katharina.

"She belongs to Baumgartner." He stepped to the door and thumped it with his fist. "He'll marry her. I'll make sure of it."

Katharina absently slapped at the flea on the back of her hand. The tiny pests were everywhere now that she had beaten them out of the cushions and woven mats. Her hope was that the fresh alder leaves she'd strewn about the room would catch most of the vermin. She'd kill the rest when they landed on the white wool blanket she'd spread over the bed.

She detested the job but was careful to hide her feelings from Elsa. The mayor's wife derived unnatural pleasure from giving her the most degrading work. Katharina knew Elsa did it out of jealousy. The woman was spitefully envious of the fact that Jerome cared about her and planned to marry her.

At least she *hoped* he still planned to marry her. He'd left Wittenberg without saying good-bye. Although it had been nigh onto a month since his departure, Katharina could think of nothing else.

She swatted the dark specks dotting the white blanket.

If only she'd gone to meet him as she'd promised. If only she hadn't made all the excuses after stitching up Doctor Luther that afternoon. She'd told herself that she was too late, that the bells had long past rung Terce. She'd convinced herself he wouldn't wait in the grove but instead would find her and tell her everything would work out anyway. After all, he'd promised to marry her whether she went through with the consummation or not. He'd promised he would marry her the very first day he returned to Wittenberg.

If only he would come soon. With a sigh she reached for the twig broom. She didn't want to think about the possibility that he might be angry with her, that he might be ignoring her.

She stretched the broom under the bed and reached for lingering dust and fleas. In the small chamber she shared with another serving girl, she'd assembled two trenchers slimed with glue. At night she lit a candle in the midst of each trencher, which attracted fleas to the sticky mixture, trapping and killing them. She had learned the flea-catching method and how to make the glue at the abbey. She'd hesitated about sharing her knowledge with Elsa, although part of her knew she ought to show the woman charity whether or not she deserved it.

She reached farther under the bed and aimed for the far corners, capturing the elusive contents: balls of dust, straw, and a crumpled sheet of paper. For a moment she stared at the wadded paper. The right course of action was to incinerate it without meddling. She picked it up and blew the dust from it. No one would know if she took a peek. With a quick glance around, she folded back the layers and straightened it.

Her heart slammed to a stop at the sight of her own handwriting. She scanned the first line. *Dearest Jerome . . .*

She stared, hot fingers of anger gripping her. It was one of the letters she'd written to Jerome. And she could think of only one way it could have gotten under Elsa's bed. The woman had intercepted it.

"She's despicable. Absolutely despicable." Katharina skimmed over the words — an outpouring of her heart, the declaration of her affection for Jerome and her desire to be his wife. She didn't doubt Elsa had laughed over every word.

And just how many of her letters had Elsa stolen? What if Jerome hadn't received any of them? What if he thought she didn't care about him anymore? How else could he interpret her silence, especially after she'd neglected to meet him in the quince grove? He would think she didn't care about marrying him. He would surely feel betrayed and abandoned. And if he hadn't been angry before, he would be now.

Fleas forgotten, she searched the rest of the bedchamber for any other letters but found none. Finally, with the wrinkled letter in hand, she stomped through the house until she located Elsa in the kitchen snapping instructions at the servants who were in the midst of preparing the midday meal. Steam rose from a large kettle over the massive hearth and along with it the smell of parsnips and turnips.

"How could you?" Katharina stormed around the baskets of bread and fish and cheese recently purchased at the market. She halted before the mayor's wife and waved the paper in her face.

Recognition lit the woman's eyes.

"You stole my letter." Katharina struggled to keep her voice calm.

"I was merely protecting Jerome."

"Protecting him from what?"

She sniffed and lifted her chin. "You're not an appropriate match for a man of Jerome's status."

"I'm his equal if not his better." Katharina's tone turned icy. "However, I hardly think *you* are in a position to know about status."

Elsa's gaze lowered to Katharina's gown

and lingered over the stains and the frayed edge. Katharina fought the urge to bunch up her skirt and try to hide the worn linen. "Jerome's parents will not want a penniless bride for their only son, especially one as old as you."

"You've no right to interfere."

"Whether I like it or not, you're my servant. I have every right to do with you as I see fit."

The frustration that had been growing over the weeks suddenly unleashed itself. Katharina knew she couldn't abide living with this woman another day, another hour, another minute. She forced a thin smile. "I'm no more your servant than you are my mistress. One cannot change the natural order of life by wishful thinking."

With her mind made up, she didn't linger. She went directly to her room, packed her meager belongings, and walked out of the Reichenbachs' house.

Since Doctor Luther had erred in placing her with the Reichenbachs, she would require him to undo his mistake. He would have to find her another place to live. She walked the short distance to the Black Cloister and was disappointed when Wolfgang informed her that Doctor Luther was gone from Wittenberg. She failed to persuade the servant to tell her where Doctor Luther was or when he might return. Instead, Wolfgang instructed her to go back to the Reichenbachs' and obey Doctor Luther's orders regarding her stay there.

Katharina decided she would rather live at the Black Cloister in abject poverty and under Wolfgang's constant suspicion than subject herself to more of Elsa's disdain or meddling.

When Wolfgang closed the door on her, she wandered down Collegienstrasse. The anger that had taken hold of her earlier seeped out and left a hole in its place. She had no one — no family, no husband, no one who would care if she was homeless. Her father, her brothers, her sister — none of them had responded to Doctor Luther's letter. Of course they lived in Duke George's territory, and she wouldn't be safe if she went to live with them.

But even if she couldn't live with them, they could still make an effort to contact her, perhaps just to visit. Why wouldn't they want to see her after all these years? Weren't they curious about her? Didn't they wonder what kind of woman she'd become?

In her mind her father was rejecting her all over again, and this time the rejection had a finality to it that cut deep. Hadn't it been enough that he'd given away his own flesh and blood — the sweet, innocent five-year-old girl who'd wanted nothing more than for him to wrap her safely in his arms?

O my God, relying on Thy almighty power and infinite mercy and promises, I hope to obtain pardon for my sins, the help of Thy grace, and life everlasting . . .

She'd once prayed the traditional prayers with such confidence. But their power seemed to be slipping from her fingers much the way her status was. No matter how hard she clung to all that was once important, she was losing her grasp.

Her pace slowed as she turned onto Schlossstrasse and neared the front of the Cranach residence. The Act of Hope prayer trailed into nothingness, unable to give her the hope she desperately needed at the moment.

She trailed her fingers across the rough bricked arch around the doorway. The urge to voice her deepest needs pulsed through her. What if she talked to God without a traditional prayer, the way the pastor did each Sunday? Would God hear her?

Part of her wanted to try, wanted to believe she could shed the old customs and beliefs just as she'd shed her nun's garments. But if she did, what would she have left?

SEVENTEEN

Katharina stepped slowly over the broken stone pathway that led to the monastery garden. Tall weeds straggled through the cracks and climbed the crumbling wall of the Black Cloister's unfinished chapel.

Wolfgang's glare from the refectory burned into her back. When she turned and looked at the narrow window, he ducked away. Only a dilapidated building stared back at her. With its peeling paint, broken shutters, and missing roof tiles, it looked just as abandoned on the outside as it was on the inside.

Wolfgang was better than a watchdog.

She turned her attention back to the garden, to the unpruned apple and pear trees, the withered and wormy fruit hanging from gnarled branches. If only Wolfgang would take care of the monastery as well as he did his master.

He hadn't wanted to tell her where Doctor Luther was working, but since this time Doctor Luther had summoned *her* to the monastery, Wolfgang had eventually pointed her in the direction of the garden.

Doctor Luther wouldn't have called for her unless he was displeased with the arrangements she'd made for herself. After two weeks of living with Margaret and Eva at the Cranachs', she'd managed to convince Master Cranach and Barbara that she could be an asset to them, especially in the herb garden and apothecary shop. They hadn't sent her away — yet.

Now that Doctor Luther had finally returned to Wittenberg, would he ruin her plans and force her to return to the Reichenbachs'?

She steeled herself as she wound through the raised herb beds until she reached the level plot used for growing vegetables. She wouldn't go back. And she'd make sure he understood that.

"Doctor Luther?" She peered past the rows of pole beans.

"Here," came his muffled reply.

She tiptoed through the overgrown vines until she came upon Doctor Luther kneeling in the middle of the cabbage patch. The basket next to him was half-filled with dirt-covered carrots, onions, and turnips.

"Herr Doctor?" She studied his wide shoulders and the strong line of his jaw and couldn't stop the leap of her pulse at the sight of him again. "You're praying?"

He gave her a weak smile, his face leaner than it had been the last time she'd seen him. "I'm composing: No! No! Their ashes shall not die! But borne to every land, where'er their sainted dust shall fall, up springs a holy band." Perspiration covered his brow, and he held a bouquet of crushed violets.

"You should take your composing to the shade, Herr Doctor."

He held up his finger in an urgent motion that told her not to speak until he finished. "Though Satan by his might may kill, and stop their powerful voice, they triumph o'er him in their death, and still in Christ rejoice."

He pressed the violets to his nose and sucked in a breath. She waited a moment, unsure if he would continue. Then his gaze collided with hers. The anguish in his eyes turned them to bottomless black. "The song is in memory of the two boys burned to death in Brussels."

She had an urge to smooth her hand over his cheek to bring his tortured heart some small measure of comfort, to help ease his guilt. "Your song will be a powerful testimony to their death."

He held her gaze for a long moment, giving her a glimpse of the burdens a man in his position carried day after day. The balance of his own life was so precarious, but now so too were the lives of his followers.

"I'm always astonished," he said, "that the songs and praise intended to glorify God have the dual role of benefiting us, of lifting us out of our mire and muck to renew our spirits."

She didn't know much about singing except Latin chants in the prescribed format within the traditional liturgical ceremonies. "I have to admit, the common singing of the psalms in your church services has been rather unusual."

"The precious gift of music has been given to man alone so we might remind ourselves that God has created us for the express purpose of praising and extolling Him. Would that we all could use our voices in joyful songs rather than being content with only the chants."

Her heart thumped harder in resonance to his words and the wisdom they contained. And yet how could she deny the validity and importance of the sacred Latin texts that had been chanted for centuries?

"The riches of music are so excellent and so precious that, next to the Word of God, the noble art of music is the greatest treasure in the world." In spite of his wilted condition in the sun, his voice had grown stronger with the power of his conviction.

"You're a persuasive man, Herr Doctor," she admitted. She'd fallen under the power of his words from the teachings she'd read while at Marienthron, and she could see now why so many others were embracing his words. "I'm still struggling to know how far to allow myself to be persuaded by your teachings. Certainly not everything about the church needs reforming."

"Correct," he said. "But we must reclaim true worship, which comes when we hear the Word of God and then unite as a congregation in thanksgiving."

She could imagine him having heated discussions about such matters with his friends and felt a small thrill that he'd taken time to discuss the issue with her, as though her opinions were worthwhile. But as much as she longed to continue the discourse, she knew she couldn't avoid the real reason he'd requested her to come.

"Did you see Greta during your travels?" she asked. After his trip to Mansfeld earlier in the summer, he'd informed her about the peasant camp and the young woman he'd spotted there, a young woman he believed was Greta.

"I'm sorry, Katharina." He shook his head reluctantly. "I didn't see her anywhere. The peasants have had to stay on the move recently to avoid capture."

Her fingers brushed against a prickly cucumber vine that had snaked through the fencing. The sting moved from her fingers to her chest. "I don't understand why she left. At least with me she was safe and comfortable."

Doctor Luther's brow rose. "Was she really safe?"

His insinuation poked the tender flesh of her heart. She'd always thought that Greta had been lucky to be her servant. The girl had been plucked from a life of drudgery and poverty and illness. She'd had a relatively easy life in the convent compared to what life was like for most young peasant girls. But after discovering what had happened with the abbot, Katharina wondered if she had been too presumptuous. Perhaps Greta would have had a better life elsewhere.

When Doctor Luther pressed the wilted violets against his face again, she silently rebuked herself for not attending to him when he was clearly tired from his travels and work. "Come, Doctor Luther. You're in need of respite and a drink." She reached for the basket of vegetables. "I shall fix you a soothing drink."

"I've already sent for one." He peered around her. "There it is now."

Katharina turned. A tall nun dressed in wimple and habit approached with a steaming mug. At the sight of Katharina, the nun stopped and smiled. "Good day." The smile lit her face and gave it an angelic glow.

Surprise stole Katharina's voice, and she could do nothing more than nod and glance at Doctor Luther, who seemed to be drinking in the sight of this woman. A sharp pang shot through Katharina. Who was the newcomer and why was she here?

"Katharina, meet Hanna von Spiegel," Doctor Luther said in answer to her unspoken question. "God helped her and several other sisters recently escape their convent. They're staying here until I can make arrangements for them."

"Welcome to Wittenberg." Katharina nodded a greeting at the young woman and offered her a smile — albeit a weak one. The nun's wimple couldn't hide her beauty or her youth. From the admiration in Doctor Luther's eyes as took the mug from Hanna, it was apparent he found her attractive.

"Doctor Luther, you're generous as always, letting the nuns stay here." Katharina tried to keep her tone steady. "But with all the rumors that resulted from our stay, you should consider other options."

He shifted his attention from Hanna and quirked his brow at Katharina. "Do I sense jealousy, my dear Doctor Kate?"

The taunt in his eyes and the truth of his words sent a hot flush straight to her face. "Don't be ridiculous . . ." Of course *she* was ridiculous for protesting his hospitality with this nun when he was only extending his usual kindness, the same he'd given her.

If she was jealous, it was only for Margaret's sake. Poor Margaret was still infatuated with Doctor Luther and was waiting patiently for him to notice her.

"If only each of the liberated nuns was as docile as Hanna. Then I wouldn't have to return to Wittenberg to learn that my devoted supporters, the Reichenbachs, have been deeply offended and their gracious hospitality rejected."

Katharina glanced pointedly at Hanna. Thankfully, the young woman took that as her cue to leave. She bowed her head and departed as silently as she'd arrived.

Once the nun was out of sight, Katharina

squared her shoulders and prepared for battle. "If anyone has been offended, it is I."

"I want you to return to the Reichenbachs and apologize."

"I shall do nothing of the sort."

Doctor Luther tossed the violets to the ground. With his gaze piercing her, he pushed himself up until he was standing. "I won't tolerate open defiance, Katharina." His voice was low and brimming with anger.

She met his gaze without flinching. "Elsa Reichenbach is a thief and a meddler."

"Elsa claims you're lazy and disrespectful."

"She stole at least one letter I'd written to Jerome — if not more — and readily admitted to her crime."

Doctor Luther wiped his sleeve across his forehead. His hand shook with the effort. "Perhaps she was doing you a favor."

"Her interference is abominable."

"And have you heard from this lover of yours? When is he returning to finally take responsibility for you?"

She glanced at the faded, wilted flower petals at his feet. Jerome hadn't contacted her yet — not even once during the long six weeks. She'd written several more letters to replace the one Elsa had taken. Perhaps he'd only now received them and was in the process of responding or maybe even on his way back to Wittenberg. Surely once he read of her devotion, he would hurry to get her.

"Jerome will return for me any day now." She took a deep breath and then tried to exhale all her doubts.

"Let's hope for both our sakes you're right."

"I shall remain with the Cranachs."

He started to shake his head.

"Eva von Schonfeld is betrothed to the apothecary, Basilius Axt," she said quickly as she'd rehearsed on the walk over. "And they'll soon leave for Prussia. Barbara has granted me permission to fill Eva's position until I'm wed to Jerome."

"*If* you're wed."

"I'll wed him, Doctor Luther. You'll see." She only hoped she sounded more confident than she felt.

Her thread of confidence grew thinner as harvest came and with it the celebration of Michaelmas. The thread unraveled to the breaking point when the Feast of All Saints came and went, and finally Christmas and Epiphany passed without a word from Jerome. Through the long, dark hours of winter, she told herself that he would come in the spring, that he was waiting for the warmer weather to make travel easier for a man and his bride.

As more accounts of persecution began to trickle into Wittenberg, she convinced herself Jerome wouldn't travel, nor would he want her to, when danger lurked at every turn. He would wait until the storm of turmoil had abated and then come for her.

The terrible tales made her cower under the blankets on her pallet at night. In the dark, bitter cold of the third-story room she shared with Margaret, she couldn't stop thinking of the new dangers that awaited those who followed the teachings of Doctor Luther and his friends. She had no doubt the persecutors would consider her one of Doctor Luther's followers. The day she left Marienthron she had joined his side, whether or not she agreed with everything he taught.

Invariably, in the deep of night her thoughts would stray to Doctor Luther and the strain that had grown more evident in his face over the past months. She could only imagine the pain each new report of torture or death brought him.

One night in the midst of a deep sleep, Katharina's eyes flew open. The sound of a strange noise lingered in her head. She lay motionless and listened.

Silence mingled with Margaret's soft breathing on the pallet across from hers.

Perhaps she'd heard the noise only in her dream . . . the horrible dream about the reformed preachers in Württemberg who'd recently had their tongues nailed to a post. She couldn't stop thinking about the pain they'd experienced trying to liberate themselves. And now because of their mutilated tongues, their persecutors had ensured the preachers would never speak again.

She shuddered and pulled her blanket up to her chin.

The brutality unleashed by the pope and his clergy was spreading everywhere, and she trembled to think it might find its way to Wittenberg. They'd begun to hear reports of retaliation — by peasants and even those of the burgher class, claiming to act in the name of Doctor Luther and for the benefit of the reforms. Groups of Bundschuh had begun attacking monasteries, pillaging, destroying relics, raping nuns, and hanging clergy who refused to join their cause.

The creak of a board sounded in the room, and this time she knew she hadn't dreamed it. She silenced her tumbling thoughts and strained to listen.

After a long moment came another sound

— the friction of cloth against planks, almost as if someone were crawling across the floor.

Her blood turned to ice, and she strained to see through the night. What if Abbot Baltazar had sent his men after them again? His threat to get them back continually stalked her.

A hand slipped over her mouth. It was cold and thin and pressed hard, muffling her startled gasp. She arched her back and twisted to break free. Panic raced through her and filled her with only one thought: she had to save herself and Margaret from capture by Abbot Baltazar's men. Once had been enough. She couldn't fail Margaret again.

She thrashed her legs and tried to pry the hand from her mouth and wished Margaret wasn't such a heavy sleeper.

"Don't struggle," came a hoarse whisper next to her ear. It was followed by the prick of a blade against her neck.

The pain deepened and forced her to lie completely still, so she couldn't attempt to identify her attacker. A ragged sleeve brushed her face. The stench of fish and excrement ingrained in the fabric assaulted her nostrils.

Ave Maria. Her mind whirled in a crazy

spiral of fear. Tortured priests without tongues lined up before her. *Glory be to the Father, and to the Son, and to the Holy Spirit . . .* She leaned back on her pallet and ordered her body into a calmness that betrayed her thundering heart.

"Sister Katharina," the attacker whispered. A hooded face appeared over hers. "I have news for you."

She squinted and tried to see past the shadows.

"If you pay the right price, I'll give you the news."

This surely couldn't be one of Abbot Baltazar's men. Who was this, and what did he want?

"You can't alert anyone else that I'm here."

Katharina nodded.

The attacker removed his hand from her mouth but didn't move the blade. "It's me, Greta."

"Greta?" Relief poured through Katharina, relief so swift that tears pooled in her eyes. She tried to sit up, but the blade bit her flesh, and she fell back. "Greta, where have you been? How are you faring?"

Margaret stirred. "Katharina? What is it?" Her voice was groggy with sleep.

"Greta's back." Katharina wished she

could wrap her arms around her prodigal maidservant and was confused that the girl was threatening her with a knife.

"Greta?" Margaret sat up, all traces of grogginess gone from her voice. "After all this time? Oh, how wonderful."

Katharina could hear Margaret fumbling to open the shutters. Within seconds the room was illuminated by the faint moonlight of the clear winter sky.

"Oh, Greta, we thought you were dead." Margaret turned and smiled at Greta, who was still kneeling next to Katharina. However, when Margaret glimpsed the knife against Katharina's throat, she gasped and hopped backward.

Greta tossed the hood away from her face, and Katharina couldn't contain a murmur of surprise. Her relief at her reunion with her servant was chased away by horror. Greta's face was that of an old woman: sunken cheeks, hollow eyes, brittle skin, only a skeleton of the beautiful young girl she'd once been. She could see gaping black where Greta was missing her top front teeth.

Katharina pushed aside the knife and sat up. Sobs gathered like storm clouds in her chest and pushed for release. Before Greta could protest, Katharina grabbed her into an embrace. The girl didn't fight her but held herself stiff. At the thought of all Greta had gone through these past months, Katharina had to stifle an escaped sob into Greta's foul-smelling cloak.

After several moments of Katharina's embrace, Greta pulled back.

"How's your baby?" Margaret asked.

"Dead." Greta's voice was emotionless.

"Oh, Greta." Katharina had to swallow hard to keep the rest of her sobs at bay. She'd tried to ignore the troubling possibility that she was partly to blame for the girl running away. But the guilt swirled with the agony of seeing the young woman so deformed and decimated.

"I have news about Marienthron," Greta whispered hoarsely. "Do you want it or not?"

"What kind of news?" Katharina asked.

"The worst kind."

Katharina's pulse slowed, and she swallowed past the tightness of her throat. "What is it?" What if Abbot Baltazar had done something more to Aunt Lena? Her heart couldn't bear the thought of the dear woman suffering further. Many times during the past months, Katharina had wished she'd tried harder to make her aunt leave the convent so she'd be safe. But then at other times, she was glad Aunt Lena was somewhere useful. If she, Katharina, couldn't find a home of her own, what would have become of Aunt Lena out in the world?

"You have to promise to pay a price first."

"But I have no money and nothing of value." Nothing except the indulgence her mother had given her, but she'd never part with that, not for any reason.

"I don't want money. I want Thomas freed."

"Thomas?" Margaret said, wrapping her thin arms across her shivering torso. "Isn't he dead?"

"He's still in the elector's prison in Torgau." Greta waved the knife. "If you guarantee his release, then I'll give you the news."

"Greta, I cannot release him." Despair rolled through Katharina. "I don't have that kind of power."

"But you know Doctor Luther. He could get Thomas out." Greta's lifeless eyes lit for a moment with a silent, desperate plea.

"Even if I ask Doctor Luther to petition for Thomas's release, I couldn't guarantee it."

Greta was silent, her gaunt face streaked with grime and bruises. The girl's thin shoulders formed sharp peaks through the ragged linen of her cloak.

Every pitiful part of the girl's condition ripped at Katharina's heart. "Greta, you must stay and let me help you."

She shook her head and started to rise. Katharina reached for her. But the hardness in the girl's eyes stopped Katharina. It was clear that Greta wanted only one thing from her, and Katharina knew she had to at least try to win Thomas's release. It was the only thing she could do for Greta now. "I shall ask Doctor Luther, Greta — regardless of whether you give me the news about Marienthron. Thomas doesn't deserve to be locked away."

Greta was silent for a long moment. Finally she spoke in a harsh whisper. "The Bundschuh are planning to attack Marienthron. They'll have no mercy."

EIGHTEEN

Luther pulled the hood of his heavy woolen cloak down again and tried to shield his face from the biting wind. It did little good. His eyebrows were already caked with ice. His hand upon the reins was numb, frozen into position. Worse were his toes. The only part of him still warm was his back, where Katharina had burrowed against him.

He should have forced her to stay in Torgau when they'd stopped to thaw themselves. It was too cold and too dangerous for her to be with them. Who knew what they would find when they reached the abbey?

Fresh anger rumbled through him. Why did he have such a difficult time saying no to her royal majesty? Actually, he *had* told her no; he'd ordered her to stay behind. But she'd been as insistent and as stubborn as a headache.

"You should be married to Baumgartner

by now," he growled over his shoulder. "Then I wouldn't have to be responsible for what might happen to you."

"And you should be married to Hanna von Spiegel." Her voice was muffled under a layer of scarves.

He snorted. "Hanna von Spiegel is betrothed to the swineherd at the Wiederstedt convent. She was betrothed before she ran away."

He felt Katharina's sharp intake of breath more than he heard it. His frozen lips cocked into a half grin. "I know exactly what you're thinking, empress Kate. That it's unthinkable, unacceptable, entirely unpardonable for a woman of noble birth to love a commoner and want to marry him."

"It's unheard of."

"Her relatives agree with you. They won't heed a word I've written to them. They've hired lawyers to prevent her from marrying out of her social class."

He couldn't hear Katharina's response, but he knew it. She was as proud as the rest. "One man is equal to another if only they want and love each other."

She didn't respond.

He knew she'd heard him. "One man is equal to another" — he raised his voice anyway — "if only they want and love each other."

She lifted her head. "An uncommon match only breeds discontent and gives birth to unhappiness."

He shook his head. "Let's hope your *common* match with Baumgartner doesn't do the same."

She stiffened and held herself rigid so she was no longer leaning into him.

He kicked his horse, urging it faster. The motion forced her to snake her arms around his middle to keep from toppling. Her body flattened against his again, sending a shiver through him. Even though layers of cloaks and robes separated them, he couldn't keep from relishing the pressure of her, the closeness.

Was that why he had allowed her to come along? Was he growing weak? When it came to women, he'd always been able to look away, deny his flesh, and fill his mind with other thoughts. Why then did he have trouble with his self-control when he was with Katharina?

He put his head down. It would be better to pretend she wasn't there.

They rode in silence as they had most of the day. The others in their party were equally somber. He hoped they could arrive in time to warn Marienthron and prevent the attack that Katharina had learned about. But he feared that they would be too late, that their mission would fail.

Lately there had been many such attacks against convents where rebelling peasants looted and killed in retaliation for all they'd suffered. Even if the tyranny of Rome and her followers was unbearable, he couldn't justify the common man taking the law into his own hands. He firmly believed that it was the exclusive domain of the princes, knights, and other secular rulers to hold authority, that it was ordained by God they should keep the peace, protect the innocent, and punish evil.

No matter how justified the Bundschuh peasants were in their complaints, he couldn't condone their violent means. Brute force was the weapon of mindless animals — whether peasant or prince.

Winter's early nightfall was upon them by the time they reached Grimma. From there it was only a short ride to the Marienthron convent. When they arrived, they saw one of the front gates hanging at an odd angle, and eerie stillness greeted them.

Luther slowed his horse. His dread increased with each step they took.

They entered the compound, and the

clopping of their horses' hoofs echoed like that of an army in the silence of the empty abbey. The destruction that met them was evidence the battle was already over. Before he'd even brought his horse to a standstill, Katharina slid down. Without a moment of hesitation, she sprang forward toward the main cloister building.

"Aunt Lena!" Katharina shouted.

The desperation in her voice tore at his heart, the same way it had when she'd shown up at the Black Cloister at dawn to awaken him to the plight of Marienthron.

He slipped from his horse, determined to follow her, afraid of what she might find.

Melanchthon's hand on his arm stopped him. "They've destroyed the relic boxes." His friend held up a handful of bones.

Through the fading light Luther could see the battered chests, their contents strewn, jars broken, shrouds ripped, bones crushed. Marienthron had been home to perhaps four hundred relics: particles of Christ's table, cross, crib, robe, blood, the stone and soil where he had wept, along with a various assortment of bones from apostles and saints.

"There are enough pieces of the true cross here to build a house." He fingered a rough plank in disgust. It was all rubbish as far as he was concerned; none of it had enough power to save a gnat. Such relics might be useless and worthy of destruction, but he could support neither the iconoclasm nor the use of unrestrained strength in rebellion. There were more peaceful methods of fighting a battle, and he'd become the master of their use.

"Doctor Luther, over there." One of the men who had joined them in Torgau pointed to a cage swinging from a tall elm in the middle of the cloister yard. Despite the growing darkness, the sight was gruesome. Inside sat the mutilated body of a priest, hands and feet cut off, his corpse left to rot. A single peasant shoe hung from the cage by its long leather strip.

Luther could only shake his head in frustration. Why wouldn't the Bundschuh listen to his admonitions? He knew the church had mistreated them, had caused them untold pain over the years. But such vindication wouldn't solve the problems.

He picked his way around the debris and entered the cloister building. The inside was as ransacked as the outside. He stopped to peer into each room that he passed. The peasants had overturned and smashed tables and benches in the refectory, broken the expensive glass windows in the common rooms, and shredded the sheets and sliced the pallets in the dormitory.

Anger swirled through his gut. The peasants might believe they were on a holy mission, but they were doing the work of the devil. He could explain it no other way.

"Kate?" His voice echoed in the unlit, narrow hallway.

"Here."

He followed her voice into one of the small cells.

She was kneeling before an older nun and wrapping a strip of sheet around the woman's head. In the deep shadows of the room, he could distinguish a spot of bright blood already seeping through the linen. Katharina's face was pale, but she worked deftly to tear another strip of linen with her teeth. Her hands shook as she fumbled to wrap the piece of cloth around the woman's head.

Luther knelt next to her, the blood-slickened floor dampening his hose. "Is she your Aunt Lena?"

Katharina nodded without pausing in her work. "She's alive, but barely."

The woman's face was ashen except for the purple welt that had swollen closed one eye. The other eye gazed into an unseen oblivion. Her habit was ripped past her knees giving him a glimpse of dark blood smeared up her legs onto her thighs.

Nausea gurgled in his stomach and rose into his throat. The peasant men were doing nothing more than satisfying their own lusts in the name of revolution. What did raping nuns have to do with gaining the freedoms they desired?

He swallowed several times and then took a deep breath. "Where are the others?"

"Sisters Maltiz and Pock are in the next cell." Her voice cracked. "They're dead."

"And the rest of them?"

"I don't know." She finally turned to look at him. The horror in her eyes made him want to pull her into his arms and hold her and shield her from the nightmare.

"How could anyone do this?" she whispered.

He could only shake his head and thank God from the depths of his heart that Katharina hadn't been there when the peasants had attacked.

NINETEEN

Katharina had no choice. She would stay in Grimma even though everything within her screamed in protest at the thought of living on the doorstep of Marienthron. She couldn't forsake Aunt Lena, not now, not after all that had happened to her.

Katharina smoothed a hand across the older woman's cheek. Aunt Lena hadn't spoken a word in the three days since they'd found her. Katharina had spent every waking moment by the woman's side, doctoring her wounds, revolted anew at the evidences of abuse the woman had suffered.

"I've decided not to return to Wittenberg — not until you're better," she whispered.

Aunt Lena stared at the ceiling, unblinking, unmoving.

Katharina touched the pulse in her aunt's neck. A steady thump against her fingers reassured her of life — a small flicker of something in the battered body. She straightened the bandage covering the woman's scalp and the deep cut, which she'd sewn closed. If only the gash had been the worst of her injuries.

"Sister Katharina?" Magdalene von Staupitz's gentle voice came from the doorway. "Doctor Luther is waiting for you."

Katharina reached for Aunt Lena's hand and hesitated.

"I'll stay with her for a little while." Sister Magdalene's voice was a whisper as she stepped to the bedside.

Her aunt's hand was cold and heavy. Katharina pressed it and hoped for the merest of responses.

There was nothing.

"Go now. You need a break." Sister Magdalene helped Katharina to her feet and turned her toward the door.

Weary from lack of sleep, Katharina stumbled into the main room of the small house.

"How is she?" Doctor Luther's dark gaze searched her face. He stood near the door and stooped under the low ceiling. He'd spent the past days meeting with the leaders of Grimma, making arrangements for the care of Aunt Lena. He'd secured the house, which had recently belonged to an Augustinian monastery but had been deserted when the monks had abandoned their vows. Now Doctor Luther had gained permission for Aunt Lena to stay there with the promise that Sister Magdalene would start a school for the girls of Grimma.

Sister Magdalene hadn't spoken a negative word about her stay with her brother Gunther at his Motterwitz estate, but the former nun had been more than eager to accept Luther's offer not only to teach the girls of Grimma but also to help care for Aunt Lena.

Katharina rubbed a hand across her eyes. When she had managed to sleep during the past nights, her dreams had always turned into nightmares of Aunt Lena. "She's still not speaking."

Luther's expression was sober and his eyes deep wells of sadness. "Then you still insist on staying?"

She nodded. Fear prickled through her again, as it did every time she thought of being close to Marienthron and to Abbot Baltazar. In her secret thoughts she was ashamed for wishing Abbot Baltazar had been in the cage hanging from the oak instead of one of the priests who'd resided in the Predigerhaus. But the abbot had been safely away at his primary residence, the Cistercian Pforta monastery.

She'd heard that he'd returned to the abbey after the attack and had begun the arduous task of restoring it for all the nuns who remained, the sisters who'd been able to hide and avoid attack. The peasant uprising hadn't deterred him from his duties. Instead, rumors had reached her ears that he was more zealous than before.

But she'd decided if Sister Magdalene was brave enough to live within the shadows of their former abbey, then she could do the same, at least until Aunt Lena was well enough to move.

"I must stay," Katharina said, rubbing her hands across her arms to bring warmth to her limbs. The hearth fire across the room barely flickered with light, much less with heat. "I cannot leave her in this condition."

Doctor Luther's weary expression spoke more than words could. He knew, as she did, that Aunt Lena and Sisters Maltiz and Pock had sacrificed themselves to protect the other women. If the three hadn't hidden the younger sisters in the cloister prison cells, and if they hadn't taken the brunt of the abuses themselves, the others would have fared far worse.

"I'll pray for her healing both in body and in mind." His voice was low. "And I'll pray for you, Katharina, that the Lord will keep you safe."

"And I shall hope that God answers your prayers, Doctor Luther." She was grateful for all his help over the past days. Not only had he spoken out against the violence, but he'd also provided for Aunt Lena, rallied the support of the townspeople for her and Sister Magdalene, and gathered assurances that the men in the area would watch over them. If anyone deserved God's mercy, Doctor Luther did.

"Will you promise to stay close to the house?" he asked.

"I'll do my best. And you must remember to write to the elector about freeing Thomas."

"It's as good as done the moment I arrive in Torgau."

She wanted to instruct him to watch for Jerome's return to Wittenberg. Should he arrive while she was away, she needed someone to deliver the news of her whereabouts.

But his eyes had grown blacker and were regarding her in a way that seared her insides like a hot tonic. Without breaking his gaze, he stepped away from the door and crossed the bare room toward her. Each of his heavy footsteps escalated her heartbeat.

When he stood before her, his body exuded a strength and warmth that made her heart race too fast. He was near enough that she could see the shadows under his eyes and the layer of scruff over his cheek and chin.

"Katharina." His whisper was tinged with something she couldn't identify. When his attention flickered to her lips, her breath caught in her throat. Did he want to kiss her? Surely he wouldn't.

"Will you promise to return to Wittenberg?" He lifted ink-stained fingers to her face.

"I'll try."

His fingers skimmed her cheek.

Her legs quivered.

"You won't return to a wasted life in the abbey, will you?"

"Of course not." Her voice was only a whisper now too.

A glimmer in his eyes illuminated the deep darkness and gave her a glimpse of the power of his desire.

He would kiss her, and she had no wish to resist him. Quite the opposite. She had a sudden, sharp need for him that tightened her entire body.

As his head lowered toward hers, her stomach flipped, and she leaned forward in anticipation.

"Martinus, are you ready?" From the doorway, Melanchthon's question cut through the room.

Katharina stumbled a step back and slipped her hands over her warm cheeks.

"I'm saying good-bye to Katharina." Doctor Luther didn't turn to look at his friend.

"We need to be on our way." Melanchthon blew into his hands and then rubbed them together.

"I'll be out in a few minutes." Doctor Luther didn't budge. His attention was focused upon her with an intensity that burned into her and made her want to forget all reason. "Can I have one moment of privacy? Is that too much to ask?"

Melanchthon cleared his throat, and his slender red face seemed to grow redder until it nearly matched the unruly hair that had wrestled loose from his winter cap. "I don't want to be the one to remind you that Katharina von Bora is promised to Baumgartner. And it's in everybody's best interest to leave it that way."

Doctor Luther leaned closer, the warmth of his breath taunting her. His eyes seemed to plead with her to dispute Melanchthon.

For an instant she longed to make Doctor Luther happy, to keep the peace, to hold on to his pleasure. Past experience had taught her that any mention of Jerome would only gain his scorn.

But her hesitancy was all it took for his eyes to fill with disappointment. "Then it really is time for me to say good-bye."

How could she respond? She didn't want to anger Doctor Luther, and yet she had promised herself to Jerome.

"You're right, Philipp." Doctor Luther stepped away, taking his warmth and solidness, leaving her cold again. "I need to accept the facts."

She braced herself for Doctor Luther's usual onslaught of derision toward Jerome. And she desperately wished that they didn't need to talk about him, that they could ignore everything and everyone else for a moment.

He stared at her, sadness deepening the lines of his face. "Good-bye, Kate." The words sounded permanent.

"I'm sure I shall return to Wittenberg soon."

"No, this must be good-bye." After a final search of her face, he turned. The cloak covering his habit swished decisively as he strode to the door.

She started after him, then stopped. What else could she say?

Without a glance back he pushed open

the door and stepped outside.

Melanchthon nodded at her. Although his eyes were kind, something in them warned her not to come after Doctor Luther but to accept the fate that had been handed to both of them. It was no secret that some of Doctor Luther's advisors cautioned him against marriage. Apparently Melanchthon was one of those.

She swallowed hard and pushed down an ache in her throat. She couldn't begin to make sense of the sudden feeling of rejection that swept through her.

Melanchthon turned to go.

"Wait." She stepped toward him.

With his hand on the door, he paused and looked back at her expectantly.

"When Jerome returns to Wittenberg, I must have someone explain to him my absence and where he can find me."

He nodded almost too eagerly. "Have no fear, my lady. I shall share the tidings with him the moment he arrives."

As he left, Katharina stared at the door. A sense of abandonment spread like a heavy coverlet over her face and suffocated her. She could hear a five-year-old girl crying and begging. For an instant she could feel the scratch of the blanket mingling with heat and tears and could breathe the odor of dust and horseflesh. Why hadn't her father listened to her pleas? Why had he thrown a covering over her head and ignored her?

She took a deep breath and exhaled the memories. "I shall marry Jerome." Her voice wavered in the silent room. He would come for her, and when he did, she would finally have a family again, and this time she wouldn't let anyone take it away from her.

Katharina had begun to wonder if Aunt Lena would ever speak again. As the winter days thawed into spring, her aunt's physical wounds healed. Only puckered scars on her back remained. They were evidence of an earlier beating, likely received for having aided their escape from the convent, and Katharina blamed herself every time she smoothed salve over her aunt's skin.

The emotional wounds, however, went deeper. Aunt Lena was lost in another world in the far recesses of her mind. Katharina could only surmise that the shock of what her aunt had seen and experienced had killed her spirit and taken away her will to live.

Day after day Katharina labored to pull her aunt back to the world of the living, but her despair festered when she could find no concoction, no tincture, no salve — nothing to help. The only comfort Aunt Lena seemed to draw was from a dagger Doctor Luther had left with Sister Magdalene. Her aunt carried the weapon with her at all times and even slept with it at her side.

Katharina stayed within the confines of the house and yard, the busy town of Grimma providing a safe wall of protection around her. On the rare days when the sunshine poured warmth over the greening grass and blossoming pear trees, Katharina couldn't stop herself from wandering a bit farther into the deserted convent gardens, which hadn't been pruned recently.

Sister Magdalene always fussed about Katharina straying too far from the main house, but the months of peaceful living had lessened her fears. She knew she was secure as long as she stayed within the confines of the town. Besides, she was sure the abbot had more important things to worry about than her.

The raised herb beds were completely safe, and she'd gone there numerous times in recent days with the excuse of gathering ingredients for the syrups, infusions, and salves she administered to Aunt Lena. It would be a month or more before many plants were in full bloom, but she'd located flowering cowslip and bistort.

She knelt next to the cowslip. The flowers dangled like golden keys, and she pressed her nose against them to take in their sweet smell. Had it really been almost a year since she'd made her escape from Marienthron and left this area?

A lot had happened in that year . . . except for the one thing she'd wanted most. She sighed and sat back on her heels. By now Jerome would have received her letters alerting him to her whereabouts. And it was spring; he could come for her if he truly wanted to. She'd begun to quietly resign herself to the fact that he didn't want her anymore. Perhaps he hadn't wanted her in the first place except to use her.

In recent days she'd found herself thinking more of Doctor Luther, of his dark eyes and the way he'd leaned into her and almost kissed her before he'd left. But he'd been silent too. Although she knew nothing could develop between them, she couldn't deny that she missed him more than she did Jerome.

With a startling flap of wings, a pair of cardinals and a dozen other birds disappeared into the expanse of blue sky.

Katharina silenced her thoughts and listened. In the distance she could hear the giggling of the girls Magdalene had assembled to teach. Their tinkling laughter wafted on the warm breeze.

A crunch of footsteps sounded in the dry leaves and twigs that littered the garden behind her. She'd thought she was alone, had expected the privacy she'd had every other time she'd come to the herb beds.

"There she is, Cal, just like Abbot Baltazar told us, sitting in the garden."

At the mention of the abbot, her pulse began to pound a wild and unsteady rhythm. She jumped up but her legs tangled in her skirt, causing her to lose her balance. A glance over her shoulder at a short man with a missing earlobe and scar along his jaw told her she was in desperate trouble.

Ave Maria. She stumbled forward. If she could outrun the men to the gate, she might have a chance. She jerked her skirt free of her legs and started to sprint. *Our Father in heaven.* But she made it only a few steps when a crushing blow to her back sent her sprawling forward. Her body slammed into the ground, and the impact knocked the breath out of her.

TWENTY

One of the convent laborers stepped on Katharina and pinned her in place. He twisted her hands behind her back and then jerked her upward to her feet. The pain ripped through her arms, and she cried out.

"It's not polite to leave without saying a proper greeting, is it, Cal?" The woodcutter spun her around.

She gritted her teeth. "You won't get away with this."

He laughed. "You've got it backward. You're the one who won't be getting away."

She struggled to pull free of him.

His grip tightened. "She's not getting away this time, is she, Cal?"

The tall laborer with his balding head covered with scant strands of black hair pulled out his knife and flashed it in front of her. The blade glinted, and she only had to think back to the slice he'd made in Margaret's chin to know he wouldn't hesitate to use it.

Except for the anxious twitters in her nerves, she held herself still. "I have important friends who will come to my aid, just as they did previously."

"We get paid after you're locked behind the prison door. That's all we care about, right, Cal? Getting the payment we've been promised."

They tied and gagged her and then carried her to an alley that bordered the garden. There waiting in a secluded hedge was a wagon that belonged to the convent. It was loaded with barrels and bags. To her dismay, the laborers stuffed her into one of the barrels, and then she could feel them lift the barrel into the back of a wagon.

In the dank cramped container, she crouched uncomfortably, unable to move any part of her body. She wanted to scream out for help, cry, pound her hands, do something. But she was trapped. Cal and the woodcutter would be able to ride through the main thoroughfare of Grimma and out the town gates, and no matter her efforts to draw attention to herself, no one would be able to hear her or even begin to suspect that she was inside the barrel.

The men didn't have to tell her to which prison they were taking her. She knew. As the wagon bumped along, her mind spun frantically, trying to figure a way to save herself. But this time all she could think about was the irony that she was returning to the convent much the same way she'd left, in a wagon bed of barrels.

When the wagon finally came to a halt and she heard the clang of an iron gate closing, she tried to push down her escalating fear. Vivid memories of the destruction and gore she had seen the last time she was here assaulted her.

The men lifted her from the barrel, and she could see that although the convent was neat, it was still in disrepair — windows boarded where there had once been stained glass, doors ripped from hinges, and broken benches. They dragged her past the kitchen and the smell of baking bread to the narrow stairwell that led to the underground cellar. She tried to catch the attention of several lay sisters at work behind large kettles and beg them for help. But Schwester Walperick turned her large backside to Katharina and signaled to the cook's maids to focus on their work.

The cook had never been a part of the more privileged community of noble nuns. The servants had their place in the social order of convent life. They lived separately, and no one questioned their God-ordained places — at least that's what Katharina had always believed.

She stumbled down the steps and realized no one would be able to help her. The sisters were attending the sacred hour of Sext. Their liturgical chanting from the choir carried through the cloister yard, breaking the stillness. It was a familiar chant, one she had sung countless times, but the words brought her no comfort now.

She had little hope of getting any assistance from the sisters, even later after they finished the recitation of the divine office. The rumors of her arrival would soon spread, but when they learned she was being held in the prison, who would risk their safety for her? Her closest allies at the abbey were gone. And even though the abbess was her aunt, her mother's own sister, the Reverend Mother had never shown her any affection or special treatment, unlike Aunt Lena.

The woodcutter pushed her through the dark passage of the cellar. She staggered along, hopelessness growing within her. When they reached the first prison cell door, he led her inside, locked her feet in stocks, then left her in utter darkness.

After the key turned and the footsteps

faded, Katharina leaned back against the cold brick wall. The dirt floor was damp, and the air had not yet been touched by the spring thaw. With no windows and only a small sliding opening in the door, the blackness of the room imprisoned her as much as the bonds on her mouth, hands, and feet.

Her heart pounded with a ferocity that shook her body. She wasn't afraid of the underground cell. She'd seen it before by candlelight. It was damp and dirty but safe. And she wasn't afraid of the cold or dark.

No. What she feared most was what would happen to her next. Sooner or later Abbot Baltazar would call for her. She would have to face him.

What would he do to her?

Her mouth dried at the remembrance of the jagged pink slices across Aunt Lena's back.

What torture would Abbot Baltazar devise for her? She had no doubt he would make her an example to the entire convent, an example of what would happen if they dared to defy him.

Holy Mary, full of grace, the Lord is with thee. Blessed art thou among women, and blessed is the fruit of thy womb, Jesus.

Would the Holy Virgin Mother really intercede for her?

O God . . . Her body trembled uncontrollably. Her mouth hurt from the tight cloth gagging her. Her wrists were chafed by the rope binding them. And the wooden stocks elevated her feet awkwardly, making her whole body slide to an awkward angle.

Everything within her longed to pray, really pray. But what should she say? What *could* she say in a situation like this? She'd heard Doctor Luther preach that one would never pray well from a book, that written prayers can teach *how* and *what* to pray for and could kindle a desire to pray, but ultimately prayer must come freely from the heart, without any made-up or prescribed words. It must form the words that are burning in the heart.

Before now she hadn't felt the need to give up the comfort of the old prayers, but at that moment with the cold blackness of the cell pressing on her and the uncertainty of her future tormenting her, how could she do anything but pray freely from her heart?

Help me, God. O God, I need Your help.

She hesitated, but fear pulsed through her and pushed out the burning words.

I believe I shall die right now just thinking about what Abbot Baltazar has planned for me. O God, please save me. Please help me.

She lost track of time. Occasionally she

heard the bells sounding in the distance. And yet she prayed in a way she'd never before dared. She wasn't sure when or how, but calm began to penetrate the frenzy of her anxiety, and she had an awareness of God's presence.

Eventually Sister Agnes, as cellaress, brought her bread and water and untied the bonds on her hands and mouth. Sister Agnes didn't speak to her or answer her whispered questions, but she was gentle, and Katharina drew comfort from that.

Hours blended into days with only Sister Agnes's ministrations breaking the monotony. And finally, just when she had begun to hope she might not have to face Abbot Baltazar after all, Sister Agnes arrived with Sister Illssee. They unlocked the stocks and pulled her to her feet. Weak and stiff from lack of use, her legs couldn't hold her. Each sister took one of Katharina's arms and half dragged, half carried her out of the cell and up the stairs to the cloister yard. After days of complete darkness, she squinted at the light, the brightness bringing painful tears. She knew without asking where they were taking her, and she began to shake uncontrollably. The moment of reckoning had finally come.

Fresh fear squeezed her chest as they led

her to the lone elm at the center of the yard, the same elm where the mutilated priest had been hung by the Bundschuh. The well-groomed shrubs and lawn were alive with spring and immaculate in spite of the evidence of the attack. Through a blur she saw that all the sisters had gathered. They stood quietly along the edge of the grass with their eyes down and their hands folded and tucked into the cuffs of their habits. They wouldn't savor her torment any more than she had the Zeschau sisters'. But they were compelled to watch or face the same consequence.

Sister Agnes and Sister Illssee stopped in front of the elm. They pushed Katharina to her knees, then stretched her arms around the trunk and bound her hands. Katharina rested her cheek against the rough bark, trying to still her shaking limbs.

The minutes dragged. The silence stretched tighter. Only the whistling song of a finch echoed in the overwhelming hush of the courtyard. Finally low voices could be heard. Abbot Baltazar's nasal tone came closer, along with the soft responses of the abbess and prioress.

A chill swept through Katharina. She closed her eyes and whispered a prayer like the ones she'd already prayed, except more desperate.

"Sisters." Abbot Baltazar finally spoke behind her. "You're here to witness the discipline of our wayward Sister Katharina."

Protest rose within her like bile.

"She's broken her vows to Christ, her Bridegroom. She's fallen prey to the heresy of that rebellious monk who has been stirring up dissension against the true church of Christ and the doctrines established by the holy apostles."

Why hadn't Doctor Luther come to her aid? He would have heard of her capture by now and would have had time to act on her behalf.

"To save her from the torments of hell and eternal punishment," Abbot Baltazar continued, "it's our sacred duty to restore her to the convent and to her vows of chastity, poverty, and obedience. Her salvation, her very life, depend upon her restoration."

She couldn't bear to think that Doctor Luther was purposefully ignoring her plight, especially in light of the finality of his goodbye the last time she'd seen him. Surely he was too good a man to let that stop him from attempting to procure her release.

"The Holy Scriptures instruct us to discipline." Abbot Baltazar's voice rang with holiness and conviction. "It clearly speaks to us: 'No chastening seems to be joyful for the present, but painful; nevertheless, afterward it yields the peaceable fruit of righteousness to those who have been trained by it.' "

A deep sense of loneliness welled up within Katharina. Her family hadn't wanted her and wouldn't protect her. Jerome had left her with promises but little else. Doctor Luther had walked away from her. Dear Aunt Lena had abandoned her to go into a world of silence.

She had no one. If she died today, would anyone care?

"Sister Katharina must be punished for her sins." Although she couldn't see the abbot, she could feel his presence behind her. "And this must be done publicly so that all who witness and hear of her punishment will be deterred from erring as she has. If we can save even one soul from repeating her sins, then we will be rewarded by God."

The abbess silently moved behind Katharina, tucking her hair out of the way and fumbling to untie her collar and expose her shoulders.

"No, Abbess Margareta." Abbot Baltazar approached. "We'll need to bare more than shoulders for this discipline."

Katharina winced when Abbot Baltazar

sliced the threadbare linen of her bodice and ripped it down the length of her back. He attacked her underbodice next with his knife, struggling to tear the material.

She sucked in a breath and waited for the knife to slice her skin.

"There." He finished and stepped away. "She'll never wear these unholy clothes again."

Cool spring air prickled the exposed skin of her back.

"We'll burn them as a sign that she's putting heretical ideas to death. And when she has received due punishment, she'll don her habit and perform acts of penance until she has abolished every thought of adultery with the world."

His cold fingers grazed the smoothness of her back with an intimacy that made her shudder. "Sister Katharina," he said in a low voice, "you'll learn to accept me. And someday in heaven you'll thank me for saving your soul."

"I shall not be able to thank you in heaven, for you won't be there." Her response slipped out before she thought of the ramifications.

She heard a startled gasp from the abbess, but the whistle of the rod slicing through the air and the connection with her bare flesh took away all thought. The fire of the strike across her skin reached inside and tore a scream from her chest.

"Your defiance is from the devil." Abbot Baltazar brought the rod down upon her skin again, then again, and again. Her agonized cries spilled out as he beat her over and over. Fire raced up and down her back until she thought her body would burn up altogether and she would find herself a heap of ashes. Finally he stopped. His heavy breathing filled the air where her screams still echoed.

Her throat was hoarse, and she was sure she was in hell with a demon on her back torturing her flesh with a flaming torch.

"Your turn, Abbess Margareta. You and the prioress will alternate disciplining now."

"But, Abbot Baltazar, hasn't she —"

"Abbess Margareta, I would not like to report any further obstinacy to the bishop."

There was a brief moment of silence before the abbess responded in a resigned tone. "How many more lashes?"

"You may not stop until Sister Katharina says, '*Mea culpa*, I will amend.'"

Katharina closed her eyes, dizzy, weak, and wishing she could fall into oblivion so she could be freed from the torment where her back had once been.

"Sister Katharina." The abbess spoke firmly behind her. "You must repent of your waywardness at once. Then we shall be finished with your discipline."

Katharina couldn't remember a kind word the Reverend Mother had ever spoken to her. In fact, Katharina had decided she reminded the abbess too much of the family she'd been denied. Perhaps the abbess had resented her sister for her freedom and normal life the same way Katharina had resented her sister.

"Quick repentance is always best," the abbess said.

"Forgive me, Reverend Mother," Katharina managed to croak. "My conscience will not permit me."

"Resume the lashes," Abbot Baltazar called.

The rod connected with her inflamed flesh, and she screamed. Although the abbess didn't have the same strength as Abbot Baltazar, the pain radiated as though ten more demons had descended upon her.

The rod fell again and again until she couldn't breathe enough to scream. In her agony she could think of nothing but death.

"Say the words, Sister Katharina." The abbess's plea penetrated the haze in her head.

Did she have the strength to utter the words they wanted to hear? Would they beat her to death if she refused?

"Repent." The abbess's tone was urgent and angry. "It's not so difficult to claim responsibility for your sins."

Would she be able to live with herself if she uttered the words? Or would she save her outer body only to kill her inner spirit and end up a shell of a woman like Aunt Lena?

"If you cannot repent for leaving" — her aunt's voice dipped to a harsh whisper meant only for her ear — "then repent for anything. But just do it or he'll kill you."

Katharina wasn't ready to die, not when she'd just begun to live. She still had too many hopes and dreams that she wasn't ready to let go of.

But could she find anything for which to repent?

The metallic taste of blood trickled from her cracked lips where the bark had chafed her. What about her pride? Surely her pride and callousness had hurt Greta. She'd taken her maidservant too much for granted. She'd presumed to think she was superior to the girl in every way simply because of their respective birthrights. If she'd truly loved Greta, not just as a master for a servant but as a friend, perhaps Greta would have confided in her. Perhaps she never would have run away.

"Mea culpa," she said. "I will amend." The hoarse voice that spoke didn't resemble hers.

"She has said it." The abbess expelled a tremulous breath and dropped something into the grass. It was the rod, slick and bright red.

TWENTY-ONE

When Katharina awoke, she desperately wished to return to the unconscious world, where she could escape the horror and pain of what had befallen her. Although her beating had finally ended, someone had moved her into the misericord, which meant one thing — her discipline would continue.

At least they hadn't returned her to the cloister prison. She didn't have to view her back to know her wounds were too serious to leave untreated. The unending pain and warmth of oozing blood told enough.

They had laid her on a pallet and exposed her tortured back to the ministrations of the infirmarian. No one spoke to her as they entered and left the room, not even in the sign language they used for communication. The sisters took turns acting as deputy and watched over her day and night, guarding the door to her room.

Over the following days Katharina had too

much time to think and sleep. Since idleness had never agreed with her, in her mind she wrote and rewrote a letter to Doctor Luther. She'd smuggle it out of the convent the first opportunity she had. In the letter she'd beg his forgiveness for anything she'd done to anger him, and she'd plead with him to come to her rescue — again.

Prayer was her one comfort. Her efforts to pray without recited words grew steadily easier and more natural. The calm she'd felt in prison returned to her. She'd reached the worst point in her life, where everything that could go wrong had, and praying kept her from sinking into the pit of despair.

When her back had finally healed enough for her to begin sitting up, the sisters dressed her in the customary habit, tied a belt loosely around her, then draped the long, wide scapular over her shoulders. As they wrapped a wimple around her head, she wondered how long it would be before they cut her hair. Over the past year it had grown until now it reached well past her shoulders. Sooner or later they would shear it short. She could bear the nun's habit; she could even endure the monotony of silence. But she would greatly miss her long hair.

One morning after Prime, the abbess came to her. With bowed head Katharina knelt and kissed her outstretched hand. The abbess stood silently for a long moment until Katharina wondered if her aunt might actually speak to her. But when she finally did, she only gave whispered instructions for penance. She made Katharina prostrate herself on the cold floor with arms outstretched and then required her to recite the Divine Office, two Pater Nosters, three Hail Marys, four creeds, five confessions, the Ten Commandments, and finally the Act of Faith.

After she finished, the abbess gave her a sheet of paper, ink, and quill. At first Katharina hoped she might be able to write a letter to Doctor Luther and somehow sneak it out of the abbey, but the Reverend Mother stood over her as she wrote her confessions, watching each stroke she made.

Every day the abbess came to oversee her penance and read her confessions. Katharina guessed the woman was waiting for her to admit she'd sinned by running away from the convent, but she determined never to write it. She would readily confess her sins of pride, anger, and covetousness, but she'd never admit she'd been wrong to leave the abbey.

Katharina knew she would eventually have to face Abbot Baltazar again. She dreaded the prospect, but she was unprepared for the fear that filled her when the door of her cell opened one evening, and instead of the abbess, he stepped inside.

The memory of the beating drenched her like icy water and made her back ache again.

"Sister Katharina." He rubbed one hand across his protruding middle and held out the other fleshy hand with his long fingernails for her to kiss. His bulging, bloodshot eyes regarded her with the same look he'd given Greta that day he'd arrived in Wittenberg.

It sent revulsion into her stomach. Nevertheless, with downcast eyes she knelt, took his hand, and gave him the respectful greeting required of her.

"I gave Abbess Margareta one week to attempt to restore you. She's asked for more time, but it's doubtful that you'd repent even if she had a full year." He motioned for Katharina to prostrate herself.

Trembling, she lowered herself until she was flat on the floor, nose touching the plank and arms outstretched.

"The time is past due for you to repent, Sister Katharina."

What would he do to her this time? Beat her again? She didn't know how her back could survive any more. The fresh scabs would easily break and bleed at the first strike of the rod.

"You must see the error of your ways." He stepped over her. "I'm convinced that painful punishment can turn many a wayward sinner back to the truth."

Holy Lord, have mercy. She swallowed and tried to push down the lump of fear wedged in her throat.

He circled near her feet. "Such small feet. I'm sure the skin is quite tender."

She suddenly pictured Thomas's crisp, blackened feet, blood oozing from bright pink cracks. Terror circled her neck like a noose and choked her breath. Was Abbot Baltazar planning to roast her feet as he had Thomas's?

"Yes, you won't resist the truth for long." He hooked his foot in the hem of her habit and began slipping it up.

Her mind shrieked, and her heart refused to beat.

"You must learn to submit to my authority." He slid her habit higher, exposing her stockings tied by garters and the bare legs above them. "A submissive spirit is what God Almighty requires of His children, and He has appointed me to train you in this endeavor."

A new fear seized her. What if he planned

to abuse her in another, more sinister way? All the years of overlooking, of denying the sordid rumors regarding the priests came back to laugh at her, and the reality of what the abbot was capable of doing mocked her.

Chills ran up her bare legs. Whatever discipline he was intending, she wouldn't let him. She'd fight. "No." She pushed up and tried to scramble forward.

His rod slapped against the wounds on her back. The pain radiated with such intensity that a scream slipped from her lips and filled the small cell. She fell back to the ground, immobilized and nearly blind from the torment to her skin.

He jumped on her, and his heavy weight pinned her legs under his knees. "You'll fare much better, Sister Katharina, if you learn submission quickly."

"No!" She struggled against him, twisting and turning to free herself.

Again the rod slashed her back.

She screamed again. The shrillness echoed off the walls.

"Abbot Baltazar?" The door to the misericord opened wide.

In a haze Katharina saw the abbess with the wooden stocks in one arm and a large candle in the other. The woman refused to meet her gaze.

Hot hatred pulsed through her — a hatred for her family so intense that she suddenly wanted to weep with the pressure of it. She hated them for abandoning her, for not loving her, for doing nothing to help her at her moment of greatest need. And now her aunt, her own flesh and blood, was planning to aid in her torture.

"Abbess Margareta." Abbot Baltazar stood hurriedly, smoothing his habit. His voice was tight with anger. "I thought I told you to wait outside the door and that I would call you when I was ready."

"You did call, didn't you?"

"No," he growled, "I did not."

"I beg your forgiveness. I thought I heard you call for me. Please forgive me."

"Very well. Now take your leave. And next time don't enter until I bid you."

The abbess hesitated and glanced down the hallway outside the misericord. "Are you sure you're not ready to begin?"

Katharina lifted her head and tried pushing herself off the floor. Dizziness from the pain in her back weighed her down, but she realized this was her chance. If she wanted to escape Abbot Baltazar, she must get away now.

"I'm ensuring Sister Katharina's submission." Irritation dripped from Abbot Baltazar's voice. "Now take your leave and close the door. You've interfered enough this week in Sister Katharina's discipline."

The abbess didn't reply but instead stepped into the hallway and peered out expectantly.

Katharina struggled to her knees. Warm rivulets trickled down her back.

"I don't think you'd like me to report any insubordination to the bishop, would you, Abbess Margareta?" Abbot Baltazar asked. "We both know what he'd do to you."

Before the abbess could reply, a tall, dark-hooded figure filled the doorway.

Katharina scrambled to sit up and suffocated a whimper of pain with her sleeve.

"Who are you?" Abbot Baltazar turned a withering glare on the intruder.

The abbess rushed toward Katharina, jerked her to her feet, and began to tug her toward the door. Confused, Katharina couldn't make her legs work even though she knew she should. Instead she watched the stranger slip a long dagger from his belt.

Abbot Baltazar quickly took a step back. "I demand to know who you are and what you're doing here."

The abbess wrenched Katharina's habit and motioned for Katharina to come with her. But Katharina couldn't turn her attention away from the blade. The hand gripping the hilt was missing several fingers. The stubs were ragged and uneven and deeply scarred.

"I vowed I would kill you," a rasping voice said. "And I always keep my vows."

Abbot Baltazar's eyes narrowed. "Abbess Margareta, call the gatekeepers to arrest this man."

The abbess grabbed Katharina's arm and ignored the abbot.

The stranger threw back his hood and revealed a disfigured face with an empty eye socket. "Remember me?"

Abbot Baltazar's face blanched.

Katharina stared. Was it Thomas, Greta's Thomas, the one the abbot had so hideously tortured?

"Sister Katharina, come with me," the abbess whispered, her face grave with urgency.

Abbot Baltazar stepped back farther, his eyes reflecting fear. "How did you get out of prison?"

"Martin Luther." Thomas thrust out the knife. "At least there's one monk in this world who's decent, who doesn't take out his lusts on helpless servant girls."

"Katharina, you must come with me now." The abbess's whisper was harsh, and there was something in her aunt's eyes that

Katharina had never seen before — concern. The concern loosened Katharina's body. She lurched forward against the abbess, letting her guide her away from the abbot.

"Abbess Margareta, I told you to get the gatekeepers." Abbot Baltazar's voice had a ring of panic.

Thomas stepped to the center of the room.

The abbot shrank back, bumping into the writing desk and rattling the ink bottles and quills that lay abandoned. "How did you get in here without the gatekeepers seeing you?"

Thomas threw off his cloak and then nodded at the wooden stocks and candle sitting where the abbess had placed them. "Those are for you, Baltazar."

Abbot Baltazar turned a stunned gaze upon the abbess.

"Quickly, Katharina." Without a glance back the Reverend Mother dragged Katharina from the room into the long, silent hallway.

"By the time I'm finished with you," Katharina heard Thomas say, "you'll beg me for mercy. But you won't get what you wouldn't give."

"Abbess Margareta, you'll be punished for this." The fear in the abbot's voice followed them. "Severely punished."

The abbess glanced at another cloaked figure, smaller and more womanly, and nodded. The woman stepped forward, closed the door, and lowered the wooden bar that would trap Abbot Baltazar with Thomas.

Katharina tried to peer past the woman's hood, but the abbess's grip tightened, and she hurried Katharina down the hallway.

"Greta?" Katharina strained to look over her shoulder.

The woman's dirty face was illuminated by the fading evening light that came from the one window at the end of the hallway. "I'm sorry, Greta," Katharina called. "I'm so sorry for not understanding, for not protecting you."

Greta's blank gaze shifted away.

"Please forgive me, Greta. I was naive and wrong and —"

"Hush now." The abbess's whisper was sharp.

Katharina cast one last glance at Greta and wanted to weep at the injustice of the girl's life all those years at Marienthron and what it had now become.

"You couldn't have protected her even if you'd tried." The abbess spoke matter-of-factly and slowed down only when they reached the stairway that led away from the dormitory. "Your own safety was purchased with a high price. You need only ask your Aunt Lena."

Katharina shuddered to think of what lengths her aunt may have gone to in order to protect her over the years, what sacrifices she had made to keep her safe from Abbot Baltazar. She owed Aunt Lena her life.

A scream like that of a swine in the slaughterhouse came from the misericord and echoed down the hallway.

Katharina's skin prickled. But the abbess pressed her down the winding stairway. When they reached the bottom, the woman shoved her toward the garden, deserted at the late hour. "Hurry now."

Katharina stumbled and almost fell.

"Use the back gate."

At that moment Katharina understood the depth of sacrifice the abbess was making for her. Katharina started forward but then glanced at her aunt one last time. She was surprised at the stark guilt in the woman's severe face.

Although the abbess had never shown her any love or kindness, Katharina realized that now, when it mattered most, her aunt had put aside her jealousy of her sister and was setting Katharina free — free to have the kind of life that she'd envied.

"Go." The command was harsh.

Katharina nodded. Then without further hesitation, she turned and ran.

TWENTY-TWO

The light of the candle fell across Katharina's back, revealing the welts and bloody slashes in the otherwise pure and creamy skin. Even from across the room, Luther could see every mark, and his own skin burned as though feeling the beating too. Fresh rage rampaged through him, and his fingers clenched into a fist with the unfamiliar urge to slam his hand against something or someone.

"How is she?" he whispered.

Sister Magdalene gave a start from where she knelt beside Katharina. Her eyes widened. "Doctor Luther?"

Katharina faced the wall, but he still heard her soft gasp and whisper. "Cover me, Sister Magdalene. Immediately."

Sister Magdalene groped for the blanket already half covering Katharina and draped it gingerly over the rest of her back.

As Luther crossed the short distance to

the pallet, Magdalene moved away. The scent of onion and an assortment of strong spices told him she had recently applied poultices to Katharina's wounds.

As he lowered himself, Katharina shifted her head to face him. Her hair cascaded over her flushed cheeks and down her bare neck. The flicker of candlelight danced on the copper tints that mingled with the silky blond. He'd never seen it down and loose. It was beautiful, and he was strangely relieved that it hadn't been sheared.

She peered at him from beneath the thin veil of her hair, her blue eyes luminous.

A strong force clutched his gut and twisted it. He'd told himself a thousand times he was through with any desire for Katharina von Bora. He was absolutely finished. But now that he was by her side, the pull was too strong. He couldn't deny that something about her drew him irresistibly. He wasn't sure what it was. All he knew was that he had to be with her and make sure she was all right.

He lifted his fingers and brushed at the soft strands.

She sucked in a breath.

He shouldn't. But the silkiness beckoned to him like gold to a treasure seeker. He twisted a long piece against his thumb, marveling at God's handiwork in a woman. These past years when his friends had started marrying, he'd tried to convince himself that he didn't need a woman. He'd tried to cut off any longings before they'd had the chance to begin. But now he couldn't imagine why he'd tried so hard to resist his natural urges, not with Katharina lying before him so exquisite and womanly.

The light in her eyes warmed his insides. Was she happy to see him?

"How are you?" he asked.

"I'm alive."

"Are you in a lot of pain?"

"Magdalene's poultices are a godsend."

He let go of her hair and trailed his fingers down her cheek, finally letting himself exhale the breath of relief that he hadn't been able to expel in the weeks since she'd been taken.

From behind him Sister Magdalene gave a slight cough.

Luther pulled his hand away and frowned at the woman. Couldn't he have a moment alone with Katharina?

"I didn't think you'd come," Katharina whispered.

"I've been in Torgau this past month, pleading with the elector for your release." Elector Frederick, as usual, hadn't wanted to involve himself in the case. With the conclusion of another Diet of Nuremberg, the pressure on Elector Frederick had escalated too high. A new pope, Clement VII, and his nuncio had demanded the elector begin at once fulfilling the Edict of Worms — rounding up the followers of the reforms and putting them to the sword.

Luther was still a hunted man, wanted dead or alive. But this time at least the German princes had taken a stand for him. They were angry that the new pope had ignored their list of one hundred grievances, the *Centum Gravamina*. In fact, the new pope had not just ignored their grievances; he'd scoffed at them and said that such a paper could never have emanated from the princes, that it only could have originated from someone who hated the court of Rome.

Luther no longer thought the princes would hand him over to the pope. God was bringing more of them to his side. But the pope's nuncio had stirred up the church's persecution of those who dared to defy him. If the nuncio couldn't get the princes to squash the reforms, then he would incite his faithful bishops and religious dignitaries to fulfill the edict.

Officials like Bishop Petrus were on a holy

mission to cleanse the church. He'd vehemently opposed Luther's efforts to get Katharina released and had made Luther's life a nightmare over the past weeks.

"Word of your escape reached me only two days ago," he said bending closer. "I thought you'd be safe with Sister Magdalene here in Grimma. But now we've reason to believe your life is in jeopardy again."

The light in her eyes faded and was replaced by fear.

"That's why I'm here." He wouldn't tell her he'd been frantic to get to her and had barely slept since he'd received the news. "I've come to take you away before it's too late. We must leave as soon as possible, before dawn."

"She's in no condition to travel," Sister Magdalene said quietly.

"Tell me the trouble." Katharina looked at him without wavering, although a haunted fear lingered in her expression.

He'd traveled all night, telling himself he'd do the same for any other nun in trouble. But the fact was, he'd panicked when he'd heard the news. After weeks of not knowing Katharina's condition inside Marienthron, he didn't want to lose her to the convent again.

"Bishop Petrus is accusing you of murdering Abbot Baltazar. He's asking for your arrest."

"No one will believe him. How could they?"

Luther had heard enough about the hideous condition of Abbot Baltazar's body when it had been discovered to know that Katharina couldn't have inflicted such torture upon the man. "We both agree you couldn't possibly have had the strength or the fortitude to murder Baltazar in the way he was. But without any other suspects, they're concluding you murdered him."

She shook her head. The movement shifted the blanket, revealing the curve of her shoulder.

He started to raise his fingers to the spot of flesh but then folded his hands together and looked away from the tempting stretch of skin. "Are you willing to identify the true murderer?"

"I can't." Her face said everything. She knew who had killed Abbot Baltazar, but she would never divulge it. She probably owed that person her life.

"I had a feeling you wouldn't tell anything. That's why we're leaving. Now."

"But Aunt Lena." Katharina strained to see past him to the opposite side of the bedroom, where Aunt Lena lay asleep on her pallet. "I can't leave her."

"She'll be safe here. The officials won't interfere with Sister Magdalene, not as the sister of one of their own important leaders." Doctor Johann von Staupitz, Magdalene's older brother, had been one of the most important figures in Luther's life during his early monastery days. Even though they weren't close anymore, Luther still thought of him as his spiritual father. Staupitz had been the first to distribute copies of the Bible to the monks of his monastery. The reading of Scriptures was usually strictly controlled and rationed, but Staupitz had encouraged them to study their Bibles. And Luther had obeyed him with more zeal than anyone else.

"Aunt Lena will be safe here with Sister Magdalene. Besides, she's lost her faculties. They won't seek her return to the abbey."

Katharina's eyes glossed with tears as she gazed at the thin, slumped form of her aunt. "She protected me all those years in ways I never dreamed of. I cannot abandon her."

Something in Katharina's expression ignited a flame in him. "What did that devil Baltazar do to you?"

She closed her eyes and shuddered.

"What did he do? Tell me. Did he violate you?" His entire body burned with a rage so intense he was certain that if Baltazar had been in the room, he would have plunged his knife into him.

Katharina opened her eyes. The despair in them tore at his rationality. He reached for her hand and pressed it between his.

"No. Not me," she whispered. "But how many others?"

He knew far too many others had suffered, but he couldn't hold back the surge of relief that it hadn't been Katharina this time.

"We need to go, Martinus." Jonas's irritated call came from the other room. "We can't afford to ride out of Grimma in broad daylight."

"Are you ready?" Luther didn't know how he could leave her if she refused to come.

She hesitated, then sighed in resignation. "Very well."

He pushed himself up to his feet. "Sister Magdalene, will you help Katharina get ready with all haste?"

Sister Magdalene hesitated, her expression one of disapproval, before she finally nodded.

As Luther closed the bedroom door, Jonas pursed his lips. "You're pathetic." He stood in front of the low, crackling fire on the hearth, drinking a mug of ale.

Luther crossed his arms. "I brought you along this time instead of Melanchthon so I wouldn't have anyone nagging me about Katharina."

Jonas snorted. "You told me we were only coming here to rescue her from danger."

"And we are."

Jonas's thick eyebrows furrowed into a frown. "You're an old fool. She doesn't want someone like you, and she never will. You're only torturing yourself to think she'll ever have you."

Luther glared back. Why did Jonas have to be right about everything? Couldn't he ever be wrong?

"Get her back to Wittenberg," Jonas groused. "Find her a noble husband. Then forget about her."

Luther shook his head but then grabbed the wall as dizziness swept over him. If he wasn't suffering from one thing, it was another — dizziness, constipation, stomach cramps, melancholy. He *was* an old fool.

"Ach." Before leaving Torgau he'd resolved to rescue Katharina, but to consider her nothing more than a sister in the Lord. However, every time he got near her, all his willpower melted away like ice in a spring thaw.

"If you've finally changed your mind

about wanting a wife," Jonas said, his hard, aristocratic expression finally softening, "you'll have to set your sights on someone else."

Luther stomped across the room and grabbed his cloak from the bench where he'd discarded it in his haste to see Katharina. "I haven't changed my mind. I don't want a wife."

Jonas just shook his head.

Luther slung his cloak over his shoulders and refused to look at his friend again for fear of what Jonas might see in his eyes. Silently he resolved that after they returned to Wittenberg, the first thing he'd write was a letter to that rogue Jerome, insisting he follow through on his promise to marry Katharina. If Jerome was the man she wanted, then he'd do his best to make sure that's who she got.

And after she was married, perhaps he'd finally have peace of mind. Then he could get back to the work God had given him without thoughts of Katharina distracting him.

TWENTY-THREE

When they arrived back in Wittenberg, Katharina was grateful that Doctor Luther returned her to the Cranach household with nary a word about her remaining there. Although he didn't waver in his kindness and consideration toward her, she was more than a little disappointed that he left her again without a good-bye.

Margaret informed her that Jerome had not visited once during her long absence over the winter and spring. But after all that had happened to Aunt Lena with the Bundschuh attack and then her own capture by the abbot, Katharina couldn't find the energy to care overly much about Jerome's return.

As the days of summer passed, she stuffed down mounting despondency. She wanted to ignore the possibility that Jerome had rejected her. Not only was it humiliating, but also deep inside was the real fear that she might never find anyone at all.

"Perhaps it's time to consider another man," Margaret whispered as they arose from their pew in the Stadtkirche after the conclusion of the Sunday morning service on the day of the Exaltation of the Holy Cross.

"Perhaps." Katharina smoothed the folds of the voluminous skirt Barbara Cranach had given her when she'd returned from Marienthron. The skirt drew tight at the waist, as did the lacings of her bodice, showing off her bust and hips much more than she was comfortable with. "I just need to be patient. That's all."

But time was hammering her patience away to nothing. She was nearing twenty-six and was rapidly approaching the age when she would be too old, when no man would want her. Then all chances of having a family, of fulfilling her deepest desire would vanish.

"Dr. Glatz has been watching you." Margaret cocked her head in the direction of the stall where important members of the University of Wittenberg often sat. "He came at the beginning of summer and has served as the rector of the university," Margaret continued quietly. "From the rumors I've heard, Dr. Glatz is a very eligible bachelor. He's wealthy and of the patrician class."

Katharina glanced in the direction of the white-haired rector. Even though he was talking with another professor, his attention slid to her as if he'd been waiting for her to look at him. Through the dimly lit church his expression was hard to read. With a vaulted ceiling and stained-glass windows, the church was rarely penetrated by sunlight. Even so, she could see that he wasn't smiling.

Turning away, Katharina took hold of Margaret's arm and then steered her past the other townswomen, who glanced at them sideways and still regarded them as outsiders. "Dr. Glatz looks as though he has a pike pressed against his spine. Moreover, he appears old enough to be my father."

"I'm sure he's a nice man once you get to know him." Margaret allowed Katharina to lead her down the aisle toward the nave. "And who are we to complain about age? We're nearly old maids ourselves."

"I'm well aware of my age. I would thank you not to say anything more regarding it."

Seemingly undaunted by Katharina's sharpness, Margaret smiled and leaned down to whisper in her ear. "It's rumored that Dr. Glatz will become the next pastor of the university's patronage parish in Orla-münde."

Despite Margaret's high praise, Katharina couldn't muster any enthusiasm for the man, although she knew she should. "If you think so highly of him, perhaps you ought to marry him yourself."

Margaret's smile only widened. "You know I'm still waiting to marry Doctor Luther." The young woman's sparkling eyes sought the object of her affection through the crowd of parishioners milling around him at the base of the high pulpit. "Doctor Luther had another wonderful sermon today," Margaret continued. "And the new hymns are divine."

Katharina pressed her lips together to refrain from the negative comments that would serve no purpose but to hurt Margaret. The reformed Mass, the sermons in the common language, and the singing of simple songs — the changes were still difficult for her to accept. She understood the benefits in the changes to the prayers; she'd experienced them firsthand. But everything else seemed too ordinary for worship of the holy God.

She also wasn't sure how she felt about Doctor Luther's preaching against indulgences. Of course, she agreed with his accusation that the pope was overcharging for his own profit. But that didn't change the fact that the indulgence absolved the buyer from punishment for sins and provided eternal glory. Doctor Luther claimed that the pardon of the church was in God's power alone. But certainly God worked in and through mortals and mortal things for His purposes. If her mother believed in the power of the indulgence, that it would someday bring them together again, then Katharina had to also hold out hope that it would.

"Oh, Katharina, *he* is divine." Margaret's tone was worshipful. "He looks so handsome in secular clothes. I wonder what finally made him put aside his habit and cowl?"

Katharina followed Margaret's gaze to Doctor Luther. He did make a handsome picture in the new clothes. Like the other scholars, he'd donned a black pleated cloak with a plain flat collar and wide sleeves. Beneath a black beret pulled low, his eyes flashed with fervor, and his face radiated passion as he spoke to the friends who surrounded him.

He was a complex man with a depth of emotion that was hard to ignore, especially when that emotion was directed at her.

Thankfully, he wasn't angry with her anymore, even though he hadn't shown her any attention in the many weeks since her return to Wittenberg, since the day he'd delivered her to the Cranachs without a backward glance.

Not that she wanted his attention.

"So this is Katharina von Bora?"

A voice at her side startled her, and she turned to find herself face to face with Dr. Glatz. To stand eye level with a man was a rare occurrence since she was petite. Yet the rector, though far from petite, was not much taller. With his wide girth he barely fit in the narrow side aisle. His head had a flat, squat shape that matched his body, and his jowls sagged, giving him a double chin.

He scrutinized her from her face down to the shoe poking out from the edge of her skirt.

Pastor Bugenhagen stood next to Dr. Glatz. He rubbed a hand down his beard and watched Dr. Glatz's reaction. "What do you think? Comely enough?"

Irritation flittered through Katharina. Did they think she was a mare for purchase?

Dr. Glatz didn't say anything. Instead he turned his sharp gaze to Margaret and perused her also. "What about this one?"

Pastor Bugenhagen shook his head. "No.

This is Margaret von Schonfeld. Doctor Luther has recently arranged for her to be married to Garssenbuttel from Brunswick."

Margaret gasped. "What? I haven't heard this. It can't be true." Her panic-filled eyes sought Katharina's.

Katharina was as surprised by the news as her friend, but before she could question the pastor further, he spoke again.

"You may have Katharina von Bora." Pastor Bugenhagen directed Dr. Glatz's gaze back to her. "Katharina's lineage is also nobility. She'll make a fine wife."

"She's handsome enough. But I don't like the ugly business regarding the murder of the abbot at the Marienthron convent. It could be a blemish on my reputation."

"Everyone knows that Bishop Petrus made false claims. Doctor Luther pursued the matter thoroughly and cleared Katharina's name."

"Still, it's a serious charge."

Katharina's mind reeled. "Pastor Bugenhagen, I'm not sure exactly what you're presuming. But let me make it perfectly clear that I'm not available for marriage to this man or anyone else."

"Oh? I'd heard the opposite —"

"Then you heard wrong." Although she knew that she shouldn't protest, that she should be grateful for the making of a new match, she couldn't stop herself. "I'm promised in marriage to Jerome Baumgartner."

"I assumed," Pastor Bugenhagen said, "since Baumgartner hadn't responded to Doctor Luther's letter telling him to hurry back to Wittenberg and marry you, that you were in need of a new match."

Letter? Katharina's attention swung to Doctor Luther. Had he written a letter to Jerome? The smile on his lips, though directed at another, warmed her heart. Had he actually told Jerome to hurry back to Wittenberg to marry her? After all his resistance to Jerome, why had he done such a thing for her now?

"If Doctor Luther has written to Jerome, then he'll surely arrive soon." She smiled at Pastor Bugenhagen, with renewed hope springing to life inside her along with gratefulness to Doctor Luther. How could anyone resist his summons?

"But," Pastor Bugenhagen said, gentling his voice, "Baumgartner hasn't responded."

"At least not yet. He won't ignore Doctor Luther."

"I've heard enough, Pastor." Dr. Glatz frowned at Katharina. "Find out the status of this other arrangement. If it isn't viable, then perhaps I'll consider taking Katharina von Bora as my wife."

He spun away from her, leaving her no choice but to swallow her tart retort.

Pastor Bugenhagen hesitated as though he wanted to say more, but then he turned and hurried after Dr. Glatz.

Katharina became aware of Margaret standing next to her, trembling.

"Garssenbuttel from Brunswick?" Margaret's eyes were windows to the shock and despair crushing her soul. "I don't know who that is." Her whisper spoke loud enough. If the man wasn't Doctor Luther, she didn't care who he was.

Katharina reached for her friend's hand and pressed the long, shaking fingers. "I'm sure Pastor Bugenhagen is mistaken. We shall go speak with Doctor Luther this instant and clear up this misunderstanding."

Doctor Luther was walking along the edge of the nave toward the stairway that led to the vestry. She started toward him, pulling Margaret along after her. "Make haste, Margaret."

When she reached the bottom, he was rounding the first bend of the stairway with Jonas and Melanchthon ahead of him.

"Doctor Luther?" Katharina called.

Their laughter and boisterous voices echoed in the narrow stairwell.

"Doctor Luther," she said louder.

He stopped and turned. His gaze alighted on her, and he smiled. "Katharina."

She moved to the first step and stared up at him with a shyness she didn't understand. She hadn't spoken with him since their return trip many weeks ago. And seeing him up close in his secular clothes, suddenly she didn't know what to think. Without the habit and cowl, he had shed the appearance of a poor peasant monk and had acquired a distinguished air.

She tried to smile, but the darkness of his eyes and the way his gaze caressed her face left her breathless.

"What is it, Katharina? No more midnight rescues, I hope."

"No. Most certainly not."

"You're healing?"

"Yes. Master Cranach has provided me with every remedy imaginable from his apothecary shop." The scabs on her back itched more than hurt. They would soon fall away, leaving only scars. In time she hoped she could shed her haunted dreams too, for the blackness of the night awakened visions of pain and abuse, of Greta and Aunt Lena and countless others. And with it came an overwhelming guilt that she had survived, that she had somehow been spared when others hadn't.

Doctor Luther's gaze probed deeper and seemed to see the pain in her heart. "Have you read the Gospels yet?"

Katharina shook her head. Margaret had the German New Testament that Doctor Luther had translated, and her friend worshiped it as she did everything of Doctor Luther's. But Katharina hadn't wanted to test God any more than she already had.

"You must read them. I'll get you a copy of the New Testament. The words will give you great comfort."

"If you go to the trouble to give me a copy, then you'll force me to try."

"Force you?" His voice hinted at humor. "I've learned that no one can force her ladyship to do anything she doesn't want to do. At least not if he desires to live in peace."

She smiled at his teasing. "You're a wise man, Herr Doctor."

"Then apparently my dealings with wayward nuns has been to my benefit as I'm all the wiser for it."

"Perhaps that's why God created women in the first place," she jested in return. "Without women to direct the male species and keep them in line, men are all too apt to wander in their own foolishness."

At her quip Jonas guffawed and slapped Doctor Luther on the back. "She put you in your place, old man."

Luther grinned and elbowed his friend back. For a moment they were almost like two overgrown schoolboys teasing each other.

With a final shove at Jonas, Luther beamed down at her. "So what is it you really need, Katharina? You certainly haven't stopped me simply to proclaim the foolishness of my gender."

She hesitated, but Margaret nudged her from behind. "I want to thank you."

Standing on the stairs above Doctor Luther, Melanchthon shared none of his companions' humor. Although his expression was softer than the darker, more aristocratic Jonas, something in his eyes warned her not to encourage Doctor Luther further.

She wanted to order Melanchthon to continue on his way, but she bit her tongue and focused on Doctor Luther. "Thank you for writing a letter to Jerome."

His smile vanished. The light in his eyes disappeared, and coldness filled the space between them. "You're welcome. Now we'll have to pray diligently that he finally comes, won't we?"

The sudden change in his tone slapped her, taking her by surprise, filling her with unexpected hurt. She stared at him, not knowing how to respond.

He gave her a curt nod, then he spun and started up the steps again.

Margaret pushed her.

"Wait!" Katharina called after him.

He paused and glanced over his shoulder, his eyes shuttered, the window to his feelings closed.

Confusion rendered her speechless for a brief moment. He was the one who'd written the letter to Jerome. Why would a simple word of thanks anger him?

"Please ask him." Margaret's desperate whisper prodded her.

She forced herself to meet Doctor Luther's sharp gaze. "A mistaken rumor is spreading about Margaret's future — something about an arranged marriage to a man from Brunswick."

"The arrangement isn't a rumor or a mistake."

"It most certainly is."

Doctor Luther descended a step. He towered above her like an imposing fortress on a hillside. "Margaret's a very fortunate woman. Dietrich von Garssenbuttel is an aristocrat sympathetic to our cause. His wife recently died, and he's in need of a mother for his young children."

"She won't marry a complete stranger."

"She has no choice." He glared at her. "She must marry. And since she's still my responsibility, I've made the arrangements. They're final."

Margaret's trembling fingers poked Katharina's back, prodding her to continue. "You've not had the decency to consider her desires. You must take her choice of a marriage partner into consideration first."

"Just who is the lucky man?"

"You."

His jaw tightened and his eyes narrowed. "Let me make this very clear. I will never get married. Never."

The finality of his words slid down the stairs and punched Katharina in the stomach. "But Margaret —"

"Never." His voice was a low growl.

"You preach of the goodness and naturalness of marriage. You encourage nuns and monks to forsake celibacy. But you yourself are unwilling to entertain the slightest possibility of such, even to a woman as kind and caring as Margaret?"

He opened his mouth as if to give her a rebuttal but then clamped his lips shut. With a shake of his head, he turned and started up the stairway again. "Margaret will marry Garssenbuttel," he called, a measure of sadness in his voice that Katharina didn't understand. "Accept it."

Jonas followed his friend. But Melanchthon shuffled his feet for a moment before addressing Margaret kindly but firmly. "Rest assured, there's no fault with you, Fräulein. If Doctor Luther were in a position to take a wife, you'd be a fine candidate. However, he's too busy right now, and marriage would only be a distraction from the greater purposes he's attempting to accomplish at this critical time. I hope you understand."

Margaret hung her head resignedly. But Katharina's heart stubbornly refused to concede.

TWENTY-FOUR

"The peasants' demands have merit." Luther rubbed his frigid hands together vigorously. Despite a fire crackling upon the hearth and his friends surrounding him, he was cold all the way through to his bones.

"Their demands may have *some* merit," Pastor Bugenhagen said, "but you can't take their side."

"If I support the peasants, the princes will have to take them more seriously."

"You'll offend the princes who have worked hard to defend you."

Murmurs of agreement made the rounds of the men.

Wolfgang added another log to the fire and fanned the embers. But Luther couldn't stop shivering even in the warming house, the room in the monastery where the monks had always gathered to keep warm on winter days.

"We've all heard the reports." Pastor Bugenhagen stopped his pacing to stand before the fire. "Thomas Müntzer has returned to Mühlhausen and is stirring rebellion. Karlstadt is in Rothenburg, causing trouble with his preaching. Open revolt will come next, perhaps in the spring. The princes will be forced to act against the rebels."

Luther buried his face in his hands. Some days he wished he could bury his whole head and take a break from the problems that overwhelmed him. His only comfort came when he immersed himself in God's Word or composed songs. "You know I've been the first one to speak out against the violence." Weariness made his voice sag. "I've condemned it on both sides. But I cannot stay silent when my brothers ask only for fair treatment."

Brother Gabriel reached for his mug and poured him a refill. Luther nodded his thanks. With just Wolfgang and Brother Gabriel to help, the convent was too big and costly for him to maintain. A smaller place would give him fewer headaches.

He'd asked the elector to give him a house between the monastery and Holy Ghost Hospital, but the elector had done nothing. It was clear now he was stuck at the Black Cloister indefinitely. Sometimes the elector's indecisiveness benefited Luther, bought him time, even saved him from his enemies. At other times, like now, the elector's inability to act gave him a headache.

In the meantime he struggled to get monastery debtors to pay their interests. Other than a small honorarium from the city for his preaching, he had nothing, which wasn't out of the ordinary. But after housing and feeding the runaways, his situation had grown even more desperate, and he couldn't afford to stay there any longer.

"The elector's health is failing." Pastor Bugenhagen held out his mug to Brother Gabriel's jug. "And Duke George is waiting to destroy him. We'll need the support of the other princes if the elector dies."

"But if we side with the peasants," Luther argued, "perhaps we'll eradicate the influence of some of the devil's handymen, like Müntzer and Karlstadt. The peasants need a voice of reason, of peace. We can be that voice."

"But we can't afford to alienate the princes."

"Ach!" Luther shook his head with growing resentment. At times like this he wished he didn't have to worry about pleasing the princes or needing their support.

The door of the warming house opened, ushering in a draft of cold winter air that swept along the stone floor and swirled around his toes, which were already numb.

"Finally," Pastor Bugenhagen said. "It's Justus."

Melanchthon stood and offered Jonas his bench.

But Jonas threw off his hood and stalked across the room. He flung aside his cloak and held his hands to the fire. Brother Gabriel poured him a mug of Obstwasser.

"What news have you for us from the Count of Mansfeld?" Pastor Bugenhagen resumed his pacing in an effort to stay warm. Melanchthon lowered himself back onto his bench, his deep-set eyes grave and his thin face reflecting the serious nature of the decision awaiting them as the conflict escalated. Should they side with the peasants or with the princes?

"No more hangings," Jonas said after he'd guzzled half of his mug.

"You've won him to our side then?"

Jonas shrugged. "Can a fox like him ever really be persuaded?" He slid a glance at Luther. The sharpness gave Luther a sense of foreboding. Jonas had news for him, and he wasn't sure he wanted to hear it.

"Any more news of the peasant uprisings?" Pastor Bugenhagen asked.

"Much of the same," Jonas replied. "Peasants are moving in the areas of Schwarz-wald and Lake Constance. Their numbers are growing. The nobility can't withstand the attacks. They're either bowing their heads to the Bundschuh banner or having them cut off."

"There you have it." Luther sat straighter. "If we support the peasants, we'll already have half of the nobility on our side."

Jonas snorted. "If you support the peasants, you'll plunge the sword through all we've worked for. The princes will turn against you faster than you can blow wind."

"Exactly!" Pastor Bugenhagen shouted. "That's what I've been trying to tell Martinus all morning."

Luther leaned back against the wall, letting the bitter cold of the stone punish him for the predicament in which he now found himself. He was in the middle of a conflict, and no matter what he chose to do, he would anger many people.

Jonas took another long swig from his mug.

Luther watched him and waited with growing unease.

His friend stared into the fire, his gruff scowl more pronounced than usual.

Pastor Bugenhagen's voice carried through the room, but Luther wasn't listening anymore.

"Come now, Justus," Luther said. "Get it out. What's the real news?"

Jonas shifted to look at him. "I've word from Nuremberg."

"More skirmishes with the peasants?"

"Baumgartner's betrothed."

"Of course he is." Something hot rolled through Luther at the mention of Jerome's name. "That scoundrel's engaged to Katharina von Bora."

"Not anymore." Jonas's stare measured him. "He's pledged to Sibylle Dichtel von Tutzing."

The room fell silent except for the crackling fire.

Confusion swirled through Luther. What exactly was Jonas saying? He met his friend's sharp gaze. Was Baumgartner giving up his claim on Katharina?

Jonas's eyes answered him before his words could. "Sibylle is fourteen and has a rich dowry. What nobleman can turn up his nose at that?"

Luther's heart sputtered with an unexpected surge of victory. Jerome wouldn't get Katharina. He hadn't deserved her in the first place.

"I'm sure his parents had a large part in choosing the girl." Pastor Bugenhagen stopped his pacing. "After all, they'd want someone young, rich, and beautiful for their son."

"They wouldn't care if she was as ugly as a sow," Jonas retorted, "as long as she brings her big dowry and gives them a baby a year."

Luther grinned. "Baumgartner deserves a sow."

Melanchthon's face grew more troubled. "Baumgartner should have fulfilled his promise to Katharina von Bora."

"Lighten up, Philipp." Luther suddenly felt years younger. "Baumgartner wasn't good enough for Kate, and you know it."

Jonas pretended to cough and spoke through his throat clearing. "I doubt anyone will ever be good enough for your Kate."

"*My* Kate?"

Jonas rolled his eyes. "Don't play the idiot now."

Luther stared back, trying to make sense of his friend's insinuations. Yes, perhaps Kate had earned a place closer to his heart than some of the other nuns he'd helped. It was natural after their interactions — her doctoring him and his rescuing her. But that didn't mean he had any claim on her.

"That settles it then." Pastor Bugenhagen folded his hands across his chest. "Katharina von Bora must marry Dr. Glatz. He's shown some interest in her."

"Glatz?" Luther choked on the name. "That old *Geizhals* —"

"Now, Martinus." Pastor Bugenhagen frowned. "Dr. Glatz is well respected, wealthy, influential. He'd make Katharina a fine husband."

"He's cranky, tight fisted, and old —"

"You're cranky, poor, and old." Jonas leaned back and gave him a knowing look.

"I don't see what difference all this makes," Pastor Bugenhagen said. "You've damaged your reputation enough by involving yourself with these nuns. The rumors surrounding you and your various women have grown to epic proportions. At least now with Katharina you have the opportunity to put to death one of the rumors."

Luther shook his head adamantly.

Melanchthon interrupted his protest. "She must marry someone. Why not Dr. Glatz?"

"Because . . ." He had no valid reason. But he felt compelled to argue anyway. "Because . . . I know Katharina won't like him. He wouldn't bring her happiness."

"Happiness?" Melanchthon's question was laced with disbelief. Although they'd tried to make favorable arrangements for all the nuns, happiness wasn't their primary concern.

It was a poor excuse. It was true, but it was still poor. The muttering from the others indicated they agreed.

"She needs a husband, not happiness," Pastor Bugenhagen persisted. "As long as the partnership benefits both of them, that's what matters."

Luther rubbed his stiff fingers and wished he could find some words to contradict Pastor Bugenhagen. But he could find nothing.

The pastor continued. "Did you consider the happiness of Margaret von Schonfeld when you made her marry Garssenbuttel?"

He pictured Margaret's pale, resigned face as she'd ridden away with Garssenbuttel. If Katharina was right, Margaret had been heartbroken. He shook his head and growled. "What other choice did I have for the woman?"

"And what other choice do you have for Katharina? Do you have someone better in mind for her?"

Luther closed his eyes and remembered all the times Katharina had looked at him, the times she'd clung to him, the times her fingers had gently soothed him. Just the memory of it warmed his body. But more than that, he craved her untamable spirit, her vibrancy, her energy. The conversations he'd had with her stimulated him in a way his friends couldn't. Had she ever felt more for him than a passing flutter? Was it possible she could harbor any affection at all for him?

He shivered, the perpetual chill just one more sign of his old age.

There was no way in heaven he would ever ask her how she felt about him. Only a desperate man would expose himself to the possibility of rejection and humiliation at the hand of a woman like Katharina.

He wasn't desperate.

Katharina von Bora was compassionate, but she was also proud and, like so many of her class, wasn't open to change. She'd probably agree to wed old miserly Glatz before breaking tradition and marrying outside the nobility.

Besides, he was never getting married. He would put a wife in as much danger as he was in himself. The thought of doing that to Katharina sent a ripple of coldness through him.

He exhaled a long, noisy sigh. "Fine. Give her to Glatz." At least with Glatz she'd be relatively safe, even if she wasn't happy. "Make the arrangements."

Katharina couldn't breathe. She couldn't

move, not even to smooth the delicate curls off Ursula's overly warm forehead. Katharina was suddenly as listless as the youngest Cranach girl she'd been cradling in her arms.

From across the study, the hard gleam in Jonas's eyes declared his morbid news again. She could understand why he'd been appointed to bring her the tidings. He'd had no trouble delivering it.

The iciness of the room crept off the wooden floor and slithered under her skirt. Jonas's news certainly wasn't unexpected, but the finality of it hurt nonetheless.

Sitting at the counting table next to her, Barbara Cranach laid down her quill pen and pushed aside the household ledgers she'd been studying while Katharina held the sleeping child and looked on. Barbara was an efficient manager of the estate. She worked ceaselessly, often far into the night. Although she was big boned and full of figure, she always moved rapidly and with purpose. Early gray threaded through her earthen-brown hair, and her face was aged with dark circles and lines, all attesting to her tireless labor to manage the enormous bustling household.

"Justus, you must be mistaken." Barbara gently squeezed Katharina's arm. "Jerome is betrothed to Katharina."

"I've spoken with Herr Dichtel von Tutzing," Jonas said without blinking. "He's promised Jerome a large dowry for his daughter."

"But Jerome is practically married to Katharina —"

"Did you consummate your union?" Through the soft flickering of the candlelight on the dark winter day, Jonas probed Katharina and demanded honesty.

Katharina quickly dropped her attention to the little girl in her arms, relieved to see that the child was still asleep and wouldn't be subject to a topic not meant for young sensibilities.

"You're out of line, Justus." Barbara patted Katharina's arm again. "You don't need to answer him, Liebchen."

Katharina shook her head. "Thank you, Barbara. I wasn't planning to respond except to ask the same question in return." She lifted her chin and glared at Jonas. "Do you think I consummated my relationship?"

Jonas stared at her intently. Then finally he shook his head. "No, I don't think you did. But it doesn't matter anymore. Even if you had consummated it, Baumgartner wouldn't have married you. He just liked the challenge of getting a vestal virgin into his bed."

No! She wanted to scream at Jonas, to deny everything he was saying. She wanted to lash out at him for his calmness, but she forced herself to answer with the measure of control appropriate to a noblewoman. "I believe he had only the best intention of marrying me but that something unforeseen has prevented him from his obligation."

"He wants money and prestige. Sibylle Dichtel von Tutzing will give him both."

Her name was Sibylle?

"She's fourteen."

Jonas's words twisted the knife deeper into her chest. She wanted to double over with the pain, but she held herself rigid in the chair. Suddenly the room with its thick carpet and the heavy tapestries against the walls couldn't hold out the winter chill.

"She has time to give Baumgartner all the children he could ever want. But you . . ."

"No." Katharina shook her head and fought the urge to cover her ears. Instead she smoothed her fingers across Ursula's silky curls and told herself that one day she'd do the same to her own offspring.

"Arrangements will now move forward for you to marry Dr. Glatz —"

"I have no wish for such arrangements."

Jonas sat silently for a long moment. "Your

problem is your pride, Katharina," he finally said. "You need a dose of reality."

Barbara stood, nearly tipping her chair in her haste. "I think it best if you refrain from saying anything else."

Jonas stared at Katharina as though he hadn't heard Barbara. "Jerome didn't want you and there's no guarantee that Dr. Glatz will have you either."

"Justus," Barbara chided, "you're being unkind."

Katharina met Jonas's gaze calmly even though her body trembled with the urge to run from the room. She then stood and was grateful when Barbara took Ursula from her, as though sensing the turmoil warring within her.

Jonas's eyes finally softened. "Maybe it's time for you to stop putting so much stock in outward qualifications and consider other marriage arrangements beneath your class —"

"You'd have me marry a butcher or a tanner or some other common laborer?"

"If he loves you, what would it matter?" Jonas regarded her with a raised brow.

She shook her head. It was too much to ask of her, too radical. She stepped around the desk and clasped her hands together to keep them from trembling. "I shall continue to trust that God will provide the right husband for me at the right time. Now if you'll excuse me."

She couldn't listen to another word. She needed to get away. The urge rose with such swiftness she would embarrass herself with an outburst if she didn't leave immediately.

"Take all the time you need, Liebchen," Barbara called after her as she settled her sleeping child against her bosom.

Katharina walked with measured steps, the carpet muting the heaviness. She passed Jonas without another word or glance in his direction. And when she reached the thickly carved door and entered the dark hallway, she wanted nothing more than to lift her skirts and run. But she had nowhere to go other than the small dormer room she shared with another woman now that Margaret was gone. The herb beds were dead and the day too cold to lose herself in the garden.

Even though she'd already resigned herself to the probability that Jerome wasn't coming back for her, the news that he was marrying a fourteen-year-old girl with a sizable dowry made the ache in her chest burn as if someone had tied her to the stake and set her on fire.

She had no dowry. That had been her

problem long ago, and apparently it still haunted her. Now that she was out of the cloister, nothing had changed. She still didn't have anything to offer. And as Jonas had said, what nobleman would want her?

The burning in her chest rose to her throat.

She would end up old and alone . . . without the one thing she wanted most.

A family.

Twenty-Five

Katharina stood behind the cluttered counter next to a gangly apprentice with only a few facial hairs to claim and watched him crush the dried herbs with a pestle and mortar. She'd been organizing the many dusty, overcrowded shelves that lined the wall, but her fingers twitched to snatch the tools away from the boy and grind the herbs properly. Instead she took a deep breath to steady herself, inhaling the scents of the Cranach apothecary shop, which reminded her of the cloister garden at Marienthron. The sweetness of lavender, marigold, and rosemary made her heart constrict with a sudden pain.

What would her life have been like if she'd never read Doctor Luther's pamphlets? Before her exposure to the seditious material, she'd lived a contented life at the abbey. She hadn't felt the dullness of the routines, the constriction of the silence, or the severity of the rules because she'd had nothing to which she could compare that life. She'd valued the protection of a cloistered life. At times she'd even agreed with the others that at least there she didn't have to worry about an arranged marriage to a temperamental man twice her age or about the real possibility that she would die during childbirth. She'd lived in quiet and gentility with uninterrupted time to devote to prayers.

But even as Katharina longed for the oblivion of cloistered life, another part of her rebelled. She knew deep in her heart that the peace and protection were really a mirage, that they masked the deeper flaws that existed in abbeys and monasteries all across the Roman Empire. In fact, shouldn't she work, as Doctor Luther had, to rescue other victims of such a system? How could she turn a blind eye to women who were possibly suffering the same fate as Aunt Lena and Greta?

"I shall finish for you." She reached for the pestle.

The young apprentice relinquished it without a word.

She pounded the pestle against the mortar and crushed the marigold with a swiftness that made the boy stand back, bumping the shelves and rattling the lids on the clay pots.

She'd told Barbara she'd make a healing broth for Ursula's lingering chills, and although the apprentice had insisted on making the concoction for her, Katharina missed the luxury of doing so herself.

The front door of the shop opened, and a gust of cold air whirled into the small room, shaking the bunches of dried herbs hanging from the ceiling. Two men entered. Their heavy, loose-fitting Schaubes were trimmed in wide collars of fur and ornamental chains.

When they glanced to the counter, they grew silent.

The shorter man cocked his head toward Katharina. "The very girl of whom we were speaking."

The man's companion surveyed her. "She's comely enough. A bit thin perhaps but still young enough to bear children."

Katharina bristled. "I beg your pardon."

The shorter man took off his beret, revealing his stark white hair that now rose in a fuzzy disarray of static. "We've met before. I'm Dr. Glatz, rector of the parish of Orlamünde."

As soon as he mentioned his name, she remembered him, though she hadn't seen him since autumn. In the dim light of the shop, she could distinguish the sharpness of his gaze. It pierced through her and made her stiffen.

"May I help you?" she asked, surveying his square face and the fleshy chin. The first time she'd met him, she hadn't wanted to consider the possibility of a union. Her initial impressions hadn't been favorable, largely because she'd still been clinging to the slight chance of having Jerome. But now with that hope gone, ought she to consider the possibility of marrying Dr. Glatz? Aside from being older, he met all the other standards she held — wealth, title, and power.

As she mentally posed the option, Jonas's rebuke earlier in the week came back to her. He'd told her not to put so much stock in outward qualifications. She wasn't that shallow, was she? To care more about a person's wealth and nobility than his character?

In fact, she had despised the way the noblemen were doing that very thing to her — considering her outward qualifications rather than the strength of her character. Was she guilty of the same?

Dr. Glatz ambled toward the counter. When he stood across from her, he coughed, and the movement shook his bulky body. "I need something for my cough," he told the apprentice.

"You'll want betony mixed with pure

honey." She turned to the boy. "Mix a tonic for Dr. Glatz."

The apprentice hopped up on a stool and squinted at the labels on the jars that lined one of the high shelves.

"Where's your master?" Dr. Glatz asked the boy. "What does a nun know about directing the business of an apothecary shop?"

"She knows more than me." The apprentice shoved aside several jars.

"Go get your master. If I'm to pay for the medicine, I want to make sure it's what I really need."

Katharina resumed crushing the marigold. "He'll tell you the same thing I have."

"Then you think you're always right?" His tone had a bite.

She didn't look up from her work. His question didn't deserve an answer.

"I suppose you thought you were right about Jerome Baumgartner?"

Her heartbeat seemed to stutter to a stop, and her hands ceased their work. Over the past few days since Jonas had delivered the news, she'd surmised she'd been one of the last to learn of his engagement to Sibylle Dichtel von Tutzing. The entire town and surrounding community had apparently heard of the slight before she had.

"I guess he won't be coming back to Wittenberg for you after all." Dr. Glatz pulled a crusty linen from his pocket and blew his nose into it with the reverberation of a lumbering cart. "What a shame he ignored the great Doctor Luther's letter."

"I don't see that the matter is any of your concern."

Dr. Glatz loosened the strap of his cloak and then leaned against the counter, clearly getting himself comfortable. "In young Baumgartner's university days, the students were much wilder than they are now. They were known for their drinking and dancing with the daughters of Wittenberg."

"Dr. Glatz, I don't wish to listen to any gossip."

"Baumgartner had earned quite a reputation by the time he finished, hadn't he?" The rector tossed a smile at his companion, who stood behind him, waiting patiently. "Quite a number of the local girls ended up wearing Baumgartner's hat and he their chaplets. In fact, he wore many a girl's *chaplet,* if you catch my meaning." Dr. Glatz and his friend both chuckled.

But Katharina could only stare in mortification at the man's audacity to speak of such matters around a lady. No matter his title, wealth, and position, how could she marry him?

Maybe Jerome hadn't made her swoon, but at least she'd known she could enjoy amiable companionship with him. But with Dr. Glatz . . . She could hardly carry on a simple conversation without it turning her stomach. How could she spend the rest of her earthly life with such a man?

She turned to the apprentice. "Are you almost ready with Dr. Glatz's concoction?" She would get it ready herself if it would speed the man's departure.

The apprentice nodded and finished measuring the betony.

Dr. Glatz leaned more heavily on the counter. "Of course our great Doctor Luther put an end to the drunken parties once he returned from Wartburg Castle —"

"I don't care to hear any more," she interrupted.

"Word around the town is that Baumgartner got your chaplet too."

"How dare you —"

"Of course I'd prefer a virgin." He leaned close enough that she could catch the leftover sourness of a cabbage dinner on his breath. His eyes had a look that made her want to hug her arms across her bosom. "But I've hardly ever met a nun who is."

Mortification was swirling through her

stomach as fast as the Elbe River at spring thaw. "You've completely overstepped your bounds."

He lowered his voice conspiratorially. "Sometimes I like a woman with a little experience too."

The conversation had gone from bad to worse. Burning with embarrassment, she grabbed the pestle and mortar and turned away from him. "You're entirely inappropriate, Dr. Glatz," she said over her shoulder. "I shall not subject myself to any more of your lewdness." She rapidly retreated into the closet-like back room of the apothecary, closed the door, and shuddered.

She hoped the Blessed Virgin would help her should she ever have to be in the same room with that man again.

TWENTY-SIX

"This is the perfect place for another garden." Barbara leaned against the oak that identified the plot outside the walls of Wittenberg. "Once it's cleared, we could fit ten, if not twelve raised beds. Don't you agree?"

"You're likely correct." Katharina studied the shriveled plants surrounded by soggy leaves left from winter. They reflected the melancholy of her heart as did the gray sky overhead.

Barbara nodded at the edge of the plot. "We could cultivate an orchard on the far end by those apple trees."

"You would do better to cut down the old ones and transplant younger trees." The spring breeze was chilly and penetrated Katharina's cloak. The edges of winter still lingered in the dampness of the air, in the barren gray branches overhead, and in the yellowed grass that was matted from recent thaws.

"Why don't you do it, Katharina?" Barbara watched her two youngest children playing chase through the remnants of the gnarled orchard. "If I convince Master Cranach to buy this plot, will you take charge of the planting?"

Katharina knew what Barbara was trying to do — help her forget about her bleak marriage situation. Over the past weeks she had done little else *but* think about how she was nearing two years since leaving the abbey and was still utterly single. In fact, she was the only Marienthron nun who hadn't found a marriage partner or at least a home.

She was grateful to Barbara for befriending her and for elevating her position beyond that of a servant. But lately she couldn't summon the energy to find enthusiasm for the pastimes that had once delighted her, especially after receiving the news from Margaret that she was expecting a baby. Her friend hadn't written much, but Katharina had read between the lines. Margaret was learning to accept her new life, and having a baby would make it easier.

Katharina slid a hand over her flat stomach. The emptiness ached with the barrenness of lost dreams. Not only should she have been married by now, but she also should have been holding a baby with perhaps another on the way. What had happened to all her hopes? Where had they gone?

"We'll have to get to work on it right away." Barbara stepped into the tangled growth and tugged at one of the plants, pulling it easily from the soil. She shook off clumps of dirt clinging to the dead roots and then tossed it aside. "I don't believe we'll have too much trouble clearing it."

"Probably not."

"We just can't supply all we need anymore with our little garden at Marktplatz."

Katharina looked away in the direction of the Elbe and the circling of swallows above it. Her presence in their household had not made things easier. She was just one more person to feed and clothe.

"Apprentices. We have too many apprentices," Barbara rushed to explain, as though sensing the direction of Katharina's thoughts. "With the apothecary shop, the printing presses, and the art studios, we have more than enough apprentices. And now Master Cranach plans to open a bookshop . . ."

"I'm sorry. I must be a burden on you as well —"

"*You* are not a burden, Liebchen." Barbara reached for her hands. "You're my friend."

Katharina looked at Barbara's chapped, red fingers and then at her face, to the creases at her eyes and across her forehead. The woman was Katharina's elder by only ten years, but the aged and tired face had the appearance of an older woman. Lucas Cranach was one of the wealthiest men in Wittenberg. Katharina couldn't understand why Barbara did so much of the work when she had servants to do her bidding.

"You're welcome to stay with us as long as you need." Barbara squeezed her hands. The reassurance poured over Katharina; it soaked into her and softened her like goat's milk over hard rye bread.

"You've been so kind to me. I cannot thank you enough." Katharina pressed the hands holding hers, wishing she could summon a smile, but there was nothing inside except a tangle of wilted weeds.

Compared with her time at the Reichenbachs', her months with the Cranachs had suited her much better. They recognized her as a noble-woman and treated her with the consideration due her status. In fact, Barbara had taken it upon herself to educate Katharina in the various tasks required to run a large household, assuming Katharina would someday have an estate of her own to manage.

But doubts had clamored increasingly louder along with the despair. Katharina couldn't keep from thinking that perhaps she was destined for singleness after all. Perhaps all the teaching on managing a household was for naught.

The clomping of horse hoofs on the rutted lane nearby drew their attention.

"Good afternoon!" Pastor Bugenhagen called from atop a mare. He lifted a hand in greeting, his shaggy beard and hair and his flowing robe giving him the appearance of one of the holy apostles returning from a missionary journey.

"Why, Pastor, we didn't expect to see you." Barbara smiled warmly.

"I'm returning from Orlamünde." Pastor steered his horse through the weeds and tangled plants. "In fact, I was planning to ride past your residence to deliver news to Katharina."

"Well, then we've saved you the effort." Barbara bent and dislodged another tall weed. "We've ventured outside the city walls because I'm considering buying a field for Master Cranach's ever-growing household."

Pastor Bugenhagen reined next to them. "You'll very soon have one less in your household to worry about."

Katharina didn't like the way his eyes narrowed on her as if she was a problem he was about to solve.

"Not this one, I hope." Barbara grabbed her arm. "Katharina has just promised to oversee the planting of my new garden. Haven't you?"

"Of course." Katharina's insides tightened with a growing sense of unease.

"I'm afraid you'll have to find someone else," Pastor replied.

"I couldn't," Barbara insisted. "Katharina knows so much about herbs, more than the apothecary or any of the apprentices."

Pastor Bugenhagen slid from his horse and pulled a withered apple from the leather pouch at his waist. He held it out to the mare, and she neighed softly before taking the treat. "I've just returned from visiting with Dr. Glatz."

Katharina had tried not to think about Dr. Glatz over the weeks since talking to him in the apothecary shop. But his insinuations about Jerome's past behavior had taunted her. She realized now that Doctor Luther had been justified in disliking Jerome. It was no wonder he'd grown angry every time she mentioned Jerome's name, especially if the rumors about Jerome's promiscuity were true. In fact, she could see now that Doctor Luther had hinted at Jerome's less-than-stellar reputation, but she'd been too enamored to pay heed.

"Doctor Luther has put off settling the matter with Dr. Glatz for far too long," Pastor Bugenhagen continued. "So I finally took the situation into my own hands."

"What matter, Pastor?" Katharina asked, although she had the sinking feeling that she already knew.

"He's agreed to marry you in two weeks' time."

Even though the news was unwelcome, it didn't entirely surprise her.

Barbara's brows furrowed. "Is this what you want, Katharina?"

She started to shake her head, but Pastor Bugenhagen cut her off. "The arrangements have already been made."

"It seems so soon," Barbara said. "There's certainly no rush —"

"He doesn't want to wait. With all the peasant uprisings and all the unrest —"

"What do such things have to do with a marriage?" Barbara looked at Katharina, and the concern in her eyes reached out to her. "Give Katharina more time."

"I shall be fine." Katharina forced herself to smile, fighting a swell of irritation. "It doesn't matter how much time I have. I'm not planning to marry Dr. Glatz."

Pastor Bugenhagen folded his arms across his rounded chest. "Dr. Glatz has finally consented to marry you. You should be relieved and honored that such a prominent man will have you, considering all the gossip that follows you."

"I shall be relieved only when I learn Dr. Glatz has put all thought of marrying me from his mind." She didn't know Dr. Glatz well, but she'd seen and heard enough to conclude that a union with him would bring only discord.

Pastor Bugenhagen's face clouded with worry. "You don't have many marriage options available to you."

"Someone will come along, Pastor," Barbara said, distracted by her children, who had begun to climb one of the scraggly apple trees. She started toward them but cast a comment over her broad shoulder. "Someone younger and kinder, a man more suited to Katharina."

After two years Katharina wasn't so sure if anyone suitable would come along. But she was grateful to her friend for speaking on her behalf.

"We've waited long enough." The pastor's voice turned thin. "She's the last of the

Marienthron convent nuns and a blemish on Dr. Luther's reputation."

"I'm sure Doctor Luther won't mind if Katharina stays with us," Barbara called back to them as she strode swiftly toward her little ones. "What harm can come to him if she continues as my companion?"

"Haven't you heard what people are saying?"

"I do my best to avoid salacious talk, Pastor," Barbara commented before calling to her children to get down from the tree.

Pastor Bugenhagen diverted his attention to the nearby robins hopping about the damp soil and plying for insects, then he lowered his voice in obvious embarrassment. "They're saying that Doctor Luther has sabotaged your prospects of marriage because he doesn't want to give up his dancing girl."

Katharina uttered an appalled gasp.

"So you see why it is urgent for you to marry, Katharina. We must silence the rumors once and for all."

The idea of serving as Doctor Luther's dancing whore burned her with shame. And yet it was only one of the many rumors she'd endured since she had arrived in Wittenberg. She couldn't let such tales force her into an unhappy marriage.

"I shall not marry Dr. Glatz." She met the pastor's gaze, determined not to give in to his demands. "Say what you will, I absolutely shall not marry Dr. Glatz."

Pastor Bugenhagen rubbed the back of his neck and shook his head. "I knew this was going to be difficult. You're as stubborn as Doctor Luther."

"I'm not stubborn," Katharina interjected, trying to calm the roiling in her stomach. "I simply won't marry a man that I don't like."

Pastor Bugenhagen sighed. "You're under Doctor Luther's protection; he's your master. And since he's approved this match with Dr. Glatz, you have no choice but to submit."

Katharina wanted to argue more but knew it would do little good. Pastor Bugenhagen wouldn't change his mind. He'd already invested too much effort to make the arrangements.

She would have to go directly to Doctor Luther himself. She pulled herself up and braced for battle.

Luther wiped the beads of sweat from his brow. His stomach had started gurgling, and he knew all too well what that meant. It wouldn't be long before his gut would clinch with the grip of pain he dreaded, doubling him over, squeezing everything out of him until his very life seemed to drain away.

"Tell me again what you've written." Luther leaned his cheek against the cool wall of the narrow cell he called his study. In the overcast spring day, the chill in the air soothed his overheated skin.

Jonas held the ink quill above the paper. "Your title: Admonition to Peace: A Reply to the Twelve Articles of the Peasants in Swabia."

Luther closed his eyes and fought back a groan. He was tired of dealing with peasants and princes alike. They were like two naughty children who wouldn't stop fighting no matter how many times he rebuked them.

"You said: 'We have no one on earth to thank for this mischievous rebellion, except you princes and lords,'" Jonas read. "In your temporal government, you do nothing but flay and rob your subjects, in order that you may lead a life of splendor and pride, until the poor common people can bear it no longer. The sword is at your throats, but you think yourselves so firm in the saddle that no one can unhorse you."

"And you do not think my words too harsh?"

Jonas sat back in the desk chair, which squeaked under his weight. "Of course they're harsh. But they're necessary."

"If only the princes would set aside their devilish pride and consider the peasants' demands." Luther rubbed his thumbs into his eyes to ward off the pounding. "Who can blame the peasants for wanting village lands and commons returned to the ownership of the village or for wanting labor services reduced to a tolerable level?"

"The Twelve Articles are too radical, and you know it," Jonas countered. "The feudal lords in Upper Swabia depend on serfdom. They'll never tolerate its abolition."

The knot of pain tightened in Luther's gut, and he bent over, trying not to cry out.

"Go on," Luther said through clenched teeth. "Read the rest."

Jonas began reading. They'd spent most of the day drafting the document, and it was long overdue. The spring thaw had awakened the dormant fury of the peasants. Every day new reports reached Wittenberg of their rampages through the south, entire villages rebelling, Imperial cities forced to submit to the roving bands of peasants.

The Twelve Articles had listed the peasant demands. Luther couldn't deny their justification. The peasants asked for nothing more than common decency. They wanted to break the chains of oppression not only from the nobility but also from the pope. They were spreading Luther's reforms throughout the countryside.

Now they wanted him to declare his support for their cause. More than anything he longed to denounce the princes and stand together with the peasants for freedom from tyranny. His father's peasant roots reached deep into his being. If not for the providence of God, he might have lived a peasant's life himself.

Luther tried to straighten and listen to Jonas, but the pain in his stomach doubled him over again. "Ach!"

Jonas fell silent.

"The devil take the peasants and princes," Luther roared. He couldn't side with the peasants; he would risk alienating the protection of the princes and jeopardize all the work he'd already accomplished. His friends made sure he didn't forget it.

Of course the peasants were wrong for using force to amend the situation, and he planned to let them know it. But if he had to choose sides . . .

Bile began to rise at the back of his throat.

He covered his mouth, gave Jonas a nod to excuse himself, then turned from the study. He stumbled down the flights of stairs, sped through the tower door into the courtyard, and then fell to his knees.

Heaves racked his body. His muscles tightened until he couldn't move. Blackness swirled through his head. He was getting too old for such stress day after day. It would surely kill him before his enemies did.

He wasn't sure how much time had elapsed before Wolfgang found him in a miserable heap on the ground and pulled him up. The servant wiped his face and gave him a hot drink. Then after his legs stopped shaking, Luther shuffled back up the stairwell to his study. When he reached the top dormer hallway, the sound of voices stopped him.

"Since Doctor Luther isn't available, you may tell him of my refusal when he returns."

Katharina had come. The thumping in his chest was so loud it seemed to reverberate in the barren passageway. It had been long weeks since he'd seen her other than just in passing at the Stadtkirche, where he could only admire her from afar in the comely garments of bright color she wore. The soft curls of her golden hair now hung well past her shoulders. It had been even longer since he'd spoken with her. Although there were times he'd longed to cross the nave and merely have a word with her, he'd always allowed his friends to steer him away, knowing the rumors would only escalate if he was seen talking with her.

He glanced down at his tunic, at the stain of his vomit. The bitter odor lingered around him. He ran his fingers over the unshaven scruff on his face and then through his hair. He was certain he looked worse than he smelled. What would Katharina think of him if she saw him in his condition? Of course, she'd seen him at his worst before, but perhaps that was part of the problem. She'd had so few opportunities to see him at his best.

He took a step back. Before making his presence known, he'd change his garments. Quickly he slipped into his dormer room adjacent to his study. He pulled the door behind him and reached for the habit he'd discarded months ago.

Her voice penetrated through the thin wall. He didn't need to listen to know why she'd come. She'd heard the news about Dr. Glatz, the news Pastor Bugenhagen had brought him — that Dr. Glatz had consented to marry the last Marienthron nun.

Glatz, the old miser.

"I shall not marry the man," he heard her say. "I absolutely oppose the match." He smiled and retraced his steps to the door so that he could hear better, stalling in his plan to change his garment. Hadn't he warned Pastor Bugenhagen that Kate was a hissing Katzen, that she wasn't suited for Dr. Glatz?

"You don't have a choice." Jonas's voice was calm and unemotional, and Luther was relieved his friend was dealing with Katharina instead of him. Jonas wouldn't let her goad him to the brink of murder.

"I most certainly do have a choice. If I'd wanted to remain under the yoke of oppression, I would have stayed at the convent. I didn't earn my freedom only to give away control of my life again."

Luther wished he could see her face. Her blue eyes would be flashing by now.

"I suppose Dr. Glatz is not good enough for you?" Jonas asked.

"You must dissuade Doctor Luther from the arrangement."

"Dr. Glatz is a doctor, professor, and pastor. He's wealthy and prominent. Surely these are the things you want." Luther's body tensed in anticipation of her answer.

"He may be endowed with the proper qualifications," she replied, "but I don't like him. Not in the least."

Luther released a shaky breath. He couldn't deny that he was relieved Katharina was rejecting Dr. Glatz.

"You'll tell Doctor Luther that his arrangements are unacceptable."

"As I told you once before, you're too proud, Katharina von Bora." Jonas's chair squeaked, and Luther could picture him leaning back, arms crossed behind his head, a scowl on his brow. "You couldn't find a man to please you unless he was the emperor himself."

"That's absolutely false."

"Then who? Who could ever possibly please you?"

She was silent for a long moment.

Luther leaned closer to the door and accidentally bumped it, making it rattle. He steadied it with trembling fingers.

"I haven't had contact with many men," she finally said. "But surely we could find someone better than Dr. Glatz. Even you, though you are disagreeable, are preferable to Dr. Glatz."

Jonas snorted.

"At least you have a heart and care about people," she said, "though you often try to hide behind your sarcasm."

His friend was silent for a long moment before speaking loudly. "What about Doctor Luther? Is he preferable too?"

Luther's pulse crawled to a stop.

"Even Doctor Luther would be better than Dr. Glatz."

Even? Was he that close to the bottom of her list of acceptable matches?

"Then you would consider marrying Doctor Luther?"

She didn't say anything.

Suddenly he couldn't breathe, couldn't move. He needed to hear her answer, and at the same time he wanted to bury his head.

"Doctor Luther is one of the most esteemed men in the Holy Roman Empire," Jonas said. "Surely you wouldn't reject him."

"Doctor Luther has made it quite clear he never intends to marry."

"Very well. *If* he decided to take a wife, would you marry him?"

Luther leaned forward, his body tight. Again he bumped the door. "Ach," he whispered harshly. What was he doing? Why did he care about her answer? He knew he ought to march out of there, go down the stairs, and walk outside without a backward glance.

But he couldn't. She had a spell over him he didn't understand and couldn't break.

"If," Jonas said again. "Hypothetically."

"*If* Doctor Luther ever decided to marry, and *if* he ever asked me, then how could I say no?"

"Then you would marry him?"

"Yes, I guess I would."

Luther's knees wobbled, and he braced himself against the wall.

"But he won't ever marry," she said in a rush. "So let's not concern ourselves with such matters."

"You'll marry him if he asks?"

"Yes. I said yes once, and you've no need to ask again."

"I'm just making sure we're clear about your agreement." Jonas's voice rose a decibel.

Luther's heart had started beating again at twice its normal speed.

"If you promise," Jonas said, "then I'll make sure Martinus cancels the arrangement with Dr. Glatz."

"You could sway him?"

"He listens to everything I say — eventually."

Luther grinned wryly, knowing the truth of his friend's statement.

"Exactly what am I to promise?" Katharina asked.

"*If* Dr. Luther ever asks you to marry him, you will agree to the proposal."

"Then I give you my word."

She didn't linger. Her soft steps passed by

him in the hallway. Part of him wanted to chase after her, grab her, and ask if she really meant what she'd said. But the other part of him was too scared.

He didn't move until he was sure she had reached the bottom of the stairwell and beyond. Still he hesitated.

"You can come out now," Jonas called. "She's gone."

Luther opened the door and glanced up and down the hallway before sliding out of the room and crossing to his study.

Jonas had pushed away from the desk and propped his feet upon it. With arms crossed behind his head, he narrowed his eyes.

Luther grinned at him. "You knew I was in there all along, didn't you?"

"You're a scared old goat."

Luther held up his stained tunic. "I smell like vomit. I couldn't let her see me like this."

"You're a she dog with her tail between her legs." Jonas's gaze didn't waver. "What the devil are you doing, trying to coax and force the good Kate to marry that stingy old Glatz? I thought we'd given up on the idea weeks ago."

"Since when has she become *good Kate*?" Luther asked, his amusement rising.

"I like her well enough," Jonas replied. "I

just haven't liked the way she's spurned you. The fact is, she doesn't desire Dr. Glatz, nor will she ever consider him for a husband. Cancel the arrangements."

"If she doesn't like the old man, she may have to wait a good while for another match." Luther would gladly cancel the arrangements with Dr. Glatz, but he couldn't let Jonas think he was too eager. "Who would want to have her, then?"

"I know very well who will have her." Jonas's lips curved into a wicked, teasing grin.

Luther leaned back against the wall, unable to deny Jonas, unable to deny his feelings any longer. He liked Katharina too much. Time and distance had never been able to extinguish his thoughts and desires for her.

Heat sliced through his middle with the suddenness of a swift blade. Although he'd tried to fight against the new feelings she'd awakened in him, the battle had grown harder. She'd brought to life the deep, God-given longings for companionship and love he'd denied all the many years he'd lived as a monk. Now that his desires were alive, he had to war against his flesh, his thoughts, even his dreams in an attempt to keep them pure and blameless before the Lord. Some days he felt as if he fought a losing battle.

"What will you tell Pastor Bugenhagen?" Jonas asked. "You need a plan, or that old rooster will cook himself with worry."

"What do you suggest?"

"Marry Kate yourself."

Jonas's words ignited the heat in his gut again. "I can't get married, and you know it."

"I don't believe your excuses anymore."

"I'm not a sexless log or stone, but every day I expect the punishment and the death of a heretic."

"You've been saying that for the past two years." Jonas shifted his feet on the desk. "You're still alive."

"Barely." He looked at the stain on his tunic. "Besides, she doesn't really want me. I know she said she'd marry me if I asked her, but she doesn't expect me to ask. That's why she agreed to your deal."

"I've seen her reaction to your presence. She has more affection for you than either of you realizes."

Luther wanted to believe his friend. Whenever he'd held Katharina, he'd wanted to think she was reacting with the same longings he had. But he wasn't sure if he'd only projected his own desires onto her.

He finally sighed. "I'll never be the kind

of man she dreamed of having."

"No man will ever measure up to her standard," Jonas conceded. "Kate's a proud woman, and she'd keep you humble."

"I've no doubt she would." Did he dare follow Jonas's advice? When had his friend ever been wrong about something?

What would it be like to share one night, to have even one kiss with Katharina? At the merest thought of sharing intimacies with her, the heat in his stomach shot to the rest of his body. He couldn't deny he wanted to sate such longings. And not with just any woman. He finally had to admit it: he wanted Katharina von Bora.

And now she'd promised she would marry him. Surely she wouldn't have agreed to such a vow if she didn't see something desirable in him. Now was his chance to have her. She would have no excuse to deny him. He could ask her without worry of rejection.

Then he shook his head. "No." The old arguments came crowding back, although with less power. The pope and princes still hunted him. God had called him to reform the church, and a wife would only distract him from his mission. At least that's what Melanchthon would tell him if he were there.

"God may change my heart if it be His pleasure." He knew his voice was too loud, but he needed to convince not only Jonas but also himself. "But now at least, I have no thought of taking a wife."

"You can try to fool yourself," Jonas said, picking up the quill pen, "but you can't fool me. I know you love her and want her. I've known it all along."

Luther ducked his head. Yes, he wanted her. But did he love her? If so, then how could he chance putting her in danger? For by marrying her, he would be signing her death warrant, just as he had his own.

He swallowed the swell of his desire even though it pained him to do so. "It's no good, my friend. I won't do it."

"Say what you want." Jonas sat forward and dropped his feet to the floor with a thud. "You're a man who feels things deeper than most, not only in your work and writings but in your personal life too. Such a man cannot resist taking a wife forever."

Twenty-Seven

Luther closed his eyes but couldn't block the nightmare of the past days from his mind — the blackened walls, the rivers of blood, the piles of severed limbs. The suffocating odor of thick smoke and the sickening stench of charred flesh permeated his senses and the fibers of his garments. The destruction he'd witnessed throughout the countryside reminded him of the Marienthron convent after the attack by the Bundschuh. Only this time the violence and cruelty had spread everywhere.

Anger and hopelessness and frustration bubbled in the pit of his stomach like boiling water in a cauldron. He pressed against the cold walls of the Church of Saint George in his boyhood parish and longed to soak in the calm strength the ancient stones offered.

Outside the wide double doors, thunder rumbled in the low clouds of the morning.

The few parishioners who'd attended the morning service had dispersed. Anxiety ruled as dictator over Mansfeld, as it did over most of the surrounding provinces.

Luther's gaze strayed inside to the great stained-glass window that graced the sanctuary. How ironic that its many colorful glass pieces portrayed a sword-holding, thunder-visaged Christ, so unlike the Christ he'd studied in the New Testament.

"The peasants' power has spread to Spires, the Palatinate, Alsace, and Hesse." Vicar Johann Ledener spoke warily to the few men who remained. He directed his conversation mostly to Melanchthon, who had insisted on accompanying Luther on his tour of Thuringia.

Luther knew his friend had wanted to monitor his speeches and make sure he said nothing to offend the princes, had worried he would lend the peasants too much support in their cause. But Melanchthon and all his advisors had been anxious for nothing. He couldn't support the peasants anymore. Not after what he'd seen over the past days of travel.

The ranks of rebelling Bundschuh had swelled like newly thawed rivers overflowing their banks, leaving a wake of destruction in their path. Everywhere he'd gone he witnessed one atrocity after another. They'd destroyed and burned the palaces of the bishops, castles of the nobility, and abbeys of innocent men and women. They claimed that they were seeking liberation from their oppressors, that they were ridding the church of corruption and spreading the true gospel. But their gospel wasn't truth. It belonged to none other than the devil himself.

The rising violence was worse than anything he'd seen before. He could still see the priests swinging from the trees, their heads drooping, their bodies listless. He'd seen the remains of some who'd been roasted alive and others who'd been mutilated and decapitated. The senseless brutality had overwhelmed him. The memories still made his stomach churn.

"The cities have been unable to resist," Vicar Ledener said. "To survive the roaming hordes of peasants, they've been forced to open their gates and join them."

Luther sighed. He'd heard the same story in every town, the same fear in every voice. The peasants had taken their grievances too far.

Yet when he'd rebuked the peasants for their methods, they hadn't wanted to hear condemnation of their rebellion. They only wanted to hear that they were justified in their actions. They'd wanted his open declaration of support against the tyranny of the nobility.

Instead he'd told them, " 'Vengeance is Mine,' says the Lord."

They'd shouted at him and asked why he was justified in declaring war against the pope and yet expected them to submit to their oppressors.

He'd reminded them that their battle was not flesh and blood, but spiritual. That prayer and submission are the Christian weapons.

But his words had incited them to anger. The threats had grown violent, the words murderous. So Melanchthon had cut short his tour. Now they would head back to Wittenberg, and he would have to face the growing pressure to side with the princes.

"Müntzer has inflamed the peasants of Mansfeld and all around the countryside," said Ruhel, a representative of Count Albrecht, who had joined their discussion. "They're flocking to Mühlhausen, and their numbers grow stronger every day."

"And what has the count done?" Melanchthon asked.

"He has issued a call to the knights, to the *Landsknechts*. They're assembling and preparing for battle, along with Duke George of Saxony and Duke John."

"No." Luther pushed away from the wall. Fresh dread pulsed through him as he stepped out of the cool shadows into the unadorned church. "There must be a peaceful resolution. No more bloodshed."

"The peasants won't listen to negotiations," Vicar Ledener said, shaking his head sadly and casting his sights to the dark corners and thick pillars of the nave as if peasants bearing knives would spring out at any moment.

"The vicar's right," the count's representative responded. "The counts of Lowenstein were taken prisoner, dressed in smocks, and forced to carry white staffs. The peasants compelled them to swear to the Twelve Articles and told them they were peasants and no longer lords. The rebels don't want any man over them, and they don't want to submit to anyone."

"Müntzer has unfurled a white banner," the vicar added. "It has a rainbow in its center and the words 'This is the Sign of the Eternal Covenant with God.' "

"A rainbow?" Luther couldn't keep the derision from his voice. "Does he think he's Noah? Is he building an ark in Mühlhausen? If so, we'll have to send him a few choice animals, a couple of donkeys, perhaps?"

Melanchthon frowned at him.

"What?" Luther raised his brow. "That donkey has called me much worse. Spiteful raven. Godless rogue. Brother Fattened Pig. Dr. Easy Chair. Dr. Pussyfoot. Brother Soft Life."

"We get your point, Martinus." Melanchthon was the most moderate of his friends, the one who always sought peace — especially with the princes — using every possible means.

But Luther feared they were beyond peace, especially with Müntzer. "The man is nothing more than an evil spirit. He's always had a rebellious bent, even in the early days of the reforms."

"Müntzer has pleaded with the mine workers to abandon their shafts and smelters to join him," Ruhel said.

"Will they?" Luther thought of his father, brother, brothers-in-law, and the many other men he'd grown up with. Surely they wouldn't listen to a radical like Müntzer.

"The count has been negotiating with them." As the spokesman for the count, Ruhel had something in common with Luther — he could rarely please anyone. "If the count releases the pressure for them to pay their debts, then they'll agree to ignore

Müntzer's plea for help."

"Müntzer should be put to the sword." Anger swirled through Luther. He opposed violent means, but this was a time when drastic measures were needed.

Everyone nodded.

"As long as he's alive," Luther continued, "he'll continue to stir the peasants toward rebellion."

"He's not the worst," Vicar Ledener said. "We've gotten reports that close to three hundred thousand peasants are armed in the Franconia area."

Luther took a sharp breath. "Surely not."

"No one knows the exact number, but it is indeed large."

His stomach turned with a sickening twist. He'd seen the devastation left behind by the smaller bands of peasants. He shuddered to think of the carnage a much larger army could wreak.

"Time to write another letter." Melanchthon caught Luther's gaze. The seriousness in his expression communicated the gravity of the situation. "We must stop the peasants from further rebellion."

"If you give the princes and nobles your support," Ruhel added, "they'll be able to put a stop to this bloodbath before it threatens us all."

"If we don't put an end to the lawlessness," Melanchthon said, "then Müntzer, Karlstadt, and others like them will undermine all the reforms we have begun."

Luther stared out the doors to the dark clouds rumbling closer, the flashes of lightning streaking the sky. Three hundred thousand peasants prowling about the country, burning, looting, murdering?

Someone had to stop them. He obviously hadn't been able to. Were the princes the only ones who could?

Did they have any choice now but to use force?

Luther lifted his niece into the air, blew bubbles on her stomach, and earned a round of giggles in reward. He laughed and set her back on the floor next to her sister, who then lifted her arms. "My turn, Uncle Martin! My turn."

At the trestle table his brother, Jacob, watched unsmiling from where he sat on the bench next to their father, who was conversing with Melanchthon about the peasant uprisings and the count's response. Their mother was removing the remains of their meal of cold partridge, bread, and figs. Her shoulders were stooped, the result of many years of carrying firewood from the forest beyond the village. Day after day the heavy load had bent her back under its weight, as it did the many other women whose lot was to carry wood.

After hearing the tales of horror Melanchthon had shared too freely with his father over their meal, Luther could see his mother glancing frequently at the crucifix on the wall above the stove. Her lips moved in silent prayer with the petitions and appeals she fervently offered to Saint Anne, the protectress of the miners. She still believed, as she'd once taught him, that the saints would help them if called upon, and they would intercede on behalf of mortals before the great Judge.

Luther peered at the high window of his father's house and listened to the patter of rain. He and Melanchthon would be on their way once the storm exhausted itself. As anxious as he was to leave, he was grateful for a few extra moments with his nieces.

With a grin he scooped up his second niece and tossed her above his head into the spacious open ceiling of the front common room. His niece squealed with delight, a sound that was sweeter than any tune on the lute. It plucked at the taut strings of his emotions, drawing out a longing he didn't want to name for fear he'd find discontentment in the course set before him.

As he placed her next to her sister, both girls clamored for more of his attention, but their mother quietly admonished them to finish their work scraping and washing the dishes. Only then did Luther notice that his father and Melanchthon had joined Jacob in staring at him.

"They're good girls," his father said with an affectionate glance toward his grand-daughters. "It's just too bad they're not boys."

Jacob didn't say anything. The grooves of his younger brother's face were lined with the grime of the mines, the constant re-minder of his lot of hard labor. And Luther wondered if Jacob felt the same way he did — that he hadn't lived up to his father's expectations, that he would forever be try-ing to ease the disappointments he caused.

His father rubbed his sleeve against his large nose. His shaggy brows were perpetu-ally angled in recent months, and his face had a new look of weariness. "It's clear you like children, Martin. I don't understand why you won't heed my advice to settle down and finally give me an heir."

Luther's muscles tightened, and he glanced at his cloak hung on a peg near the hearth to dry. He'd rather depart in the pouring rain than have a conversation like this again with his father.

As though sensing the shift in Luther's mood, Melanchthon rinsed his greasy fingers in an ewer at the center of the table and spoke. "Martinus has other important matters that need his attention, especially with the surge of peasant uprisings. He'd do best to stay focused on the reforms."

"It would seem he's caused enough trouble with all his meddling in the affairs of both princes and paupers," his father remarked dryly. "Perhaps my son will have learned his lesson this time and finally return to his work as a distinguished professor."

Luther could feel the heat of his ire rising no matter how strongly he wished to remain calm. "All I've tried to do is mediate peace between the two sides. Surely you can't fault me for that."

His father shrugged. "You've done what you can to change the corruption. And now the rest is out of your hands." Luther knew that was as close to an admission of praise as he'd ever get from his father. For the rest of his accomplishments, Luther suspected he'd always fall short.

Perhaps responding to the turmoil between them, his father lifted his mug of beer and shook his head in weary resignation. "Maybe you're too old now for any woman to want you."

Luther's frustration mounted once again, "There are women who will have me. One former nun, Katharina von Bora, has promised to marry me if I but ask." Once the words were out, Luther regretted his rashness in speaking them, especially when his father sat up straighter on the bench.

"Then I would like to see you ask." His father narrowed his eyes in challenge.

Melanchthon frowned at Luther, his face sharp with a warning against saying more. "Martinus isn't going to ask." Melanchthon had heard all about Jonas's conversation with Katharina and the bargain by which she'd weaseled her way out of a marriage to Dr. Glatz. Melanchthon had been none too happy to discover the promise.

"You're married," his father said, pinning Melanchthon with a piercing glare. "You somehow manage to have a family and balance your work. Why can't Martin be like you? Why must he remain single?"

"It's my choice." Luther's voice grew louder.

"Actually, we've decided for you, Martinus." Melanchthon waved his hand as though the matter were dismissed. "We

415

know you're not inclined to take a wife. But should you change your mind, we decided this wouldn't be the right time to begin thinking of marriage."

Luther's body stiffened in rebellion at his friend's declaration. Did his advisors believe they could plan his life for him? "*We?* Nobody makes decisions for me."

"We all gave our input," Melanchthon said, "and we only want what's best for the cause."

"No one's going to tell me when I can or can't get married." He glared at his young friend, who had it all — a beautiful wife and now two children. How dare his friend deny him the same. "If I want to marry Katharina, I will."

Melanchthon shook his head.

His father folded his arms across his broad chest. "This Katharina von Bora. I think I like her."

Luther had half a mind to ride back to Wittenberg and marry Katharina tomorrow just to prove to Melanchthon that he could do what he wanted, that no man could control him.

Besides, if he married her, maybe he'd finally earn his father's approval.

Katharina knelt in the freshly tilled soil of

the box garden. She dug a shallow hole, dropped the feverfew seeds into it, then smoothed dirt over the top.

She sat back on her heels and brushed her hands together. It did little good. Her fingers were dark and her nails crusted. After days of planting she didn't know if they'd ever be clean again.

She'd soaked her hands every night in lady's mantle water and applied an oil made from water lilies and roses. Yet no matter how hard she tried, she couldn't keep her hands as soft and white as they'd been when she'd lived in the abbey.

Squinting against the sunshine that was bathing her in blessed warmth, she glanced around at the four gardens she'd already designed. The pathways between them formed the pattern of a cross. She'd grouped them so that in each bed the tallest plants grew in the farthest corners and the other plants diminished in size toward the center and pathways. When she finished, the garden would have twelve beds that formed three crosses, the perfect number, one for each of the Trinity.

Barbara had assigned several servants to build the raised boxes and till the soil. They had also helped her transplant many of the herbs from the Cranachs' town plot. But

Katharina had claimed the sole duty of laying out the garden and arranging each plant.

Barbara had been right. The project had been the dose of medicine she needed. The days working outside in the fresh spring air, the freedom to create, and the hard labor had brought her a new sense of purpose. Although her singleness haunted her, at least among the gardens she could forget about it for a time.

And she was grateful that no one had pressured her anymore regarding Dr. Glatz. Two weeks had come and gone with not another word about the man. Apparently Jonas had followed through with his half of the bargain and had convinced Doctor Luther to cancel the arrangement.

Would she have to carry through with her part of the bargain, with her promise to marry Doctor Luther should he ask? A tremor in her chest made her suddenly breathless, as it did every time she considered the possibility. She was quite sure Doctor Luther would never ask her, but even so the thought sent strange anticipation through her. What would it be like to marry him?

Her mind flashed to the time in Grimma when he'd leaned in to her, his dark eyes trained on her lips and full of longing. At just the thought, a responding heat flushed her cheeks, and she ducked her head in embarrassment. She couldn't deny an attraction to Doctor Luther. But marry him? It was preposterous to entertain such a thought, not when he'd been so adamantly opposed to marriage. And not when she'd held on to the hope of marrying within her patrician class and being restored to a life-style that should have been hers by birth-right.

"Katharina!"

She peered down the grassy lane and spotted Barbara Cranach waving at her, half running, half walking, her linen head covering flapping behind her like a goose in pursuit.

"Katharina," Barbara called breathlessly again, "gather the servants."

The urgency in the woman's voice propelled Katharina to her feet. She shook her skirt, dislodging dirt that clung to the linen.

"You must come back inside the town walls." Barbara's round face was ruddy from her brisk pace and lined with more tired grooves than usual. "It isn't safe for anyone to be outside."

Katharina glanced to the orchard at the far end of the plot, to the pig market down the road, then to the rolling fields beyond and the laborers hard at work.

Barbara stopped at the cross path, breathing hard and holding her side. "The peasants are revolting."

A breeze lifted a loose strand of hair and sent a chill down Katharina's spine. The wind brought with it the moist manure odor of the swine farm.

Katharina returned her attention to the fields, to the peasants weeding the recently planted barley and wheat and others plowing the fallow field to prepare it for the next season of planting. Their backs were bent every time she looked at them; they showed no sign of revolt.

Barbara's eyes were wide with fear. "They appear peaceful, but at any moment they may strike out at us."

"Why would they do that?" Katharina watched the men and the few women. Like her, they'd worked hard all week; they'd barely given her a glance. "We've done nothing to them." The memory of Aunt Lena's torn habit and the splotches of blood on her thighs haunted her. What had Aunt Lena done to deserve their brutality? What had Sisters Maltiz and Pock done to deserve death?

"We just received news" — Barbara lowered her voice — "of the horrible, horrible death of Count Louis of Helfenstein in Weinsberg."

The name didn't sound familiar to Katharina, but she swallowed her mounting fear and nodded for her friend to continue.

"The peasants besieged his castle and captured him and seventy of his men, his wife, and infant son. They formed a gauntlet with their pikes, played their fifes gaily, and pushed the count and those with him to their deaths."

Katharina couldn't hold back the question that begged for release. "The wife and son too?"

Barbara shook her head. "They spared her since she is the natural daughter of Emperor Maximilian. But they refused to listen to her pleas of mercy for her husband and instead forced her to watch them butcher him. Then they threw her on the back of a dung cart with her wounded infant."

Katharina shuddered at the image of that poor woman having to witness such brutality.

"The peasants are out of control." Barbara's shaking fingers grasped Katharina's. "I'm afraid for you out here by yourself. Come back to the safety of town."

"But the garden. I cannot desert it now . . ."

Barbara tugged her. "The peasants are savages, Liebchen. There's no telling what they'll do next."

Savages? Some, perhaps. But was it fair to assume they all were? What about Greta and Thomas? She hadn't seen them since the day she'd escaped from Abbot Baltazar. She didn't know where they'd gone or even if they were still alive. But she couldn't ever think of them as savages.

Abbot Baltazar deserved the title of savage more than anyone else she knew. Whenever she thought of the way he'd abused Greta and likely many other women, she could understand Thomas's rage and the anger of all the others who'd been unjustly treated by those who'd been appointed by God to rule them kindly.

The abbot had failed. She'd failed. So many others had as well. But it didn't justify what the peasants had done to Count Louis of Helfenstein. Or what they'd done to Marienthron and Aunt Lena.

The nobility had grown too proud. She, Katharina von Bora, had grown too proud. And somehow things must change. She must change.

When she'd escaped from the convent, she'd thought that would be enough of a transformation. But she realized now that it had only been the start.

TWENTY-EIGHT

"Slow down, Martinus," Melanchthon said, jogging alongside Luther to keep up.

Luther's stride lengthened, and he didn't pause to return the greetings of those he passed on the street. He scowled through the summer sunshine, blinded by the fury that had possessed him since the courier had arrived at the Black Cloister.

"The news of the battle is harsh," Melanchthon said, his breath coming in gasps. "I realize that. But there's nothing we can do about it now."

"Don't tell me there's nothing I can do! I'll do something even if it kills me." Luther's blood boiled through him, scorching his very soul.

"Let's take some time to cool off first." Melanchthon's footsteps slapped against the stones of the street.

"I wish I'd never written the letter in the first place!" Luther's roar made the women ahead of him pull aside in fright. He knew he ought to explain that he was not a madman, but he would only frighten them more with his angry ranting about how both prince and peasant looked to him as the cause *and* the solution to the problems.

"I told you the wording was too harsh against the peasants," Luther said through clenched teeth. "But everyone agreed it was necessary."

He'd titled his latest letter "Against the Murderous, Thieving Hordes of Peasants." He'd written it shortly after returning home from his trip through Thuringia. He'd known he needed to speak out against the rebellion. It had become all too clear after his tour through Thuringia that the peasants wouldn't listen to reason, that they wouldn't stop their senseless rampages unless forced at the point of a sword. Even though he hated the use of physical force, in his letter he'd told the princes to stop the peasants, with violence if necessary.

But he hadn't planned on the princes butchering them.

"I'll make sure Cranach stops printing the letter!" Luther roared. "Today. And I'll write another, telling the princes what fools they are."

They crossed Marktplatz and hurried past

the vendors in the market square, past the tubs of eggs and butter, past baskets of beets and cabbage and onions, past wagonloads of goods brought in from the countryside for sale. The strong odor of salted fish mingled with the yeast of fresh-baked bread. The clamor of voices, the squawking of hens, and the squeals of children at play filled the morning air.

Luther ducked his head in shame. Most of the vendors were peasants. They would have heard the news of the battles too — thousands of peasants massacred, chained, and beheaded. And they would blame him as surely as he blamed himself. If only he could slip past the market without their noticing him.

He was sure they hated him now. After being their champion for so long, he'd failed them. He forced himself to move faster until he was nearly running. He couldn't face them.

"I should have known this would happen if I threw in my lot with the princes." He stumbled over a crack in the stone street and caught himself. "They're a bunch of idiots."

"*Idiots* that we need if we want the reforms to succeed."

Luther shook his head. "Ach!"

When they reached the gate of the Cranach home, Luther barged through.

"Cranach, stop your presses!"

He strode across the bustling courtyard to the ground-floor room Cranach used as his printing shop. Without knocking he pushed open the door. "Don't print any more of the pamphlets!" His voice boomed against the walls.

The typesetter at his low bench jumped up and bumped the tray of letters on the desk before him. The tray crashed to the floor, spilling his hours of labor into a scattered mess.

The room grew silent.

Cranach rose from his bench, a half-bound book lying on the table in front of him. Concern filled his eyes, and he raised questioning brows at Melanchthon, who'd entered and was bent over trying to catch his breath.

Luther crossed the room and stopped in front of a string of wet papers hanging to dry. He reached for one and ripped it down.

"That isn't one of yours," Cranach said calmly. "It's Melanchthon's."

Ink from the paper smeared Luther's hand. "I'm sure Melanchthon doesn't have anything good to say either." He balled the paper into a wad and threw it on the floor.

"Why don't you settle down and tell me what's going on." Cranach started toward him, smoothing a hand down his forked beard.

"I can't settle down! Not when five thousand peasants were slaughtered at Frankenhausen."

Cranach exchanged glances with Melanchthon. He knew they thought he was overreacting, but he didn't care.

"The princes massacred the townspeople, then beheaded three hundred rebels!" Luther pounded his fist on the worktable. "They even raped Müntzer's wife."

One of the journeymen shook his head. "That isn't the worst, Doctor Luther. We just got the news of the battle near Alsace. Eighteen thousand dead peasants."

"No." Luther looked to Cranach for confirmation.

Cranach waved a hand to silence his worker, but his sad eyes testified to the truth of the statement.

Pain shot through Luther's chest as if someone had slashed it with a searing hot poker. The intensity took his breath away.

"They had no chance against the knights," the journeyman continued. "The peasants broke formation in the face of the charging cavalry. Their farm equipment was no

match for the long pikes of the Landsknechts."

Luther heard a drumroll of death begin in
his head. He could picture the battlefield,
the pikes slicing through the peasants, the
horses trampling them underfoot.

"Don't say any more." Cranach's sharp
command stopped the journeyman's next
sentence. But the man's words of horror
already hung in the air.

Cranach started toward Luther. "You look
pale. Maybe you should sit down."

The drum in Luther's head pounded
louder. He gripped his head and groaned.
The pressure was too much. "What have I
done? What have I done?"

The peasants had trusted him, had believed he would help deliver them from their
oppression. When he'd allied himself with
the princes, he'd betrayed them, his people.
Now the guilt of their deaths fell upon his
shoulders.

Cranach reached for his arm. "Come with
me. We'll go get a drink."

Luther brushed him away. The room
swayed under his feet, and he stumbled like
a drunken man. "When will the princes
stop?" he shouted, throwing out his arms,
trying to balance himself.

Cranach grabbed him.

"Will they stop when they've finally murdered every peasant in Germany?" Blackness hovered before him. It was the dark hole of melancholy. He hadn't fallen into it recently, but this time his body pulled him toward it, and he couldn't resist.

His knees buckled and darkness swallowed him whole.

Visions of headless peasants filled his dreams. They chased after him and reached for him with their bloody hands. He couldn't escape even though he never stopped running. His chest heaved with the effort of breathing.

We know that all things work together for good to those who love God, to those who are the called according to His purpose. The verse from Romans drifted in the distance. He raced faster and tried to grasp it, but it slipped from his fingers.

The princes laughed at him from atop their horses.

He wanted to yell at them, to tell them that he didn't care if they supported the reforms anymore. But his voice rumbled in his throat, and no matter how hard he tried, he couldn't make a sound. They'd gagged him and left him to take the brunt of the blame and anger for their brutality.

"We've done everything we can." Voices sounded above him.

Cool fingers brushed against his forehead. "The physician bled him?"

"He thought if he drained the melancholy blood out of him —"

"Bring me the cool rag and the Obstwasser."

The fingers lifted his hair, gently like a heavenly breeze.

He strained upward, craving more, but his body had turned to bronze.

Faint strains of music called to him.

"Schlaf, Kindlein, schlaf. Sleep, child, sleep." A sweet voice beckoned him. "Sleep, child, sleep. Your father tends the sheep. Your mother shakes the branches small. Lovely dreams in showers fall. Schlaf, Kindlein, schlaf."

"Katharina?" he mumbled, trying to open his eyes and sit up.

The music stopped. "I'm here."

He fought through a dizzy wave of darkness but couldn't pull himself out of the deep pit into which he'd fallen.

The soft plucking of the lute started again. This time she hummed the tune of the lullaby.

His body began to relax. Slowly the dizziness cleared and the blackness dissipated.

He opened his eyes and found himself looking at the drooping canopy of bed curtains above him. The thick burgundy layers had been pulled open to the confines of a strange bedroom.

Where was he? What had happened?

"Katharina?" He reached out a shaking hand.

Her fingers met his. The feel of her cool skin was a balm against his hot flesh. With a sigh he laced his fingers through hers and then lifted her hand to his cheek and pressed it to the heat of his face.

In the dimness of the room, her pale face, framed by her golden hair, hovered near. "You look like an angel. Am I in heaven?"

She smiled. Perched on the boarded edge of the bed, she held the lute and appraised him with concern.

"You're not dead yet, Doctor Luther. Although with as much blood as the physician drained from you, I'm quite surprised you're not."

He took in the black slit on his lower arm, still oozing blood, and became conscious of the sting of the wound.

"So they couldn't bleed the melancholy out of me?"

"They tried. But then Wolfgang begged Master Cranach to send for me."

"Wolfgang?" His trusted old servant had actually asked for Katharina? "Wolfgang must have been really worried about me to send for you."

"Maybe he has finally realized I'm not going to kill you."

"Or maybe he's going senile."

Katharina's smile widened, softening the worried lines in her face. "I guess he knew I could beat the devil from you."

"If anyone could beat that old Enemy, you could."

Wisps of her hair floated about her like a golden crown. The tilt of her head, the bearing of her shoulders — she could have been a princess except for the smudge of dirt on her high cheekbone.

"Did they find you in the garden?" He touched his thumb to her cheek and rubbed it against the dirt.

At his stroke she stiffened and glanced over her shoulder at the others in the room.

His gaze followed hers. Cranach, Melanchthon, Jonas, and other friends and servants watched them from the dark fringes of the room.

"What is this?" he croaked to them, dropping his hand. "I'm not dying, not yet."

Jonas stepped to the edge of the bed. "You're sure? Because we've got the parish box waiting outside the door."

Luther rolled his eyes at his friend's poor attempt at humor. "Will you send everyone away? We'll postpone the laying out for another day."

As the others exited the room, Katharina rose to leave too.

He grabbed her hand and pulled her back down. "Don't leave yet. I still need my Doctor Kate."

She looked at her hand held captive by his, a flush spreading up her neck.

He was embarrassed to admit that she was the reason he wanted everyone else to leave. He couldn't explain why, but he needed her there without everyone else looking on.

"Please stay." His whisper was hoarse.

She trembled slightly but didn't meet his gaze. "Then you must promise to be a good patient and do everything I say."

"Don't I always do what you say?" he asked, trying to infuse his voice with a lightness that would disguise the longing coursing through him.

She extracted her hand and shoved the jug toward him. "Sit up and take a drink."

"Yes, lord Katharina." He tried to push himself up, but the jolt of pain in his head made him bite back a groan.

"Let me help you." She slipped an arm

behind his neck, and the warmth from her body drew nearer. The scent of herbs he couldn't name filled the air between them. God help him, but he didn't believe he could resist her another moment. A glance to the doorway told him that they were finally alone, save Jonas. She tried easing him up. He cooperated for only a moment before collapsing backward, leaving her little choice but to fall against him.

Her startled gasp melted against his cheek.

"I beg your pardon, Herr Doctor." She started to lift herself up, sounding mortified.

"Wait, Katharina," he whispered, fighting the urge to wrap his arms around her and make her stay. "Don't go yet."

She pushed up so that her face hovered above his. Her eyes were wide and dark as the evening sky. She glanced over her shoulder, and he followed her gaze to Jonas, who quickly pivoted and feigned an interest in the tapestry on the wall. Luther would have to thank his friend later for his help in orchestrating a moment alone with Katharina.

"Talk to me for a minute," Luther whispered, drawing her attention back to him. He couldn't keep his gaze from sliding over her high cheekbones and down her long neck.

Her quick intake of breath told him she sensed his perusal. "What do you want to talk about?" she whispered.

"You." He couldn't think straight. "You smell of flowers and sunshine."

"I've been busy with the new garden plot Master Cranach purchased."

He slipped his arm around her waist so that his palm rested on the small of her back. It fit there perfectly. And when she again didn't resist him, his confidence soared. "Tell me, are you as bossy with your plants as you are with your people?"

"More so." Her lips quirked.

"Then they obey your every demand?"

"I give them no choice."

"I have no doubt you'll have the best garden in all of Saxony."

She rewarded his compliment with a smile that took his breath away. He would marry Katharina von Bora. He couldn't resist his desire for her any longer. He'd tried. The Lord knew he'd tried.

His body craved her the way his mind craved the gospel. And the plain fact was that he was too old to fight against himself and everyone else any longer. If he married Katharina, he'd finally stop his father's nagging, he'd set a good example for the priests and bishops who were still resisting marriage, and he'd prove to the world that he was human, a man of the flesh just like every other man.

So what if his enemies captured him and burned him at the stake in a week, a month, or a year? At least he would have experienced the gratification of knowing a woman, of being with Katharina for whatever time he had left on earth. The war against the peasants had all but obliterated the efforts of the reforms anyway. The pope wouldn't have any reason to hunt him down now.

As if sensing his train of thought, her breathing turned ragged. Her lips were only a hand span away. Her soft, beckoning lips . . .

"Doctor Luther, you promised to be a good patient —"

He touched her lips with the tips of his fingers, cutting off her breathy whisper. Then he slid his hand upward to the back of her neck and gently lowered her face toward his.

She trembled but didn't resist.

In all his forty-one years, he'd never kissed a woman. But his body seemed to know exactly what to do. His lips grazed hers, lightly. Her softness brushed against him like the petals of a spring flower. He tested, teased her lips with his own, his breath mingling with hers in a growing intensity.

"Kate." Then his fingers on the back of her neck guided her so that their lips had no choice but to meld. She hesitated for only an instant, and then he felt her lips responding to his, matching his fervor.

A loud clearing of someone's throat caused her to jump. She broke away and struggled to push back from him.

Luther wasn't ready to end the kiss. He yearned for more, but somehow he found the will to release her.

Clearly flustered, she quickly made a move to stand, but he reached for her arm and stopped her. He didn't want this moment with her to end quite yet. And although he knew he should be grateful for Jonas's presence, he frowned at his friend who peered at them over his shoulder from where he still stood in front of the tapestry.

"Save it for the marriage bed." Jonas grinned.

"Get out."

"Not unless you want me to get Pastor Bugenhagen so we can make this official right here and now."

Luther groused under his breath at his friend but was half tempted to have Jonas do just that.

"You're quite well, Doctor Luther." Katharina's cheeks were pink, and she looked everywhere but at him. "You don't need me any longer."

"But I do need you." He watched the way her lips curved and wanted nothing more than to taste them again. Suddenly he knew with startling clarity the truth of all he'd preached about marriage during the past several years. In fact, he'd recently written to two leaders of monastery orders, supporting their consideration of marriage. He'd expounded on Genesis 2:18 and the interrelationship between woman and man in marriage. "It must, shall, and will not be any other way," he'd written. "Forget about your concerns, enter into marriage joyfully; your body demands and requires it; God wants it and wills it."

He reached for Katharina's hand and brought it to his lips. The delicate fingers were streaked with dirt. He found the soft skin of her palm and pressed his lips there, savoring the warmth and moisture his breath made against her.

Her eyes were bright, and she didn't resist the intimacy. Was she feeling the same pull to him?

He trailed his lips to her wrist and felt the

thumping of her pulse.

When her eyes met his, he knew he had her. The deep pools of her eyes shone with a desire that equaled his. Pleasure rushed through him.

Surely if he asked her to marry him now, in this instant, she wouldn't want to say no.

"I meant it, Katharina. I need you."

Jonas coughed.

"I'm pretending you're not here, Justus." Luther shot his friend a glare and then pushed himself up on the bed until he was sitting. His head pounded, but the pain was faint in the surge of his other emotions. He brought a hand to her cheek and stroked her warm skin. "You'll make a good wife to an old man."

She stiffened. "I thought you understood that I wouldn't marry Dr. Glatz."

"Dr. Glatz?"

"Didn't Justus tell you? He agreed he would —"

"He did sway me." Luther smiled. "Of course you won't marry that old miser."

She studied his face a moment before a small smile curved her lips. Heaven have mercy on him. She was irresistibly beautiful when she smiled.

"When I said you will make a good wife to an old man, I was referring to myself. I

440

am the old man."

Her smile froze.

His heartbeat stuttered. She'd promised Jonas she would marry him if he asked. All he needed to do was ask. "I've decided that instead of old Glatz, you shall have old Luther instead. What do you say to that match?"

She didn't say anything. Instead she pulled her hand away from his, hesitated, then looked at her lap.

His pulse resumed its beating, growing louder. So he still wasn't good enough for her?

"Well, I don't want to marry you either." He rushed to get the words out.

Her gaze snapped back to his. "What?"

"If I have to marry, then I'd prefer someone like Eva von Schonfeld or Ave Alemann. Both are young, beautiful, and docile, unlike you — always the hissing Katzen."

Her wide eyes filled with hurt.

He was suddenly too angry to care. "But they're both married. Everyone is married. Except for you."

"I didn't plan this."

"Neither did I. But you're a forsaken woman. Now I'm stuck with you, and you have become a burden to me."

The delicate features of her face hardened,

and for a long moment the pain in her eyes almost made him stop.

But the hammering ache in his chest propelled him forward. "Since it appears my father and the entire Holy Roman Empire will not rest until I have married, I have decided that I'll take a wife."

He could see Jonas shaking his head and waving his arms, but he refused to heed his friend's attempt to keep him from sliding further into the gutter.

"It looks as if neither of us has much choice these days. You have Glatz or me. And I have —" He paused and took a breath. "Well, I have only you, a poor refugee and a domestic aid."

Anger sparked to life in her eyes. "I'm much more than that —"

"Oh yes, I forgot. If I marry you, then I am practically marrying royalty. What a bargain for me."

She jumped up from the side of the bed and stood facing him, her petite body tight. "You're impossible." Her eyes flashed, and her fingers twitched as if she would like to slap him.

"You'll marry me. You must agree to it since you promised Justus you would."

Her blazing gaze met his.

Every nerve in his body strained for her answer.

When she didn't say anything, a rage of blood pounded through his head. "You can't stay single any longer. You'll either marry me, or I'll send you to Dr. Glatz."

"I won't marry that man. You can't make me."

"Then I guess you'll marry me."

"Then I guess I will."

She handed him his lute. Then she spun away from him and crossed the room. She nodded at Jonas and left.

When the door had closed behind her, Luther blew out a frustrated breath and fell back against the bed.

"That went well," Jonas said, stepping over to the edge of the bed.

"I don't want to hear it."

"You sure know how to sweep a girl off her feet."

"She doesn't want me, so why should I care?"

"It looked to me like you *both* wanted each other."

Luther closed his eyes. His entire body sagged with exhaustion, and the fire of his anger smoldered into embers.

"Justus, what have I done?" He groaned and turned his face to his pillow.

Had he really just bound himself to Katharina? To a woman who didn't return his love? To a woman who'd agreed to marry him out of obligation to a promise and not because her heart desired it?

That wasn't what he'd wanted. He'd wanted her to return his desire and affection in the same measure. And he was crushed and angry that she hadn't.

More than that, he was scared. He'd finally done the one thing he'd said he never would. He'd pledged himself to a woman.

And in doing so, he'd just put a target on her back.

"What have I done?" he moaned again.

No matter how angry Katharina made him at times, he would die before he saw her come to harm.

TWENTY-NINE

"You will look beautiful in this." Barbara pulled the laces on the bodice and tightened them. "Once we shorten the skirt, it will fit you perfectly."

Early summer sunlight streaked into the bedchamber, filling it with brightness, but it couldn't lift Katharina's melancholy. She studied the folds of silk brushing against her legs. The trimmed skirt opened in the front from the waist down to reveal an underskirt.

She'd never worn anything so exquisite. The bodice sleeves were tight but fashionably puffed and slashed at the shoulder and elbow. A stand-up collar draped her shoulders. Its silk and trimmed fur hugged her in a perfect fit.

"Doctor Luther won't like it," Katharina said, touching the braided rings that adorned the neckline, marveling at their delicacy.

"He'll love it," Barbara said. "He won't be able to keep his eyes off you."

She'd be surprised if he looked at her ever again. In fact, she was surprised he was actually going through with the betrothal.

"Maybe I should just wear my Sunday skirt." Would she displease him even more if she arrived at the betrothal ceremony dressed like a princess? "You're more than kind in offering to let me wear your dress, but I don't think I should —"

"Nonsense. I have more dresses than I can use. Consider it my wedding gift to you."

Katharina bit back the rest of her protest. She couldn't refuse her friend's gift. Her fingers slid over the smooth, creamy material. If her father had been able to provide a dowry for her, if he'd been arranging her marriage to a nobleman, she would have worn a dress like Barbara's — or one even more elaborate.

A man like Jerome would expect such attire and not just for a betrothal ceremony. But Doctor Luther?

"Perhaps Doctor Luther would prefer a plainer style," Katharina said.

"The man is a boar when it comes to knowing anything about personal grooming." Barbara held the hem while one of the servants measured and pinned. "Now no more about it, Liebchen. I want you to wear this dress."

Maybe he would cancel the plans. There was still time. The betrothal ceremony was more than a week away, set for June 13, the feast day of Saint Anthony of Padua. She'd heard tales that Melanchthon and some of his other friends were angry at him for making marriage plans while the entire countryside was still in turmoil from the rebelling peasants. Perhaps they would convince him to stop.

And yet she'd heard the other rumors circulating about her and Doctor Luther, rumors that would surely force Doctor Luther to marry her. The stories differed, but most said she had seduced him with his lute and had lain with him in Master Cranach's bed.

Embarrassment rushed through her at the thought of people repeating the tale. Of course this time she *had* overstepped the bounds of propriety, and the rumors bordered on half truth.

Her stomach dipped at the remembrance of the moments with him and the kiss they'd shared. It had been unlike anything else, not even remotely like the one kiss Jerome had given her. In fact, just thinking about the touch of Doctor Luther's lips twisted a

447

ribbon of heat through her middle and up around her heart.

"Do you know what to expect after the betrothal ceremony?" Barbara bent her head and focused on the hem.

Katharina fidgeted with the delicate linen ruffle at the edge of the sleeve. Had Barbara read her thoughts? Was she remembering the rumors too?

"After the betrothal you will consummate your union," Barbara said softly.

Katharina felt the heat make a path to her face, burning her cheeks with the naiveté of a twenty-six-year-old virgin. Like all young noble-women, she was familiar with the ancient German customs. The betrothal ceremony was considered the official contract of marriage, and afterward the union was consummated in the required presence of a witness. Such customs, especially among the patrician class, ensured that no one could interfere with a union once the betrothal had taken place.

But the marriage bed itself? She ducked her head in another flush of embarrassment. No one ever spoke of the intimacies between a man and a woman, especially behind the cloistered walls of the convent.

"You don't have a mother to instruct you about the marriage bed." Sunlight highlighted the gray strands in Barbara's hair, which was twisted back into a fashionable knot. "So I thought if you have any questions about — well, about anything . . ."

Katharina could only think back to the way Doctor Luther had held her on the bed, the way he'd pulled her against him. She'd lost all sense of reason when he'd kissed her just briefly. What would happen if she spent an entire night with him?

Her body felt suddenly too hot, as if someone had closed all the windows and set the hearth fire burning.

Barbara cleared her throat. "You can always talk to me if you think of something later."

Katharina nodded, unable to speak.

"Of course you must stay the night in our guest chamber. It's only natural since you'll have the betrothal ceremony here." Barbara stood up and faced her directly. "Besides, you don't want to spend your first night at the Black Cloister. It's in such a state of disrepair; I fear you'll have much work to make it livable."

"I'd be grateful for all the guidance you can give me."

"After the betrothal I'll help you bring order back to the monastery. But we can't do anything until your union is official." She reached for Katharina's head cap and unpinned it. Then she began to unravel Katharina's hair out of the tight braids she wore coiled beneath the head covering.

She hadn't cut her hair in the two years she'd been gone from Marienthron, and finally she could revel in the glory of having it long.

"You and Doctor Luther must host a lunch for the witnesses the day after your betrothal. You'll need to have it here too."

"We cannot impose —"

"You won't be imposing. I'm happy Doctor Luther has come to his senses and is finally marrying. And I could pick no one better for him than you."

"But you're doing so much already."

"Katharina." Barbara's fingers stilled against her hair. "Master Cranach has never paid Doctor Luther for any of the works he's printed and sold."

Katharina nodded in acknowledgment. Not only was she marrying out of her class, but she was marrying a poor man, quite possibly one of the poorest men in all of Saxony.

She couldn't deny that she cared for Doctor Luther. Nor could she deny the strong passion his presence seemed to draw from deep inside her, a passion she'd never known existed. Nevertheless, doubts waged war inside her. There was a part of her that didn't care about their differences or his poverty, the part that swelled in anticipation of finally being with Doctor Luther, of getting to spend her days and nights with him. She wasn't afraid to admit that she enjoyed his company, that she admired his intellect and appreciated his strong beliefs.

But another part of her couldn't stop questioning whether she was doing the right thing in relinquishing her title and status. Surely Doctor Luther could understand that this was a momentous, life-changing decision for her?

As she tried to make excuses, she knew her hesitancy at his proposal of marriage had hurt him. And she wished she could redo those moments in the bedroom, wished he had at least allowed her to explain herself.

"You must let us help with the betrothal and wedding plans," Barbara said. "It is the least we can do to repay Doctor Luther for all he's given us. He does so much for others without asking for anything in return."

Katharina looked down at the shimmering dress, which grew blurry behind a sudden veil of tears. He'd done so much for her even though he hadn't needed to. He'd sheltered her, provided for her, and given to her when he'd had nothing to give. He'd even saved her life more than once.

Barbara shook Katharina's hair, letting it cascade down her back. "He gives until he has nothing left to give, and then he'll give his life if need be."

What if his offer of marriage was only an attempt to rescue her again — this time from her life of singleness and the rumors that were ruining her good name? Maybe he was marrying her out of obligation and charity.

Barbara combed her fingers through Katharina's hair. "He may not be everything you thought you'd find in a husband. But he's a good man, Katharina. He's been good to you."

"You're right," she whispered, unable to keep the wobble from her voice. "He's a good man."

"Every maiden has doubts before the wedding. But you shouldn't worry about anything." She stepped back and examined Katharina. "When he sees you like this, he won't be able to resist you."

Katharina looked down at herself. Waves of hair tumbled around her face and over her shoulders. He'd told her she looked like an angel when she had a smudged face and clothes soiled from the garden. What would he think of her like this?

Would she be beautiful enough to make him forget that she'd hurt him? She could only pray that eventually they'd be able to put aside their reservations and find happiness together.

The day of Saint Anthony of Padua arrived too quickly. Katharina waited for someone or something to intervene. Even when she stood next to Doctor Luther in the Cranachs' parlor and Pastor Bugenhagen took his place in front of them, she expected one of his advisors to barge in and tell them this was all a mistake and they shouldn't do it.

The small group of witnesses, however, stood behind them, and Pastor Bugenhagen began to read the special ceremony he'd prepared for the occasion.

She glanced at the dark paneled walls and the closed door and then back to Pastor Bugenhagen. A part of her wanted to run from the room, away from Doctor Luther's displeasure. He hadn't paid her any attention since she'd arrived except to cast an irritated glance at her shimmering dress and long hair, making her wish she'd followed her intuition and worn her everyday clothes.

She focused straight ahead on the beam

of sunlight slanting in the window that illuminated one of Master Cranach's oil
paintings of the Madonna and Child. She
tried to draw in a steadying breath, but she
couldn't seem to find any air. If only Doctor Luther would look at her with kindness
and reassure her that she was doing the
right thing, that no matter what happened,
they would be happy.

Pastor Bugenhagen's words couldn't penetrate the heavy layer of uncertainty and
insecurity surrounding her. She went
through the motions of listening and praying and reciting the words that officially
pledged her to Doctor Luther.

How had she reached this point? She had
risked her life to escape from Marienthron
for the opportunity to experience love and
family. And somehow she'd ended up with
an uncertain marriage to Doctor Luther,
the very man whose teachings had awakened
her desires for marriage. The irony of the
situation taunted her.

When the ceremony finished, Barbara
elbowed Master Cranach. He gave a start,
then fumbled in the pouch at his belt. After
a moment he stepped toward Doctor Luther
and handed him a ring.

Doctor Luther held it up to the scant light
coming in the window. "What's this?"

"Remember?" Cranach wiped a hand nervously over his beard. "We talked about it."

Doctor Luther squinted at it.

Cranach cleared his throat and nodded toward Katharina. "I engraved your names and today's date on the inside."

Doctor Luther studied the ring for a moment, then nodded at his friend, who was watching him expectantly. "It shows your fine workmanship, my friend. I thank you."

Master Cranach smiled with satisfaction.

Then Doctor Luther turned to her and held out the ring.

She wavered, unsure if he expected her to take it or if he planned to put it on her.

"I see you're still hesitating," he mumbled, reaching for her hand. His fingers were warm and firm against hers. The merest touch, as usual, was enough to spark something deep inside her stomach. She glanced at his face to see if he had the same reaction to her. But his face was schooled in passivity, and he kept his focus on her hand and the process of putting on the ring.

He slipped it down slowly, almost like a caress. When it moved over her knuckle and he let go, she finally dared to breathe. With all eyes on her, she spread her fingers out and studied it. She was sure Master Cranach had spent countless hours over the past week crafting it, believing it to represent the love she and Doctor Luther would share.

"It contains all the symbols of the Passion of Christ," Master Cranach rushed to explain. "In the center is the crucified Savior with spear and rods on one side and the leaf of hyssop on the other."

A bittersweet pain squeezed her heart. A ruby, the emblem of exalted love, topped the intricate goldwork.

"Underneath are the three nails and the dice the soldiers used to cast lots. Everything is grouped to make a large cross with the jewel in the center."

Passion. She was sure Master Cranach had intended the ring to remind them of their passion not only for Christ but also for each other. Again regret caught in her chest. Everything about the ring was exquisite. Had she and Doctor Luther shared mutual affection for each other, the ring would have been perfect.

"It's beautiful." She mustered a smile for Master Cranach and Barbara. "You're so kind to honor me with such fine workmanship." They beamed at her, and she felt a small measure of relief that she'd given them the response they'd expected.

With the betrothal ceremony complete,

the conversation switched to the recent news of the death of the elector and of his brother, Duke John, succeeding him. Rumors abounded of Duke George wanting to invade and take control of Electoral Saxony. But at the moment the nobles were too busy fighting the peasants to have the luxury of fighting each other.

After dinner and amid the perpetual talk of politics, Barbara finally led her away from the others to the guest bedchamber. She helped Katharina unlace the beautiful skirt and bodice and peel away the layers of clothing until she wore only her undertunic. Feeling naked and mortified, Katharina could only stand and stare at the bed with its covers already pulled back, revealing fresh sheets.

"The men will be here soon," Barbara warned when Katharina resisted her tug toward the bed. At her friend's words Katharina practically hopped into the bed and pulled up the covers as far as her chin.

Barbara smiled at her sweetly as if it was perfectly normal for Katharina to be unclad in bed, waiting for Doctor Luther's arrival. "God be with you," she said tenderly. Then she kissed her on the cheek and left the room.

Katharina lay stiffly and looked around.

The richly embroidered bed curtains hung loosely. Someone had strewn fresh alder leaves on the floor, along with rose petals. The shutters were closed, candles lit, and goblets of wine poured and waiting on the bedstead.

The room was a lover's paradise, the perfect place for a betrothal night.

If only they were more suited for each other . . .

The door creaked open. Laughter and echoes of bawdy wishes came from the hallway.

Doctor Luther stumbled into the room, followed by Jonas, who laughed and shoved the door shut on the others.

She clutched the sheet and shivered. She really had no idea what to expect. Why hadn't she asked Barbara more about the consummation when she'd had the chance?

When Doctor Luther's gaze alighted on her, his grin faded and he took a step back.

"This isn't the time for shyness, Martinus." With a chuckle Jonas shoved him from behind.

Doctor Luther tripped to the end of the bed and caught himself against the bedpost and curtain. His gaze landed hard upon hers. For the briefest moment she thought she saw something soft there, but then he scowled.

She shifted her gaze to the candles flickering in the wall sconces.

"Go on. Get into bed," Jonas said with a fierce glare of his own. "I know you want her. You can't fool me with your tough act."

"You don't know what I want," Doctor Luther growled.

"Just get in bed."

He didn't move.

"So you've had a little fight. Time to get over it and move forward."

Doctor Luther grunted.

"Besides, I can't leave the room until you prove to me you're well on your way to consummating this marriage."

"You won't make this easy on me, will you?"

"You asked me to be the witness, and I'm taking the responsibility seriously."

Katharina peeked at Doctor Luther. A strange pang pinched her chest. She seemed to have a knack for offending him at every turn.

"Of all your friends, I alone understand that you need Katharina," Jonas continued. "You have from the moment she arrived in your life. And you will until the day you die."

Doctor Luther didn't deny Jonas, and for that Katharina was relieved.

Could he hear the pattering of her heart and know she didn't want him to be irritated at her? Although neither of them was entirely sure they were doing the right thing, couldn't they make the best of the situation and attempt to live in harmony with each other?

She heard him shuffle and glanced at him in time to see his gown rise above his head. An expanse of his bare flesh met her gaze.

She sucked in a gasp and pulled the sheet over her eyes.

The coverlet lifted and the bed dipped. The weight and heat of his body slid next to her, not touching, but close enough that a slight move would bring them into contact.

Her body tensed.

"Now I can tell everyone I saw the happy couple on their marriage bed." Jonas knelt at the foot of their bed and bowed his head. "Let me pray over you."

Katharina couldn't focus on anything but the warmth of Doctor Luther's body next to hers and his ragged breathing near her ear.

When Jonas finished his prayer, he stood and tugged the bed curtains closed as far as they would go, allowing them privacy in his presence.

For a long moment neither of them moved.

Finally Doctor Luther sighed and pushed himself up so that he was leaning on one elbow and looking down at her. The sheet fell away, revealing his chest. In the scant candlelight that came through the slit in the bed curtains, she saw his shoulders and torso were smooth and taut. And completely bare.

She tried to find someplace else to focus and settled for the canopy above them.

"Kate Luther," he whispered.

Her heart skipped a beat. "You have a common name now." His whisper had an edge to it. "You lost your title today."

She didn't want to think about it. She didn't want to think about anything.

"No more *von* Bora, the knight's daughter. I guess that means you're a commoner, like the rest of us."

Was he trying to rile her? If so, it was working.

"But I don't suppose that'll stop you from acting like an empress."

"And I don't suppose you will stop acting like an oaf."

He snorted. "So I'm an oaf, am I?"

Her emotions swirled together and stirred the calm waters of her self-control. Everything she'd wanted in life had spun away from her grasp.

"You're a big oaf." The words wouldn't stay inside.

"Then that makes you a big oaf's wife."

"Surely you must know how difficult a day this is for me. Why must you make it harder?"

"Difficult?" His whisper was harsh. He rolled against her.

The impact of his body against hers tore a gasp from her.

"Am I that despicable?" His face was so close she had nowhere to look but into the fury of his dark eyes.

For an instant she could see his pain, the hurt from her careless words. "I didn't mean —"

"You *did* mean it."

"You misunderstand me."

"So I'm stupid too?"

His breath was hot against her cheek, and she was suddenly conscious of the solid feel of his body against her.

And the fact that he wore absolutely nothing.

"Doctor Luther, please." She couldn't keep the tremor from her voice — all the nervousness and stress of the day finally overwhelming her. "I don't wish to have strife between us. Could we call a truce at least for today?"

He didn't say anything.

She shifted away from him, so that she was facing the opposite way. Her throat tightened. She didn't know exactly what she longed for, but she certainly didn't want his anger.

He was still for a long moment. Finally the tip of one of his fingers slightly grazed the dip in her shift on her back. At the feathery touch her breath caught in her throat. "Your scars," he whispered, tracing one of the puckered lines, "do they ever hurt you?"

She swallowed past the constriction. "Not much now."

His fingers halted at the edge of the thin linen. With a sweep he brushed her hair away so that the upper part of her back and neck was laid bare to him.

"If I'd been there that day you suffered your beating," he whispered, "I would have taken the stripes in your place."

His words poured over her like warm wine.

The edge of his thumb made a slow path across her shoulder. She closed her eyes at the pleasure his touch brought. And when his lips and breath quickly followed the trail of his thumb, she gave a startled gasp.

His lips left a tingling trail, and his fingers dug into the long waves of her hair. "I'd like a truce today too," he murmured against her ear. "Otherwise you'll surely win the battle. I'm much too overcome by your beauty to speak coherently any longer."

She tilted her head back, giving him access to the full length of her neck.

"Maybe you'll win even here in our marriage bed," he said hoarsely. "You make me weak with desire."

His mouth dipped closer until his lips brushed against the corner of hers, tickling her. Her lips chased his, wanting the kiss he'd almost given, but he tilted out of reach, leaving her breathless.

"Doctor Luther," she pleaded.

"Call me Martin."

"Martin." His given name came out a caress. "Kiss me, Martin."

His chest heaved against her back, and his mouth brushed against her ear again. "Are you ordering me or begging, my empress?" His tone was tender and teasing.

"I'm begging." She twisted so that she was facing him.

His eyes sparked with passion and something more, something that set her heart on fire in a way that his kisses didn't.

Suddenly his mouth covered hers, cutting off further words. And she was helpless to do anything but respond. Her arms found their way around him, and she became lost to everything but him.

THIRTY

Katharina nibbled at the cut of venison that dripped with the sweetness of grapes and the tang of sauerkraut.

With the garden in full bloom, the colors were vibrant, especially with the June sunshine shining brightly over every flower and bud. Barbara had prepared a lavish feast in the center of the Cranach courtyard for their betrothal lunch. The servants had roasted venison and mutton and served it with ale-flavored bread, red currants, and stewed cabbage. They brought out shining platters filled with strawberry tarts and pale yellow custards, and they went from table to table filling silver goblets with spicy mulled wine.

It was the kind of feast Katharina faintly remembered eating in her father's home before she'd gone to the convent. The scent of exotic spices swirled in the air, taking her back to the dark, candlelit hall of her childhood manor, to the warmth of her mother's arms and the sweet cinnamon of her breath.

Katharina lowered the venison back to her plate and wished she had an appetite to enjoy the bounty. But her body was too keenly aware of the man sitting beside her, and her head was swimming with memories of the night they'd shared.

If only she'd been able to sit anywhere except at Doctor Luther's side at the center table. Every time his leg bumped her or his arm grazed hers, her heart would start beating erratically, and heat would swirl to her face. Even without that contact, his presence alone overpowered her. When he drank from his goblet, she imagined his lips kissing hers. When he broke apart his food with his hands, she could feel his fingers skimming across her skin.

More than anything, she wanted him to hold her and cherish her the way he had when they'd been alone. Although he hadn't spoken often during the night, he'd made her feel loved in a way she couldn't begin to explain.

But now, in the daylight, in the middle of the garden, she wondered if she'd only dreamed everything. He certainly acted as if nothing had transpired between them. How could he eat? How could he laugh and talk with his friends as though this day was like any other?

She didn't dare chance their gazes colliding. She was afraid he'd see just how much he affected her. And he didn't meet her gaze either or attempt to converse. Why did it have to be so awkward between them?

In addition, she couldn't make eye contact with any of the guests. If she did, she was sure they would see what she had done with Doctor Luther during the deep hours of the night. In fact, she was sure everyone already knew about the intimacy, which was the reason for the sly smiles and lifted brows that Doctor Luther easily laughed off.

Of course she and Doctor Luther had eventually fallen into an exhausted slumber. Then in the early hours of the morning before the bells chimed for Prime, she'd dressed and tiptoed out of the chamber and made her way to the garden. She'd needed time alone to process all that had happened, the plethora of new feelings and sensations. She wasn't quite sure what had changed about her feelings for Doctor Luther; all she knew was that she couldn't spend a night like that with a man and be the same afterward.

"The Wittenberg city council has just heard about your betrothal," Barbara said, approaching the center of the table, carrying a bottle of wine, "and they have sent you wine to help celebrate the occasion."

"So the whole town has heard the news?" Doctor Luther ran his thumb around the rim of his goblet. Katharina caught her breath and could almost feel his thumb grazing her neck. Warmth stole through her belly, and she forced her gaze back to her uneaten food.

Doctor Luther sat up straighter, and any hint of indulging in pleasantries vanished. "Then I assume Melanchthon has heard now too."

Katharina looked up to see the young professor crossing through the flower beds toward them. His face sagged with a frown.

"Here we go," Doctor Luther said under his breath.

Except for the chirping of birds, the garden grew quiet.

Melanchthon nodded at the others, but he wove his way through the maze of servants and guests until he stood directly before Doctor Luther. "Martinus, may I have a word with you in private?" His voice was tense.

"I'm in the middle of a glorious celebration. You wouldn't have me leave the side of my beautiful bride, would you?"

Melanchthon gave Katharina a curt nod, but his eyes narrowed with accusation.

She lifted her chin. Was this lofty friend of Doctor Luther's daring to blame her for the betrothal? Did he think she had seduced Doctor Luther or somehow trapped him into marriage? She pressed her lips together to keep from reminding him that she hadn't planned any of this.

Melanchthon's gaze flitted back to Doctor Luther. "I need to speak with you."

"Not today." Doctor Luther lifted his goblet and took a drink.

"Only for a moment."

"I couldn't bear to be away from my dearest Kate for even a minute." Doctor Luther reached for her hand and slid his fingers into hers, bringing her hand to his lips and pressing a gentle kiss there.

For the first time since the feast started, his gaze met hers. The brown of his eyes was lighter than usual, with flames that licked her insides and set her on fire. Their sensuousness told her that he remembered every intimate detail of the previous night and that he hungered for more.

Under the heat of his gaze, she could only flush and pray no one could see the response that leapt to life inside her.

Melanchthon looked back and forth between them, and his glare deepened. "Then it's true?"

"What's true?" Doctor Luther kept hold of her hand as he moved it underneath the table and rested it on his leg.

"Rumors are spreading —" Melanchthon glanced at the other guests and then lowered his voice. "People are saying you consummated your betrothal. Tell me it's not true."

"Of course it's true. Why wouldn't it be?" Below the table his thumb swirled a small circle on the pulse point of her wrist.

She trembled at his caress, and his lips lifted into a half grin.

"I can't believe you did this," Melanchthon said between gritted teeth, as he leveled another glare at Katharina.

Her normally loose tongue was tied today. She had no longing to join the disagreement and voice her opinion. It was hard to think coherently about anything with Doctor Luther's fingers stirring her passion in secret under the table.

"If you don't believe me, then ask Justus." Doctor Luther tossed a grin down the table toward Jonas. "He was there. He witnessed everything for this very reason — so that my well-meaning friends wouldn't be able to cover up what's happened."

Melanchthon frowned at Jonas, then at

Pastor Bugenhagen. "I thought we all agreed that if Martinus wanted to get married, he should wait until order is restored to the empire."

"Katharina needed a husband," Pastor Bugenhagen replied. "We had to stop the rumors. Better sooner than later."

"Martinus was incessant with his pining over Katharina." Jonas leaned back with a scowl at Melanchthon. "If I'd had to listen to any more of his lovesick whining, I was afraid I'd go mad."

Doctor Luther's fingers tightened within hers, and with his other hand he grazed her lower arm, letting his fingers linger with an intimacy that made her breathing quicken.

Melanchthon leaned onto the table and lowered his voice. "We had decided this was an inopportune time for you to take a wife. It'll only provoke more turmoil."

"*You* decided," Luther said tersely. "Besides, how could there possibly be any more turmoil than already exists?"

"Just wait. If you thought it was bad, it's going to get worse."

The two friends locked eyes.

She was relieved Doctor Luther was taking a stand for their marriage. But a deep part of her wished he would declare that he wanted her in his life and couldn't bear to live without her, that she was more than just an obligation for him to fulfill.

Melanchthon's shoulders slumped as if in defeat. "You know when word of this reaches our enemies, they'll flay you alive —"

"They already flay me —"

"And now they'll be after your wife." Melanchthon's brows drew together above grave eyes. "What happens if they kidnap her and demand your life for hers?"

Doctor Luther's grip on her hand tightened. He opened his mouth but after a moment closed it.

For once, the man who'd changed the Holy Roman Empire with his words was speechless.

Luther stared at the barren wall of his study and wished he could block out the clattering of pails and constant chatter that seemed to arise from every corner of the monastery. He had long ago given up any thought of writing. The ink on the tip of his discarded quill had already dried.

In one short week since the betrothal, Katharina had taken control of the Black Cloister as if she were lord of the manor. The day after their betrothal celebration, she'd arrived with Barbara Cranach and several Cranach servants. They'd begun cleaning and repairing the building.

Of course they hadn't bothered to ask his permission or his opinion. Katharina's forthrightness had started another battle between them. She claimed she was only making much-needed improvements. Even though he privately agreed with her, he knew the place would never be worthy of her, not even with all the improvements in the world. And that thought rankled him more than anything. The Black Cloister would never be like the manor, castle, or large estate that she could have lived in had she married someone else, someone more worthy of her.

She arrived every day well before Prime, before the sun rose, and worked until long after dark. He'd taken to hiding in his airless study to avoid her. He told himself he needed to stay out of her way because he didn't want to see the condescension in her eyes as she surveyed her new living situation.

But that was only half the truth. The other half was he was afraid that if he was alone with her, he'd disgrace himself with his need for her. Tradition dictated that they wait for further union until they were officially wed. But after having spent one night with her, he was loath to spend one without her.

Instead of making an utter fool of himself, he'd isolated himself. And now he was beginning to feel like he was back at Wartburg Castle in exile. Truthfully, this time he didn't mind the exile. He'd been working on the translation of the Old Testament into common German so he could finally complete the entire Bible.

At least in his closet room he didn't have to face criticism from all fronts. The peasants hated him because they thought he'd turned against them and had allowed the princes to slaughter them. The princes hated him because of his latest harsh words, rebuking them for their ruthless treatment of the peasants during their battles. He'd heard recent rumors that they were thinking of handing him over to the pope and enforcing the Edict of Worms once and for all.

As usual, Duke George hated him and wanted him dead, but he was still too busy fighting the peasants to concern himself with other matters. The peasant rebellion was the only thing stopping the duke from riding into Electoral Saxony and attempting to forcibly oust their leader, Duke John. Luther's friends were doing all they could to ingratiate themselves with Duke John. As

Saxony's new elector, he had the power to hand Luther over to Rome if he so chose. Melanchthon had gone to Torgau to negotiate with the leader, but Luther figured it was a wasted trip. The reforms had failed.

Everyone despised him. They wouldn't listen to anything he had to say anymore. And now some of his friends, including Melanchthon, were upset that he'd gotten married. He might as well hand himself over to the pope.

"Ach!" He pushed away from his desk and stood. The rumbling in his stomach told him he was due for a break. He couldn't avoid Katharina forever.

As he descended the tower stairway, the overpowering scent of lime assaulted him. The servants had applied great amounts of lime to whitewash the walls. They weren't finished yet, but he could see the progress they'd made in a week.

No one had cleaned or repaired the cloister since he'd returned from Wartburg, when he'd found the place empty and the brothers married. It was overdue. And yet, as long as it was suitable for the wedding banquet they would host, what more did they need? The date for their public wedding ceremony was only a week away. He'd already written letters to his parents, inviting them to Wittenberg. At the urging of Jonas, he'd invited many of his friends as well.

He asked himself again, as he had a hundred times since the betrothal ceremony, why he had done it. Why had he gone forward with the betrothal when Katharina clearly had been hesitant to marry him?

Melanchthon's warning at the betrothal dinner always lingered at the front of his mind. Luther had known that if he took a wife, he'd be putting her in danger. But the thought of something happening to Katharina paralyzed him with fear. He didn't want to admit that his own selfishness and lusts had driven him and that now he'd quite possibly put Katharina in the worst danger of her life.

With a growing sense of dismay, he walked past the servants working in the hallway and headed toward the kitchen. He didn't know if Wolfgang would have a meal ready, but he'd fasted long enough.

As he stepped into the kitchen, he was surprised to find the delivery door leading to the side alley open and two strange men filling the doorframe and staring openly at Katharina as she examined the contents of several crates on the floor. Their faces were dirty, their eyes narrow, and something about them caused Luther's heart to gallop. What if one of his enemies had sent them to his doorstep? What if they planned to kidnap her? It had happened before and could very easily happen again.

"What are you men doing here?" he bellowed.

Katharina jumped, and the strangers took a step back, clearly not expecting to see him.

Luther barreled across the room, past the center worktable that was piled high with cheeses and vegetables of all sorts, apparently in preparation for the wedding feast. "Get out!" He didn't care that he looked like a stampeding bull.

Katharina's eyes widened, and she stepped aside.

"If you want to do business here at the Black Cloister, you'll do it with my manservant, not my wife." He swung the door shut, letting it slam in the faces of the strangers with a reverberation that rattled the kettles hanging from hooks in the ceiling beam.

"Doctor Luther!" Katharina finally said with a gasp. "That was completely unnecessary."

He let the bar on the door fall into place with a thud, fear blazing through his blood. "It was absolutely necessary."

"I didn't have the chance to pay them."

"You shouldn't have been in here alone with them in the first place."

"They were selling me grain."

"Let Wolfgang buy the supplies from now on."

She huffed. "I'll do no such thing. He won't have the slightest idea what I need —"

"I don't care!" he roared.

She pressed herself against the wall and eyed him with both caution and irritation. "If I'm to manage this home, I shall do the buying and selling."

He moved in front of her, close enough that the hem of his cloak brushed against her skirt. "I'm your husband, and you will obey me in this matter."

She lifted her dainty chin and pert nose. Her glorious summer-blue eyes flashed with anger. "You're not my husband. Yet." Her words were hard and challenging.

With the outer door closed, blocking the daylight, the dimness of the kitchen cloaked them. The faint clink of a chisel and the distant chatter told him they were completely alone in the privacy of the kitchen. He was alone with Katharina. And his body reacted with a heated longing so intense that he braced an arm on one side of her to keep from crushing her to himself. He couldn't take his eyes from hers. He didn't care if she saw how much he wanted her.

He heard a soft intake of breath, which told him she wasn't immune to his presence.

Drawing courage from her reaction, he leaned down and placed his mouth next to her ear. "You're mine."

Her breathing grew choppy.

His gaze lingered over the span of her neck near his hand. It beckoned him, and he was helpless to do anything but lower his lips to the silkiness below her ear. He took a deep breath of her sweet, spicy scent and leaned against her.

She trembled. Instead of repelling him, her fingers slipped up the arms of his cloak, and she clung to him.

Her reaction made him want to groan. He brushed his lips against the softness of her skin. She was his. God had given him his desires. They were natural and good. Hadn't he preached that very message to others for years?

He shifted so that his nose brushed hers and his mouth hovered above hers, mingling their ragged breaths.

"I'm just worried about you," he whispered, grazing his lips against her cheek. "I don't want anyone to hurt you."

She nodded and chased after his lips. "Then I'll make sure Wolfgang or Brother Gabriel is with me from now on."

He pressed the full length of his body against her, not sure how he could wait another week to be with her. "Kate . . ." He laid a kiss on the silky hair near her temple.

"Take it to the bedroom, you old randy dog." Jonas's voice, laced with wry humor, jolted him away from Katharina.

Luther scowled in the direction of the hallway, where Jonas stood behind Brother Gabriel, peering over the old brother's tonsured head with a wicked grin.

"I'm sorry, Doctor Luther," Brother Gabriel whispered. He ducked his head but not before Luther saw the mortification filling the old monk's face. "I didn't know you were with Sister Katharina."

Katharina had slipped around Luther and had quickly turned her back on the newcomers to hide her blush of embarrassment.

"Go away," Luther growled at Jonas. "Don't you have better things to do than spy on me?"

"I've been given the joyful task of helping you draft your rebuttal," Jonas said dryly.

"What rebuttal?"

"Every bishop and archbishop between here and Rome has accused you of finally succumbing to your lust." He nodded to Katharina, now bent over one of the crates near the alley door. "And even though they're right, I've been given the task of helping you write a letter to explain otherwise."

Luther rubbed his temples. The pressure in his head and behind his eyes began to increase. He'd long known that if he took a wife, his enemies would accuse him of giving in to his lusts. They'd said from the start that his desire to get married had driven his reforms. Even the King of England, Henry VIII, had written against Luther, claiming that his uncontrollable manly urges had prompted his desire to change the church.

Now they were gloating. They thought he'd proven them right. The lawyer Schurff had summarized the position of his enemies well. They believed that if he got married, he'd make all the world and the devil himself burst with laughter and would destroy the work he'd begun.

"Let my enemies laugh at me." Luther took a deep breath to try to relieve the storm brewing inside his head. "Let them think my marriage will hurt our cause and further my demise. They'll soon see otherwise." At least he prayed it was so.

Jonas snorted. "I don't know how much

lower you could sink when you alone are being held responsible for the thousands of headless peasant bodies that litter the roadways."

Luther didn't want to think about the massacre or the trip through Thuringia his friends wanted him to take. They reasoned he could begin to repair relations with the multitudes of peasants and help restore order. But he'd told them he wouldn't travel until after the wedding.

Truthfully, he didn't know if he'd ever want to leave Katharina again, not when he longed for her more than the breath of life.

Brother Gabriel slowly backed out of the room and disappeared. Luther wished Jonas would follow. But his friend leaned lazily against the doorpost as if he planned to stay a while.

"The entire world is waiting with bated breath for the real reason Martin Luther is getting married," Jonas continued. "And now we must give them the answers they want."

"They'll have to wait."

"It should be an easy answer," Jonas said, glancing at Katharina's bent back. "You'll tell them you've fallen in love. It's as simple as that."

The sounds of Kate digging through the

crate stopped.

A peal of embarrassment resounded through Luther as loud as the bells in the Stadtkirche. "It's not about love," he quickly protested. From the corner of his eye, Luther saw Kate suddenly swivel and fasten her intense gaze on him, but he couldn't bring himself to look at her.

"If not for love," Jonas said in exasperation, "then what's your marriage about?"

"I'm making a statement."

"What kind of statement?"

"To Archbishop Albrecht of Mainz and others like him who've been hesitant about taking wives. If I get married, then they'll follow my example."

Jonas crossed his arms. "That's never motivated you before."

Luther sensed Katharina's stillness as if she too waited for his response.

"And I'm doing it to please my father so I won't have to listen to him nag me about it every time I see him."

"Since when do you care about pleasing Hans?"

Luther shrugged.

"You know you haven't cared since the day you threw away your lawyer's robes and donned the monk's habit."

"He wants an heir."

"So what."

Luther met Jonas's glare with one of his own. "So what. What do you want me to say?"

"Tell the truth. Tell everyone the real reason you're marrying Katharina."

Katharina's gaze was unwavering.

He refused to look at her and instead frowned at Jonas.

"Aren't you finally willing to admit you've fallen in love?" Jonas asked.

"Absolutely not!" The words fell from his mouth in a roar. "We haven't married for love. Katharina is too proud for love."

Luther turned to see Katharina stiffen. He caught a glimpse of dismay in her expression before a flash of defiance erased it. "I most certainly am not too proud."

"You're only marrying me because I'm your last option," he stated, daring her to defy him.

"And you're only marrying me out of obligation." Her eyes flashed again, drawing a new battle line between them.

Jonas rolled his eyes. "The problem, Martinus, old man, is that you don't want to admit to anything."

"We've both stated our motives. So as you can see, we're together for convenience, not love."

"Then, my deluded friend, let's be off to write this letter. We need to give the world some kind of logical explanation for this crazy marriage."

Luther glanced at Kate, but she'd turned her back to him again and held herself stiffly.

Swift regret rippled through him. His muscles tensed with a sudden need to go to her, pull her in his arms, and tell her he hadn't meant anything he'd said.

He didn't want to act like a donkey every time he was around her, but he couldn't help it. Somehow whenever it came to Katharina, his heart and his body reacted before he could rationalize his behavior.

Jonas gave him a furrowed glare, one that branded him a coward. Luther could face an inquisition comprised of the holiest men in the land, and he could accept the possibility of a slow and torturous death at the stake. But he was too scared to face love.

Thirty-One

Barbara kissed Katharina's cheek. Then she opened the door and swung it wide. A cheer rose from the crowd that was waiting outside the Black Cloister.

Katharina's heart tapped an anxious beat as she gazed over the swell of townspeople and wedding guests, most smiling, others curious, all straining to see her. Had the entirety of Saxony come to witness the Kirchgang?

Barbara fidgeted with the garland of roses that crowned Katharina's head, untangling several ribbons wound through the flowers so that they streamed down through her loose, long hair. Then her friend nudged Katharina from behind, leaving her little choice but to move forward into the morning sunshine to meet the excited crowd that would escort her and Doctor Luther to the church.

Doctor Luther stepped to her side. His

dark cloak was brushed spotless, and his hair was trimmed and combed into submission underneath his beret. The fact that he'd clearly taken time with his grooming for this special day brought her a small measure of comfort after the tension of the past week.

As he took in her appearance, his eyes warmed with appreciation. He leaned in and whispered so that only she could hear, "You look lovely, Katharina."

The words took her by surprise and sent a ripple of pleasure through her. "You happen to look rather nice yourself."

He grinned, which momentarily took the edge off the strain that had resided between them since he'd made his declaration in the kitchen regarding their marriage being one of convenience rather than love.

She hadn't been able to soothe the sting since she'd learned the real truth about why he was marrying her. Their marriage was just one more of his efforts to reform the church, to set an example for other monks who were still reluctant to take wives. She meant no more to him than one of his pamphlets or sermons.

But perhaps for today they could call another truce? Before she could make her suggestion, several musicians started a merry tune with the whistle of their fifes and the tapping of their drums.

"They're calling for you to begin." Doctor Luther gently steered her forward, leaving her little choice but to join the musicians and the group of young maidens bearing garlands of finely gilded wheat, and the young Cranach daughters, who carried branches of rosemary decorated with rainbows of silken ribbons. Together they led the procession down Collegienstrasse.

Doctor Luther followed several paces behind with the men and guests of honor. They strolled along the street until they reached the portal of Saint Mary's Church. There Doctor Luther tumbled forward against her amid the shoving and laughing of his friends.

Pastor Bugenhagen stood in the arched entryway and lifted his hands to signal that he was ready to begin. The townspeople and guests grew silent. The pastor smiled. "Let us begin this union with prayer."

The warmth of sunshine spilled over Katharina's bowed head, but she couldn't focus on anything except Doctor Luther's arm brushing against hers and the wild thumping of her heart. She would share the marriage bed with Doctor Luther again this night and every night thereafter.

Her thoughts went back to their brief moment of intimacy in the kitchen before Jonas had interrupted them. Doctor Luther had been tender and passionate. Warmth spread its fingers through her stomach as it had every time she remembered his body pressed against hers. If there wasn't to be love between them, at least there would be something.

Pastor Bugenhagen cleared his throat. "Now for the exchange of your vows."

Doctor Luther shifted.

"Martinus, do you desire Katharina as your wedded wife?"

The muscles in his arm flexed against hers. For a long moment he didn't say anything. A cloud drifted in front of the sun and covered her with its shadow. A cool breeze lifted the tendrils of her hair and skimmed over her back.

"Martinus," Pastor Bugenhagen hissed through his teeth.

Surely Doctor Luther knew what was expected of him next. He was the one who'd written the marriage liturgy.

She glanced at him, at the hard lines of his jaw, at the granite in his eyes. Apparently this final step in the marriage process was more difficult than he'd imagined. She wanted to reach for his hand and squeeze it and reassure him that everything would be all right. But would it?

The whispers in the crowd behind them escalated.

"Yes." The word was forced. "I take Katharina as my wife."

Pastor Bugenhagen released a breath and wiped the moisture on his brow. Then he turned to her. "Katharina, do you desire Martinus as your wedded husband?"

"Yes." What else could she say? What other choice did she have at this point? She twisted his ring off her thumb and held it out to him.

He looked at it but didn't make a move to take it.

"For you," she said softly.

His eyes widened and lit with a question.

"From Master Cranach."

Barbara had given it to her earlier when she'd come to help her prepare for the wedding, informing her that Master Cranach had wanted to honor Doctor Luther with the gift.

Doctor Luther took the ring and studied it. It didn't have the same intricate engravings as the one Master Cranach had designed for her. But it was equally stunning. It was a double ring, each one passing through the other to cause them to remain permanently interlaced. A diamond was mounted on one and a ruby on the other next to their engraved initials. Both rings also contained the motto "What God doth join no man shall part."

Doctor Luther nodded his thanks at Master Cranach standing nearby and slipped the ring on the fourth finger of his left hand. Traditionally the ring was worn on the right hand, but Barbara had already instructed Katharina that followers of the reforms wore their rings on their left hand as another sign of their rebellion against the ways of the Church of Rome. The fourth finger had the vein that carried blood to the heart, signifying undying love. She didn't pretend that Doctor Luther had undying love for her, but she was surprised, nevertheless, at the longing that pierced the emptiness in her heart, the longing for real love.

Pastor Bugenhagen's gaze shifted between them nervously. "Time to move inside for the blessing at the altar. Shall we proceed?"

She followed the pastor inside. Once at the altar she knelt next to Doctor Luther. The coolness of the nave soothed her, as did the gentle flickering of the candlelight. Except for a few close friends, they were alone. Pastor Bugenhagen recited a lengthy blessing and then ended with a prayer. Without the usual traditions of the Church of Rome, the service was short. Doctor Luther had done away with ancient customs: the sharing of Mass, the nuptial veiling, and the distribution of Saint John's wine, the love drink.

After they finished, Pastor Bugenhagen led them back to the portal of the church. When they stepped outside, the crowd cheered, and the musicians started their song.

"You'd better take hold of my arm" — Doctor Luther held out his elbow — "or we may get separated."

The townspeople pushed in around them with wide grins, and well wishes were showered on them. Hands reached out, and bodies jostled against Katharina. She slipped her hand into the crook of Doctor Luther's arm and allowed him to lead her through the maze. He spoke kind words to the people and returned greetings as they paraded down the street toward the Black Cloister.

The guests of honor followed in their prescribed order of importance. And in that brief walk, as she saw the admiration for Doctor Luther shining in the eyes of the townspeople, Katharina was surprised by her own growing esteem for him. Even more, she was unprepared for the honor they showed her: the kind words, the genuine smiles, the warm congratulations.

When they reached the garden gate of the cloister yard, the townspeople turned away and only the guests followed them to the inner yard. She and Barbara, with the help of the servants, had removed the tables and benches from the cloister refectory and had assembled them in the courtyard for the wedding feast.

Now the servants brought out platters laden with venison and hare, cheeses and breads, fresh strawberries and wild blackberries, boiled cabbage and beets. Barbara had orchestrated a feast fit for royalty.

They sat at the head table with the guests of honor, which included Doctor Luther's parents. Although she and Doctor Luther drank from the same cup and ate off the same plate, as tradition required, they were in separate worlds, she making conversation with the women and he with the men.

When the banquet finally ended, they followed the musicians to the town hall. She relished her dance of honor with Doctor Luther, the nearness of his presence, the touch of his hands, even though he avoided looking into her eyes. Then they sat next to each other and watched the slow marches that allowed for the introduction of all the prominent guests.

After the dances the guests gave their wedding presents. Even though the gifts were obligatory, joy shone in their faces as they gave. She realized they wanted to bless Doctor Luther in return for the countless ways he'd given to so many of them.

He received the gifts gratefully but was more interested in the people presenting them than the gifts themselves. Even the sizable cash donation from the new elector through his representative didn't elicit more than a nod before Doctor Luther changed the conversation. She smiled graciously at the representative to make up for Doctor Luther's lack of enthusiasm, knowing they would need the outpouring of generosity to help them in their poverty.

Finally, after the guests had presented their gifts, the Wittenberg city council added a last token in the form of twenty Gulden and a barrel of beer.

When the formalities were finished, Doctor Luther joined a circle of his closest friends and sipped from a tall tankard. The men's laughter rang against the walls of the town hall and drowned out the chatter of the women, who sat around Katharina. She found herself leaning forward, waiting for Doctor Luther's boisterous voice to rise above the others. And whenever she stole a glance at him and saw the smooth, carefree lines of his face, her heart beat faster. What would it be like to share a pleasant conversation with Doctor Luther — one with laughter, one in which his face was free of all worries?

"I'd like to speak a word about my son." Hans Luther had risen from his bench and was holding up his mug. He was shorter and stockier than Luther, but they shared the same strong carriage and broad shoulders. She'd also noticed that Hans Luther's dark eyes swirled with innumerable emotions in much the same way his son's did. The noise tapered to silence, and everyone's attention was fixed upon Hans — except Doctor Luther's. Instead he stared at his tankard, wariness creasing his forehead.

Hans Luther cleared his throat. His cheeks and wide nose were flushed a purplish red, and the heat of the room had left wet rings on the armpits of his shirt sleeves. There was an almost imperceptible tremble in his mug before he thrust it higher. "I never thought I'd live to see this glorious day," he started, "the day my son would finally take a wife."

A soft ripple of laughter followed Han's declaration, but Doctor Luther sat stiffly and stoically, as though bracing himself for his father's next words.

Hans glanced around the crowded room, the open doors and windows allowing in the evening sunlight but little breeze to cool the stuffiness. His attention alighted on her for only a moment before returning to Luther. He seemed to be waiting for Luther to look at him but then continued anyway. "This son of mine has always had a mind of his own. He's always tested the limits of my patience, even as a boy."

Doctor Luther's head drooped as his father spoke. Although he'd never spoken to her of his relationship with his father, she knew in that instant that he felt as cast off as she did. Perhaps he hadn't been rejected in a physical sense, as she had been by her family, but he'd obviously felt the sting of rejection, and her heart ached for him.

Hans stared at his son's bent head. Sadness flickered across his features for just an instant before he seemed to push the gloomy thoughts aside. "I may not have seen eye to eye with my son on many issues over the years," Hans said, his voice loud in the strange silence of the hall. "But I want him to know . . ." He stopped and took a deep breath. "I want my son to know that in spite of our differences, I'm proud of the man he's become."

At his father's words Doctor Luther's head snapped up. His tumultuous dark gaze met his father's. Something seemed to pass between the two — a father giving a blessing to a son who'd likely craved it his whole life.

Hans cleared his throat again and looked at his mug for a long moment before finishing in a voice tight with emotion. "My son, I wish you many happy days with your new bride."

Doctor Luther's Adam's apple strained in a swallow before he then nodded at his father. Doctor Luther didn't speak, but gratitude radiated from his eyes.

Katharina's chest expanded with a swell of happiness that he could experience a measure of reconciliation with his father, even if only for this moment.

After Doctor Luther's friends rose and joined in the congratulations, he finally made his way to her. "Time to go." His voice held a note of embarrassment, especially in the midst of the rib poking and ribald remarks of his companions. As she rose and followed him from the hall, they bade their guests farewell. She felt the scrutiny of a hundred pairs of eyes, and she knew what every single person there was thinking — that Doctor Luther was taking her home to bed. She was glad for the June warmth that could explain her heated cheeks.

When they exited onto the quiet street, only Doctor Luther's closest friends accompanied them. They had no need of the bawdy parade to the marriage bed. Doctor Luther and his followers had discouraged the rowdy revelry that traditionally went along with the bedding rite.

The evening air smelled sweet and clean after the hot, dank town hall. The low sun reflected against the clear blue of the sky, with threads of purple and pink beginning to lead the procession of the coming night. Katharina took a deep breath, then she pointed her face into the summer breeze and let it caress her cheeks.

They walked side by side, the crunch of their footsteps filling the space between them. The chatter of Doctor Luther's friends went before them and prevented them from having to make small talk. When they came within sight of the Black Cloister, Doctor Luther spoke. "Merchant Koppe has finally arrived." He nodded to the wagon parked in front of the gate.

Katharina stopped and stared at the covered wagon bed. Her heart picked up speed as her mind raced back to the long, cramped ride that had brought her to Wittenberg.

"Brings back memories, doesn't it?" Doctor Luther asked softly.

She nodded and tried to push them aside. It was too hard to think of the decision she'd made that night so long ago, the decision that had altered her life in a way she'd never foreseen. "Regretfully he's too late for the festivities."

"I expected him yesterday," Doctor Luther said, as he opened the front door and nodded his farewells to his companions.

As they ducked into the parlor, the room was empty except for one person — a frail nun hunched over and sitting on the wall bench. She didn't move; it was almost as if she hadn't heard them enter.

Katharina raised a brow at Doctor Luther. "Is Koppe smuggling out more nuns?"

He nudged her. "You'd better go see."

With hesitant steps she approached the nun. The woman's veil hung askew and hid her face. "Sister?"

The woman didn't budge.

Katharina looked back at Doctor Luther. He cocked his head at the woman. "Who is it?"

She shrugged, then shifted her skirt and

lowered herself until she was on her knees. "Sister?"

The nun still didn't respond. "My name is Katharina, and I'm here to help you." She waited. Was the woman deaf? Slowly Katharina pushed aside the veil. The woman made no move to stop her.

As the material slid from the nun's face, Katharina's pulse stopped. Then a gasp slipped from her lips. "Aunt Lena?" The old woman looked at her with wide, blank eyes. Not even a sliver of recognition was visible within the depths.

Katharina didn't care. With a sob she threw her arms around her aunt and pulled her into an embrace. Aunt Lena's body fell against her like a limp rag doll.

Katharina hugged her tighter and pressed her face into the woman's shoulder, this dear woman who'd loved and protected her more than she'd ever realized at the time. "Oh sweet, sweet Aunt Lena," she murmured into the woman's veil. "How I've missed you."

An ache deep inside pushed upward, demanding release. For a long moment she could do nothing but rock back and forth and squeeze the woman. The rounded pommel of her aunt's dagger poked into Katharina's ribs — an all-too-painful reminder of the fear that still tortured the woman.

Who had brought Aunt Lena? Had Merchant Koppe delivered her?

She pulled back enough to see that Doctor Luther still stood in the same spot. His expression had softened with tenderness.

"You did this?"

He nodded. "I'm just sorry Merchant Koppe didn't make it in time."

The tightness in her chest moved to her throat. She didn't trust her voice to work. He couldn't begin to understand how much his effort meant to her.

"Thank you," she managed.

"She hasn't recovered yet, has she?"

She pressed Aunt Lena's head against her bosom. "I shall care for her now. It's the least I can do after . . . after . . ." The words caught in her throat.

"She can live the rest of her days here with us at the Black Cloister."

Katharina kissed the wimple and brushed her tears against the linen. "Doctor Luther, you are a good man." Doctor Luther might not be perfect, but there were not many as kind and generous as he was.

His gaze probed her, as if he was trying to see deep into her heart. He *was* a good man. She wanted to reassure him that no matter their differences she admired him, but when his focus dropped to her lips and sudden desire tightened the lines in his face, words and reason fled.

He seemed to give himself a mental shake and straightened his shoulders before tearing his attention from her. "I'll leave you now to care for Aunt Lena. You'll need to spend time with her and settle her in." He started toward the door.

She couldn't keep her longing from following after him. "Shall I . . ."

With his rigid back facing her, he stopped. "Would you like me to . . ."

He pivoted slowly and cocked his head. Although his face was unreadable, something in his expression made the heat in her middle cascade to her fingers and toes.

How was a woman supposed to ask her husband about the marriage bed without sounding eager? Did he expect her to sleep with him or not?

"Barbara instructed her servants to prepare a fresh bed in your room."

"That was kind." His voice was low, and the darkness of his eyes deepened.

"I don't know if . . . that is, I don't know your intentions . . ."

"I'll be waiting for you."

A whisper of delight trailed through her. "Then I shall not keep you waiting long."

"Good." A slow smile curved his lips.

Katharina leaned against Aunt Lena's wimple, which was blessedly cool on her cheek. Somehow she'd managed to please Doctor Luther, and she suddenly wished she could please him more often.

But how?

All her life she'd been rejected and forsaken. Even though Doctor Luther had already rejected her in some ways too, was there still hope she might earn his acceptance?

She was surprised by how much she hoped there was.

Thirty-Two

Maybe she wouldn't come to him.

Luther sat at his desk and stared at the half-written hymn.

Katharina was taking much longer than he'd expected with Aunt Lena. Maybe he'd only imagined her interest. She'd certainly been pleased by his long-overdue effort to transport her aunt to Wittenberg. He thought he'd even seen respect in her eyes, but perhaps he'd just been swept up in the moment.

He let out a long sigh that was a half groan and leaned back in his chair. It seemed to groan too.

His friends had all gone, and the cloister was quiet except for the pounding in his head. If only the men hadn't reminded him again of all the troubles. Couldn't he have at least one day when he didn't have to think about the peasant rebellion?

At the town hall his friends had informed

505

him that Duke George was stirring up trouble against him again. The old prince was spreading word that he was to blame for the revolt, that his teachings had stirred up the peasants. The duke was calling all of Germany to return to the old faith. Worse, the man had appealed to the new Elector John, and was poisoning his mind against the reforms.

Luther kneaded the back of his neck. Tension stole through him as it always did when he thought of the ways he was failing.

"God, where are You?" he whispered. "I thought You were with me. I thought these reforms were a part of Your plan."

He waited, wanting — needing — to hear from the Lord.

A door squeaked down the hallway. He listened as soft footsteps padded toward his study. His heartbeat sputtered to life. Was she finally coming?

The footsteps paused outside his closed door.

A shiver of nervousness rippled through him and turned his body into a statue. Forgetting to breathe, he stared at the door and waited for her to open it.

He could picture her as she'd looked all day, her long hair in lovely waves fluttering in abandon about her face, beckoning him.

The shimmering of her blue eyes had weakened him. The creamy skin revealed by the dip in her bodice had tempted him.

She was beautiful. And she was finally his.

His nerves tingled, and he realized he'd been waiting for this moment all day — the moment he could finally be alone with her.

After a minute her footsteps sounded again, this time retreating. He sprang to his feet and exhaled a shaky breath. He didn't know why he felt nervous. In fact, he was more anxious now than on their betrothal night.

He hurried toward the door, flung it open, and held the candle high. "Katharina. Wait."

She stopped and turned. The flicker of the candlelight danced across the delicate lines of her face. Her hair hung loose and swished across her back. The strands beckoned him with their gentle dance.

Her skin flushed the same shade of pink as the roses in her wreath. "I thought you were busy. I didn't want to disturb you . . ." Her gaze shifted to the door, to his tunic, to his hands — everywhere but his eyes.

"I'm never too busy for you." The words came out before he could stop them.

Her eyes lifted to his. The depths reflected clear blue, and for once he could find nothing within them to rile him.

"Is Aunt Lena settled?"

"She's finally asleep." Katharina lifted a hand to her hair and combed it away from her face.

Longing pierced him with a swiftness that took his breath away. He stepped across the hallway to the small cell he'd used as his sleeping chamber since the day he'd arrived in Wittenberg. He pushed the door open wide and held out a hand to her.

Without taking her gaze from his, she glided toward him. Each step she took made his blood pump faster. When she reached him, all he heard was the thudding of his heart.

Her fingers slid into his outstretched hand. That one single act of placing her hand in his spoke louder than her words ever could. She'd come to him because she wanted to, not because anyone was forcing her.

His chest swelled with gladness. He closed his fingers around hers and then led her into the cell, pushing the door shut behind them. A sweeping glance told him the Cranach servants had cleaned the room and had made a new pallet big enough for both of them. He stood for a moment, holding her hand, suddenly not sure what he should do next. He had no experience talking with women and even less wooing one. His palm started to sweat. Should he just lie down and pull her next to him? He glanced at the pallet. Surely he could think of something more tender than that. If only he'd thought to have a bouquet of flowers to give her.

She turned to him with a shy smile. "I want to thank you again for bringing Aunt Lena here today."

"Maybe you'll be able to help her regain her wits."

A shadow crossed Katharina's face. "She's so lost. She doesn't recognize me at all."

"Give her time."

"She's had so much time already. I think I must accept that she'll never return to this world."

He placed the candle on the narrow ledge that jutted out of the wall. Then he turned to face her. He hesitated for a moment, not sure if he dared to be so bold as to reach for her.

Katharina gazed up at him earnestly. "If she hasn't come out of this spell by now, will she ever?"

"We'll pray she will in God's time."

She studied him. "I'm still learning the new ways of prayer, Doctor Luther. And I find it difficult to believe that God would care about something so insignificant when

He has much bigger problems to attend to."

Luther lifted a hand to her cheek. He couldn't resist touching her any longer. "Our Lord always gives us more than we pray for. If we pray properly for a piece of bread, He gives us an entire field. Yet we rarely begin anything with genuine prayer and thus miss out on so much of His blessing."

She leaned her head into his hand. Her breath came in a short burst before she pressed her lips to the palm of his hand. The soft moisture of her lips against his skin sent a shudder of warmth through his insides.

He slid his hand into the hair at the back of her neck and dug his fingers into the strands. The richness glided across his fingers like fine gold silk.

All day he'd longed for the moment when he could touch her hair, but he quickly realized he needed more. He wanted to connect with her, to share with her, to feel her love.

Gently he tugged her toward him.

She came to him with a soft sigh. Her body melted against his, and her arms circled him.

"Doctor Luther?" Wolfgang's voice rang from the stairwell.

Luther lowered his face toward hers. Nothing would stop him from kissing his wife on their wedding night. Nothing. He locked Katharina in his embrace. "Let's ignore him." His mouth hovered near her ear, and he pressed his lips against the hollowness of it.

"Doctor Luther, I'm sorry for disturbing you." Wolfgang's voice came from directly outside the cell. "But you must come right away."

Katharina tried to wiggle out of his grip.

"Don't worry about him," Luther whispered. "If we ignore him, he'll learn not to disturb us." He buried his nose in Katharina's hair and took a deep breath. She smelled as fresh and sweet as the roses of her wreath. He peeled back strands of her hair until he exposed the creamy skin of her slender neck. Then he nuzzled it with his nose and breathed in more of her, feeling her tremble beneath his touch.

"Doctor Luther!" Wolfgang shouted through the crack in the door. "This is urgent, Doctor Luther."

He swept his lips across her neck. The sweetness of her was like a taste of heaven.

The pounding grew more insistent.

"Martin," she whispered, "I don't believe Wolfgang is planning to leave until you answer him."

"Ach!" Luther pulled back, frustration plowing through him. "Go away, Wolfgang!"

"I'm sorry to disturb you, Doctor Luther." Wolfgang spoke breathlessly.

"This is my wedding night! Whatever it is, it can wait. Now go away." He bent back to Katharina's neck.

She arched out of his reach. "See what he wants. I'll wait."

Luther couldn't keep from growling. "What is it, Wolfgang? Be quick about it."

"I need to speak with you privately."

Luther shook his head. "I can't believe this."

"You must go." She smiled, desire shining in her eyes. "I shall wait for you."

He hesitated but then finally released her. "This better be good, Wolfgang, or I'll hang you out the tower window by your feet." He swung open the door and glared at his manservant.

Wolfgang slumped his shoulders and took a step back. "It's Professor Karlstadt. I have news of him."

"You've interrupted me over news of Karlstadt?" Luther's voice came out in a roar. "I'm spending time with my bride on my wedding night, and you interrupt me with news about a man I detest?"

Wolfgang lowered his head, and his shaggy black hair fell forward. "He's here."

Luther's next sentence stuck in his chest. "Karlstadt is here at the Black Cloister?"

"He's alone and he's hurt."

Katharina came to his side.

"Why did he come here?" Luther asked. His one-time friend and fellow professor had turned into his enemy the day he'd resorted to violence. Karlstadt had incited the students to riot during the days Luther had been in exile at Wartburg Castle. He had claimed that he was only taking the reforms to the next level, that they needed to rid the churches of all the images and statues of the Virgin Mother, which he believed were nothing more than idols.

Luther had returned to Wittenberg to restore order and to squelch Karlstadt's radical ideas. At that time Luther had tried to reason with Karlstadt, but his friend had already come under the influence of the devil. The man had developed new ideas about communion and had rejected infant baptism. He'd become nothing more than a troublemaker, and Elector Frederick had ordered him to leave Saxony.

Luther had encouraged the elector's decision. At the time, the fledgling reforms hadn't needed any further threats, especially from within the ranks. Karlstadt had lived in poverty and disgrace since his banishment.

"Why is he here now?" Luther asked. "Has he come back to kill me?"

Wolfgang shook his head. "Melanchthon is with him and says to tell you that Professor Karlstadt is a changed man and begs for your forgiveness."

Luther snorted. "I don't trust Philipp today any more than I trust Karlstadt." Melanchthon had resisted his feelings for Katharina all along. Since their angry exchange at the betrothal dinner, Melanchthon had hardly spoken two words to him. And now Melanchthon had shown up at the Black Cloister on his wedding night with one of his greatest enemies. "Philipp is exacting revenge because I didn't invite him to the wedding."

"Do you want me to tell them to leave?" Wolfgang's face filled with worry.

"He knew I'd be busy." Luther shook his head. "That snake."

"I'll tell him to take Professor Karlstadt somewhere else."

Luther shouldered past Wolfgang. "I'll tell him." He'd give Melanchthon a tongue thrashing, and then he'd boot everyone out of the cloister for the night, perhaps even

Wolfgang.

"This won't take long," he told Katharina over his shoulder.

Katharina listened to Doctor Luther argue with Melanchthon while she pressed the poultice against Karlstadt's filthy forehead. She had cleaned and sewn the gash, and now the warm paste of comfrey and calendula wrapped in clean linen would ease the pain.

She couldn't help but overhearing the sharp exchange Doctor Luther was having with Melanchthon and his other advisors. They were all urging him to travel to Torgau to meet with the new elector.

She didn't understand the situation but had heard enough to know that if he didn't go, Duke George would likely convince Elector John to join with the other princes in suppressing Doctor Luther and the reforms once and for all. Without Elector Frederick there to provide a shield from the attacks, perhaps the arrows would finally reach their target.

Katharina watched Doctor Luther's dark eyes flash with anger, and compassion stirred within her. Ever since she'd met him, the princes had wavered in their support of him and the many changes he'd wrought in the Church of Rome. She couldn't imagine living with such inner turmoil and uncertainty — never knowing which day would be his last.

"Then apparently I have no choice." His irritated voice carried through the small room. "I must fall prostrate before Elector John and kiss the ground he walks on, or he will reinstitute the old faith."

No one said anything.

Finally Melanchthon spoke. "You must go. And you must also write another letter, one that will placate the princes."

"After they've butchered the masses, I'll do no such thing —"

"You must." There was a strange challenge in Melanchthon's words, as though he was asking his friend to prove him wrong, to prove that he would still be loyal to the cause even though he'd taken a wife.

"I refuse to leave until the morning," Doctor Luther said, but without conviction.

"It's nearly morning. We need to leave now."

Luther let out a noisy sigh. Then he turned toward her. Candlelight showed the frustration on his face.

Was he disappointed that their night together had been interrupted? Her heart fluttered with the thought that he wanted to be with her enough to fight with his friends.

He started across the room in her direction. She glanced down to the tattered rags Karlstadt claimed for clothes, trying to hide the strange passions Doctor Luther's merest glance stirred within her.

Karlstadt had long since fallen asleep. After weeks of running and hiding and avoiding marauding bands of peasants, somehow he'd finally made his way to Doctor Luther for help. He'd promised Doctor Luther that he was a changed man, that he would never again write, preach, or teach. On his knees and with tears wetting his cheeks, he'd begged Doctor Luther to appeal to the elector to spare his life and let him return to Saxony to live in peace.

Doctor Luther stood above her, silent and unmoving for a long moment. "I regret that I must go," he finally whispered. "All my friends are convinced that if I'm to save our cause, then I must leave for Torgau at once."

She lifted her face. "I shall never try to stop you from doing what God's called you to."

He lifted his fingers and made a slow, tender trail around her face. Her insides flipped with a sharp need for him.

"I want you to stay away from Karlstadt," he said, with a glance of disdain toward the sickbed. "I've instructed Brother Gabriel and Wolfgang to move him to the barn."

"I shall need to tend his wound."

"Only with their assistance. I don't trust him. He's lived too long as my enemy. I fear that he may offer the hand of friendship but stab me once my back is turned."

"Then I shall use caution."

He brushed his thumb across the high ridge of her cheek. "I don't know how long I'll be gone. But while I'm away, use the wedding money to purchase whatever you need."

Katharina leaned into his touch and nodded. Suddenly she had a vision of her future, of the kind of life she would lead, forever saying good-bye to the man she had married and wondering if it would be the last time she would see him alive.

A hard lump settled into her chest. She'd known Doctor Luther traveled extensively to preach and spread his new teachings. He'd always done so. But she hadn't expected her reaction, hadn't expected she'd care so much that he was leaving or that his life would be in jeopardy with each leg of the journey.

"Good-bye, Kate." His words were soft, and his eyes filled with regret.

"Good-bye, Martin." Regret whispered

through her too. She'd anticipated their night together, and now she would have to wait for his return — if he returned.

He shot a glance at his friends, then leaned down and bent his face toward hers.

She felt the warmth of his breath as his lips brushed against hers for an intensely sweet moment.

Then he was gone.

THIRTY-THREE

Katharina didn't know what was wrong with her. The empty place in her heart pained her as it never had before. No matter how hard she tried to busy herself with other tasks, her thoughts came back to Doctor Luther, to memories of his touch, his kiss, the look in his eyes when he'd said good-bye.

With each day he was gone, her longing to see him and be near him swelled until she felt that she might make herself sick with the pain of it. Work was the only distraction from her heartache. She cared for Aunt Lena, attended to Karlstadt's wound, and busied herself bringing order back to the monastery. She finished cleaning the rooms and spent the majority of her time extending the garden.

Several other preachers arrived at the cloister gate, seeking help from Doctor Luther. She allowed them to stay with Karlstadt in the barn. When they offered to work for their stay, she began to think of all the opportunities she had to make the Black Cloister function to her advantage.

She knew Doctor Luther's financial situation was bleak. He had nothing in the way of worldly wealth or even a steady income. As she walked through the empty but freshly cleaned rooms of the dormitory, she realized if she housed and fed university students, monks, and refugee preachers, she could possibly earn money.

Katharina discussed her plans with Barbara Cranach. Finally with Barbara's guidance she hired two servants. She used a majority of their wedding money to buy provisions, bedding, fabric, grain, malt, wood, pots, and all the other supplies she would need to provide for boarders.

Of course Wolfgang protested her initiative and grumbled each time she asked for his help. But Brother Gabriel was more willing, and she turned to him often for assistance, especially since the new boarders were men.

At Barbara's suggestion she decided to use the second floor of the cloister as the main living space for Doctor Luther and herself. She converted one of the smaller rooms into a bedroom and had one of the pastors build them a bed.

While she worked, thoughts of Doctor Luther lingered in her mind. She had hoped for a letter, for news of his well-being, but the days passed with nothing.

Her worry mounted when word reached Wittenberg that Duke George had beheaded two men merely for having Luther's pamphlets in their houses. It seemed now that the duke was done fighting the peasants, he planned to continue the bloodshed but this time in an aggressive war to suppress Doctor Luther and his followers. At night Katharina shivered on the new bed, thinking about the never-ending danger her husband faced.

When the day of Saint Mary Magdalene came and passed, and he'd been gone for nearly three weeks, Katharina started to fear that she would never see him again. Her heart jumped with anticipation every time she heard the clomp of horse hoofs on the street outside the cloister. Her eyes would dart to the gate whenever anyone entered. But disappointment became a constant companion as each day passed without his return.

It wasn't until one afternoon toward the end of July that she looked up from the garden and saw Doctor Luther striding toward her. She took in the sight of him — his strong, purposeful step, his wide shoulders, his dark, passionate eyes. And suddenly she knew what was happening to her.

She was falling in love.

Her breath stuck on the edge of a sob. Relief weakened her knees so that even though she wanted to run to him, she could only kneel in the freshly weeded soil and watch him approach.

He was safe — for at least one more day.

The late afternoon sunshine had already plastered her bodice to her back, but a fresh warmth breezed over her skin. She tilted up her wide-brimmed straw hat and smiled at him.

He was darkly handsome, his face chiseled and strong. He came directly toward her, but he didn't return her smile.

Everything inside her wanted to jump up and throw her arms around him and tell him never to go away again. But when he stopped in front of her and towered above her, something in the tight lines of his face made her heartbeat falter. The brown of his eyes flashed with a spark of anger.

Her smile wavered.

He glanced over at Brother Gabriel weeding the rows of beans. "I need to speak with Katharina. Privately."

Brother Gabriel nodded, stood, and brushed the dirt from his gnarled hands.

"You may finish tying the grapevines," Katharina said to him.

He bowed slightly, then shuffled toward the end of the garden where she had recently pruned the vines. They had been neglected for years and were in need of cultivation before they would ever be productive.

Doctor Luther's gaze followed Brother Gabriel. Once the old monk reached the vines, Doctor Luther turned his attention back to her.

She smiled at him again. "Welcome home. I've missed you."

"Exactly what do you think you're doing?" His voice was a terse, low growl, and his eyes narrowed on her.

Her heart pattered to a stop. No warm greeting. No platitudes about how much he'd missed her too. He had nothing to offer but his censure. "I'm not sure what you're referring to."

"I think you know."

Her smile faded in the scorching heat of his glare. Was he angry at her already?

She studied his face, the gauntness of his cheeks, the crevices in his forehead, and the dark circles under his eyes. The trip had taken its toll on him. "You're tired." She pushed herself off the ground and straightened. "Let me fix you a soothing drink and prepare you something to eat."

He planted his feet and folded his arms across his chest. "I lost my appetite once I stepped into my home and heard what you've been doing during my absence."

Her mind began to whirl. What had Wolfgang told him? Every day she'd labored from before first light until well after dark. How could Doctor Luther find any fault in the things she'd accomplished while he'd been gone? "I thought you'd find satisfaction in all my hard work to make the cloister livable and sustainable."

"Quite the opposite. I'm very disappointed."

His words were like a bucket of cold water on a hearth fire. "I don't understand —"

"Yes, you do." He took a step nearer, close enough that she could detect the lingering scent of horseflesh on his clothes. "I'm still not good enough for you, am I? And the cloister isn't good enough either."

"Martin," she pleaded. She reached for his arm.

He leaned away from her touch.

Sudden tears stung her eyes, and she pulled back.

"Too bad you don't have a wealthy husband who can give you a house full of servants and land and fancy clothes and all the things a noblewoman wants."

"Why would you say such a thing —"

"You've turned my home into a business!" he roared. "Apparently you're not satisfied with what I provide. So now you're charging people to stay here."

"I'm simply trying to find a way to have a steady income."

"Why? Because you're not satisfied with the kind of life I can provide you?"

"No . . ." Was she dissatisfied? She looked around at the bigger garden, the pruned trees, and at Brother Gabriel working quietly with his back to them, clearly trying to ignore their argument. Why had she worked so hard over the past weeks? Was she trying to make more of her life here than possible?

"The fact is, Kate, you've never thought I was good enough for you." Through the flashes of anger in his eyes, she glimpsed a deeper hurt. "You're still trying to be a noblewoman."

She wanted to deny his words, but she didn't know if she could. "I thought I was helping."

"You? *Helping?*" He snorted. "You used the wedding money to hire servants. How is that *helping*?"

"I've worked every bit as hard as the servants."

"Sure." He started to stride away. "You worked hard spending the wedding money."

"That's not true." Certainly he could appreciate her efforts to fix and clean up the cloister. "If you look around, you'll see how much progress I've made since you've been gone."

He reached the edge of the garden, then halted. "I've never made anyone pay to stay at the Black Cloister. Never."

"But it will help bring us an income —"

"When you were homeless, did I ask you for anything?"

"No."

His gaze burned into her. "I've opened the doors of the monastery to everyone — runaway nuns and monks, friends, and now even Karlstadt, one of my enemies."

He was right. He'd provided a refuge for her and countless others. And he'd done so out of the goodness of his heart, even though it had put him in greater danger and poverty.

"I've never charged anyone for staying here in the past, and I'm not planning to start now."

She shook her head in mounting frustration. "But we need some way to provide for the upkeep of the buildings and to buy provisions —"

"God will provide. He put fingers on our hands for the money to slide through them so He can give us more. Whatever a person gives away, God will reimburse."

"But surely God's not opposed to us finding a way to earn money."

His glare narrowed. "If anyone comes to the Black Cloister for help, we give it freely." He turned to go.

"If we had an income, just think of how many more people we could help."

"No." He walked away. "My answer is no. Don't ask me again."

Katharina watched him until he turned past the raised herb beds and disappeared behind a wall of tall ferns.

She let out a long breath and blew at a loose strand of hair dangling in her face. "That didn't go well."

Down the path Brother Gabriel kept his focus trained on the vines in front of him, and his face was impassive, as usual. Nevertheless, Katharina couldn't keep from feeling humiliated that the old monk had witnessed her disastrous reunion with her husband.

Katharina kicked the trowel she'd left in

the dirt. She'd only thought to make their lives better. She'd wanted to please him with her improvements, to make him proud of her initiatives to earn money. Instead, all she had done was anger him. Again.

What was wrong with her?

She'd missed him, had longed for him, had dreamed of seeing him again. And now she'd pushed him further away when the only place she wanted to be was in his arms. Was she simply destined to face rejection?

Her throat tightened with the pain of a lifetime of being discarded by the people she'd loved. She wasn't sure how she could bear one more rejection, especially by the man she'd grown to love.

Katharina sprinkled more lavender water on the sheets she'd turned down. Then she dried her fingers in her hair.

Maybe he would like the scent of lavender in her hair too.

She checked the candle on the ledge. The puddle of melting tallow had grown steadily since she'd arrived in their new bedroom. She listened for his footsteps. Had he forgotten and gone to his old his cell?

After dinner she'd told him about moving their living quarters to the second story. He hadn't appeared happy with the news, but he'd nodded his acknowledgment before he resumed his discussions with their visitors.

With a sigh she lowered herself to the edge of the box bed and smoothed a hand across her undertunic. Her gaze sought the safety of her discarded skirt and bodice draped over the chest at the end of the bed. Perhaps she'd been too bold to presume he would come to her when he was clearly displeased with her management of their home.

Her heartbeat wavered but only for a moment. She must hold out hope that he would not let a petty disagreement stand between them. Surely he remembered their wedding night with as much longing as she did. Surely he would want to come to her and continue what they had begun.

She leaned over and reached for the pouch draped across her clothes. She pried open the string and pulled out the rolled paper her mother had given her. It was wrinkled and smudged and the red wax seal all but gone. But it was still her greatest treasure. If everything else failed — if she failed–she would always have her mother's gift to rely on.

The door creaked.

She sucked in a breath and jumped up.

Doctor Luther stepped in and closed the door behind him. He leaned back, his face hidden by the shadows of the room. For a long moment she could feel his eyes burning into her.

The air was suddenly charged. A shiver of delight whispered through her body, and she hugged her arms across her chest.

Finally he stepped away from the door and crossed toward the bed. He studied the barren room, only slightly bigger than the other cells. It was just as plain except for the bouquet of lavender she'd placed in a crock on the bedside table.

He fingered the end of the box frame and the freshly filled straw mattress. "I suppose you required one of the guests to build the bed as payment?"

"Pastor Bremer offered."

"And I suppose you thought that my simple cell wasn't good enough, that you needed a bigger, fancier room?"

So he was still angry. She watched the muscles in his jaw work up and down. What could she do to win his favor again? Dare she approach him and hold him? Would her touch work to bridge their differences? Then would he realize how much she'd grown to care for him?

"As a matter of fact" — she took a step toward him — "I wanted to move here so we could have a little more privacy."

Her fingers moved to his arm. She skimmed upward.

His muscles tensed, but he didn't pull away.

"I thought about you while you were gone," she whispered.

He drew in a sharp breath. And then he leaned into her and wrapped his arms around her waist, drawing her against his chest.

The rapid thump of his heartbeat resounded in her ear, and she hoped it meant that he wanted to be with her as much as she did him. "I'm sorry for my harshness earlier," he whispered. "I was a donkey, as usual. All I dreamed about every minute I was away from you was doing this . . ."

Lowering his mouth to hers, he took her with a passion that left her breathless with desire. His lips crushed hers, demanding and devouring until they were both panting with need.

Finally he broke away, pulling her more fully against his body, his heavy breaths sizzling in her ear. "God is my witness, I've been miserable without you —"

He suddenly stiffened and peered over her shoulder at the bed.

Slowly, almost ominously, he released her and reached for the rolled parchment she'd left on the bed. "What's this?"

Katharina's pulse raced at double speed as his fingers closed around the paper she'd carelessly discarded when he'd entered the room.

"It's nothing." She tried to pull it from his grasp.

His grip tightened, and he backed away from her. "Tell me, Kate. What is it?" His voice was low.

"Please return it this instant." She lunged for it.

He held it up high out of her reach. His eyes flashed with accusation. "Why in the name of all the saints do you have an indulgence?"

"How do you know it's an indulgence?" She tugged on his arm, needing to get the paper away from him before he had the chance to look at it more closely.

"I know an indulgence when I see one." He yanked away from her. "Am I to be mocked in my own home by my wife?" His voice pounded her. "I have defied the pope and put my life in danger every day because of my stand against indulgences. And you — you dare to bring one into my home?"

Her legs trembled as she bumped against the bed. His anger was like a physical force slamming against her, pushing her away from him. "My mother gave it to me before she died, when I was just a little girl."

"I don't care who gave it to you! I've fought against every adversity to eradicate indulgences. You know I hate them. Everyone knows. And yet you've harbored this idol anyway." He waved the paper with such disgust that it could have been the very devil himself.

She stared at the sheet, her last link to her mother, to her family, to her nobility.

"Tell me, Kate." His tone sagged with disappointment. "Do you really think this indulgence has the power to help you in any way?"

She hesitated. Did it? She didn't know anymore. Her title and her nobility hadn't helped her. Perhaps the indulgence was just as worthless.

"You don't need to say anything." He started across the room to the window. "I already know your answer."

Before she could move to stop him, he held the paper toward the flickering flame of the candle.

"No!" she cried. "I know you don't like them, but I've already given up so much for you — my status, my safety, my title. Must you demand this of me too?"

Flames burst to life at the edge of the

sheet. Her heart stopped, and she could only watch it burn as a deep sense of loss seeped through her. The fire spread, its ravenous appetite consuming every word until it touched Doctor Luther's fingers. Only then did he let the flaming remnant flutter to the floor. Once it reached the ground, he stomped on it until only ashes littered the floor. Then he turned and stared at her with sadness. "Maybe it's time for you to stop holding on to your pride and your past."

She tried to take a breath, to say something, anything, but she couldn't. The scent of burned paper chastised her.

He crossed the room and yanked open the door but then stopped. "Don't ever bring another indulgence into my house." With a flap of his robe, he walked out and closed the door behind him.

She stared at the door and dragged in a slow, painful breath. Tears sprang to her eyes.

His anger and disappointment lingered in the air just as thick as the smoke.

She fell back onto the mattress and squeezed back hot tears. Blessed Virgin Mother, she'd angered her husband again. Was that forever to be the course of her marriage to Doctor Luther? She didn't want it to be, but apparently their differences were too large to surmount.

Her eyes grew blurry with the pool of tears that pressed for release, and yet she could clearly see the blackened remains of paper scattered on the floor. The acrid stench of the burning paper swirled around her, taunting her, reminding her once again of how tightly she'd clung to traditions, the old ways of doing things. She hadn't wanted to give up everything — the prescribed prayers, her title, her indulgence. But gradually they had been tugged from her grip whether she wanted to relinquish them or not. Was it finally time to let go of her own volition?

Luther stared at the murky liquid in his mug. It was as black as the night sky. He sloshed it around and then took another gulp. The Obstwasser burned a trail down his throat to his stomach.

He leaned back against the garden bench and closed his eyes. A soft breeze fanned his hot face. The chirping of the crickets sang to him, and the lingering perfume of violets wafted over him. Yet the balm of the summer night couldn't reach the tortured spot deep inside him. It couldn't calm his anger, the anger that had ignited when

Wolfgang had reported to him all Katharina's activities during the weeks he'd been gone.

He'd ridden into the cloister needing her more than food, drink, or even another breath of air. He'd nearly fallen off his horse in his haste to reach her. In fact, during his entire trip to Torgau, he'd fought his constant thoughts of her. Whenever he'd been tempted to leave early, Melanchthon had reminded him of his calling to God's work and the need to prove himself faithful to the reforms.

Luther had tried to convince himself of the truth of Melanchthon's words. In the aftermath of the peasant revolts, he was doing all he could to appease both sides. Their cause needed his devoted attention now more than ever. He didn't need thoughts of Katharina interfering with his work.

"Ach." He sat forward and took another sip from his mug.

His attention strayed to the dark window on the second story, the room where she'd waited for him. The candle was long extinguished. But the flames of his desire to be with her couldn't be doused, not even by his anger. And how could he stay angry with her when she'd said she'd missed him and thought about him when he was gone? The light in her eyes had welcomed him. She'd opened wide her arms for him. Even the bed . . .

Had he been too severe in handling the indulgence? Should he have gently instructed her in the ways of truth? She, like so many others, still had much to learn about the grace of the gospel.

He wrenched his gaze from the window.

Even if he could impart truth to her soul, they would always be at odds. He would remain a simple, poor man who could never shed his peasant roots. And even without her title, she would always be a noblewoman. Her blood would demand more wealth and prestige from him than he could give. How could she ever be happy with a man like him?

Luther tipped up his mug and drained the last of the liquid. Perhaps those who had opposed his marriage had been right. Maybe he'd been a fool to marry Katharina. And perhaps he'd been a bigger fool to think she would ever be content to live a simple life with him.

His stomach lurched with a sudden sharp pain. His body tightened, and nausea rose with a swiftness that propelled him to his feet. Heat rushed through his body, and dizziness followed on its heels. He was going to be sick. It had been a while since he was ill, and he was due for something. Only this time he'd been too distracted by his thoughts of Kate.

His stomach clenched, and he bent over. He heaved, the motion racking his body with such force he was sure his back would break. When he finished, he fell onto the bench and wiped his trembling arm across his mouth. That was all he had time to do before his stomach wrenched again. Pain coiled around him and squeezed tighter until he could hardly breathe. *Help me, O Lord. Help me.*

He slipped off the bench into the puddle of his vomit. His mind swirled, and he struggled for a gasp of air. He slumped facedown on the ground. The pain was so intense he could almost embrace death to escape it. Almost.

And yet the thought of parting with Kate, the thought of never seeing her or holding her again was a torment far worse.

His moans echoed in the night and reverberated through his mind as if they belonged to another person. Grass filled his nostrils and mouth as he attempted to suck in air, but the constriction in his stomach wouldn't let him breathe.

He'd always known his days were numbered. He'd pictured himself burned at the stake or tortured on the rack but never dying alone in the cloister courtyard.

Lord, have mercy. It was finally happening. He was going to meet his Maker.

THIRTY-FOUR

A beating on the door awakened Katharina from a fitful sleep. She sat up in bed and pulled the sheet around her body.

The pounding echoed through the bedchamber again and rattled the door.

"Who is it?" she demanded.

"It is I, Wolfgang. You must come quickly. Doctor Luther needs your help."

Katharina's heart clattered to the bottom of her chest. "Tell me what happened."

"He's almost dead."

"Dead?" The chill of the night crawled over her skin and made her shiver. She threw back the cover and slid her feet over the edge of the bed.

"I found him outside hardly breathing."

Katharina reached for her bodice and skirt. She shoved her arms into the garments and tried to her make her shaking fingers work quickly at tightening the front laces.

"Tell me his symptoms."

Wolfgang listed them as she pulled on her skirt. Her mind went to work preparing a list of the herbs she would need. "The physician is already here, but Doctor Luther isn't responding . . ."

"You should have come for me first," she said as she opened the door.

Wolfgang's bushy black brows pressed together. "He was angry with you. So I thought —"

"If you want to serve your master best" — she brushed past him — "then you have to learn to trust me more."

"I'm realizing that." He scurried after her. "I'm sorry for not coming to get you right away."

Katharina pushed down her irritation. Wolfgang was only trying to protect Doctor Luther, but when would he learn she was no more the enemy than he or Brother Gabriel?

She pressed her lips together to keep from berating the manservant further. They raced through the dark monastery hallways, the light from Wolfgang's candle casting eerie shadows on the stone walls. With each hurried step she tried to convince herself that Wolfgang was over-reacting, as he was prone to do, and that Doctor Luther would be just fine. And yet she couldn't ignore the feeling of foreboding.

When they reached the infirmary, she elbowed her way through the guests and friends who hovered near him. Fresh irritation swept through her. Why had no one notified her sooner? Did they not realize how much she cared about him and would want to be with him?

She lifted her chin and ignored the eyes turned on her. She and Doctor Luther might not have a love match, but she had every right to be here, more so than they did. For too long they'd had Doctor Luther to themselves, and now they needed to give her the place she deserved in his life.

At the sight of his face, gaunt and pale, she swallowed hard to push down a burst of panic. His breaths came in shallow, short gasps through blue-tinged lips, and his eyes were glazed and unseeing. The long slits on his arm oozed blood, and the physician had filled a bowl already.

"No more bloodletting." She reached for a towel and wrapped it around Doctor Luther's arm to stanch the blood flow.

"We don't know what ails him." The young physician moved away, the worry on his face only adding to her own.

She prodded Doctor Luther's stomach,

and he moaned at the touch. Her fingers found the pulse in his wrist. It was sluggish beneath her fingers.

Wolfgang hadn't exaggerated. Doctor Luther *was* dying.

For a moment panic paralyzed her so that all she could do was stare into his eyes. The light within them was fading. "Herr Doctor? Can you hear me?" she asked, kneeling beside him.

He didn't respond.

She reached for one of his hands. It was limp within hers. The clammy coldness of his skin made an icy trail to her heart. Somewhere, at some point, she'd fallen in love with this impossible man. Would she lose him before she had the chance to try to make things right between them?

She smoothed a hand over his forehead, attempting to brush away the deep grooves that pain had etched there. She moved her hand to the bristly scruff that covered his cheek and jaw. Usually her touch had the power to calm him, to pull him from the abyss. But this time he didn't move, didn't even seem to recognize her. She wanted to cry out, to shake him, to keep him from slipping away. But fear choked her and cut off all but the whispered "Ave Maria."

"What can we do to help you?" Melanchthon spoke softly at her side. His face was devoid of disapproval for the first time since the betrothal. Instead, his expression spoke of humility. It wasn't an apology, but it seemed to be his acquiescence to her permanent place now in Doctor Luther's life.

And Doctor Luther's life was at stake. If she wanted to help save him, she would need to draw upon all her resources, all the knowledge she'd gained during her years at Marienthron, all the experience she'd accumulated.

Her fingers trembled as she combed a stray strand off his pale forehead. Could she save his life?

"Do whatever you must, but please don't let him die," Melanchthon whispered hoarsely, his deep-set eyes brimming with tears.

"Then pray," she said in return. She would do all she could, but ultimately only God could save him now.

Katharina used every concoction she'd memorized, the treasured medicinal recipes that monks had copied and passed on for centuries.

At the end of the first day, Doctor Luther was still breathing. She sat by his side all night and spooned as much medicine into him as she could and pressed warm cloths against his abdomen. His friends also took turns staying with him and praying. They encouraged her to take time away from her doctoring to rest, but she wouldn't leave him.

By the second day, the blue rim around his lips had faded, and he rested easier. On the morning of the third day, he finally awoke. He was too weak to move or to speak, but for the first time since Wolfgang had knocked on her door, her heartbeat steadied its rhythm. His thrumming, warm pulse beneath her cold fingers made her want to cry with weariness and relief.

The devil would not get Doctor Luther yet, not while she was on duty.

Doctor Luther's eyelids fluttered open, his gaze rested on her for only a moment, and then he closed his eyes again.

"Kate," he mumbled.

She reached for his hand and squeezed it. "I'm here." Was God giving her another chance at love? Suddenly she knew with certainty that she didn't want to think about life without him. She'd been prideful to believe they weren't suitable for each other. He was *more* than a suitable match. He challenged her and made her think deeply. He was interesting to be with, talkative, stimulating. He was blunt but never dull. He was wise but never puffed up with his own importance. She connected with him on so many levels — physically, emotionally, intellectually — in a way she never had with Jerome. She'd never felt the same passion or depth of emotion with Jerome. In fact, if she was completely honest, she had to admit she'd wanted to use Jerome just as he'd wanted to use her. She'd thought he could give her the perfect life with his titles, prestige, and wealth.

But none of that mattered anymore. Not in the face of losing this man before her. What mattered was loving him, being with him, and perhaps one day having a family together.

Wasn't that what she'd missed all those years away from her family? Wasn't that why she'd clung so tightly to her mother's gift? Because she'd longed for the deep emotional connection that only relationships could bring? She'd had a glimmer of that kind of loving relationship with Doctor Luther, and she didn't want to lose it, not before they really had the chance to work through the issues that stood between them and held them apart.

If only she could find a way to show Doctor Luther that she truly valued him, that his life was more important than where they lived or what they had or the name she owned.

He fell back asleep, and this time she could see he was resting peacefully. Only then did she allow herself to leave his side and finally sleep for the first time in days.

When she awoke, the shadows of the room alerted her to the passing of time. She was anxious to return to Doctor Luther but went to Aunt Lena's cell first. Brother Gabriel had assured her that he'd taken care of Aunt Lena during the past days, but Katharina couldn't bear to neglect her aunt any longer.

She doubted Aunt Lena had noticed her absence and lack of attention, but Katharina knew she must continue to care for her. Katharina led Aunt Lena to the winding steps and down to the first-floor refectory. She settled her at one of the tables, then pressed a kiss against her wimple. Her heart ached at the sight of the old woman slumped over with her clothes hanging loosely on her frail body, her bony fingers folded in her lap, her eyes staring unseeingly at the table.

Over the few weeks since Aunt Lena had arrived, Katharina had lost hope that the woman would ever escape the world of oblivion into which she'd fled. She'd tried to pull her aunt out, tried to engage her, but the only time she'd gotten a response was when she attempted to take away Aunt Lena's dagger during a bath. Aunt Lena had grown so agitated by not having it at her side that Katharina had finally relented and given it back. All she could do was resign herself to keeping her aunt secure, especially from those who might try to label her a witch.

Katharina started toward the kitchen to find leftovers from the evening meal for Aunt Lena, but a commotion in the infirmary drew her across the hallway.

"I'm ready to get up," Doctor Luther said hoarsely. "And nobody can stop me."

She stepped into the dank room that reeked of onion poultice and saw him struggle to sit up while Jonas and Brother Gabriel worked to hold him down on the narrow bed. "Doctor Luther, you're ill and must stay in bed," she said as she crossed the room toward him, her relief mounting with each step. His fight had returned, and that meant he would survive.

"Ach, and here comes my lord and master, Kate, ordering me around like she usually does." He glared at her with eyes that were black against his pale face.

She couldn't keep from smiling. "You may

not get out of bed, but you may sit up for a short while."

He grumbled under his breath but fell back against the straw mattress. He closed his eyes, and weariness flitted across his face.

"We shall prop you up." She nodded to Brother Gabriel to help her lift him. "And then perhaps you'll be able to eat something."

"It's about time," he muttered. "I've survived another attack of the devil only to die of starvation."

She bent near him and slipped her arms under his back to help pull him to a sitting position. His cheek hovered close to her mouth, and she suddenly had an intense longing to brush her lips against the unshaven roughness.

He turned and met her gaze head-on.

Her breath caught in her chest. She was close enough to see the dark inner circles of his eyes widen. Was it with desire?

He lifted his hand and pressed his palm against her cheek. "Be still and let me look at you," he croaked. "You're a much better sight than Justus."

Jonas guffawed. "She's a much better sight than you too, you cantankerous bear. And I do believe your wife is the only one who has the power to tame you."

"She has no power over me," Doctor Luther said, but weakly, even as his gaze feasted on her face.

She wanted to bend down and kiss him full on the lips, to reassure herself that he was living and breathing. But Brother Gabriel's hovering presence and the censure in his old eyes stopped her.

"I think you're the one with power over me, Herr Doctor," she said, knowing it to be truer than he realized.

"I have no power over you, my lord and master," he said, his voice taking on an edge. "You'll do what you want. You've made that quite clear." Was he referring to the changes she'd wrought in the monastery while he'd been away? Surely he could see some good in them. If she must relinquish her grip on her old way of life, certainly he could do likewise so they could find a compromise in a life that would suit them both.

"I'm a strong-willed woman," she admitted, "and God is teaching me to let go of my pride. But perhaps you'll have to learn to accept me as I am. And I shall need to do the same with you."

"Don't you think you're asking for the impossible, Kate?" He leaned back into his mattress, dropped his hand away from hers, and closed his eyes. "After all, weren't you the one who once uttered the wise words 'An uncommon match only breeds discontent and gives birth to unhappiness'?"

She recoiled at his statement even though the words had once been hers. She wasn't sure if she believed them anymore. She wanted to think she'd changed enough, grown humbler, so that their match was no longer entirely uncommon. Of course she still had remnants of pride to battle and probably would all her life. But perhaps her pride would always be too great for him; perhaps he would always view their marriage with discontentment whether she did or not. Perhaps she would always remind him of the noble class he despised, the princes he needed but loathed.

"Brother Gabriel," Doctor Luther said, "my mouth is parched for your Obstwasser."

Brother Gabriel started toward the door.

Katharina rose and stopped him with the touch of her hand. "I shall fetch it."

The old monk started to shake his head.

She pushed down the ache in her chest and held up a hand to stop him. "I've need of a brisk walk and fresh air."

Brother Gabriel hesitated. "You won't

know where to find it —"

"I know exactly where you keep it." Katharina hurried from the room before he could protest further. The ache rose to her throat and made her want to cry with frustration.

She made her way outside and strode across the cloister yard, past the stable and the storage barn toward the brewery. When she reached the door, she stopped and leaned her head against the grainy wood. Was her marriage with Doctor Luther doomed to failure?

She blinked back tears and then pushed open the rickety door of the brewery. The darkness of the shack beckoned her. She released several deep breaths of pain. "Ave Maria. Ave Maria." Which was worse, living an empty noble life without love, or loving passionately but being denied love in return? Without a doubt she knew it would have pained her less to continue a loveless life at Marienthron, for her unrequited love for Doctor Luther was tearing out her very heart.

She wanted to sink to her knees, bury her face in her hands, and sob. Instead, she swiped at the tears on her cheeks. She'd never given in to self-pity and wouldn't start now. She took a shuddering breath, then skimmed the sandy grit of the clay jars on the shelf. Her fingers found the tall one in which Brother Gabriel stored the Obstwasser.

It was lighter than usual. She shook it, and from the sloshing she guessed it contained enough for one mug. She couldn't fault Brother Gabriel for not keeping up with the demands of the brewery. He'd stayed as busy as she had the past days, tending to Doctor Luther's needs.

She stepped out of the brewery into the fading evening. With a deep breath she began to slowly retrace her steps to the infirmary. Somehow she must gather the courage to keep going. And maybe one day she would finally win Doctor Luther's love.

Perhaps if she learned to brew the sweet Obstwasser herself, a special Obstwasser just for him. She lifted the jug and pried off the lid. Then she lowered her nose to the opening and took a whiff. An odor like that of a dead mouse filled her nostrils, not the fruity tang she'd expected. She sloshed the jug again and stared at it. This was most certainly not Obstwasser. What was it? She took another sniff of the contents, and the bitterness filled her mouth and throat and made her gag. The jug slipped from her fingers and fell to the ground. Some of the murky liquid splashed out and formed a dark stain on the grass.

She reached down and dipped her fingertip in it. Cautiously she touched the drop to her tongue. It was wine, but it had the bitter taste of hemlock and possibly henbane. She spit several times to get the bitter residue out of her mouth, then she rubbed her mouth against her sleeve to rid her body of any traces of the herbs.

If she didn't know better, she'd suspect that the drink was a poisonous potion. Such a concoction mixed with belladonna or cowbane was a poison commonly used by witches and assassins. An average dose could cause convulsions, vomiting, and sometimes paralysis and loss of speech. It would close the lungs and make breathing difficult. A large enough drink would lead to death.

Why would Brother Gabriel have such a deadly concoction sitting on the shelf in the brewery? She corked the lid and secured it tightly. She'd need to admonish him to be more careful. With determined footsteps she crossed the courtyard. In fact, she would encourage him to do away with the poison altogether. What if someone discovered it in the brewery and decided to use it for evil intentions?

As she stepped through the door, she

gasped as a sudden thought struck her. What if someone had already used it to poison Doctor Luther? His symptoms — the trembling, vomiting, and difficulty breathing — were the very symptoms one would expect of a poisoning.

Who would do such a thing?

Her mind spun with the possibilities and landed on a suspect without hesitation. It had to be their guest Karlstadt. After the past few years of being enemies with Doctor Luther, why would he now seek friendship — unless he wanted to get close to Doctor Luther and kill him?

Katharina raced down the hallway. She had to share the news with the others, and they would have to send Karlstadt away before he made any more attempts on Doctor Luther's life.

"Look what I discovered." She burst into the infirmary and held up the clay jug. On a stool next to Doctor Luther, Jonas started. And behind the worktable, with pestle and mortar in hand, Brother Gabriel froze and his eyes widened.

"It's about time," Luther growled. "Pour me a tankard."

"You don't want to drink any of this," she said. "It's poison."

The room grew so quiet that the only

sound Katharina heard was her heavy breathing.

"I found it in the brewery, and I'm quite certain this is what made Doctor Luther sick."

Doctor Luther's face blanched. "Someone is trying to poison me?"

"Someone is intending to kill you."

A sudden somberness drew the lines of his face together into a frown.

"And I believe I know who the assassin is," Katharina said.

"Who?"

A sharp prick against her spine made her yelp. Before she could turn to discover the cause, someone wrenched one of her arms behind her and yanked upward. The movement forced her to her knees with a dizzying cry of pain.

"Don't try anything, or I'll slit her throat," Brother Gabriel said.

Thirty-Five

The cold edge of metal now pressed against the vein in her neck, paralyzing her. She couldn't breathe or blink or even begin to process what was happening.

"Let her go." Doctor Luther's voice was calm, but his face had turned as ashen as a corpse. He struggled to the edge of the bed. At the same time Jonas jumped to his feet, the stool clattering to the floor. With a scowl he started across the room toward her.

The blade sliced into her skin. Burning heat took the place of the cold metal, and she screamed at the sharpness of the pain.

Jonas froze midstride.

"Stop!" Doctor Luther's voice was hoarse. "Don't hurt her."

"If anyone moves again" — Brother Gabriel's voice was as soft as always — "I'll kill her."

Kill her? A warm trail of blood slid down her neck and pooled at her collar. How could Brother Gabriel say such a thing? Sweet, quiet Brother Gabriel, who'd been her friend these many months she'd been in Wittenberg.

"Why are you doing this?" Doctor Luther pleaded. "What reason could you possibly have for hurting Katharina?"

Brother Gabriel yanked her arm again, and she couldn't keep from crying out again.

"Gabriel, let her go!" Doctor Luther lunged to his feet unsteadily.

"Stay where you are, or she dies." Brother Gabriel lifted the knife and repositioned it higher so that it forced her chin up and exposed her neck.

Dizziness swept through Katharina. *Hail Mary, full of grace, the Lord is with thee . . .* Her desperate plea suddenly felt hollow. How could the Virgin Mother have the power to save her? What assistance could any of the saints offer her now?

Brother Gabriel twisted her arm and pulled her to her feet and toward the door. She didn't resist for fear she would again feel the bite of the knife against her skin.

"So you're the one who poisoned me," Doctor Luther said, watching them with panic flashing across his taut features. "Who are you working for? Duke George?"

Brother Gabriel's silence was all the answer they needed.

"If he hired you to kill me, then why wait until now? Why didn't you try earlier?"

"I only agreed to spy."

"Ach, so now I finally know who's been alerting my enemies to my whereabouts and the routes I travel." Doctor Luther swayed on his feet and would have fallen if Jonas hadn't grabbed him and held him steady. "What's happened to turn the spy into a murderer?"

If Doctor Luther thought to stall Brother Gabriel, the tactic wasn't working. He continued backing to the door with his unrelenting grip on her.

"You're not a murderer, Brother Gabriel," Doctor Luther said, his voice gentling. "Please put the knife away."

Brother Gabriel's old hand was frigid against her arm, but he didn't falter. "The Duke has promised me my own parish as a reward for my service to God and the pope."

"You could have given me a lethal dose of the poison if you'd really wanted me dead." Doctor Luther spoke as though reasoning with a child. "But you're not a killer, are you? You couldn't go through with murdering me, and you won't kill Katharina now either."

Brother Gabriel didn't respond except to pull her into the hall. He started toward the parlor, but at the sight of several guests headed their way, he rapidly backed into the open door of the refectory. His grip was so tight she felt sure her arm would be dislocated.

He kicked the door closed and dropped the bar to latch it in place.

Her blood pulsed hard. What did he intend to do with her now? "Brother Gabriel, please. I don't understand what I've done to anger you." Her voice shook. "I thought we were friends."

He directed her toward the chair in front of the lectern. "Sit."

She lowered herself, and only then did he release her arm.

"I don't wish to hurt you, Sister Katharina." He took off the cincture at the waist of his tunic. His eyes remained calm and steady, even slightly apologetic, but he exuded a strength that belied his stooped shoulders and slight frame.

"And I think deep down you don't wish to harm Doctor Luther either, do you?"

He didn't acknowledge her.

"We don't have to let this go any further. You don't have to let the duke bribe you into something you know in your heart is wrong —"

"Be silent," he said. He jerked her hands around the back of the chair. The motion was so swift and painful that it cut the words from her lips with a gasp. How ironic that he was requiring her to be silent while she sat in the seat assigned to the monk appointed to read from the Gospels or necrology of the saints while the rest of the monks ate in silence.

Katharina's gaze landed on the figure of Aunt Lena sitting on one of the long trestle benches across the room. The old woman stared at the table in front of her, exactly as Katharina had left her. Katharina quickly shifted her attention, hoping Brother Gabriel wouldn't notice her aunt, but his attention had already shifted to the old nun. He stared at her for a moment as though trying to decide what to do with her. Katharina was relieved when he resumed wrapping and binding her wrists, apparently deciding not to disturb Aunt Lena.

He tightened the belt until it twisted into her skin. She wouldn't be able to loosen its hold without a utensil. But the long room was bare. The plank tables were smooth and clean, just as she'd left them earlier that day. Not a plate or goblet or knife in sight.

Brother Gabriel had left her no chance of

escape. *Lord, have mercy.* Her heart cried to God this time.

"Brother Gabriel." Doctor Luther's voice came from outside the door. "It's me you want, not Katharina. Release her and take me in her stead."

Brother Gabriel started closing and locking the shutters on the windows.

Unlike most of the other reformed monks, he had continued to wear his monk's habit and tonsure. He'd also faithfully continued to follow the divine prayer schedule. She'd simply thought him too old and set in his ways. But what if he hadn't wanted to change? What if he stood opposed to Doctor Luther's reforms?

A shudder started up her spine.

"Please." Doctor Luther's voice had a desperate ring. "I know this isn't how you had it planned. You never expected to be caught with the poison. But if you let Katharina go, then this whole incident doesn't have to go any further."

Brother Gabriel walked over to the door and made sure the bar was securely in place. Then finally he stood back and tucked his hands into his flowing sleeves. He stared at the door, hesitating as though he was figuring out what to do next.

"If you release her," Doctor Luther

pleaded, "I'll allow you to take me to the duke yourself. Then *you* won't have to kill me. The duke will relish doing the deed himself."

"Are you crazy?" came Jonas's angry rebuke. "Of course you're not letting that old snake take you to the duke."

"Jonas is right!" Katharina shouted. She wouldn't let Doctor Luther hand himself over to Brother Gabriel and the duke. If he did so, it would be his death sentence.

"It's the only way," Doctor Luther called back.

"We'll break down the door and attack him," Jonas retorted.

"If you do, I'll kill her," Brother Gabriel warned in a tone that was much too serious.

"I'm turning myself over to him." Luther's voice strained against his tight throat.

Jonas grabbed his tunic sleeve. "No. Not yet. I'm sure we'll think of something else."

Luther swayed with dizziness and reached for the hallway wall to keep himself from falling. He could think of nothing but the blade pressed against Katharina's slender neck and the crimson slash in her beautiful skin. He didn't know if Brother Gabriel would follow through with his threat to kill her, but he wasn't taking any chances.

"I need to get Katharina out of there." His legs trembled under the weight of his body. His muscles were as weak as herring soup during Lent. He tried to take another step forward, but he buckled and fell to his knees.

Despair rose up like choking bile. This was no time for weakness, but his illness had left his body a mere shell, empty of strength. "Jonas, help me up. I have to get her."

Jonas knelt beside him, and Wolfgang hovered over him. Some of the monastery's guests had also gathered in the hallway. Surely all of them together could overpower one frail old monk. But with his threat lingering in the air, how could they do so without putting Katharina's life in more danger?

"What do I need to do, Brother Gabriel?" Luther rested his forehead against the door. The cool wood soothed his burning skin. "Just tell me how I can save Katharina."

"Wait," Jonas whispered. "One of the men has gone for help. Don't do anything rash —"

Luther held up his hand to silence his friend as Brother Gabriel spoke through the door. "You need to get a horse and a wagon ready at the front gate."

"We can do that." Luther nodded at one

of the men, who spun away to do his bidding.

"Then I'll bring Katharina to the wagon," Brother Gabriel continued. "I want you to be waiting for me in the back of the wagon with your hands and feet tied tightly."

"Very well."

"I will release Katharina once we're on our way."

Jonas scowled darkly and shook his head.

"Until that point, if anyone tries to stop me or come near me, I'll slice off Katharina's fingers, one at a time." The monk's voice was as quiet and calm as if they were having a conversation about buying hops instead of bargaining over her life. Luther fought off a wave of dizzying weakness. He didn't want to lose Katharina. In fact, the thought of Brother Gabriel harming her any further made his stomach churn with the strength of an attacking band of peasants.

"What should we do?" Luther asked. "We can't just sit here."

"We need to hold him off until more men arrive," Jonas whispered.

"If we try to overpower him, he'll hurt Katharina."

"But if you bind yourself over to him and allow him to take you to the duke, you'll be burned at the stake by week's end."

"It doesn't matter." Desperation clawed at Luther's insides, and he strained every muscle to pull himself up but only made it to his knees.

"Of course it matters. The reforms depend on you."

Luther looked at his friend's earnest face. "Do the reforms *really* depend on me, Justus? Maybe for too long I've believed that they do. But the truth is, if it is God's reformation of the church, it will succeed with or without the help of Martinus Luther."

Jonas's forehead furrowed, and Luther could see the turmoil in his friend's eyes and the desire to give a rebuttal. But instead his friend clamped his lips closed, too honest to deny Luther's words.

"God's in control," Luther continued, "and I'm only the dumb donkey the Almighty has chosen to speak through." God didn't need him to change hearts. The heavenly Father could use someone else to preach the good news of salvation through faith in Christ.

Luther heaved and finished pulling himself to his feet even though the weight of his arms and legs tried to drag him back down. "Katharina," he whispered. "My Kate." Her beautiful face flashed before him, and he remembered the tenderness with which she'd looked at him when she'd come into the infirmary. She'd knelt before him with such openness, such sweetness. And although she hadn't apologized, she'd made a peace offering.

All he'd done was throw it back in her face.

Because he was a coward. He'd been afraid to allow himself to love her. He'd been afraid that if he admitted how much he'd grown to care about her, he'd get hurt in the process. But whether she ever returned his love or not, he had to stop running from his fears. He had to finally admit what Jonas had seen all along — he was in love with Katharina von Bora.

"I love her, Jonas." The knowledge gathered force and tore at his heart. "May the Lord help me, but I love her."

"I know."

Luther put a hand on his chest as if he could block the ache that was pounding like a battering ram. He might as well stop fooling himself into thinking he didn't love her. He certainly hadn't fooled his friends.

Did it really matter if noble blood ran through her veins? What good would it do either of them to let their class differences separate them? Sure, her pride was difficult to bear and often stung him deeply, but maybe he'd been wrong too for harboring resentment toward her. In fact, over the past weeks all he'd managed to do was make himself miserable with his anger and unforgiveness.

He straightened. *O Lord, I'm sorry,* he silently cried out. *Won't You give me another chance?* For a moment strength surged through him, as if God Himself had touched his body and given him a burst of renewed energy. Then dizziness swept over him with a force that left him nauseous. He grabbed the doorframe to keep from sinking back to his knees.

"I won't wait much longer," Brother Gabriel said through the door. "I know you'll try to stall until you have amassed more men."

"We're doing everything you asked." Luther's voice was faint, but the urgency inside him was growing stronger with every passing moment Katharina was in the room with the monk.

He slumped against the door and slid down the length of the smooth planks. *God, help me!* He dragged in a breath and fought to scramble back into the world of the living. He couldn't lose consciousness now. He couldn't leave Katharina at the mercy of his enemies.

"If you don't cooperate, I'll have to give you more incentive." Brother Gabriel's words registered in Luther's head from a distance. He tried to answer, to yell out that he would do anything, but he could manage nothing more than a hoarse breath.

"I don't want to hurt your wife, Doctor Luther. But you might force me to start cutting her up."

"No!" A new rush of panic chased the blackness of oblivion to the back of his mind.

"Maybe I'll start with her tongue."

He heard Katharina cry out, "Please, Brother Gabriel, please let me go." The terror in her voice shredded his last reserve.

"She has a sharp tongue," Brother Gabriel continued. "Perhaps you'll think I'm doing you a favor by cutting it out."

"No!" The word tore from his throat. Luther's mind flashed to the slice Brother Gabriel had made in Katharina's throat. "Justus, I'm breaking down the door." He banged his fist against the plank. The thud echoed with pathetic feebleness.

"And since you're not cooperating," Brother Gabriel said with a low, deadly tone, "I'll start cutting now. Except I'll save her tongue for last so that you can hear her scream while I cut off one finger at a time."

Who was this madman? How could he have lived with the old monk all this time and never known the devil lived inside him? Had Katharina been right? Was he too trusting of his guests?

Katharina's frightened whimper sent chills over his skin. His helplessness, his weakness, the thought of Brother Gabriel sawing off one of her delicate fingers, the torturous pain she would endure . . . He began to tremble at the horror of the situation.

"Don't just stand there watching me," he said to Jonas and the others nearby. "Everyone help me."

He raised his hand and pounded the door again. As though finally understanding the desperateness of their situation, Jonas lowered his shoulder and rammed it into the door. It didn't budge. His friend tried again, this time harder.

"Take me now, Brother Gabriel!" Luther yelled at the door. "Take me now. Tie me up! Cut off my fingers! Do whatever you want with me! Just let Kate go!"

A scream pierced the air. The long, high pitch spoke of agonizing pain. The strength of it slashed through Luther's heart with such swiftness that his pulse slammed to a halt.

"Kate!" he shouted.

Pain radiated through his hand; he could almost feel the knife blade severing his finger. A sob swelled in his chest. "O God, have mercy."

THIRTY-SIX

Katharina shrank back into the chair as far as she could go. What was happening?

Brother Gabriel's wide eyes were fixed straight ahead, and his mouth hung open with the remnants of his scream that turned into a long, hoarse gasp. The knife slipped from his grip and clattered to the floor. He tried to take a breath but stopped short and gasped again.

Surprise lit up his eyes. He moved his lips, but all he emitted was a gurgle. He took another step toward her, but then his body jerked. His face contorted into a tight mask. He gurgled another breath, then fell forward.

She sucked in a gasp and braced herself.

His head bounced against her knees, and she was helpless to do anything but watch with revulsion as he slid to the floor in a crumpled heap at her feet. A wet stain formed a widening circle on the back of his habit. And standing in the place where Brother Gabriel had loomed only an instant before was a thin, frail figure.

"Aunt Lena?" Katharina stared at her in surprise.

At the sound of her name, the old woman faltered. For a long moment she looked at Katharina with blank eyes. Then the woman's gaze shifted to her own outstretched hand and the knife she clutched tightly. Blood trickled down the glinting blade, made a bright trail over her pale skin, then dripped to the floor. It was the small dagger she'd brought with her to Wittenberg, the dagger she never let leave her side.

"Aunt Lena, you saved my life."

The woman didn't say anything. She only stared at the knife with unseeing eyes.

Fear shivered through Katharina. What if Aunt Lena turned the knife on herself?

Katharina strained against the ropes binding her hands behind the chair. If only she was free. "Aunt Lena, look at me."

The woman didn't move.

"Aunt Lena, it's me, Katharina. Put down the knife."

The trembling in her aunt's hand was the only sign she'd heard.

"Put down the knife and free me from my restraints."

The woman's arm shook harder with a force that made her entire body quaver.

"Oh, Aunt Lena." Longing swelled through Katharina. She wanted this dear woman to come back to her, to come back to the world of the living. "I love you, Aunt Lena. And I need you in my life."

The older woman let go of the knife. It fell from her hands and hit the floor with a clank. Slowly she shifted to look at Katharina, and this time a pool of tears had settled in her eyes. For the first time in two years — since the night Katharina had climbed out of the abbey window — she found herself gazing into the clear eyes of the woman who had risked everything for her.

"I love you," Katharina said again through a throat that ached with all the loss and pain they'd experienced. "Thank you for protecting me," Katharina said, "again."

Tears spilled onto the woman's gaunt cheeks. She shuffled with stilted steps until she finally stood next to Katharina. She cast a glance at Brother Gabriel's lifeless body before she reached for Katharina's face. Her cold fingers pressed against Katharina's cheeks.

"Oh, Katharina." The words were only a breathy whisper, but they echoed through

Katharina's head as if Aunt Lena had shouted them.

The older woman pulled Katharina's head against her bosom and pressed a kiss there.

A sob swelled from the depths of Katharina's heart. The strain of the past week, nearly losing Doctor Luther, the terror of being with Brother Gabriel, and now the joy of seeing Aunt Lena return from the land of the dead — the emotions spiraled through her and overwhelmed her. She wished she could wrap her arms around her aunt and hug her in return, but her hands were still bound behind the chair, and she couldn't even wipe the tears from her cheeks.

A pounding on the door ricocheted through the room.

Aunt Lena jumped back and began trembling again.

"Katharina?" Doctor Luther's weak voice wavered with desperation. "Katharina, I'm so sorry."

"It's only Doctor Luther," Katharina quickly said.

A glazed veil fell over the woman's eyes.

"Don't leave me now, Aunt Lena. Not now that I have you back." She tugged against the ropes again.

Aunt Lena blinked.

"Open the door for Doctor Luther," she said. "Please, Aunt Lena."

Her aunt took a step, then stopped. The dark wells of the woman's eyes reflected a pain so intense that it twisted through Katharina, making her want to cry out at the unfairness of all that had happened to her.

"All I've ever wanted was to keep you safe." Aunt Lena spoke so softly Katharina could hardly hear her.

Katharina thought of Abbot Baltazar and then of Greta and the countless others who had suffered abuses at the hands of those meant to oversee their souls. Why had God allowed such hurt and heartache to so many others but spared her? "I owe you my life and much, much more. I shall spend the rest of my life repaying you for the kindness you have shown me."

Katharina suddenly became aware of the noise in the hallway. Another slam against the door caused Aunt Lena to jump. The strength of the pounding splintered the door. It was followed by another slam. In the next instant the planks cracked and crashed into fragments on the floor.

Within seconds the door was unlatched. Men armed with knives and halberds poured into the room. She searched the faces of the students and men of Wittenberg who had come to her aid. Finally, through the crowd she found the face she wanted most to see.

He stumbled into the room, sagging against Jonas, hardly able to stand even with Jonas's full support. His pale face was lined with tension. In the same instant she saw him, his dark eyes locked on hers. The force of his love reached across the room and wrapped around her with a fierceness that left her breathless.

As he hobbled toward her with the help of Jonas, one of the students cut loose her binding and helped her to her feet. She stood with trembling legs and sucked in a lungful of air.

His eyes begged her to forgive him, to come to him, to love him in return.

Her heart swelled with a new joy, the kind that made her chest tighten and her throat ache with the need to cry again. He pushed away from Jonas and stumbled forward a step. But the weakness of his legs didn't hold him, and he crumpled to the ground. Katharina rushed across the room, and when she reached him, she fell to her knees. She didn't care that men milled about them or that a dead body was sprawled on the floor in a pool of blood.

"Kate." His voice wavered. He grabbed her hands and looked at each of her fingers.

"He didn't have the chance to hurt me. Aunt Lena came to my rescue first." Katharina cocked her head at Aunt Lena, who hovered nearby.

Luther looked at her. "Thank you."

Aunt Lena nodded but lowered her head.

"I don't know how I can ever thank you enough." Luther's gaze then turned back to Katharina. "Because next to the Lord, Katharina is my greatest treasure."

Gladness flooded her heart, and even amid the tumult, she wanted to throw her arms around Doctor Luther.

He glanced at her neck then and scowled. Tentatively he lifted his fingers to the spot that still stung from Brother Gabriel's slice.

"I don't think it will need sewing." She touched the line in her neck. "It's not too deep."

His hand captured hers. He lifted the edge of his robe and gently rubbed the blood off the tips of her fingers. Then he bent his head and pressed his lips into the palm of her hand.

The warmth of his breath and the tenderness of his touch caused the joy in her heart to unfurl.

His kiss lingered in her palm before he

finally pulled away and closed her fingers into a fist. He wrapped his hand around hers. "Katharina, I give you now what I should have given you long ago."

Her breath caught in her chest.

"I solemnly give you all my heart and all my love, from this day forward and forever-more."

His gaze held hers for an endless moment, radiating a passion she'd seen only when he stood in the pulpit and preached.

"Although I covet your love and hope that one day you can come to care for a poor, old man like me, I don't need your love in return." His gaze searched her face. "I'll love you regardless —"

She lifted a finger to his lips to stop him. "I think I have cared for you since the day we met."

His eyes flickered with surprise.

She smiled. "I was a fool to let my pride stand in the way of truly loving you."

His lips curved into a slow smile. "So what exactly is my dear lord Katharina saying? Is she admitting she was wrong?"

"Maybe she is." Katharina lifted her chin in mock offense, but her smile widened.

"Then let me hear you say it."

"Say what?"

"Tell me you were wrong." His expression

danced with all the fullness of life he possessed.

A sudden and overpowering love welled up from deep within. *This* is what she had wanted; *this* is what she had risked everything for. This man . . . Martin Luther.

"Is her royal highness, the empress Katharina, still too proud to admit anything?" His voice was filled with playfulness.

She reached for his hand and opened it up. "I was wrong." She bent her head toward his palm and kept her attention focused on him.

His eyes widened, and the playfulness within them faded.

Her lips found the soft center of his hand, and without breaking her gaze, she pressed her mouth against his skin. She tasted the salty dampness of him.

His nostrils flared with desire.

Slowly she raised her head. Then she closed his fingers over the kiss she'd given him. "I solemnly give you all my heart and all my love. From this day forward and forevermore."

EPILOGUE

June 7, 1526

Katharina brushed her lips against the downy softness of the baby's head. The newborn scent was sweeter than any flower or herb she'd ever known.

"What shall we name him?" She smiled up at Doctor Luther.

Perched on the edge of their bed, he gingerly peeled back the corner of the linen blanket until a tiny, wrinkled, red forehead appeared. Reverence and wonder widened his eyes. "So we've not birthed the two-headed, antichrist monster that the pope predicted?"

"You have a beautiful son, Doctor Luther," Aunt Lena said. She combed through Katharina's long hair with her fingers and pushed it away from her face.

Katharina squeezed Aunt Lena's hand, grateful the woman had been the one to deliver her baby into the world and the first to hold him.

Aunt Lena had become such an integral part of daily life at the Black Cloister, Katharina didn't know how she'd managed without her, especially with the continual trickle of guests coming and going. And Aunt Lena had a special way of relating to the runaway nuns, a gentleness and understanding that the women needed.

Aunt Lena's cool fingers grazed her cheek. "I'm proud of you."

"During all those many years in the convent, did you ever think I'd be a wife and a mother?"

"It suits you perfectly." Aunt Lena began plaiting the long strands of her hair. "Doctor Luther suits you perfectly."

Aunt Lena was right. Even though she didn't always agree with him, especially over how to handle their money, God had indeed brought her exactly the man she needed.

In fact, God had brought her more than she had ever dreamed possible: a husband, a family, now a child. But first she'd had to let go of her own stubborn expectations. She'd had to shed not only her habit and cowl but everything else that had been comfortable and familiar until finally God had her in a place where He could use her.

It hadn't been easy to let go of the traditions. But she was reading through Luther's German Bible, and slowly the words were unlocking a wealth of treasure she'd never imagined.

As though sensing her thoughts, he slipped his fingers through hers and brought her hand to his lips. "I'm a fortunate husband. The best and dearest wife has presented me with a son, and I've become a husband and father by the wonderful grace of God." He leaned forward. His gaze shifted to her lips.

Her insides melted at the thought of one of his kisses. Even after a year of marriage, he could still command her heart with the slightest look or the merest touch.

She lifted her face gladly to his and breathed a small sigh of pleasure as the warmth of his lips melded over hers, gently at first, then harder, with all the passion that resided in the fibers of his being.

Pastor Bugenhagen cleared his throat next to them and fingered through the pages of his Bible.

Jonas chuckled. "I think we better leave these two alone and come back later for the baptism."

Doctor Luther released her and grinned at his friend. "Can't I ever have any peace, even to congratulate my wife on the birth of our son?"

"You weren't born to bring peace," Jonas retorted.

"You were born to change the world," Katharina added. Every day she feared for his life and lived with the knowledge that any one of their guests could be the next assassin. But she had accepted his calling and loved him for his commitment to it.

He bent forward and pressed a kiss against the fuzzy head of their son.

"You haven't answered my question," she said. "What shall we name him?"

He sat back and cocked his head. "My hissing Katzen is asking *me* for input? I find that difficult to believe."

"Of course I am. You're the father."

"I'm sure you already have him named."

"I wouldn't ask for your input if I already had —"

"What is it?" His eyes danced with mirth.

"Herr Doctor, *you* must decide."

"My Katharina, my lord, tell me his name."

She smiled. "Very well. His name is Johannes, but we shall call him Hans, after your father."

He was silent for a long moment, his eyes upon the tiny bundle in her arms. When he didn't say anything, her heart slowed to an unsteady patter. Had she been wrong to assume he was learning to forgive and love his father?

Finally he met her gaze. And this time she could see a new kind of love burning within the depths of his eyes, the kind of love only a parent can have for a child.

"And so, if I agree to the name you have picked out, what will you do for me?" His tone was serious, but the corners of his mouth fought a smile.

Katharina's heart started again. "Dear husband, I shall do whatever you wish."

He guffawed. "Whatever I wish? Then I'll have to think of something very special." He paused for a moment, and the dark desire of his eyes collided with hers. "I would like another kiss from my beautiful wife."

"It will be very difficult to obey you in this matter," she teased. "But I shall endeavor to try."

He bent his head toward hers once again. "I love you, Katharina Luther."

"And I love you, Martin Luther."

AUTHOR'S NOTE

I would like to be able to tell you that Martin Luther and Katharina never faced any more hardships together. But the pages of their twenty-plus years of marriage are riddled with one difficulty after another, including poverty, plague, and the threat of war against the Turks. Two of their five children died, and those losses affected both of them very deeply. Katharina's biggest challenge was in doctoring her husband. He continued to suffer from a myriad of illnesses, including bouts of depression, attacks of dizziness, and kidney stones.

In addition to the personal losses and health issues, Luther and Katharina faced continual religious persecution throughout the rest of their lives. The pope and the Holy Roman Emperor thought that the blood of the Peasants' War had extinguished the fire of the Reformation. However, it wasn't long before the flames burst forth again throughout Germany with greater power and brightness than before.

In 1526, not long after the birth of their first son, Hans, the elector and a number of other princes formed the Evangelical Alliance. They finally gave the Reformation and the gospel their allegiance in a move that likely wouldn't have happened had Luther sided with the peasants during the Peasants' War. He had alienated himself from the peasant class but in doing so had preserved the success of the Reformation.

Also shortly after the birth of Luther's son, the princes declared that it was absolutely impossible for them to execute the Edict of Worms because of their fear of the turmoil it would bring throughout their provinces. They asked the emperor to dispense with the edict once and for all. Although the edict of death against Martin Luther was not done away with altogether, it was suspended. For the next few years, while the emperor Charles V was busy fighting to suppress France, the pope, and the Turks, finally the Reformation had a respite from the intense persecution it had faced earlier. During these years most of northern Germany became Lutheran.

Although Luther gained the support of the leaders, the followers of the Reformation still faced perils and threats every day. In response to the dangers, Luther said, "Our chief labor is prayer; let the people know that they are now exposed to the edge of the sword and to the rage of Satan, and let them pray."

After reading a book like this, you may be wondering how much of the story is true to history and how much I added for interest. In any work of historical fiction, a writer must start with the framework of facts and then add many more details to bring about an enjoyable, entertaining story. So what really happened?

Most of it! Katharina did escape from her convent in the back of a wagon. She made it to Wittenberg and was placed in the home of the Reichenbachs, where she met Jerome Baumgartner. He promised to marry her but then left, and she never heard from him again. In the meantime she went to live with the Cranachs and learned from Barbara how to run a large home. Eventually she was the only one of the Marienthron nuns left in Wittenberg. The pressure for her to marry increased until Luther arranged the match with Dr. Glatz. Katharina opposed the match and declared she would rather marry Doctor Luther. Amazingly enough, their betrothal night was witnessed by Jonas. They had a separate church ceremony two weeks later, and their wedding night was interrupted by the arrival of Luther's old friend-turned-enemy, Karlstadt. They took in many guests and lived in constant danger, and Luther truly believed he would be captured and burned at the stake any day.

Most of the characters, including Melanchthon, Jonas, Pastor Bugenhagen, Wolfgang, Aunt Lena, Abbot Baltazar, and the Cranachs, were real people, who are recorded in history. I invented only a few for this story, including Greta, Thomas, and Brother Gabriel. I've also tried to the best of my ability to portray the essence of Martin Luther's personality and have used many of his famous quotes throughout the book. In addition, I've attempted to capture the social, political, and religious climate of the tumultuous times surrounding the Reformation and the Peasants' War.

Was Katharina kidnapped and returned to Marienthron for a short while? Were attempts made to poison Luther? Did Aunt Lena suffer such horrible abuses? These are from this writer's imagination. We will never know all the details and intrigues of their lives, but it is certainly interesting to imagine what could have happened. Avid medieval and Lutheran experts will need to forgive me for the select liberties I took for the sake of creating the plot as well as condensing time and events.

Through all the hardships, Martin Luther and his wife, Katharina, enjoyed more than twenty years of marriage together. Luther truly did love Katharina with all his heart. In a letter to one of his friends, Luther said of his wife, "Kate, my rib, greets you, whom, in my poverty, I would not exchange for all the wealth of Croesus."

Katharina stood beside Luther, strengthened him, and helped forge him into one of the greatest heroes history has ever known. May her story encourage and inspire you to treasure those God has given you.

READERS GUIDE

1. Katharina and the other nuns risked their lives to leave the convent. What were some of the factors that motivated them to attempt such a dangerous escape?
2. Like the nuns, have you ever faced a tough choice between staying safe in the life you've always known versus moving out of your comfort zone into something unknown, risky, and perhaps even scary? What was the experience like?
3. Luther encouraged other former monks and nuns to get married, and he proclaimed the goodness of marriage. Did you respect Luther's reasons for not wanting a wife or family for himself? Why do you think he changed his stance?
4. As you think about the prevalence of cloistered life in the Middle Ages and of all the many men and women who became monks and nuns, what were some of the benefits of such a life? And what were

some of the problems?

5. What expectations did the nuns have about what life would be like for them in the "real world"? What were some of the realities they faced once they left the convent?

6. Sometimes we have high expectations for what our lives should be like, but the reality of our experiences doesn't always live up to those expectations. Have you ever faced disappointment when something didn't turn out the way you thought it would?

7. Luther was torn over who to support during the Peasants' War: the peasants or the princes. Whom did he eventually side with? Do you think he made the right choice? Why or why not?

8. Have you ever made a tough choice that you later questioned or regretted? What kind of repercussions did you face as a result of that choice?

9. Katharina and Luther had their own battle of the classes going on — one that mirrored that of the princes and peasants. During the Middle Ages, class differences were often considered "God-ordained" so marrying outside of one's social class was rare. Did anything surprise you about the class system of that time? Why is such a

rigid system difficult for us to understand in our modern times? What examples can we see now of class differences in society?

10. What were some of the abuses of the Church of Rome (the Catholic Church) at that time? What were some of the ways Luther and his followers tried to make changes?

11. Luther felt like he was a disappointment to his father. He didn't think he could live up to his father's expectations. Have you ever disappointed anyone in your family or failed to live up to expectations? How did that make you feel?

12. Were you surprised by the very last scene, either by the person who was sabotaging Luther or the person who ended up rescuing Katharina?

13. Katharina struggled to let go of customs, traditions, and titles. She was accustomed to the accepted way of doing things, both socially and religiously. Why is it so hard for people to accept new ways of doing things?

ABOUT THE AUTHOR

Jody Hedlund is a best-selling author and winner of multiple awards including the Carol Award for Historical Fiction and the Award of Excellence. Jody comes from a strong Lutheran background, having both a father and uncle as Lutheran ministers. She also attended Lutheran middle school and high school and was always fascinated by the stories of Martin Luther that she learned every year in catechism classes.

She received a bachelor's degree from Taylor University and a master's degree from the University of Wisconsin, both in social work. She lives in Midland, Michigan, with her husband and five busy children. Find Jody online at www.jodyhedlund.com.